The Historians

ALSO BY CECILIA EKBÄCK

Wolf Winter
In the Month of the Midnight Sun

The
HISTORIANS

A Novel

CECILIA EKBÄCK

HARPER ● PERENNIAL

NEW YORK ● LONDON ● TORONTO ● SYDNEY ● NEW DELHI ● AUCKLAND

HARPER PERENNIAL

HarperCollins books may be purchased for educational, business, or sales pro-
motional use. For information, please email the Special Markets Department at
SPsales@harpercollins.com.

Originally published in Canada in 2020 by HarperCollins Publishers Ltd.

FIRST HARPER PERENNIAL EDITION PUBLISHED 2021.

Library of Congress Cataloging-in-Publication Data has been applied for.

ISBN 978-0-06-304300-8 (pbk.)

21 22 23 24 25 LSC 10 9 8 7 6 5 4 3

For Silvia Hammarberg and Gabriella Wennblom

Мои любимые подружки

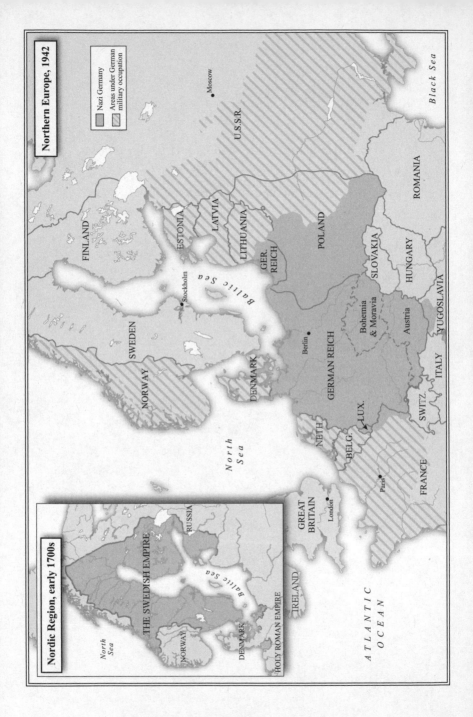

Northern Europe, 1942

Nazi Germany

Areas under German military occupation

Black Sea

U.S.S.R.

Moscow

FINLAND

ESTONIA

LATVIA

LITHUANIA

GER. REICH

POLAND

ROMANIA

SLOVAKIA

HUNGARY

Stockholm

Baltic Sea

SWEDEN

Bohemia & Moravia

Austria

YUGOSLAVIA

NORWAY

DENMARK

Berlin

GERMAN REICH

ITALY

SWITZ.

NETH.

LUX.

BELG.

North Sea

Paris

FRANCE

GREAT BRITAIN

London

IRELAND

ATLANTIC OCEAN

Nordic Region, early 1700s

North Sea

RUSSIA

THE SWEDISH EMPIRE

Baltic Sea

NORWAY

DENMARK

HOLY ROMAN EMPIRE

PREFACE

THE NORDIC COUNTRIES
DURING WORLD WAR II

Sweden was the only Nordic country that remained neutral during World War II. The country, however, accommodated the Nazi regime:

- German soldiers were allowed passage through Sweden. Over two million German soldiers traveled back and forth to Norway by Swedish rail in 1940–1943.
- Swedish iron was critical for wartime production of steel and was sold to Germany at the same level preceding the war, which the Allies argued prolonged the war. The Swedish iron was called "Hitler's Achilles' heel."
- Swedish railways allowed the transport of the German 163rd Infantry Division, together with howitzers, tanks, weapons and ammunition, from Norway to Finland.

After 1944, Sweden shared military intelligence, helped train soldiers from Denmark and Norway and allowed the Allies to use Swedish airbases.

Norway was occupied by Germany on April 9, 1940. King Haakon VII fled to Great Britain and exiled Norwegian forces continued to fight from abroad. Norway withstood a German land invasion for sixty-two days—making it the nation that held out the longest, after the Soviet Union.

Denmark was occupied by Germany the same day the occupation of Norway began, without fighting. Until April 1943, King Christian X and the government functioned as in a protectorate. An effective resistance movement developed toward the end of the war and Germany then placed Denmark under direct military occupation.

The occupations of Norway and Denmark were largely motivated by the German aim to control the mining districts in the north of Sweden. After the invasions of Norway and Denmark, Sweden found itself isolated and completely dependent on Germany for its imports.

Finland participated in World War II, twice fighting the Soviet Union, and then Nazi Germany. As relations with the Soviet Union changed, so did Finland's position in relation to the Allied forces—at one time for them, then against, then finally for them again.

Thus, the four Nordic countries, which, since the thirteenth century had been in various unions with one another, found themselves in very different situations and, occasionally, even on different sides during the course of the war.

Cast of Characters

Ackerman, Oliver, police inspector in Uppsala
Anker, Erik, Danish, history student in Uppsala, 1936–1940;
  Laura's friend
Becker, Jim, former Security Services agent
Bolander, Kristina, Jens Regnell's fiancée
Cassel, Barbro, secretary at the German trade delegation in
  Stockholm; Kristina's friend
Dahlgren, Bertil, Laura's grandfather; former military
Dahlgren, John, Laura's father; governor of the Swedish Central Bank
Dahlgren, Laura, history student in Uppsala, 1936–1940; works for
  Jacob Wallenberg on the team negotiating iron access with Germany
Ek, Abraham, Georg's son; Gunnar's friend
Ek, Frida, Georg's wife
Ek, Georg, mining worker, Blackåsen
Enander, Mr., businessman; Jens's neighbor
Falk, Birger, history professor in Uppsala; Professor Lindahl's nemesis
Feldt, Magnus, Sven's father; military
Feldt, Sven, private secretary to the minister of social affairs, Gustav
  Möller; Jens's friend
Günther, Christian, minister of foreign affairs, Stockholm
Hallberg, Britta, history student in Uppsala since 1936, originally from
  Blackåsen; Laura's friend
Hallberg, Fredrik, foreman of Blackåsen iron mine; Britta's father
Hallberg, Gunnar, Britta's twelve-year-old brother
Hansson, Per Albin, Sweden's prime minister

Helsing, Artur, Kristina's godfather; retired businessman

Ingemarsson, Pierre, doctor, Blackåsen

Jonsson, Annika, Daniel Jonsson's sister

Jonsson, Daniel, archivist, Ministry of Foreign Affairs, Stockholm

Karppinen, Matti, Finnish, history student in Uppsala, 1936–1940; currently works for Finnish Ministry of Information; Laura's friend

Lagerheim, Harald, formerly in charge of guest relations, The Hotel Kramer, Malmö

Professor Lindahl, history professor at Uppsala University; government advisor

Lindholm, Sven Olov, leader of a Swedish Nazi Party, the SSS (*Svensk socialistisk samling*)

Lundius Lappo, Andreas, Sami, theology student in Uppsala, originally from Blackåsen; childhood friend of Britta Hallberg

Möller, Gustav, minister of social affairs

Nihkko, Sami elder

Notholm, Lennart, owner of the local hotel, the Winter Palace, Blackåsen

Öhrnberg, Ove, doctor and scientist, Blackåsen

Olet, Taneli's cousin

Persson, Emil, journalist at *Svenska Dagbladet*; anti-Nazi

Regnell, Jens, personal secretary to the minister of foreign affairs, Stockholm

Rogstad, Karl-Henrik, Norwegian, history student in Uppsala, 1936–1940, then resistance fighter in Norway; Laura's friend

Sandler, Rolf, mining director of Blackåsen iron mine

Schnurre, Karl, German envoy; Hitler's messenger to Sweden

Svensson, Emilia, archivist, Ministry of Foreign Affairs, Stockholm

Ternberg, Helmuth, Major, deputy head of the C-Bureau

Turi, Javanna, Sami, living close to Blackåsen, thirteen years old

Turi, Taneli, Sami, Javanna's brother, nine years old

Wallenberg, Jacob, renowned Swedish businessman and chief negotiator with Germany

LAPLAND, JANUARY 1943

Javanna Turi's heart thumps dark and slow in her chest; her body is taut. She has been frightened before: seeing bare ground beneath the supplies in the food pit, or hearing gray-legs howl. There is a lot in Javanna's life to be scared of. Best not to think too much.

But this . . . This is different. The thought slithers through her mind that this kind of fear she ought to think about.

Javanna, Janna, Jannanita, Javanna Turi, hurry home to me— her mother's singsong voice echoes inside her mind.

Javanna Turi: Sami, thirteen years old, skiing in a forest she knows as well as her own sweet self, setting the traps she has set since she was seven.

Afraid.

She could leave it. She has already set four. But she has seen the tracks of a hare on the hill by the frozen river and she's planned to set a spring pole trap. Back in the camp, she cut the snare, carved the sticks, brought the bait. Her mouth waters at the thought of meat.

The evening is cloudy, but for a moment a cold moon shows her face. The white on the hill glows. It beckons her to come,

come closer. She sets off toward the knoll, skis hissing on parched snow.

Javanna, Janna, Jannanita, Javanna Turi, hurry home to me.

She reminds herself that she has no reason to be afraid. This is *her* land. But only one moon ago, Ámmon didn't come home. Ámmon was old. Older than the roots of the trees. His time ended. Only cold freezes your body to white stone; where wild animals have eaten, there will be scraps. Ámmon was gone as if seized by a giant hand and torn off the surface of the earth. And ever since, Javanna feels it. Something has joined them here. Something foul.

Stallo, the grown-ups whisper at night. Stallo, the giant who eats human meat. But in the tales, Stallo is clumsy. This presence feels sharp. It watches them. Waits for that one mistake.

The moon hides again, but Javanna has reached the hill. By the cluster of young trees, she puts her rucksack down on the snow and takes a while to find a pole with good spring. When she's happy, she takes out her knife and trims the branch of its leaves before tying her snare line to its end.

Was that a sound? She tries to see in the dark.

No. No, all is still. So still as only a winter forest can be in the dark. Quickly now, she scolds herself, before your fingers freeze. The tip of her tongue is out. She feels her work rather than sees it in the darkness.

From her rucksack, she takes out the forked stake. She drives it into the snow, ties the end of the trigger line to the pin she has carved and runs the line under the fork. Her fingers dig.

Last thing to do is to bait her trigger stick and for that she needs fat.

Done. She puts her hands to her mouth, blows hot breath into them—squeezes them to get some feeling back and puts on her mittens. The knife goes into its case, the rucksack onto her back. She hits her thighs with her fists a few times to get the blood flowing.

Then, beneath the big spruce tree below the hill . . . a movement. Fleeting, but she is certain; the darkness changed. It shifted. Swayed. Bulged out in her direction then pulled back.

"Hello?"

She waits.

There is no answer. But Javanna's chest feels so tight she can't breathe. She is certain. There is something there.

Stockholm, February 1, 1943

They'd decided to meet at the café in the NK department store. In the elevator, Britta stared at herself in the mirror. She didn't recognize herself: her lips were cracked, the dark rings under her eyes a faint metallic blue. And the smell. Even though she showered and showered, she still smelled of sweat. The kind you cannot wash away. The reek of fear.

She entered the empty café, looked around, and took a seat on one of the green leather sofas by the atrium.

A man and a woman walked past her. The man fell back and let the woman go before him, his hand still at the curve of her back, as he glanced at Britta. Normally she would have responded: caught his gaze and winked. Normally.

At the entrance: a tall, blond woman in a light coat, eyes searching.

Relief flooded her. She dropped her lighter on the table and rose. Then her friend was in her arms and Britta's eyes welled up and she felt she'd never let go. *Laura.*

"Hi," Laura said softly. She took a step back to look at Britta, hands on her shoulders, eyes narrowing.

"Look at me," Britta said and wiped her eyes. "I'm getting emotional!" Her face twisted.

Laura squeezed her shoulders.

They sat down. Laura took off her coat and folded it on the sofa beside her. Her face was serious. Her large gray eyes steady, unwavering.

"You've lost weight," she said. Not missing anything.

"I'm smoking too much," Britta said. "Even more than when you knew me."

"I still know you."

Britta tried to smile. "Of course you do."

Britta picked up the lighter, turned it in her hand. She didn't know how to approach the matter for which she had come. She loved this woman more than anything. How could she put her, too, in danger? How could she tell her what she had learned? She rubbed her forehead with her knuckle and narrowed her eyes to stop herself from crying again.

"How's work?" she asked, stalling.

"Brilliant." Laura sighed and lit a cigarette and signaled the waiter for coffee or its substitute.

Laura was a part of the Swedish trade delegation negotiating iron access with Germany. A dreadful war was ravaging Europe and—in some ways—Laura was having the time of her life. And Britta was the one person she didn't need to lie to. They'd never lied to each other. Never held back. Before.

"You're made for it, of course," Britta said.

"Ten years this weekend since the Nazis came to power," Laura said. "And things are just getting worse."

Sweden was on a knife's edge: there was a potential Allied invasion of Norway that would create a second front in Sweden;

there were rumors of the German forces in Norway massing for an invasion of Sweden regardless; and then the Soviet Union advancing in the east . . . Yes, the war was closing in on them.

"Have you heard from the others?" Laura asked.

Britta narrowed her eyes. Tell her, she thought, but couldn't.

"No," she said, shortly.

Laura nodded. She paused as the waiter put down two steaming cups. Then she leaned forward and put her hand on Britta's arm. "How are things really?"

This was the moment. Say it, Britta told herself. Tell her! Instead she heard herself laugh as she leaned back against the sofa.

"Same as usual," she said. "You know me; still causing trouble left and right."

And Laura didn't insist. They sat for a while longer, sipping quietly, but now Britta wanted her friend to leave. Fear was eating away at her. She couldn't bring Laura into this.

It was time. As Laura put one arm in her coat, Britta grabbed the other.

"You know I love you, right?" she said. Had to say it, one more time.

"Yes," Laura said and searched her eyes.

Britta let go of her arm, gave a flicker of a smile. "I'm going to finish my drink. You go ahead."

And so they parted, life taking them in different directions. The last thing Britta saw of her friend was that blond hair turning the corner by the counter.

BLACKÅSEN MOUNTAIN, MARCH 31, 1943

He hiccupped. He'd drunk too much. In fact, he was as drunk as a lord. But could you blame him? All day in the dark; the trolleys that had to be lifted onto the tracks; the drilling steel that jammed; the instability of the tunnel roofs; the fear of black lung from the dust . . .

No, after a week mining in hell, a man deserved to drink himself legless.

He hiccupped again and thought of Frida and their six little ones. They'd be fast asleep now. He'd been on his way home when he'd had the impulse to make a detour up to the mine.

When Georg looked back toward the town, it was pitch black. He'd snuck past the Swedish soldiers guarding the rail tracks at the base of the mountain. Tiptoed like a ballerina. A drunk one. He chuckled. Not that it had been hard. Come Friday night, they, too, were sloshed.

He slid. Hands flailing, he tried to grab onto the mountain-side, but there was nothing to grip and he went straight down onto one knee. *Jesus Christ.* Gingerly, he rose and pushed his knee out a few times. It was fine. Perhaps he should turn around.

He burped and it echoed. Sounded like a toad. A mountain toad! This made him laugh again.

No. He just had to be careful he didn't fall off the path. You'd freeze to death before someone found you.

God, how he hated this mountain; hated it even more at night. Not that he was superstitious, but you couldn't avoid hearing the stories: sorcerers and witches; curses . . . But Blackåsen had jobs and a man needed to work.

The town was booming thanks to the war. And this, in a sense, was why he was now climbing the mountainside in the middle of the night.

Manfred's fault. "Shame on us!" Manfred had wailed like he did every Friday. "Our fellow brothers are under their rule, and here we are, a bunch of cowards, working for them."

They'd patted him on the back, *hmm*ed, tried to get him to shut the fuck up.

Politics were politics, and there was not much an ordinary man could do. The Germans traveled through Blackåsen and it was dangerous to show your feelings. Who knew how things would end?

Only Georg had seen something. Something that might prove Manfred wrong. They weren't all cowards. There was a new mining shaft on the west side of the mountain. They weren't allowed to go that way, for "security reasons." The former director had had signs put up, and a chain, but necessity knows no law. Georg had sneaked off and that's when he'd seen it. A man had been going into the shaft. And Georg had figured it out. Everyone knew the Norwegian resistance had bases here and Swedes were helping them. Now Georg was only going to have a peek. He was certain he'd find a place where they gathered. Perhaps he could help them, too.

He had reached the point where the path turned, leading downward now, headed for the new galley. How dark it was: not a single star. No moon, either. The skin on his back prickled.

But then, there it was: a hole leading straight into the mountain.

"Hello?" he said.

He cleared his throat. "Hello?" he hissed. "You don't have to be frightened. I won't let anyone know you're here."

He didn't see the dark shape approaching. He didn't see the lifted baton. He only felt himself go down on all fours. I really shouldn't have drunk so much, he thought, before all went black.

The Historians

APRIL 1943

I.

LAURA

Clicking typewriter keys, muttering voices, shrilling phones
. . . the barrage of noise in the office was constant. Whenever
Laura left work, the echo in her ears made her feel for a while
that she had gone deaf. Jacob Wallenberg, Laura's boss, mentor,
and Sweden's chief negotiator with Germany, walked through
the room and they watched him, to see whose desk he would
stop at, so they could try to guess the latest twist.

"For you." Dagmar, at the desk opposite hers, was holding
up a receiver.

Laura was already on another phone waiting for a confirm-
ation of travel plans. She took the second phone from Dagmar.

"Yes?"

"Laura Dahlgren?"

"Yes?"

"It's Andreas Lundius. Andreas Lappo Lundius . . ."

Who?

"Britta's friend."

A face now, remembered from university: quiet, Sami. He
and Britta were from the same town in Lapland and had known
each other since childhood. At university in Uppsala, Laura and

3

the others had told Britta she only needed them. It'd been said jokingly, warmly, but they'd been serious. To be deemed a friend of the Sami would do Britta no favors. But Britta was loyal. Andreas was studying theology with plans to become a priest, she remembered now. But then, weren't people like him always studying theology? The priests ensuring the few Sami youths they deemed had potential got a university education. Why was he calling her? How had he even got her number?

"Yes?" she repeated.

"Well, um . . ."

She tapped her foot underneath her desk and rolled her eyes at Dagmar. Couldn't bear slow talkers.

"Britta has disappeared."

Laura hung up the other phone, turned away from the noise in her office to face the window and bent forward to create a shield against the sounds with her back. "What do you mean 'disappeared'?" She sounded angry, even to her own ears.

"We were supposed to meet for dinner last night, but she didn't come."

Last night? That wasn't a disappearance. Laura exhaled, sat up straight.

"She probably went somewhere else," she said, meaning "with someone else."

"I walked by her dormitory this morning. She didn't come home."

"Britta is not the most reliable person," Laura said. "You know this. She changed her plans."

"That's what I would have thought . . ." Andreas's voice sounded far away, and the rest of his sentence was garbled.

"What?"

4

"She made me *promise* that if something happened to her, I would call you."

LAURA TOOK THE train to Uppsala. Her carriage was empty apart from a mother holding her sleeping baby. Outside her window: a blur of fields, dark empty roads and dull trees. The sky was an insipid gray.

She imagined Britta before her—the laughing eyes, the uneven teeth, the blond hair neatly rolled at the sides and pinned to the crown of her head.

It wouldn't have surprised Laura one bit: Britta not coming to a dinner because she had met someone on the walk from her dormitory to the restaurant, and, just like that, decided to spend the night with them. It had happened countless times. Her friends had gotten used to it. But Britta never worried. She thought she was invincible. So why on earth had she told Andreas to contact Laura if something happened to her? She'd even made sure to give him her number.

And then there was their meeting in Stockholm a few months ago. Laura was certain Britta had contacted her for a reason that, in the end, she had not revealed. Her heart clenched. I let her down, she thought. She came to talk to me and, seeing me, she decided to keep quiet.

As the train rolled closer, she could see the black twin spires of Uppsala Cathedral. They pierced the sullen sky and made the world twirl around them, as if the spires held the world in its place. Her heart ached. Laura hadn't been back in Uppsala since she left university three years ago. Too many memories, she thought. Things you shouldn't be dwelling on.

There had been five of them, inseparable, until the war brought occupations of Denmark and Norway. They'd always ended up in her apartment in the early morning hours, drunk—the only difference to what degree—Laura, Matti and Karl-Henrik in the red velvet armchairs, Erik and Britta on the settee. They'd crack open one more bottle, lounge and gaze up at the painting on the ceiling, the one Matti swore must be a Julius Kronberg: a light blue sky veined with thin white clouds on which perched small golden-haired cherubs; naked women stretched on the rocks beneath, their hands in the air trying to touch the cupids. *Futile Desire*, Erik had named the artwork. Books were piled everywhere on the floor, balancing on the window sills, throwing candlelight shadows like a landscape of miniature buildings in the dimmed room.

She remembered one night in particular, a strange one, for it had been a premonition of what was to come. They'd opened a bottle of champagne, but Laura had already had too much. It only tasted bitter. She'd laid her head on the backrest and looked at the painting, which seemed alive in the muted light, the golden locks of the cupids waving in an indiscernible breeze, the hands of the women grasping at thin air.

"Now, this is more like it," Erik said. "*For helvede*, Britta, that club was lousy. A real dump."

"So was the chap," Matti said.

Matti felt like the youngest of them, always joking, teasing. But sometimes—not ill meant—he'd go too far. Laura glanced at Erik, but he was lighting a cigarette, his face blank.

"Oh, what do you know?" Britta said, but she was laughing. She took Erik's cigarette, inhaled, let the smoke out slowly and handed it back to him. "Yes," she agreed then. She swirled around, put her head in Erik's lap and her legs over the armrest.

"Now this," she said. "This is nice."

Erik seemed to relax. There was the notion of a smile on his thin lips as his black eyes rested on her, in his lap. The stubble on his cheeks glittered in the faint light. Oh, why wouldn't they get together? Laura had thought as she always did. They were perfect for each other. Anyone could see. But so far, Britta had been unwilling and hadn't gone with Erik, like she might have with someone else.

It had begun to rain outside. Raindrops tapping the window panes. Gently at first, then insistent. Against the glass, a fury of smattering waves.

"This *is* nice," Karl-Henrik said.

Laura opened her eyes. Karl-Henrik was the most distant of them. He disliked people and walked the earth as if he'd arrived here from the moon: each movement exact, a continuous frown on his face, thinly veiled disdain pulling the corners of his mouth down. At night, she left her apartment door unlocked for him. A couple of times a week, she'd hear him enter, go from the hallway to the library and the door slide quietly shut. In the morning, she'd find an empty whiskey glass on a table and a full ashtray. He needed this. To be somewhere he wasn't completely on his own when the night got too dark. A breathing body next door. Warmth. Life. How she first understood that he would come, she didn't know.

"I mean, this doesn't happen often, does it? These kinds of friendships . . . Or does it?"

He tapped his foot, looked at the ceiling, tapped again.

"Did he just say he liked us?" Erik asked.

Karl-Henrik frowned. "I wouldn't go that far. We have idiots among us." He threw a glance at Matti. They'd been arguing the value of Aristotle all evening.

Matti snorted. His hair was too long and covered his green eyes. He pushed at his fringe. An impatient gesture. He caught her gaze, winked at her. Despite herself, she blushed.

"I'm sure the other students have found each other, like us," Erik said.

"You think?" Britta asked.

Laura had never been this close to a group of people before. They had met and fallen in love. They were fiercely protective of one another. Nobody else seemed remotely interesting.

Erik shrugged. "Then let it all remain like this." He dragged on his cigarette and tipped his head back to avoid getting the smoke in his eyes. "And they stayed the same and didn't change. They never fought, they never separated, they never ever grew up and left."

Erik's voice sounded like that of a priest: solemn, chanting. As if he were reading them a spell.

"You do know things change, right?" Britta said, twisting her head, trying to catch his eye.

"Nah," Erik said. "Not us."

"Perhaps if we sacrificed to your Odin," Britta said, smiling now, "he'd allow us to stay the same. Do you think he'd have us? We strive for wisdom, like he did."

Erik's big passion was Old Norse history and Asatru, the Norse faith. They'd all become besotted with it. How many afternoons had they spent in Laura's apartment listening to Erik tell them the stories of the Norse?

Erik lifted his chin. "The only sacrifice Odin wants is one of hanging. They used to have these big feasts to the gods' honor once every nine years. It is written that they sacrificed nine of each male type; hung them in the trees. Men, dogs, even horses, hanging in these sacrificial groves; their blood used to appease the gods."

"Well," Britta said lightly, "that shouldn't be too hard to arrange."

"We could start with your man from tonight," Erik said.

It was a joke, but Laura felt cold. The room was no longer cozy, as much as dark. The flickering candles made the shadows from the book piles tremble, as if they were about to topple over.

And that was it. Their connection had, of course, toppled over. In the end, they had not been able to remain friends. And that was still impossible to think about.

THE DOOR WAS unlocked, but then Britta never locked it. Her room was as Laura remembered. It was one of the newer student lodgings: a square area with a low bookshelf, a single bed, a one-door wardrobe, a desk with a chair and an armchair, all the furniture in light wood with narrow legs and straight lines. Behind the door there was a sink and a mirror that sat too far up on the wall—fitted for male students, not female. On the floor, a light blue rag mat. Scandinavian neat and tidy. Only Britta was not. The desk was laden with heaps of books and used coffee cups, their bottoms stamped black by the residual grounds. The ashtrays balancing on the piles of books brimmed with butts, the ends red with lipstick. There was a glass vase with a bunch of parched flowers—roses—the area beneath covered with spent petals. Seashells, round stones, sticks turned silver bleached by the sun, bottle caps and corks filled an ice bucket on the window sill. The wall beside the shelf was covered with postcards—Laura recognized a couple she herself had sent—and wide-ranging newspaper clippings, about the war, Lapland, the national team in gymnastics. There was a photo: herself and Britta, champagne glasses in their hands. Britta exploding out of the picture with her wide smile. Laura, slightly behind her, also blond—hair in a straight bob, also smiling, also beautiful, but her large gray eyes serious. It was a good photo, she thought. Captured them both. Matti had taken it. *Come. On. Laura. Smile! You do know how to, right?* On the floor were stacks of newspapers and more books. The armchair was buried under clothes, several pairs of stockings thrown over its arms. On the floor behind the armchair, there was a mound of high-heeled shoes in all colors, seemingly swept together and pushed out of the way. A stray spectator pump had ended up lodged under the wardrobe door. Necklaces hung from the arm of the bedside lamp: colored glass, pearls and silver. The bed was unmade. The room smelled stale. It needed airing. Despite all the evidence to the contrary, Britta's room felt unused. Laura could not have lived like this. She needed clean lines to have space to think.

She wondered where the stray kitten had gone. Britta had found it after a night out, small and paltry, more a mouse than a cat. She'd picked it up, laughed at its tiny black paws clawing at her, and dropped it in the pocket of her trench coat.

Erik: "You are not going to take that home, are you?"

Laura: "It's not a good idea."

Britta: "But it won't make it on its own."

Britta had used to call them "her strays."

The room was warm. Laura pinched at her shirt collar and lifted her top away from her chest. Britta was Britta. She'd be back any minute and laugh at them for making a fuss.

Andreas stood in the doorway, shifting his weight from one

foot to another, as if he didn't feel comfortable being in Britta's room. Well, it was his doing they were here.

"How do you know she didn't sleep here?" she asked him.

"She'd promised her girlfriend next door a book she needed for a class this morning, and her friend waited for her last evening and kept checking to see if she'd come home yet. She tried again this morning before going to school."

Britta would have forgotten. Laura walked to the desk and looked among the books and coffee cups, but she found no scraps of paper, nothing that could give a clue as to Britta's whereabouts. And yet . . . Something about Britta's room was off, she thought. She turned to look around again but couldn't see what it was.

"Perhaps Britta went straight to school after a night out."

"I checked," Andreas said. "She didn't."

Laura could feel her nose twitch. She would have hated having Andreas ask for her.

"I went to the library, too. I asked her friends." His black hair fell over his forehead.

"What friends?" she asked. Now that we are gone, she meant.

"A couple of the other history students."

There was a sheen on Andreas's forehead. His face was ashen.

"What is going on?" she asked sharply.

"What do you mean?" He picked a book up from the bedside table, bounced it in his hand as if to feel its weight, put it back.

"Why on earth would Britta tell you to call me if something happened to her?"

He shrugged. "I don't know."

"Rubbish."

"She'd hardly confide in me now, would she?"

He was telling her he knew she had no time for him. Letting her be right. But he wouldn't meet her gaze.

"It's probably nothing," Laura said, once they were back on the pavement outside the student dorm, but now she didn't like it. "You've tried school, the library and her friends . . ." There were bars, she thought. Restaurants. Clubs. But it was early in the day. They would be closed. Before, they would have gathered in Laura's flat, but that was long gone. "We could try the Historical Society," she said. "See if they've seen her."

He nodded, hands thrust in his pockets.

They crossed the lawn leading up to the main university building. Spring had arrived in Uppsala. The grass was a thick green. Blue hyacinths were growing in the flower beds. The trees were abounding with small, bright green shoots. There was a scent of wet earth and new grass. Some students lay on the lawn despite the gray weather, reading. They had spread out their jackets; the ground would still be a damp cold. Any day now, the restaurants would move their tables outside. They'd be buzzing with people laughing and debating. There would be the beat of drums and brassy notes of jazz trumpets coming from the dance palace they called Little Perdition. You'd want to stay, to dwell. But, for now, there was still a bitter wind. She wrapped her arms around herself and picked up her pace.

The small square that held the enormous red cathedral also hosted Holy Trinity Church, the archbishop's residence, the former main university building, Gustavianum, with its round green ball on top of the copper roof, and the Dekanhouse, where the State Institute for Racial Biology had its offices. All that history weighing in on a quadrangle of cobblestones. The Historical Society having its headquarters here felt right.

She traced the black twin spires of the cathedral with her

gaze. She missed it—the five of them—and her eyes prickled. Oh, to have one more of those student days, go to dinner, drink too much and then amble home arm in arm through the streets singing silly student songs. To hear Britta's hoarse laughter, Erik swearing. To flirt with Matti. To poke at Karl-Henrik for being serious and hating everybody. For things to be easy, for any division to be unthinkable. She shouldn't be here with Andreas; she should be here with them. But university was in the past. And, since the war came closer to home, so were her friends.

The yellow Ekermanska's House that lodged the Historical Society lay opposite Holy Trinity Church. It looked smaller than she remembered it. It was the gray weather. The house, too, was folding in on itself for protection. The Society held regular meetings both during the day and at night; lectures, debates. This was also where Professor Lindahl had held his *nachspiele*, light evening meals with selected students, in the vault of the Historical Society, after the meetings.

She walked up the stairs, turned the handle, but the doors were locked. There were no notices for upcoming meetings on the silver board. She shrugged and took a step down.

"There was one thing," Andreas blurted out.

She waited.

"Before the riots . . . Before Easter. Britta met with a man named Lindholm. He's the leader of the *Svensk socialistisk samling*, the Swedish Nazi SSS."

Laura knew of Sven Olov Lindholm. She remembered his grinning face from the news reports earlier that week as he stood on the Uppsala mound with a Nazi salute while the police cut down protestors with sabres. It had been all over the news both in Sweden and abroad: the press describing the police as "Nazi-friendly."

"Did she get caught up in the riots?"

"No, she spent Easter in Stockholm. Didn't get back until after. This happened before she left."

Stockholm. Britta had been in Stockholm without getting in touch.

"Why would she have met with him?"

"I don't know. But I saw them at Kafé Centrum. They didn't seem unfriendly."

"Never," Laura said.

Britta was not a Nazi sympathiser. She could perhaps be deemed immoral when it came to her own life, but when it came to human rights and justice, she was the most moral person Laura knew. She'd remained friends with Andreas, for heaven's sake.

Andreas's eyes were large. "I'm only telling you what I saw. They were having coffee. Then she told me she was going to Stockholm for a few days. She came back Tuesday and called me to arrange to meet for dinner yesterday. I was going to ask her about Lindholm."

Before she could probe him further, the caretaker of Ekermanska's House arrived.

Laura tried her best smile.

The thin, gray-haired man scowled. Did he remember having to clean up after her and the others after their *nachspiele*?

"I wonder if you might let us in?" she asked.

"Why?"

She didn't want to tell him about Britta. It seemed ridiculous now; what would Britta be doing alone in a locked building? "I forgot a book here. In the large meeting hall upstairs." She hoped he didn't keep track of who was a student and who had left the program.

He grimaced again but unlocked the doors. Laura looked at

Andreas, signaling him to follow. In the hallway, she paused. It smelled of cold stone. The vault where they had used to have their *nachspiele* lay at the end of the corridor near the back. A few steps down, and there it would be: white stone walls, a single dark wooden table. Candles in iron holders along the walls and the rusty chandelier above the table provided the lighting and threw the arch of the room into a dusky warmth. She would bet the room still echoed with their laughter.

She felt the usual tingle of excitement.

She could envision them now, the cellar room full of smoke, the debates getting more heated as the evening went on. Lectures taught them history and methods to study. The *nachspiele* had been about playing with knowledge, debating under the supervision of the most brilliant mind Laura had ever met, that anyone of them had ever met. "Most students will be contented with the lectures," Professor Lindahl had said in his soft voice when he first invited her to the meals. "I think of such students as able artisans. We need able artisans; there is nothing wrong with being one. But other students need . . . more."

The delight of being part of those needing more! Her stomach still swooped at the thought.

Of course, the other history teachers had not liked the *nachspiele*, calling them "unorthodox," even "dangerous." Especially one: Professor Falk. He had tried to get the headmaster to shut them down. But the headmaster hadn't wanted to vex Professor Lindahl and thus they had continued.

Who had taken their places at the *nachspiele* now that they were gone? She hadn't thought to ask Britta.

The caretaker indicated the stairs. She walked up the stone steps to the room where the Historical Society meetings took place. The windowless space was gloomy. Back then, they'd never noticed. Professor Lindahl had stood at the front, his blond hair glowing white in the dimness. All eyes on him, the students' burning with admiration. The other lecturers' faces, sullen. Professor Lindahl was a legend. Rumor had it that he knew the prime minister had lied about the state of the Swedish defense program by counting the number of times his eyes blinked during the speech. People said he was called in to advise the Swedish government and that its members feared him as much as they revered him. He'd been responsible for the removal of more than one minister from his post. He'd been involved in instating a few as well. Yes, Professor Lindahl was special. There had been a lot of jealousy among the faculty.

"Where did you sit?" the caretaker asked.

She lifted her brows. Oh, the book. "Right here." She pointed to the chair beside her. "I guess I must have left it in the library after all."

They walked back downstairs to the vestibule. Behind the stairs, in the corridor leading to the vault, a movement, low down by the floor. Dark, small. A rat? Laura hesitated. "I'm just going to have a look . . ."

There was a poster on the wall in the corridor: *The Finnish Cause Is Our Cause*, depicting two soldiers dressed in white, skiing, one wearing the Finnish flag, the other, the Swedish. The poster was old; the cause had already been lost and now "the Finnish cause" was no longer the same as the Swedish; the Finns had joined forces with the Germans to fight the Soviet Union. But at least the worst fears of the Reds storming into Sweden hadn't materialized. *Not yet.*

On the floor, a short trail of brown spots. Coffee? The caretaker was losing his touch.

She came to the opening and stopped.

Britta sat in the dim room on a chair by the table, wearing a brown skirt and a brown sweater with a collar. Her head was lowered and her loose blond hair hung over her face. She hadn't put it up as she usually did, yet Laura would have recognized that mane anywhere.

Laura held her breath.

"Britta?"

She felt, rather than heard, Andreas and the caretaker approach. Her heart thudded in her chest. She took the two steps down. Britta didn't move. Was there a rope around her torso?

Britta's sweater was bloody, torn into shreds, her ravaged chest visible through the slashes.

Did she fold away Britta's hair to see her face? Put her hand under the chin and raise it?

She must have done so, for afterward she knew that there was a tiny black hole in her friend's right temple. The left side of her face was swollen. Her mascara had run and painted black shapes on her cheek. What was on the other side, you couldn't tell. It was covered by blood since her right eye had been gouged out. Later, Laura would only remember details: minutiae, vibrant, in color and excruciatingly clear, such as how white and clean the rope was that held her friend upright. Or how Britta's ankles were crossed, and one shoe had come off, displaying a stockinged heel discolored black by the leather. The tinny moan from the caretaker behind her. Andreas leaning against the wall as if broken. Her own scream that seemed to fill the small area. Or the sour tear in her throat, as she vomited on the floor.

====

A POLICEMAN LED her upstairs. Laura was standing with her arms wrapped around herself in the windowless gray room. She couldn't breathe. Her lungs had collapsed. She closed her eyes, but the image of what she had seen was imprinted on her mind. It always would be. There was a wave of nausea, and she thought she might vomit again. *Oh my God, oh my God, oh my God.* This couldn't be happening. Impossible.

A man in his forties entered. He had heavy facial features and thick black hair. His eyes were deep set and dark. "Laura Dahlgren?"

Had she told them her name? She couldn't remember.

"I am Police Inspector Ackerman. Please take a seat."

Laura sank down on the chair closest to her. Her knees were shaking, knocking against each other. Her fingers tugged at the sleeves of her shirt as if they had a life of their own. The policeman watched her for a moment, brown eyes squinting, then opened a black notebook and took out a pen.

"You found her," he stated.

Her teeth were chattering. Breathe, she told herself. Focus. Her grandfather had taught her: when panicking, focus on your breathing and the next task. Then the next. *Don't think. Whatever you do, don't think.* Her father would just say "Control yourself." Same thing.

"What is her name?"

"Britta Hallberg." Her jaws were tight, and she had to force her mouth to open. Her voice sounded distant. Not like her own.

"Where was she from?"

"Blackåsen."

"How did you know her?"

"We studied together, before the war broke out."

"And she continued her studies?"

She nodded. "Research, for her doctorate."

"What?"

"What do you mean?" She didn't understand.

"What did you study?"

"History."

"And what do you do now?"

"I work for a trade delegation in Stockholm."

"Stockholm. Why are you here today?"

"Andreas . . . Britta's friend, was worried," she said. "He couldn't find her. He called me. I came, and we searched for her together."

"Why was he worried?"

"He and Britta had agreed to meet last night, and she didn't come. That made him worried."

She inhaled and it sounded like a hiccup. *Don't think now. Later.*

"Has this happened before? Her going missing and him calling?"

"No."

"You said 'Britta's friend.'" Does that mean he's not a friend of yours?"

"Yes."

"So why did he call you?"

"I think she must have been frightened." A flash of Britta's streaked face. She had to swallow. *Breathe.* "She had told him that if anything happened to her, he needed to call me. And when I met her last time, I got a feeling there was something wrong."

"But she didn't tell you what it was?"

She shook her head. If only she had insisted! Her face twisted into a sob, but she forced it back under control. If she started, she'd never stop.

Inspector Ackerman tapped his pen against the book.

"How did you know you would find her here?" he asked.

"I didn't . . ." She sounded desperate. "Andreas had already looked for her in other places. I didn't expect to find her."

He scribbled in his book. "The young man. Was he her . . . ?"

"They were childhood friends, that's all. Where is he? Andreas?"

"We will question him at the station."

"Why?"

"It is better."

He didn't want them here together after finding Britta, she thought. He wanted to ask his questions without them having spoken to each other about what they'd seen. Perhaps also because Andreas was Sami.

Andreas knows, she thought then, with such certainty she surprised herself. He knows who did this.

No. Impossible. He cared for Britta, she had to give him that. If he knew more, he would have said. But he had been scared. Perhaps he was just worried about Britta. But that worried after only one evening's absence? It didn't make sense.

"Did she have anyone else?"

"No one in particular. Well, not that I know of."

Erik would be devastated. The others . . . She'd have to tell them. Britta, who'd remained outside the war, was the first one among them to die. It didn't feel real. Her teeth began chattering again and she shivered. She put her hands between her thighs, squeezed them, tried to calm her body down.

The policeman studied her.

"Did she have any enemies?"

"She is friends with everyone . . . Was . . . Everyone liked her."

Images of Britta flickered through her mind—Britta laughing, cigarette between two fingers, champagne glass in the other hand, her head turning right and left as she said hello to people. Everyone's gaze following her.

She blinked hard, didn't want to see.

"Who would do such a thing?" he asked.

"No one," she said.

He looked at her. Someone had.

"I don't know. Everyone liked her," she repeated. *Loved* her, she thought.

"Anything else that strikes you as strange or unusual, lately?"

"I haven't seen her since February. I don't know what was going on in her life recently." It hurt to admit that.

"Was she politically active?"

"No. She had strong opinions of right and wrong . . . of justice, but she wasn't engaged in a party or anything . . ."

She didn't tell him about Britta supposedly meeting with Sven Olov Lindholm. Andreas could tell him that himself. She still didn't believe it.

"Why did you come here to look for her?" he asked.

"Like I said, it was the only place left. We went to her dorm. Andreas had asked in class."

"Who comes here?"

"The history students. The professors."

"Who has a key to this house?"

"You'll have to ask the administration. The caretaker does. There's a key at the historical administration. It hangs on the wall. We all know this."

"All, as in . . . ?"

"Students, teachers . . . But why?" she said. "Why on earth would anyone do this? Britta was . . ." her voice broke. *Lovely. Wonderful. Harmless.*

He didn't respond.

"Is there anything else you can think of that might be important?" he asked instead. "Arguments, past lovers . . . ?"

She shook her head. There were plenty of past lovers, of course, but that had been innocent. They had fought—their group—toward the end, but that had nothing to do with this. She thought back to Britta's room. Something about it still bothered her.

The image of her ravaged friend floated up before her again. "Her upper body." Her hand flew up to touch her own blouse. "Her eye . . . What happened to her?"

He shut his book. For a moment she thought he wouldn't respond. "It looks as if she was tortured," he said then.

Laura gasped. To hear it said out loud . . . "Tortured?"

He nodded. She covered her mouth, then removed her hand. "And shot?" she asked, remembering the wound in the temple.

He nodded again. "We will know more after the autopsy."

Laura shivered. "The shot to her temple . . . It's so . . . . cold."

"I don't know," he said, rising to stand. "The coldest wounds can display the most passion, don't you think?"

2.

JENS

It's not reasonable." Daniel Jonsson, one of the archivists, followed Jens Regnell down the corridors—not for the first time—waving a bunch of papers. "You have to tell him."

"I have." Jens took the steps up to the second floor two at a time. You don't know how many times, he thought.

They were in the Arvfurstens palats, the seat of the Ministry of Foreign Affairs. The unreasonable person they were speaking about was the minister himself, Christian Günther, to whom Jens was a secretary.

"He's been doing this since the beginning of his tenure. There must be archives. Especially now, when we're changing our positions, there must be trails of what we say and do."

The civil servant's curly gray hair was standing on end as if he had thrust his fingers through it before coming to find Jens. His glasses had slid down his nose and he pushed them up with a finger as he blinked and walked sideways trying to catch Jens's gaze.

"The minister runs things the way he decides," Jens said. "And he is successful."

This was a partial truth. In his short time with Christian Günther, Jens had learned that the foreign minister was popular with the prime minister, detested by the Swedish people, mistrusted by the press, perceived as pro-German.

The archivist scoffed. "He doesn't follow the government's policies but makes up his own as he goes."

Jens slowed his steps. "I'll pretend I didn't hear that," he said.

The archivist gave him a look—*you know I'm right*—and they walked a couple of steps in silence.

Jens did know Daniel was right. He might be new in his post, but he had heard the rumors. German activities approved with no government protocols or records, least of all from Günther. Sweden might be neutral, but they'd had to acquiesce, even now with Allied pressure on them to "cut the Germans off, or else . . ." It was a balancing act. Sweden was completely dependent on German imports and although, after Stalingrad, Günther had instructed his staff that their foreign policies must now include the *possibility* of a German defeat, Germany had not yet lost. The commander of the Swedish Armed Forces, Törnell, still thought they would win.

"There are rules," Daniel said. "If he won't record the minutes of the meetings, you'll have to."

Jens wanted to laugh. Or cry. At most meetings, Günther would ask his staff to leave, despite them grumbling it was against due process. In their communications, the Germans called him an "unobjectionable friend of Germany."

Jens stopped. In the gold-framed mirror behind Daniel he caught a glimpse of himself: too blond, too blue-eyed, too bloody earnest; a schoolboy soon to turn thirty-five in some dressing-up game, wearing a dark suit and a white shirt with a darker tie. What on earth was he doing here?

"Listen," he said to Daniel. "I will do what I can. What are you missing?"

"The records show there have been several phone calls between our minister and the Danish foreign minister over the last few weeks. I spoke with my counterpart in Denmark and he said the exiled Norwegian foreign affairs minister was also involved. These contacts aren't logged at our end. There aren't any notes. I need to at least log them and list what was discussed."

"I'm sure they were just updating each other on recent events."

"There should still be records."

"Weren't they listened to?"

Calls had been monitored by the Security Services since the beginning of the war—listened to, registered. Mail was read and censored. Daniel had likely gotten his information from those registers.

Daniel scoffed. "You try getting information out of the Security Services."

"And your counterparts . . . Didn't they tell you what the meetings were about?"

"I didn't ask! What will it look like if it's revealed we have zero insight?"

The archivist looked dejected. Jens softened.

"I will find out. I promise." He touched Daniel's sleeve before turning to walk away. "I promise," he said again over his shoulder and sensed more than saw his colleague shake his head.

Günther didn't share anything with anyone. It wasn't a lack of trust, Jens thought, as much as the belief that he knew best. He simply thought himself better than the others in his department, and the other men in the government, for that matter.

The door to the large meeting room opened and the head of the Foreign Affairs' political department, Staffan Söderblom, exited, followed by the secretary to Prime Minister Hansson, Jon Olof Söderblom.

Secrets. Everywhere, secrets.

"I didn't know there was a meeting planned between our offices," Jens said.

"A brotherly conversation," Staffan said. "Well," he nodded to his brother, "see you later." With that, he walked toward his office.

Jon Olof remained, sinking his heels into the thick red carpet, his hands clasped behind his back. "It must be hard," he said to Jens.

No love lost between the two. Jon Olof, son of the Archbishop, was an upper-class snob pretending to be a friend of the workers; blond curls, scheming eyes under the nonchalant eyebrows. Jens saw him as a liar and a cheat. As for Jon Olof's brother, Staffan was the minister's chosen right hand, despite Jens being Günther's secretary. The strength of their relationship was no secret.

"What's that supposed to mean?" Jens now said to Jon Olov.

Jon Olof smirked. "I mean, there's a lot going on now in Foreign Affairs. Hard to keep track of everything, and everyone, right?"

Jens shrugged. "I feel differently."

"I thought I might see if Günther is in?" Jon Olov said, as if to prove a point.

"He's out," Jens said. "Won't be in until tomorrow." Fact was, he had no idea where Günther was.

Jon Olov smiled. "I see. I thought Staffan said he was on his way in. Well, poster boy. See you around."

As Jens got into his office, Kristina rang to remind him of the dinner that same night. "It's important," she said, meaning important for his career, for him, for them.

"I'll be there."

"Don't be late."

He sat down to sort the mail but had no peace and rose again.

For a while, he stood by the window that overlooked Gustav Adolf's Square, empty since personal driving had been forbidden. He looked at the majestic neoclassical Royal Swedish Opera behind the equestrian statue of King Gustav II Adolf; at the Norrbo bridge of arched stone stretched over the Lilla Värtan strait. On the wide sky over Stockholm, the heavy clouds were darkening purple. It might begin to rain. At least this winter hadn't been as cold as the previous few. He wished he could open the window to hear flowing water, and wind, but that was forbidden for safety reasons.

Jens had arrived at the ministry too late to have any impact. Too late to become close to Christian Günther. "You won't change that," Jens's father, the schoolteacher, had said to him, when he was considering saying yes to the minister's request to become his secretary. "Staffan Söderblom and Christian Günther have history together. You'll always be second. Can you handle that?"

No, Jens, the achiever, could not handle that, but he had thought it would change. *He* would change it. He was well educated, experienced, smart, and he had achieved this on his own without the correct family background. In fact, he had never been second best. Ever. And he had liked Christian Günther. He could see them becoming close. He'd been certain he could make it happen.

So far, he'd been wrong. He'd left a high-paying job at a company where they had loved him to become nothing more than an administrator. Worse, the more he tried, the more Christian Günther seemed to make a point of ignoring him.

Jens returned to his desk. There was an oil painting on the wall opposite, an older man, gold chain over his fat belly, deep frown, scowl, beaked nose. He seemed to stare directly at Jens

whenever Jens sat down. Judging him. *Not enough. Not enough.*
He hated the bloody thing. It was likely some masterpiece, but
surely he could get rid of it? He'd ask the administrative staff if
he could have it exchanged for a landscape. He sighed, turned
on the radio, and began sorting through the letters. His father
might have been right. How much time did you give a new challenge before you surrendered? Ridiculous. He wouldn't give up.
He never had.

The last envelope was thick. Like all the others, it had been
opened, the content checked and then taped up again. A botch
job. It was addressed to Jens, not the minister. The handwriting
was hasty, it swept across the paper. He opened it.

Inside was a lengthy typed document.

*Nordic Relations Through the Ages—Denmark, Norway
and Sweden on a New Path*, by Britta Hallberg. Jens hesitated,
thinking he recognized the author's name, but he couldn't
think where from.

He flicked through, read headlines such as *Objectives,
Introduction, Sources.* A thesis. Sent to him by mistake, perhaps?
But it had been addressed to him personally. He turned to the
Contents page:

i. *Introduction*
ii. *Objectives and Demarcations*
1. *History: The Scandinavian Unions*
2. *The Reich*
3. *The 1800s: A New Way*
4. *The 1900s: A New Threat*
5. *Behind the Scenes of the Three Kings' Meeting in 1914*
6. *Outcome from the Three Kings' Meeting in 1939*

The Three Kings . . . Danish, Norwegian and Swedish. Jens liked the title and the table of contents. It sounded interesting. The kind of thing that, once upon a time, he would have devoured, keen to perhaps discover a new way of thinking. But he did not have time to read any longer. And it was unfinished: no conclusion. He threw the document into the garbage bin underneath his desk.

On the radio, they debated whether *Ulven*, the Swedish submarine that had sunk during an exercise mid-April, should be salvaged, were they to find it. They had talked about nothing else since it happened. Radio presenter Sven Jerring's steady, measured voice summarized the pros and the cons. The crew was dead. Trying to locate the submarine, they had found mines— German mines on Swedish territory. It was likely that the vessel had hit one of those. They hadn't yet been able to pinpoint the location of the submarine. Poor men, Jens thought, waiting in the deep for a salvation that never came.

The man in the painting on the wall opposite glowered at him, face full of disgust. Jens sighed.

Stirred by some vague feeling of sadness for the waste and the futility, he changed his mind, pushed back his chair and bent to pick the thesis up from the garbage bin. He put it in his desk drawer. Then shut it with a bang.

3.

BLACKÅSEN MOUNTAIN

Where have you been?" his mother demanded. There were red spots on her cheeks. Since Taneli's older sister went missing, his mother had grown thinner and more gnarled. One hundred days since his sister vanished. One hundred days that his mother cried and that he himself walked around with an abyss inside his chest. Each day, he teetered on the edge of that abyss, tried his best not to fall in. For the first two cycles of the moon they hadn't stopped searching; all of them had been out each day, tracking, calling, spreading their circles wider and wider. By the third cycle of the moon, only Taneli remained. The others held their gazes low around him, certain his sister was dead. She wasn't. Couldn't be.

His mother grabbed his arm and pulled him along with her. Raija, Taneli's dog, followed close.

Two white men were by their fireplace. They were dressed in gray jackets and trousers. They wore hats and vests. The buttons on their shirts shimmered. The other children were already lining up. One man, red-haired and bearded, was measuring them one by one while his companion made notes in a book. The man who was doing the measuring opened their mouths, peered inside, squeezed their bones. He then placed a set of tongs on their heads and read the number back to his colleague. It was not the first time they'd been measured, just like the cattle you'd buy at market time.

Taneli lined up behind the others. Raija pressed against his shin. She was a Lapphund with a keen little face and small bear ears. Her fur was long and fluffy, beige on the legs and ruff, the rest of her black. Her soft tail curled up over her back and Taneli would pull it through his hand. She was a good dog. Brave and willing to work hard. And she was his. By their huts, the adults were standing, watching, hands open, not speaking.

The others said Stallo, the giant, had taken Javanna. But Taneli didn't think so. They'd found her trap on a knoll by the river; the prey that had been caught in it glittered blue with frost. Of Javanna there had been no trace: her rucksack was gone; her skis, too. Stallo was not that neat. No, something else had happened to Javanna.

Taneli's mother had told him how excited his sister had been about his birth. Javanna had put her hands on their mother's belly every time their mother would let her, and whispered truths into her stomach. Truths meant only for Taneli. Maybe this is why he could feel her and the others couldn't. They were tied together by that belly button as if the umbilical cord had connected the two of them, rather than stretching between mother and child. "She is the one who chose your name," his mother always said. "She said you had to be called Taneli."

Nihkko, one of the elders, had spoken with Taneli. "You have to stop," he'd said. "You have to accept."

"She is not dead."

"How do you know?"

"I just know."

"Hearing her doesn't mean she is not dead," Nihkko had responded. "The dead speak."

Taneli shrugged. He knew what he knew.

Nihkko had fallen silent, his face thoughtful. Then he said, "I wish she were alive, too. There were prophesies laid on her life. She was supposed to replace me. But it would be better now if she were not."

The way he said it sent shivers down Taneli's spine. He hadn't thought about it like that: hadn't thought about what could be happening to her if she was somehow trapped and being held.

"You!"

The man pointed to Taneli with his pen. It was his turn. He walked close. The man positioned him beside the others. Taneli focused on the man's beard. Reddish and neat, each hair seemed to have its place. Perhaps the man combed it with something. First, the man ran his fingertips over Taneli's head, pressing to feel its shape. It was not an unpleasant feeling. Then he placed the set of tongs on Taneli's head. He read out the number aloud for his friend to write in his book. He put his fingers between Taneli's teeth and prised his jaws open to look inside. The fingers tasted bitter and left an oily feel in his mouth.

He placed his knuckles under Taneli's chin and tipped it up. He looked at Taneli but without seeing him.

"He doesn't look like the others," he said, whereupon his friend approached them.

"Not a clean racial type," he added.

The second man was also bearded, but his was sparse and straggly. His eyes were light blue, like water pouring from a cup. His eyes met Taneli's and Taneli could feel his chest clench. There was nothing in this man's eyes: no emotion, no spark, just a flat surface. This was what evil looked like, Taneli thought. The hair stood up on his arms.

In the second man's book were drawings of human heads. The men studied them and Taneli. Their eyes flicked back and forth between the sketches and Taneli.

"You're right," the second man said. "Hybrid."

"Yes," the first man said and narrowed his eyes at Taneli. "And more Swedish than Sami."

Taneli turned his gaze to him, anger rising. "But I don't want to look like a Swede," he said.

He could feel his mother holding her breath over by their tent and pressing her fist against her chest. He knew his father would be rubbing his knuckle against his forehead and making a face, as if his head hurt him.

The man who had measured Taneli ignored him. But the man with the light eyes held Taneli's gaze and smiled. Taneli could feel himself going weak. There was something so utterly terrifying about this man.

Before the two men walked away, the man with the light eyes kicked Raija in the side. He wasn't looking at the dog, though. He was looking at Taneli.

4.

LAURA

Stockholm's central train station was full of people hurrying to catch their trains. Rush hour. Laura walked in the opposite direction. People bumped into her. She felt dizzy. She kept seeing Britta's body before her. She might be sick again. She had failed her best friend; the one person on earth she loved the most. During their time at university, Laura had grown to hope she and her friends would stay together after their studies and live in a big house like bohemians. She must have mentioned it to Britta, for she remembered Britta's curt answer: "You're not being realistic. Now is now. Who knows what will happen?" And Britta had been right. Matti had gone back to Finland and enlisted in the army, Karl-Henrik was in Norway, having, from what she understood, joined the resistance. Like Norway, Denmark was occupied, and so Erik had remained in Stockholm. Laura had taken the job in Stockholm and Britta . . .

In the main hall, under the curved glass roof, there was a queue for the platforms. "Excuse me," Laura said. "Excuse me."

She wanted to scream for people to move. Instead, she caught the eye of a policeman, black uniform, white hat.

Focus on your breath, she thought. Look at your feet. One step. One more.

The train ride back had been dreadful. Laura had felt nauseous. Dark yellow grass from last year still clung to the fields outside the window beyond the reflection of her white face, birch trees like dirty stripes against the gray spruce forest, all of it shouting of death and loss. Waves of realization that Britta was gone hit against her; each breaking her down.

She had planned to go home, but now she couldn't face being on her own. There was her father's house in Djursholm, but he was at work. She walked out of the train station, followed Vasagatan to the water and then continued alongside Värtan strait toward the King's Garden and her workplace. Only now did she notice the heavy sky. A storm was on its way. How was it possible that Britta was gone, and, in the world, things would simply continue as normal? Nothing could be normal again.

She opened the heavy wooden door to her place of work and her shoes made hollow taps on the reception area's marble floor. In her office, the brightness and the noise assaulted her. She remained standing in front of the door.

"There you are," Jacob Wallenberg said. "We've had a message from the Germans. Could you please take a look?" He leaned back and narrowed his eyes. "You're pale."

This was his strength. He didn't miss anything, never forgot a face, never failed to take that extra look, always had time for a conversation. That and, of course, his ability to keep everything in his head: every line in a dialogue, each number.

"A university friend of mine died," she said. My best friend, she wanted to say. My only friend.

"I'm sorry. What happened?"

"She was murdered. Shot."

"Really? Do they know by whom?"

She shook her head.

"She was still a student in Uppsala?"

Laura nodded. "Doing her doctorate."

"Was she involved in the riots?"

"No."

"Any involvement with student groups? Or people from other countries?"

She looked up. Wallenberg was studying her, a frown above his deep-set eyes. Did he think this had to do with the war?

"Not that I know of," she said.

"What was her name?" he asked.

"Britta Hallberg."

"Hopefully they'll have the time to investigate. With this war ongoing, priorities are skewed."

SHE SAT AT her desk until late afternoon without accomplishing anything. When her colleagues put on their jackets and grabbed their bags, she was startled. She, too, rose and put on her coat. She'd take the tram to her father's house. Anything but the empty apartment. The sky was still dark. The air heavy, not yet having had its release.

"Look who's here." Her father's eyes shone with contentment when he saw her.

"Look indeed," her grandfather said and beamed.

It had always only been the three of them, plus an army of servants and a governess. Laura's mother had left when she was little. She had no memories of her. Not a face, not a smell. Nothing. Her father didn't want to discuss her.

In her mind, Britta was there, asking, "Why haven't you gone to find her?" Mouth half-open, eyes on Laura's lips, interested in the response.

"She's a flapper," Laura had responded, using words she must have picked up from someone. She could hear how small-minded she sounded and felt furious with herself. There was also the usual hitch in her chest: bottled-up tears making themselves known.

Britta laughed. "So? I would probably have been one, too, if I'd been born ten years earlier."

"She left us." Laura cut her off. It was the one thing she didn't want to discuss with Britta.

More than anything, growing up, she had wanted a mother. She had looked at her friends' mothers and coveted the soft hands, the compassionate eyes. She assumed her mother looked like her. With her blond straight hair, her gray eyes, the cool expression on her face and the bump on her nose her father said made her look aristocratic, Laura did not have her father's more Mediterranean features. She used to imagine being out and about and coming face to face with her mother—both understanding immediately who the other one was. But it hadn't happened and there had been no attempt at contact. No, her mother had abandoned them. She had no mother.

"Emphasis on 'us,'" Britta had said and nodded. "It's for their sake you're not trying. For the sake of your father and your grandfather."

It was true that it could have been considered betrayal. "Why would you even be thinking about her?" her father had asked when she was younger, eyebrows knotted. "You never knew her. How could she possibly matter to you?"

Now Laura's father offered her his arm. "I'm very happy to see you," he said and patted her hand with his.

In the dining room, three covers were set out. They set a place for her each night, though nowadays, she rarely came home. She felt a sting of bad conscience as she imagined the two men sitting here together each night, in silence, her place empty. She inhaled the familiar smells of their meals: candle wax, cigar smoke, old books or newspapers. Fresh bread.

"So, how are you?" Her father poured her a glass of Riesling.

"Good."

"How's work?"

"Good."

"Wallenberg going strong?"

"Yes."

"It must be hard for him—all these moving parts, the change of direction—negotiating us out of what he negotiated us into." Her father sounded curious.

She shrugged and took a sip of her wine, even though she much preferred spirits.

"Any trips planned?"

"No."

She didn't want to talk about Wallenberg or about work.

Her father frowned at her brusqueness but let it pass. "The war is not finished yet, though. No matter how it plays out, there will be a new world order. One can only hope Sweden manages its balancing act until it's over."

She wasn't certain of her father's feelings about Germany. He'd been educated in Berlin. In the beginning, he'd openly admired Hitler and the order and vision he brought, but then, who hadn't? Everybody had been swept off their feet: the grandeur, the possibilities! Her father had seen Hitler speak live once. "He is magnetic," he'd said. Even now, when the war appeared to be turning, her father was sparing in his judgment of the man.

"I don't get the Germans," Laura muttered. "Look at Stalingrad. Hitler demanded they sacrifice themselves, no regard for the individuals. And they still follow him."

"Oh, Laura," her father said. "Then you have never felt the power of a true cause. They'd die for him any day. They *want* to die for him. They are lucky to have a genuine vocation."

She wanted to tell her father about Britta, but she didn't know how to approach it. Laura had brought Britta home once though she knew her father wouldn't like her. When she was little, he had picked among her friends, pointing out "good friend" and "not good friend," like you sort good apples from rotten ones. "People are simply destined for different things," he'd say. Or—quoting the Bible—"Iron sharpens iron." Britta had not been a "good friend," although her father hadn't been rude to her, just curt.

Afterward, Laura wanted to apologize but wasn't certain how to go about it. She felt disloyal.

"You are lucky to have a father who thinks the world of you and wants to protect you," Britta had said. "Mine always thought I was a tart."

Laura must have made a face, for Britta said, "Don't worry. He didn't exactly break me. I just wish . . ."

She hadn't finished the sentence, but there had been such longing in her voice that it had hurt to hear. Laura had hugged her.

"Thanks," Britta had said briskly, and she had never spoken of her father again.

==

LAURA'S FATHER AND grandfather continued to discuss the most recent developments. Her father was the governor of the Swedish Central Bank and now talked about the other heads of central banks he had met on his latest journey—the big dilemma for them all being how to protect their nations' gold—and their thoughts about the war. Normally, she'd engage in the discussion—that's how they had raised her; discussing, debating, arguing—but today, she had nothing to say.

The food was her favorite, sea bass with butter and new potatoes. Fish was a rarity these days. Rationed. She should eat. But she wasn't hungry. She opened her purse to look for her cigarettes, but as she stared at the empty pockets, she realized she must have forgotten them on the train.

"I ought to head home," Laura said.

Her father's face was blank. "I'd like you to stay."

She shook her head.

"Your room is still here."

"I have to get up early tomorrow, Dad," she said, but what she wanted to do was to find Erik. She had to share the loss with someone who, like herself, had known and loved Britta.

Her father kept looking at her but then nodded. "Alright. I'll have my driver take you."

Private driving might have been forbidden since the war, but her father was exempt. She rose and kissed him on his forehead. He patted her on her back.

"Come back soon, daughter."

"I will," she promised.

"I'll walk you out," her grandfather said.

Dusk had fallen while they were having dinner. The house looked a sad gray with its blackout curtains. The paved entrance gleamed black in the faint light from the porch as if it had rained when they were inside.

"What's going on?" her grandfather asked, as they stood on the porch. Of course he would have noticed.

"My university friend, Britta, died. She was killed. I found her today."

Her grandfather put his hand on her arm. She remembered how huge he had seemed to her when she was a child, towering over her. His booming voice had scared her. He'd been a general in the military; used to command. He'd ruled their house, too, until, one day, it became clear he no longer did and that her father had taken that role. Now he was smaller than she was, his hair tousled white, his blue eyes peering at her from underneath bushy white eyebrows.

"She had been tortured," she said. "Then shot."

"Tortured? Military connection?"

Laura shrugged. Her grandfather saw the military in every-thing. "She was a history student. She wasn't involved with the war."

"Most often, people are killed by those they know and love," her grandfather said, forehead wrinkled. "Only, not everyone knows where to get hold of a weapon."

The car pulled up to the stairs. She kissed her grandfather's cheek. "Don't forget to turn off the porch light."

"Be careful," her grandfather said and squeezed her arm.

"It has nothing to do with me."

He shook his head. "I know of only three reasons why you would torture a person."

"What?"

"The obvious one, of course—he wanted to find something

out. Did she know something she shouldn't have? Did she have any inappropriate connections?"

She thought about Andreas saying he'd seen Britta with the leader of the SSS.

"Or perhaps it was personal—someone wanting her to pay. An upset lover?"

It felt strange to hear her grandfather say the word.

"Or?"

"Or he's the kind who enjoys it."

DRIVING THROUGH STOCKHOLM at night felt eerie. All windows were dark, signs turned off, streetlights painted black. Shop windows were boarded over or covered by mounds of sandbags. Once, they met another car with shielded lights, just like on their own. A diplomat, perhaps, or some politician. The faint lights veered, and it was yet again dark. They drove on wet streets, crossed bridges under which water ran black. Cocooned in the car, it felt as if they were alone in a city of ghosts, normally inhabited by hundreds and thousands. When her father's driver had dropped her off, Laura waited inside the door until the faint lights were gone. The sole of her shoe was coming off. Her father could easily get her a new pair, but, somehow, she took pleasure in interacting with Germany in bad shoes. This is your fault, she would think. Your doing. Not that the people of Germany would care. And the sole was going to come off any day now and she couldn't see herself with wet feet.

Erik had remained in Stockholm. If it had been her country that was occupied, she'd have wanted to go back. Not to fight, but to live through what everyone else was living through. But she'd seen him with both Danish and Swedish officials—perhaps he was serving his country in ways she didn't know about. Everyone had secrets. A few times, he'd been at the Grand Hotel. They'd both been accompanied and had merely nodded to each other. But that's where she headed, thinking she would give it a try.

They hadn't spoken since university. It was how they'd left it, the five of them, three years ago. They had had the worst of fights, all of them screaming insults and accusations at one another. She wasn't certain there was any going back. Too much had been said. Then, before they could try to make up, Matti was drafted and Germany invaded Norway and Denmark and Karl-Henrik left, too. The only one Laura had stayed in touch with was Britta.

THE BAR WAS full of people, cigarette smoke thick beneath the meringue Swiss roof. People saved up cigarettes to be able to enjoy them on a night out. She loved the scent. She saw Erik before he saw her. He was wearing a dark suit with a gray waistcoat. A tie, too. She didn't think she'd seen him in a suit before—he was more of a trousers and crumpled shirtsleeves kind of man. He was at the bar underneath the arches, leaning on the marble counter. He pulled on his cigarette, and the narrow, unshaven cheeks seemed hollower. His nose was blunt, his chin squared off and his brown eyes almost black. He always made Laura think of a policeman on the hunt, with his face worn and pale, bags under his eyes. Yet despite his disheveled appearance, he was strangely attractive. This impression of being a pursuer, a hunter, was reinforced by his lean frame—as if he never slept or ate—and a restlessness: his fingers tapped, his head jerked. Erik had grown up in Copenhagen, with his parents and five siblings, but, from what he'd told them, he had spent most of his boyhood zipping through the harbor looking for goods to steal, or beseeching sailors for cigarettes, getting beaten up by his father when found out. He was a couple of years older than the rest of their group, and had done a short stint in the military—"bloody brutes." That he came to study at university was quite an accomplishment; but then, he was the only one besotted with history; the rest of them had ended up studying it for other reasons.

Erik hadn't been invited to the first *nachspiel* but had showed up anyway.

Professor Lindahl had been unmoved: "Mr. Anker, I believe," he'd said, when Erik had stood in the entrance to the vault and refused to leave, though the administrator had said the meal was by invitation only. "Why don't you join us? It does seem appropriate. With Laura and Britta from Sweden, Matti from Finland, and Karl-Henrik from Norway, we now have all the Nordic countries represented."

Later, Erik had become the favorite. Professor Lindahl often turned to him for his view.

There was a woman beside Erik, a blonde. He was trying to pick her up. He kept looking at her while drinking his beer . . . said something to her. The woman turned her shoulder. It made Laura laugh. A strange bark that got caught in her throat.

He noticed her now. He looked behind her, as if to see who she was with, his whole face lighting up when he saw she was on her own. "Laura!" he shouted. Not a policeman. A friend. The blonde beside him glanced up, but now he didn't notice. "Here!"

She made her way to the bar.

"*For helvede*, Miss Dahlgren," he cursed. "It's been much too long. Years!" He wrapped his arm around her, pressed her so hard against his chest she felt her earring pull out of her ear and kissed her cheek. He smelled of smoke and alcohol.

Just like before, she thought. She touched her earring. It was still there.

"What can I get you?" he asked.

"Same as you," she said.

The beer was ice cold and the glass steamed. The blonde looked over her shoulder at Erik. She was busty, lips too red. A poor copy of Britta, Laura thought.

To her horror, her eyes filled with tears. She blinked. Erik took one look at her, stubbed out his cigarette, grabbed her arm and his drink and guided her away from the bar to a table in a corner, where they sat down in the armchairs. He leaned forward, serious now.

"What's going on?" he asked.

"Britta is dead," she said. His hands on his knees twitched. "No."

She nodded.

He looked her in her eye as if to verify it was true, then exhaled and leaned back. His mouth twisted. He rubbed his cheeks, his chin, then his head—first with one hand, then two. He looked as if he might cry. He broke off in the middle of the movement and forced himself to be still. "What happened?"

"She was killed. I found her."

"You found her?"

Laura nodded again. "She'd been tortured, then shot."

"*Tortured?*" His voice was hoarse. "Are you sure?"

She nodded.

"Fuck!" he exclaimed. His eyes were large, his hair standing up. If he'd been alone, he would have thrown his glass, she thought. Broken it. A visual of a thousand shards down a wall.

He looked away, blinked, grabbed his beer and took a swig.

There was more; what she hadn't dared to think through for herself, but that she had to say now . . . something that he would understand. She leaned forward, put her hand on his arm. "Erik, her eye had been gouged out."

He inhaled. A rasping sound. "What do you mean?"

"Only one eye," she said.

She could see his mind working. He was thinking the same thing as her.

"That's a coincidence," he said.

It had to be, of course.

"Andreas said he'd seen Britta with Sven Olov Lindholm, the head of the Swedish Nazi SSS before the riots," she continued, speaking eagerly now, wanting to let it all out.

Erik scoffed. "Britta with the Nazis? Never!"

"That's what I felt," she admitted.

"Why were you there?"

"Andreas called me and said she was missing. Erik, do you know what she was up to?"

"What do you mean 'up to'?"

"She was *tortured*," Laura repeated, stressing the word. "I saw her . . . Her body was cut." She had to swallow. "And then she was shot in the temple. Executed. There must be a reason."

"I haven't seen her since we left university. I have no idea what was going on in her life now. If I ever did." He lit a cigarette, his face still pale. "What do the police say?" He spoke with the cigarette in the corner of his mouth.

"They don't know anything. But Britta came to see me in early spring."

"Yes?"

"I think she was frightened."

"Of what?" Erik caught her eyes through the smoke.

"She didn't say."

"That doesn't sound like her."

She shrugged. She was certain.

"What is he like, the policeman investigating?" Erik asked.

"He seems thorough."

She kept thinking of the missing eye and of the god Odin. Odin had sacrificed an eye to be allowed to drink from the well of cosmic knowledge. He had gouged it out himself and thrown it into the water.

"No sacrifice too great for wisdom," Britta had said that afternoon, when Erik had finished telling them that story. "I'd do it. One eye for wisdom. Easy choice."

"Interesting." Matti had leaned forward. "Traditionally, the eye represents insight. So, Odin basically exchanged one kind of insight for another."

"Mimir was the guardian of the well," Erik had said. "The name Mimir means 'the Rememberer.' His wisdom was the wisdom of the traditions, their memories. Odin traded an everyday way of seeing things for another mode; that of history."

But Britta was dead. Whatever new wisdom she had acquired was gone with her.

5.

JENS

In the hallway: "You're late." Kristina was dressed in a black silk blouse, wide silk trousers, her dark hair held back by a simple hairband, her earrings pearl.

"Just a tiny bit." He kissed her just as she turned her head and ended up kissing her ear, which left a bitter taste of hairspray or perfume in his mouth. She swept past him with a big smile on her face; he knew, even though he could only see her tall back in the shimmering blouse. She turned in the doorway to wave at him to come.

Jens inhaled and straightened up. The candlelit dining room floated with colored silk and cigar smoke. There was music: cool, smooth jazz. It was Kristina's father's apartment, but he and his wife were posted abroad.

"Ah, the wayward young man!" Artur said. "Now we can eat." Artur was Kristina's father's friend and her godfather. A former businessman, now retired; well mannered, a good conversationalist, he was invited to all Kristina's parties. He was a gentleman: approachable, generous, always ready to laugh. Together, Kristina and her godfather were an unbeatable team. They could get the most reserved people to relax and leave feeling like old friends.

Artur patted him on his shoulder. Jens smiled. Artur made the introductions: a colonel, thirty years Jens's senior, a well-dressed army man with iron-colored hair above large ears and dreamy eyes—though there was little that was pensive about him, heading up, as he did, the command expedition of the land defense working for the minister. His wife was a large woman with white hair and round cheeks. Another Mr. and Mrs.: him, tall and sparse, serious face, a director at Volvo; his wife, dark-haired, same serious long face as her husband. Employed by the Scandinavian Bank, nevertheless. There was a delightful, smiling, dark-haired young woman in a suit who went by the name of Barbro Cassel; nonchalant eyes, smoking, a secretary at the German trade delegation. Kristina's hand touched his arm.

And then, from the kitchen, a German accent, followed by the voice of Kristina's chef responding to what had been said or asked.

Out came the envoy to the German trade delegation, Karl Schnurre, the person who showed up whenever Hitler had a message for the Swedes. Between two fingers, he held a piece of ham. "*Köstlich!*" he exclaimed. "Tasty." He raised his hand above his head and dropped the meat into his mouth. A snake swallowing a mouse. "Ah, Jens!" he said, rubbing his hands together to wipe his glistening digits. "I haven't seen you for a while. It's working out with Günther, then?"

"Ah, it's true," Barbro Cassel had appeared by Schnurre's side, tilted champagne glass in her hand. "You are Günther's secretary, right?"

Jens daren't look at Kristina. Schnurre. What on earth . . . ? He managed a smile and shook his hand that a second ago had held ham.

"Yes." He nodded.

"He's a good man," the German said.

I know you like him, Jens thought. The two of them met regularly, whenever Schnurre had a message from his overlords, or Günther wanted one passed back. Though relations had soured, with Sweden now offering free entry to Jews, causing Germany to complain that the Swedes were trying to sabotage the German Jewish actions.

"Let's sit down," Kristina said.

Schnurre offered his arm to Barbro Cassel.

Across the table, Jens caught Artur's gaze. *Were you in on this?* The older man shook his head, his eyes asking back, *Will you make a scene?* No. No, of course not.

And Kristina? A diplomat's daughter, she engaged in diplomacy. Though it was an unfair struggle. They spoke of everything apart from the war: the winter and the spring that seemed to dawdle; the upcoming premier of the play *We Have Our Freedom!* God, who mentioned that? The German at the table lit Fräulein Cassel's cigarette. Quickly, they moved on to travels, though nobody moved about much these days for obvious reasons and so they found themselves back at the war again. They discussed food—and ended up with the shortages and the rationing and stopped right before anyone mentioned the German blockade on boats to and from Sweden. They talked about the prime minister and ended up lamenting the weak government, veering dangerously close to repeating the arguments of the failure of democracy. News? Oh, no—change the subject straight away. Luckily, Schnurre was focused on Barbro Cassel and didn't seem to hear much. Every time their conversation ended up on a topic that could become a problem, Jens would glance at Schnurre and exhale as the German didn't react.

And on every occasion, Barbro would catch Jens's eye, her face amused as if she were having the most wonderful time.

You had to admire Kristina, Jens thought. Nothing fazed her. Wherever the discussion took them, she would find a way to turn it onto a different subject. Perhaps she made a list of acceptable matters ahead of a dinner. He could see her sitting by her desk, the mahogany one with the leather surface, thinking through implications of various conversations, crossing topics out, adding others, planning transitions.

Jens thought about the dissertation he'd been sent: *Nordic Relations Through the Ages—Denmark, Norway and Sweden on a New Path*. He was certain the German would have a view on that. After all, they were trying to design that path.

He could feel himself drifting. Artur said something, the others laughed. Kristina's hand touched his thigh. *Stay focused.* She leaned forward. In the neck of her blouse, a glimpse of a red lace bra.

Things got better when it was time for coffee and cake. Karl Schnurre, mood lightened by excellent drink and food, entertained them with audacious stories about meetings with Hitler, though they didn't know if they dared to laugh or not.

Jens wondered about Kristina's friend, Barbro.

There were two information-gathering units in Sweden: the C-Bureau and the Security Services. Everyone knew about the Security Services, but not about the C-Bureau's existence— even people who should have. Jens wouldn't have known about it if it hadn't been for his close friend, Sven. And Sven knew because his father had been involved in financing the agency before it existed formally—set up by people who felt the government wasn't doing enough to protect the country. Stockholm was like that. Secrets floated just beneath the surface. Perhaps because the country wasn't at war and the personal risks seemed minimal, people talked. Most people knew things they weren't supposed to. Many were involved somehow: activists, spies or double agents.

Was Barbro a member of the C-Bureau? A so-called swallow? The bureau enlisted young women, put them into situations where they could acquire information.

If she wasn't already, they should recruit her, he thought.

And soon it was time to break up, and everyone began to move more quickly now. Jens wished he could hear what the husbands and wives would make of the dinner once they were out the door and certain they weren't overheard. Artur pulled Jens to his chest and rolled his eyes. *We made it.* Jens cleared his throat. There were *thank you*s and *let's do this again*s, and a brief hallway conversation between him and Schnurre:

"Talk to your boss," Schnurre said. "Tell him to stop asking about Jews. It's annoying people at the highest level."

Hitler. He meant Hitler himself. Sweden had finally declared that it would offer assistance to any Jew who reached its borders. Sweden now also actively sought out Jews with any kind of Swedish links and inquired as to their whereabouts.

"The fate of the Jews is important to us," Jens ventured. "Look at how the Swedes reacted when Norway's Jews were deported."

"But why?" Schnurre seemed truly interested.

Now Jens couldn't help himself. "They're human. We know what you're doing to them. The transportations, the concentration camps . . ."

The German was studying him. His cigar hung from his lips. "Sweden should be grateful to Germany for our sacrifice in fighting our common enemy in the East," he said then, his gaze hard.

"You think you Swedes are clean? You should have a look in your own cupboards."

Schnurre pressed a finger to Jens's chest and looked him in the eye, as if to impress his words on him, or put a full stop to the conversation. "Nah," he said and nodded, but it sounded like "I dare you."

What?

Once the flat was quiet, Jens sighed, exhausted. He walked into the living room. What had Schnurre meant? Kristina was turning off the lamps, so they came to stand in the dark. She came close and kissed him.

"Angry?" She put a finger in his tie, loosened it. He put his hands on her hips, felt them move under the silk against him. She leaned back to look at him.

He was too tired to be angry.

"It's important to keep them close to us," she said. "It is not yet certain where things will end up."

"Now you sound like Günther."

She shrugged. "He's right. We don't yet know."

Jens didn't respond.

"Besides, it wasn't my fault," she said. "I invited Barbro and she called this afternoon asking if she could bring Karl along."

Already on a first name basis with him, he thought.

"You should have said no."

"Barbro is an old friend. And it's just a dinner," she said.

That got a rise out of him. "It is never 'just a dinner,'" he said. "You know what they do to people in their country. You know what they do to people in countries they conquer. It is never ever 'just a dinner.'"

She didn't respond straightaway. She kissed him again on his cheek, on his neck. "But they are here," she whispered in his ear. "Whether we like it or not. They might win this war and we might have to learn to get on with them."

Jens withdrew. "'Get on with them,'" he repeated. "Never."

She put a finger across his lips. "The government needs people like you, but you have to learn to serve the government and not your own feelings."

"I don't ever want to have them for dinner again." He meant the Germans. All Germans, no exception. "Make no mistake, Kristina, if this happens once more, I'll leave," he threatened, though they both knew he wouldn't. There could be ramifications and he was scared. They were all scared. That was the goddamn problem.

Kristina smiled and kissed him on his mouth.

He broke away. "Did the colonel know?"

"What?"

"Did he know Schnurre was coming, or was it a surprise to him?"

"I just had the time to call him ahead of time," she said. "He alone knew."

"He wasn't bothered?"

She shook her head, kissed him again. "He said they had met before."

"Did you hear what Schnurre said? That we Swedes should have a look in our own cupboards?"

She didn't respond. Instead, she pushed him gently backward until he sat down on the sofa. Straddling him, her eyes on his, she loosened her tie-back blouse and opened it, her chest shining white in the shadowy living room, the red bra he'd glimpsed during dinner looking like the darkest wine. Impossible to remain angry. Damn the Germans, he thought. Damn the war, too. He ran a finger down her neck and farther.

She shivered, arched her back and slid her hips toward him, then back. Making room for him, he thought, and found the thought irresistible.

He circled her waist with his arm, turned her over onto her back on the sofa and pulled a tasseled pillow under her head. He kissed the white skin on her chest and then on her abdomen.

She sighed. Her hips rocked. Up and down. Up. Then her fingers were in his hair, pulling him up, her mouth against his, unzipping him, not waiting any longer. He opened her trousers and she was in his hand, wet, lovely. She jiggled to rid herself of her pants, pushed them off with one foot, then the other, lifted herself up against him, and he was inside.

Impossible to think about anything but this.

This.

Her arms around his back, her tongue in his mouth, the smell of her hair, sliding slowly, faster: thrusting. He could go on forever.

She cried out, tensed, shuddered, and he tried to wait—he could go on forever—but to no avail.

They clung to each other.

"Again," she said, when their breaths had quietened.

Yes, again.

6.

Blackåsen Mountain

Rolf Sandler hadn't been in his post for long, but already it was clear to him that he had underestimated the difficulties. *Mining director of Blackåsen mine*. He loved the sound of it. The position of mining director had looked like the perfect match for him: important for the nation and a huge step up for someone so young and ambitious.

The prime minister himself had called him on his appointment. "You have no idea how important your role is," he'd said. "The mine is what keeps Sweden out of the war. Ensure the production targets are met no matter what, and by God, ensure it remains in our hands."

On his arrival, he'd been surprised at how advanced Blackåsen had been. A model village. The workers' dwellings were shaped like inkwells; wooden apartment houses painted in red, yellow or green, with room for two families downstairs and two bachelors upstairs, looked neat and brightened the town. The large white school was magnificent; the red wooden church with its pointy gables in all directions and its unique square shape. It was a small town, but they had the amenities they needed. Plumbing, space, parks.

His own large villa with its bays could match any house in Stockholm.

There were the challenges he had anticipated: the workers were poor, despite the modernity of the town. They looked at him with a mixture of reverence and fear. The Sami workers eyed him with something akin to hatred. The ones he met were forced laborers. He didn't understand enough about their tribes roaming the forests and this worried him.

Tensions between the population and the Germans were palpable. Each time a train with German soldiers passed through, he increased security. There were Norwegians fleeing through town that he tried to avoid seeing . . . Yes, these challenges he had expected. But some things he hadn't foreseen.

Winter, for example. Winter had shocked him. The darkness didn't lift. For six months, they lived in never-ending night. It was like being in a continuous dream. He was always tired, his thinking sluggish. And the cold! He couldn't have imagined you could live in such extreme cold.

As winter proceeded, and he was getting ready in the morning, he could see how his neat dark beard grew scraggly despite his care; his skin, usually with a warm olive tone, paled; and there were dark, dry shadows supporting his blue but bloodshot eyes. It wasn't long before he looked much older than his thirty-eight years.

Then it was his relationship with the foreman, Hallberg. After eight months, they still didn't see eye to eye. They were very different people, of course. One educated, one a former worker himself. One a newcomer, the other one here for four decades. The director had a feeling the foreman still did not see him as his boss. But Sandler needed Hallberg to be on his side. If it didn't change, he'd have to replace him.

The second thing, and perhaps the most worrying, was that he hadn't expected there would be areas in this town—on his own mountain—over which he had little control.

Lennart Notholm, owner of the local hotel, the Winter Palace, had come to see him the second day after his arrival.

Director Sandler had taken an immediate dislike to the man. It was his eyes, he thought. With most people, if you looked them in the eye, you felt a connection. With this man, there was nothing. He wore the right clothing but was still unkempt. His tunic was stained and frayed. He was unshaven. There was dirt under his fingernails. All this, despite him being wealthy enough to own a hotel.

"I have just come to ensure that everything will continue as usual," Notholm had said.

"I have no idea," Sandler had answered. "What is 'usual'?"

"We are renting some land from the mining company."

"Who is 'we'?"

Notholm reached for the photo frame on Sandler's desk—a photo of his nephews—lifted it up and looked at it. "Some local businessmen."

The director could feel himself bristle. "Where? Outside town, or . . . ?"

"No, on the mountain itself."

That was highly irregular. He didn't want nonworkers on the mountain. The risks were simply too high.

"Then no. That will have to stop," Sandler said.

Lennart Notholm put the photo back on his desk and smiled a lopsided grin, his eyes still cold. "I suggest you find out before speaking. Ask your superiors. *Director*." His voice was full of scorn.

Sandler had sent him packing.

The thing was, when Sandler had called his superior, the man had said to leave it be. He had known this man for years. He had worked for him in one form or another ever since he first became an engineer. But, this time, when Sandler protested, his boss did not hear him out. Instead, he raised his voice and said, "Leave them alone. This is beyond you. I expect to hear you have given them your fullest cooperation."

"But it's not safe," Sandler had insisted. "We're setting explosives in the mine every day. They could get hurt. Or worse."

"This has been studied. You will get nowhere close to them for a while yet."

"But . . ."

"I will only say this once more. Leave him to it. Leave *them* to it. Their access has been granted from the highest levels. If you disturb them in any way, you will never work in the industry again."

And he had hung up.

The director couldn't believe his ears. This was "beyond him"? "He would never work in the industry again"?

Notholm had smiled when Sandler had told him that all would continue as usual.

"We are working on a secret project," he'd said. "Nobody can approach. And I mean nobody."

And so, there were areas on his own mountain where the director could not go, and he did not like it one bit.

OUTSIDE, THE TOWN had fallen silent. Sandler rose from his desk. In a mining town, there was always a racket: explosions from the dynamite, the crash of iron being tipped, the droning of the sorting band, the chewing of the big grinder. Quiet was bad.

He grabbed his jacket and walked out onto the porch. Already, they were coming for him on the road: the foreman and a couple of other men.

"A body," Hallberg said, grimly.

"An explosion gone wrong?"

"Not quite."

Sandler waited.

"We found him at the bottom of the mountain."

"Who is it?"

"Georg Ek."

A vague image of a man: short, heavy set, dark. Spoke with a southern accent?

"What happened?"

Hallberg was looking back toward the mountain. "I don't know," he admitted. "He's been gone since Friday night. His wife reported him missing on Saturday morning."

The director knew well what Friday evenings looked like for the miners even though nobody would ever admit it to him.

"Why wasn't I informed he was missing?"

The foreman shrugged. "We thought he might have gotten lost. We've been looking for him in the forest."

"Take me there," he said.

Dr. Ingemarsson was already there when they arrived. He was standing in the snow, bent over what looked like a rolled-up carpet. His doctor's bag was closed. It wouldn't be needed this time. Sandler took big strides through the snow to reach him. As he approached, it became clear the roll was a man.

"What happened to him?"

The doctor stood up and stretched his back. He pointed up the mountain. "I'm guessing that he was up there and fell . . . It looks to me like it might have happened a few days ago. His body is frozen solid."

He'd gone missing on Friday night.

"What on earth would he be doing up there Friday night?" Sandler asked.

The foreman shook his head. "I have no idea."

"And the night shift? Nobody saw him?"

"The night shift finished early on Friday. They needed to blow in the mine and decided to wait until daylight. And nobody comes this way any longer."

Sandler bent over the man on the ground. His head was cracked open. The edges of the wound seemed pushed in, rounded. He felt slightly nauseous. There were the usual scrapes and bruises that he would have expected.

"His neck isn't twisted," he said, hesitantly.

"It doesn't need to be. If you're unlucky . . ." Doctor Ingermarsson shrugged.

"This wound?" Sandler pointed to the open head.

"I guess that's what happened: he hit a stone on the way down."

The foreman wrinkled his forehead. The director sighed and straightened.

Two Sami men approached with a stretcher. They'd been told to take the body away, he assumed. They were not young, and yet their steps were light, their bodies supple. It was as if the snow and the ice on the ground meant nothing to them. The two stopped at a distance. There, they bent their heads. Not out of respect, Sandler thought. More like . . . keeping themselves apart.

The sun had heaved itself up over the horizon and painted

the landscape a cold gray. He was going to have to tell the widow. He sighed. He believed they had young children, too.

As he left, he looked back. The Sami were now standing by the body. One of them gazed up the mountain, then touched his forehead and his heart.

As if crossing himself.

7.

LAURA

Laura sat at her desk, staring at papers without understanding, shuffling them from one pile to another, then back again.

On the radio, they were talking about the mass graves found in Poland. Tens of thousands of Polish officers apparently killed by the Reds. Laura's chest felt tight as she listened. No one wanted Germany to win, but the alternative was horrific. They said that in the Baltic countries, during the year the Russians were in charge, eighty thousand people had disappeared. It was such an awful, awful world . . . Such a . . .

She found herself moving the papers across her desk again and forced her hands to still. Stop, she told herself. Just stop. What good did it do to get caught up in the miseries of the world?

After leaving Erik that night, she hadn't been able to sleep and then she hadn't been able to get up. Friday, she'd called in sick for the first time in her whole life. She had then spent the weekend in bed. Slowly, the walls moved closer. The room turned cold. She was shivering, but couldn't go and get another blanket. She couldn't cry—daren't cry. She daren't move. In the end, she daren't swallow. She had lain silent in bed, eyes wide open, mouth dry, heart pounding, ripped apart—for that was what the grief felt like; as if she had been cut open and left that way, never to close again.

She might be ill: she had a headache and a sour taste in her mouth. She should not have come to work. She wasn't ready. Nothing here was important today. In fact, nothing here might ever feel important again. All that mattered was that Britta, the best friend she'd ever had, was dead. What would have happened, she thought, if Britta had told her what was bothering her that day? Surely together, they would have found a solution and Britta would still be among them, alive, not tortured to death. *Tortured* . . . She shrank at the thought. If only she had forced her friend to talk.

One time, Laura had been sad. Funny how the reason had now vanished from her memory, but she remembered that at the time, it had appeared detrimental to her very existence. They'd been at a bar, Laura had tried to put on a good show, and she thought she'd succeeded. *Don't show weakness. People eat you up if you are weak.* Her father's words echoed in her mind. Britta and her date were leaving. Britta came to say goodbye and she could read the misery on Laura's face. She'd wrapped her arms around Laura. "We need to leave," her date had said, stooping over her. "We'll miss the play." The play was sold out months ahead; it was impossible to get tickets. Britta had been excited about it. And yet Britta had turned on him, despite Laura's protests: "This is my best friend," she'd said. "My best friend is hurting. If you don't get that I must stay here with her, you are more stupid than I thought." She'd sent him packing. Later, she'd mocked Laura's father. "Not show weakness? What rubbish! Weak is strong. Messy is strong. Together is strong. And your father . . ." She'd laughed. "He is old and he is dead wrong."

And she'd kissed Laura with an open mouth.

Laura hadn't said, but she had felt that her father was right. How she wished she'd been more callous. She tried her best to be strong, and to prove to him that she was, but there was something missing in her; she didn't have what it took. But Britta loved her regardless. And Britta had stayed.

Why had Laura not done the same for Britta? What kind of a selfish person does not insist on being told what is going on with their friends? Why hadn't she wanted to know what was wrong? Who was she becoming?

"The boss wants to see you," Dagmar said.

Laura sighed. She'd be no good to him today. She picked up her notebook and a pen. In his office, Wallenberg nodded to her to sit down.

"Your friend," he said, "who was killed . . ."

Britta? Why was he asking about her? Her stomach clenched. "Yes?"

"She is from Blackåsen."

"Yes."

"Her father is the foreman of the iron mine."

"Yes." Did she know this? She wasn't certain. Britta had said her father had thought she was a tart.

"Her death might not be a coincidence," Wallenberg said.

She shook her head, didn't understand, and then she did.

"No," she said. "I didn't talk to her about my work. Ever." I never talk to anyone about our work, she thought. She knew how sensitive it was, balancing demands, Swedish iron to Germany, German coal to Sweden. Wallenberg's connections with the secret opposition in Germany; she'd even been privy to some of those meetings. She had his trust and she wouldn't betray his confidence; he must know this.

"I spoke to the police this morning. She was tortured." Wallenberg picked up a paper from his desk and studied it. Had he obtained a copy of the police report? It shouldn't surprise her. The Wallenbergs were a prominent Swedish family. The two brothers, Jacob and Marcus, were helping Sweden in their negotiations with Germany and the Allies. Whatever a Wallenberg wanted, he would have no problem obtaining.

"Perhaps the perpetrator hoped you had told her about the negotiations," Wallenberg said.

Laura shrugged. She couldn't know that.

"The gun she was killed with was a Walther HP. German."

"German?"

"It doesn't tell us much," he said. "They have been imported in rather large numbers. I would expect to find them among the police and the military."

Police. Military. Nothing of this made sense.

He looked down at the papers again. "Cuts—lots of them, bruises, missing one eye and then shot . . . Her body had been moved after she was killed, placed in the Historical Society in Uppsala."

"Moved?"

"Yes, she wasn't killed where she was found."

She frowned. "How could that be? She was found in the middle of town!"

He shook his head. "I don't know. But more important is *why*. Why would they want her body at the Historical Society? What are they trying to do or say with this? There has to be a reason."

He was right: why on earth would someone want her to be found at the Historical Society? If the killer had to take the risk of moving her body to get her there, it must mean something. Why there?

He put the papers down on his desk. "It seems too much of a coincidence that you are on this project; we are trying to substantially reduce the trade with Germany, and now your best friend is killed by a German weapon and in such a manner. *And* her father is the foreman of the mine. We need to know more."

"The police . . ."

He shook his head. "The police may or may not see the connection. Do you know Britta's father?"

"I've never met him."

"I want you to talk to him. I want you to ask around among her friends, too . . . see if she had received threats, if she feared anyone. I need to know for certain this is not linked to us. I need to know if this has anything to do with Germany."

She nodded. She had no other choice.

He met her gaze, held it. "If there is a connection, I might be putting you in harm's way. I am aware of this. But there's no one who's in a better position to find out. You knew her, you are smart. You know how important our work is."

"Of course, I'll go," she said. She hesitated. Had to know. "Was she alive . . . Was she alive all along when he hurt her?"

His face was serious, and he nodded.

"I am sorry," he added.

Back at her desk, she sank down onto her chair. Her legs felt weak. She tried to imagine the events, but it was beyond what she was capable of. She mustn't go there.

She understood why Wallenberg thought the way he did. If Laura had spoken with anyone about her work, it would have been Britta. But she didn't believe this was the reason for Britta's death. If it were, they ought to have come for Laura directly. Whoever killed Britta—if they had followed her—must have known that Laura and Britta didn't often see each other any longer.

There was the gun, the *German* gun. But there was a war. A person determined enough could get hold of a gun without too much trouble.

She thought about the torture. Had Britta told the killer what he wanted to know? Had she been able to? Or had she known it wouldn't matter whatever she did? Laura shivered.

Her phone rang, and her hand shot out to lift the receiver.

"How are you?"

Erik. She exhaled.

"I've been better," she said, her voice warm.

"What you need is a drink. I could use one, too."

"I can't today. Another time, I would love to." She meant it. "My boss wants me to go back to Uppsala and ask around about Britta."

As she said it, she was already cursing herself. She shouldn't have told him.

Erik paused. "He can't ask you to do that. That's a job for the police. And why would he want it? Britta's death has nothing to do with him. Or with you."

"He's worried there's a connection to our trade delegation. He thinks perhaps the killer thought I had told her things."

"This has nothing to do with you," Erik repeated. "*You* must see that. You know what she was like. There were always hurt people around Britta."

You being one of them, she thought. Laura had been jealous of the obvious attraction between Britta and Erik, of being wanted in that way: a desire lingering on, unconsummated. The pain and delight of wanting. But it had hurt Erik, she was certain. "You're choosing not to remember," Erik said, and he did sound sad. "You didn't think her flings mattered, but perhaps those who fell in love with her didn't agree."

"Everyone liked her," Laura had told the policeman. And that was true. In general. But there had been heartbreaks. Partners who wouldn't accept it was over. Men showing up in strange places, at strange times, with pleas, demands, threats. Britta had been irresistible, and she had used it to her advantage. She rarely dated the same man twice. Her close friends warned Britta at one point, only for her to belittle their concerns. So they'd left it. They were at university—people were supposed to mess about. But it was quite possible a lover had not been able to let go.

"I remember," she said. "Her body was moved after her death, Erik, and then they left her at the Historical Society. Why there?"

"Why not, Laura?" he said, and she could almost hear him shrug. "It stands mostly empty. Perhaps the killer knew that."

Yes, she thought, perhaps.

"It's just that it was special to us," she said.

"It was special to a lot of people."

That was true.

"You're still going?" he said.

"I have to."

He sighed. "Have it your own way. But be careful. You don't know what's behind this."

"I will," she promised. "I'm only going to see if there appear to be links to Wallenberg's negotiation team. That's all."

They hung up.

There had been slighted lovers, that was true. But the

Historical Society hadn't been broken into. The perpetrator had used a key. To take a key meant planning. And he had locked the door behind himself before leaving. She assumed—perhaps wrongly—that a slighted lover would have been acting on impulse. That it would have been clumsy, messy.

This had been cold.

Erik had sounded certain, and he knew what it felt like, hurting for love. But then, he hadn't seen the body.

SHE AND ERIK should have met up earlier, seeing as they were both in Stockholm. Erik and Britta had been special, that was true, but she and Erik had been friends, too. She remembered once, after a long night out, Erik coming to her apartment wearing Laura's black feather fascinator.

"You forgot something," he'd said.

"What?" she'd asked. "Is it the bowtie?"

He'd laughed and handed her the hat.

"Surely someone like you would have a drink for a thirsty man?"

She'd opened a bottle of champagne and they'd stood by her window drinking straight from the bottle, passing it between them, looking out on students making their way home in the early morning hours.

"Fucking upper-class brats," he'd said, swaying. There had been something like hatred in his voice.

"I'm one, too," she'd reminded him, gently.

He had stirred, turned to her, smiled and toasted her. "You are a particularly lovely upper-class brat," he'd said. "A beautiful, delightful upper-class brat. A goddess, even . . ."

For a moment, she'd thought they might kiss, but a car horn honked, they both looked up and the moment was gone.

Perhaps they hadn't met up earlier because it had to be the five of them for things to make sense, she thought now; for *them* to make sense. She would have spent time with Britta on her own, of course, but the others? And now, the war had taken them in such different directions. It had taken her to restaurants, hotels and negotiation rooms. She didn't want to imagine where it'd taken Matti and Karl-Henrik.

Her head still hurt. She sighed, tasted her own sour breath and felt nauseous again.

"Ask around," Wallenberg had said. Well, the first one she wanted to talk to again was Andreas. He was there when it started and knew more than he had wanted to tell her, she was certain. She needed to find out who Britta's friends were now. She should see Professor Lindahl, too.

The phone rang again. This time it was Ackerman, the policeman.

"I want you to come in and meet with us again," he said.

Was he the one who had given Wallenberg a copy of the police report?

"I've told you what I know," she said.

"There have been developments. We need to ask you more questions."

She had no reason to feel worried, and yet she did. Perhaps this was how you felt when you were meeting the police. She didn't know; didn't have that experience. They agreed to meet again the following day.

As they hung up, she realized she felt better. How peculiar. But it was action, she thought; doing, and not just sitting and thinking. A project. Dotting the i's and crossing the t's for Wallenberg and, at the same time, helping Britta. She would find out if there were any German connections in Britta's life or other people asking questions about mines. That shouldn't be too hard. Uppsala was small: people ought to have noticed. She stood up. She'd pack a bag. Stay the night.

8.

Foreign Minister Christian Günther paced in the office to which he had called Jens. He passed his enormous desk, the gilded gigantic mirror, the statuette unidentifiable to Jens.

Staffan Söderblom had left as Jens arrived. Jens wished he knew what they had talked about.

"It will not do," Günther said to Jens, punctuating each word. *Will. Not.*

His face was drawn, but the gaze behind the round glasses was intense. He was talking about the German mines found in Swedish waters. About *Ulven*'s men dead at the bottom of the sea.

Jens thought about the German response to their protest—simply referring to a Swedish order of 1940, according to which Swedish submarines should avoid diving exercises when German ships were close. The order did exist. They had gone and found it, the minister harrumphing when he saw his own signature.

"I want you to draft a response," Günther said. "State that Swedish ships on Swedish waters can do whatever they want, and that German mines on Swedish territory are completely unacceptable."

73

Jens wrote it down.

"Send it to the Swedish delegation in Germany," Günther said. "Have them pass the message on."

Jens nodded.

"They won't need to have any meetings," Günther grumbled.

Everyone knew whatever was sent to the Swedish delegation in Berlin made its way seamlessly to the Gestapo and the SS.

"Anything else?"

"Have a word with the US ambassador—see what they are up to in Finland, with the Russians. If anything," he added. "Who would listen to us?"

Günther's warnings to the Allies about the Soviet Union had become a consistent feature since Stalingrad. He was worried; they all were. But so far, Jens had seen no proof that the warnings were being heeded.

Günther sat down in his chair. "That's all for now."

Jens hesitated.

"Yes?" Günther looked up.

"I was at a dinner yesterday." Jens hoped he wouldn't have to say it was his fiancée, Kristina, who had arranged it. "Karl Schnurre attended."

"So Hitler's emissary is back in town?" Günther leaned back in his chair. He steepled his fingertips, considering.

"He told me to tell you not to inquire about the fate of Jews. Said it was 'annoying people at the highest level.' I told him the fate of the Jews mattered to us Swedes. Said he only had to look to the Swedish response to the deportation of the Norwegian Jews to see that."

Günther exhaled. "And we will work harder than ever," he vowed. "Save as many as we can."

"Schnurre said something bizarre, though. He said, 'You

think you Swedes are clean?' and that we should look in our own cupboards."

Günther shrugged. "They'll never see they've done wrong," he said, speaking about the Germans. "I think if the entire world so judged them, they wouldn't see it. Anything else?"

Jens hesitated. "The archivist, Daniel Jonsson, had a word with me."

Günther's brows shot together. "What does he want this time?"

"He asked for notes from the recent calls between us and the Danish foreign minister and the Norwegian foreign minister in exile, to put them in the records."

"He's mistaken." Günther looked down at his calendar.

"What do you mean?"

"There have been no recent phone calls between me and them."

"Daniel said—"

Günther raised his voice. "I don't care what he said. He's wrong."

Daniel was methodical. He'd found the calls in the register of the Security Services. And hadn't Daniel said he'd checked with his counterparts?

He found the minister studying him.

"How long have you been working for me now, Jens?"

"Six months."

Günther nodded. "I'd like you to speak with Daniel and ask him to stop requesting my records—I assume this is what he has done. This time, he got it wrong. Errors can start all kinds of rumors."

"He is normally diligent," Jens said. "And I don't see how I can ask him to stop requesting information." It was the archivist's job. To document. To know what was going on.

Günther silenced him with one acidic look. "Tell him to stop," he repeated, in a low voice. "Do you know why I chose you to become my secretary?"

"No."

"I took you on because you were not one of those career civil servants entangled in their routines and petty concerns. You are here for me alone. You can be gone just as easily."

Jens found himself fidgeting with his pen and forced himself to stay still.

"Are we clear?" Günther asked.

"Perfectly."

BACK AT HIS office, Jens sat down in his chair, not certain what had just happened. When a colleague infuriated Günther, he normally displayed a nonchalant attitude and simply ignored the person in question. Jens had never seen him threaten; for that's what he had done: threatened. Daniel had struck Jens as good at his job, conscientious, meticulous. But this time, what Daniel had told him was perhaps incorrect and had gotten him into trouble. Though to ask that the archivist stop requesting the minister's records seemed an excessive response to a mistake. Documenting was the archivists' job. By law, Jens was certain. Or at least in the charter for how a ministry should be run.

He rose and walked down the corridor to Daniel's office. He found the archivist hunched over a bunch of papers on his desk, several empty coffee cups beside him.

"Oh, Jens," the archivist said, pushing up his glasses on his nose with a finger. "Did you manage to find anything out about those phone calls?"

Jens hesitated, closing the door behind him. "I spoke with the minister this morning."

"Yes?"

"He says he hasn't spoken to the Danish or Norwegian ministers for a long time."

The archivist's mouth hung open. "But he did," he said finally.

Jens raised his eyebrows.

Daniel rose, walked to another table, searched among the papers. "Hold on." He turned to the bookshelf. "I had it right here," he mumbled.

"You got me into trouble with Günther."

"Wait. Jens, I swear it was here."

Jens waited.

After a while, Daniel stopped. He faced Jens, his hands outstretched. "I get copies of the records from a contact at the Security Services. I ask for them, as I know the minister occasionally forgets to tell us what's going on."

He was being tactful. Günther didn't forget anything.

"It was on the last one. I can't find it now, but I'll find it. I'll show you. And, before coming to you, I spoke to my counterpart, who verified what I said. I wouldn't have talked to you if I wasn't absolutely certain."

Jens didn't respond. He nodded and opened the door.

"You'll see," the archivist said to his back.

Jens didn't know what would be worse: the archivist being right, or him being wrong.

9.

BLACKÅSEN MOUNTAIN

Georg was dead. Frida still couldn't believe it. What on earth would become of them now?

Frida picked among the clothes she had washed. Her hands worked automatically, folding, flattening, pressing, but her heart wasn't in it. Hadn't she always known that something like this would happen if they moved to this place?

The little one was screaming. She'd sent the bigger children outside.

"To do what, Mummy?" her daughter had asked.

"Clean," she'd mumbled.

"Clean what?"

She lost her patience. "Anything! Find something useful to do!"

The children quickly scurried outside, and she sank down into the chair and buried her face in her hands.

It was only for a minute. Then she'd fetched the laundry basket. There was always so much to do. If you stopped, you wouldn't manage. Now, she could hear her eldest, Abraham, chopping wood, the rhythm of the ax not as regular or as strong as Georg's, but not far off.

The little one was still screaming. "Hush, hush," she mumbled, but she didn't pick him up.

Oh my God, she thought. What were they going to do?

Director Sandler had come to tell her himself. The foreman had brought him. The director had perched on the edge of the chair she had just been sitting on, pinching at his trousers as he crossed his legs. He was a handsome man, she'd always thought. A different breed, of course. He had no idea what it was like in their shoes.

She'd expected his visit. Georg had been gone since Friday. Georg would never go away without telling her. He was a man who liked plans and routines. No, deep inside, she'd known something had happened.

"It wasn't a work accident," the director had said.

"Then . . . what was it?" she asked.

"A fall."

Frida had looked to the foreman, who stood just behind the director, hat in his hands.

"He was found in the open pit area," Hallberg said. "We think he was on the mountain on Friday night. Would you have any idea why?"

"No . . . He was at work. And then with the others," she said and glanced at the foreman again—drinking, she thought, but she didn't say that. "He never came home. On Saturday morning, the others said he had left earlier."

The mine. She couldn't wrap her head around it. In the middle of the night. What had he been thinking?

"I am so sorry," Sandler said. He looked around the worn cottage and at the children and sighed.

"I suppose you'll need us to leave," she said, and it was difficult pronouncing the words.

"Yes," he admitted.

"Unless . . ." the foreman began. The director turned to him. "How old is your oldest?"

Abraham's eyes turned black. Don't say anything, Frida pleaded with him in her mind.

"Thirteen," Abraham answered, his voice breaking in the middle, shooting up. He cleared his throat and frowned. He hated it when that happened, as it was a sign he was not yet a man.

"Unless you want to take your father's place." Hallberg finished his sentence.

"We'll think about it," Frida said rapidly, without looking at her son. When they'd told him about his father, he had screamed that he hated the mine and that he would never set foot inside it. But there was money. There was this house . . .

The director stood up. The foreman put his hat back on.

"Don't worry, Mummy," Abraham said, when they had left. "We'll find a way."

She had looked at him; she hadn't raised him to be naive.

The little one was screeching now, long, piercing shrieks.

"Be quiet!" she yelled and covered her mouth. "I'm sorry," she cried. She wiped her eyes with her sleeve, rose and picked the baby up, rocked him in her arms. "I'm sorry," she repeated. The baby turned, looked for her breast and she gave it to him even though she wasn't certain she'd have anything to give.

Another thing to worry about.

What had Georg been doing on the mountain in the middle of the night? Why was he there? She couldn't understand it. Had he forgotten something? She couldn't see what could be so important that he'd gone back on his own.

She walked to the window to see it: the blunt black shape that was visible from everywhere in town, the massive ditch in front of it where the ore had been mined in the open before they began the tunnels. The central point, the one reason they were all here. She'd told Georg that they shouldn't come here; told him that if they did, they'd never be able to leave. The hatred she suddenly felt for her late husband surprised her.

Her grandmother had told her the stories about Blackåsen Mountain and about the influence it had on people. "It's the iron," she'd said, chewing bread. She broke off another piece and put it in her mouth, her jaws working. "Magnetic. It pulls you in and keeps you close. Some things are just neutral," she'd said, "neither good, nor bad. But Blackåsen is not like that. Blackåsen has powers and, as far as I know, it has only ever used them to do evil."

IO.

LAURA

Laura got Andreas's address from the Department of Theology after stating it was a family emergency. She felt bad about lying, but the administrator gave her no choice. Andreas had a room in the student home managed by the Friends of Sobriety, a ten-minute walk from Britta's dormitory. His doorbell was marked by a handwritten *A. Lundius*. Nobody answered when she rang it. She had been surprised to see he lived at a student home. But she wasn't certain what she had expected. She didn't know how much of a distinction the university was making between Sami and Swedish students.

The front door opened and a young man came out, wet hair combed, book bag under his arm.

"Excuse me," Laura said.

He paused, angry. A first-year student, she thought, strait-laced, stressed.

"I'm looking for Andreas Lundius."

"He's not here," the boy said, brusquely.

"Where is he?"

"I don't know. We don't exactly socialize. I saw him leave last week. He was in a hurry."

Last week?

"Where did he go?"

The boy shrugged. "Traveling, I guess. He was carrying a big bag."

Andreas couldn't leave. Did the police know?

"Where to?"

"I have no idea. Why does everyone want to talk to him?"

"What do you mean, 'everyone'? Who else has asked for him?"

"A man. Early this morning."

"Did he say who he was?"

The boy shook his head.

"What did he look like?"

"I don't know. Dark hair."

"How old?"

"Forties?"

"Did he have an accent?" she asked. A German accent, she thought.

"Not at all."

"Could it have been a professor?"

"Maybe. He was wearing a suit. He didn't resemble a teacher, more a lawyer, or a banker."

"Or a policeman?"

"Yes." The boy lit up. "I'll bet you it was a policeman."

IN THE AFTERNOON, on the way to meet Professor Lindahl, she stood for a while in the square beneath the cathedral. Britta was dead, killed, but not where she was found. She tried to visualize it, a person carrying her past this cathedral across the cobblestone square. Or the other way, down the hill of the main university building. Or coming up along the small streets from the river? Britta was tall. She would not have been light to carry. Perhaps he had wrapped her in a rug? Perhaps there had been several perpetrators? Or perhaps he drove the body there. But in that case, would someone have noticed a car?

Three women came up the hill wearing the brown jackets and skirts of the military volunteers. The badge on their caps told what organization they belonged to, but Laura didn't know enough about it to tell. Many women had joined, but Laura had never contemplated it. She'd felt she was doing her part for Sweden in her role.

"I'd do it."

A fragmented discussion from another time. *Britta*. Hitler had just been given Sudetenland by Prime Minister Chamberlain. A war seemed inevitable.

"I'd be a soldier. I'd kill for our country." Britta rose, face grim, made a salute, hand to forehead.

"You couldn't kill a fly," Erik had said, softly. "You'd find a reason to feel sorry for anyone—regardless of what they'd done."

"I could if I had to," Britta insisted.

"Imagine actually extinguishing a life," Matti said.

"If it comes to their life or yours . . ." Britta said. "You've been a soldier." She turned to Erik.

"In peacetime," he said. "God." He rolled his eyes.

"Question is where you draw that line in the sand," Karl-Henrik said. "I think most of us would find that the line is actually further away than we had originally thought."

Britta plopped down in the armchair behind her. "Actually," she said, "the one among us who could kill is probably Laura." She raised her glass to toast Laura. "You have that steely resolve . . . You'd do it if you had to."

"Me? You've got to be joking."

Britta tipped her head to one side to look at her.

"Never," Laura had said.

Erik had been laughing. "Well," he'd said, "at least we're your friends. Likely better to be killed by someone you know."

Britta would have been more likely to enlist than her, Laura thought now. Britta had a strong moral compass. But as far as Laura knew, she never had.

PROFESSOR LINDAHL WAS late, so she sat down on the chair outside the classroom where they'd agreed to meet.

He might have been disappointed when only Britta continued their studies. Laura hadn't talked to him in person about leaving after Jacob Wallenberg asked her to join the trading committee with Germany. She had written him a letter, to which she received no response. She regretted that now. She'd been in a rush, flattered that Wallenberg wanted her—keen to get into real life and contribute to the war effort.

She should have gone to see him. He had taken them under his wing. It was at the *nachspiele* that she had met the others, including Britta. In that way, the professor had chosen her friends for her.

She pictured him in her mind. Impossible to tell his age; he could be thirty, he could be fifty. Short and slim, dressed in a black turtleneck and black trousers; a white face with the soft skin of a child and feminine features with a broad, sensitive mouth; his blond hair parted on the left, bushy, coarse, flattened to shape rather than combed and long enough to cover his ears. His eyes, too, were unusual: one green, one brown.

He'd always been ahead of them. Sometimes his comments were so far out there, it had been hard to follow his train of thought. But if you tried to trace it, you'd discover that his brain seemed to leap two or three steps at the time—simply skipping the middle. She'd never forget hearing him speak that first time.

"You have come to study history," he said in a quiet voice. "Welcome." He'd crossed his arms over his chest. On the stage, he'd looked like a tiny black figurine. Or a dancer.

"We live in the most interesting period, and you have chosen to loiter in the past. I wonder why?

"I get the impression from people I meet that history is not important. It doesn't produce anything that we buy to put in our apartments or our houses. It doesn't stand in front and lead the world. Apart from knowing the answer to the question of who invaded who in what year when playing games, the study of history has nothing to offer.

"I think to myself how they could not be more wrong.

"History is about the past, certainly, but it is far more than just that. History is knowledge. Knowledge in the most beautiful, deepest sense of the word. History brings comprehension of what came before us, as well as insight into the future, for in our past lie the seeds of what will come. As the future happens, you will be able to go back and see the roots of each conflict, the reasons, and it will be clear to you why change occurred, or, perhaps more importantly, why it didn't. It can even give us the road to follow next. And this, my dear fellows, is wisdom. Of course, it is precisely in these times that we must study our history."

SHE HEARD SOFT tapping sounds coming from the stairs and rose. Her breathing quickened and she wiped her hands on her skirt.

In the gloom of the stairway, the professor's pale hair seemed to be glowing. He was dressed in his usual black attire.

"Laura," he said, in his soft voice. "What a pleasant surprise."

She hesitated. He must know about Britta's death and understand that this was why she was here.

He took her hand and she looked into those strange eyes, one green, one brown.

He let go of her and opened the door to the classroom. He was carrying nothing: no notebook, no papers or pens. Everything was kept in his head, she thought, and felt the usual surge of admiration for him.

He pointed to a chair and she sat down. He pulled out another chair and sat down opposite her. He leaned forward in his seat, crossing his arms. She'd forgotten how small he was.

"I've come to see you because of Britta," she said.

"Oh yes, Britta." He pursed his lips. His face was impassive, but then he rarely showed emotion. He often looked at them as if studying a peculiar animal or plant he had not come across before; head tilted, eyes narrowed, pale lips pursed.

"I don't know what to say," she admitted.

"It was a shocking event."

"She was still a student of yours?"

"Yes."

"Still at the *nachspiele*?"

"Yes . . . Why are you asking about this?"

She couldn't tell him it was Wallenberg who had sent her. "She was my best friend," she said. "I guess I'm trying to come to terms with her death."

He nodded.

"I don't understand it. Why should this have happened to her? And why leave her body at the Historical Society?"

"Death is always sudden for those who remain," Professor Lindahl said. "You know this, Laura. We cannot prepare for it. It always leaves us with questions . . . as it should. It is an interruption of life as we know it."

"Aren't people talking about it? You know . . . speculating?"

"I must admit, I rarely listen to gossip." He leaned back in his chair and looked away.

Upset, she thought. Or bored?

She bit her lip. Britta was your student, she wanted to say. We all were. We were special. Britta was special. The professor could be cold and aloof in his interactions—mechanical even. She realized now that she could have mistaken the glint he got in his eyes when they said something brilliant for fondness. On the other hand, she herself had written him a letter about leaving her studies, rather than taking the time to see him. Had this upset or annoyed him? Could this be why he was being unsympathetic?

"What was Britta working on now?" she asked. As she spoke the words, she realized what had been missing in Britta's room: her notes and research papers, her work.

"She was doing research for her doctoral thesis."

"What was it about?"

"The Scandinavian countries and their relationships with other nations through the times, I think." Seeing her gaze, he added, "With Britta, it was difficult to know what she was working on. She was unstructured. She'd come to see me to discuss her work and often, she had started all over again, changed her mind as to what she wanted to focus on. I must admit, I didn't have much hope of her finalizing it."

"Where would her research be?"

He shrugged. "I guess it would have been with her."

88

Britta used to have a brown leather bag in which she kept her study material and her notebooks. She carried it around with her, slung over one shoulder. But it had not been in her room, nor could she picture it with Britta when they found her.

"Who comes to the *nachspiele* now?"

"Oh, that varies."

It never used to vary, she thought. He always invited the same students. She assumed he didn't want her to know. She was no longer one of his protégés, not part of the inner circle.

"Perhaps you could give me a name," she tried. "I would just like to talk to a student who knew Britta during her last few months."

He looked at her, eyes unblinking, expressionless. "I don't think I want them disturbed. This has been difficult for them. They have work to do. As, I am certain, do you. One has to be careful about these things, Laura. They can drag you down with them. I'm sure your father has already taught you that."

There was an odd note in his voice. Her father? The comment was so out of place that it struck her as absurd. She wasn't a child.

Lindahl rose and put out his hand to shake hers. As she left, she tried to shrug the feeling off, but she felt sad at the loss of their relationship. He had understood more about her than anyone.

As she walked down the stairs toward the ground floor, a man came up to her, half running up the steps. The gray head, the steel-rimmed glasses, the strict suit. It was Professor Birger Falk—Professor Lindahl's nemesis. She didn't want to see him. He'd always been on their case. Prying. Wanting to know what they were working on, what Professor Lindahl had taught them, with the aim of landing the latter in trouble. When they'd worked on their special project—the one that ultimately had driven them apart—he'd been so insistent they'd stopped studying at the library and kept to Laura's flat. "It's not psychology that you're supposed to study," he'd yelled at her and Britta at one point. "It's history!"

She hesitated but couldn't turn around and walk the other way. And then he noticed her.

"Miss Dahlgren," he said. "To what do we owe the honor?"

He stopped, forcing her to do the same.

"I was meeting with Professor Lindahl."

Professor Falk studied her. "Ah," he said then, as if he could read how the meeting had gone on her face.

Laura felt her cheeks heat up. Embarrassment or anger; perhaps both.

She remembered being cornered by Falk on another occasion. "Lab rats," he'd said. He'd been standing too close and she had tried to move away. "That's all you are to him. He throws things out there, sees how you react, has you fight one another for his approval. Then he studies you. It's detrimental. Even more, it's dangerous."

Now, she swallowed. "You wouldn't happen to know who comes to his *nachspiele* now?" she asked.

"After your group, it seems to have changed somewhat," Professor Falk said. "Perhaps the students are less suggestible. But I know Henrik Kallur often joins."

She nodded thank-you then continued down the stairs. He didn't move and she felt his gaze following her.

As she pushed open the door to the outside and felt the wind blow her hair, only then did she exhale.

═══

Henrik Kallur proved to be a young man with round cheeks and round glasses. His tie was askew, and he had a yellow stain on his shirtfront.

"I am a friend of Britta," she said, by manner of introduction.

"My God, what happened to her?" He pushed his library chair back with a juddering sound. The students close by turned to give them reproachful glances. Henrik didn't notice.

That he was one of Professor Lindahl's chosen students surprised her. He was nothing like the five of them, she thought. But then, what had they been like?

Smooth, she thought. Smart, funny . . . She sighed. How easy to romanticize the past.

The words *lab rats* still rang in her ears. She shrugged to get rid of the feeling accompanying Falk's words.

"Beaten, they say," the boy continued. She could imagine him doing the rounds at the university, bigmouthed: "Beaten, they say." Anger rose within her and she wanted to punch his fat face.

"Did you know her well?" Laura asked.

"Nah. She and I weren't close. Not like many others, if you know what I mean." He winked at her.

Her stomach turned. She pressed her nails into the palms of her hands.

"Besides, we were all busy working on our theses," he added.

"Do you know what hers was about?"

"Not really." He shrugged.

Hopeless.

"Who else comes to Professor Lindahl's *nachspiele*?"

He rattled off the names of four other students. She wrote them down and took her hurried leave. Well, it seemed Henrik was not impacted by Britta's death. In fact, he was the most unlikely friend of Britta she could think of. She would have found him unbearable. Why had Professor Lindahl chosen to have him in his group? But Professor Lindahl supported no fools. She assumed there was more to Henrik Kallur than met the eye.

On the advertisement board by the exit: a photo of Britta, smiling. Laura exhaled slowly. "Do you know something?" the poster read. There was a number to call—she supposed to the local police. Laura stood looking at the photo until the face of her friend dissolved into small black and white dots.

LAURA WENT TO speak with the other students attending the *nachspiele*; the names given to her by Henrik Kallur. What astonished her was how little they knew Britta. Britta seemed to have become a leftover from the past, a student who was their senior by a few years, the one they were intimidated by, and gossiped about, but whom nobody knew. When Laura lived in Uppsala, you couldn't walk anywhere with Britta without her stopping and talking to people. She would strike up a conversation with the man who sold her cigarettes, with the waitress who brought her coffee, anyone she met. Later, she'd remember their names. Laura also couldn't see how students could be in the *nachspiele* together without forming bonds. It was part of the process, she realized, Professor Lindahl's process; to pit them against one another, and then unite them. "He throws things out there, sees how you react, has you fight each other for his approval," Professor Falk had said. Kind of. But not for Professor Lindahl's own pleasure, she thought. No: to display the beauty of their brilliance, individually and jointly. They'd come to rely on each other's intelligence to push themselves further. This was why they had become inseparable. It had been immensely alluring. Together, each of them had become a better version of themselves. Smarter. More insightful.

"But what about the debates?" Laura had asked. "You must have spoken to her then?"

"Not much," one student said. "We debated but didn't speak, if you know what I mean."

Her eyes wouldn't meet Laura's. Scared, Laura thought. But then a fellow student had just been killed.

"Aloof," a boy stated. "Disdainful. She'd sit on the edge, smoke and look at you, judging." He shook his head. "I'm sorry," he said, likely for speaking ill of the dead, "but it's true."

"She worked on her thesis," another boy said. "She didn't want to share it with us. As if we would steal her material."

And this, this wasn't Britta at all. Laura wanted to scoff and convince them otherwise, but that was pointless. What mattered was how much Britta must have changed during the last year. So what would it have taken, to put Britta on the sidelines? And where was her thesis?

"I didn't know her well," another of the female students said. Laura had found her in the reading room and they'd gone outside to talk. They were standing in the hallway on the second floor, outside the heavy wooden doors. She had brought the book she was working on, as if worried another student would steal it. She hugged it against her chest. Large, round glasses, bangs, square short hair. Not Britta's type but sweet.

"But I do think she was heartbroken," she said and nodded to herself.

Heartbroken?

"There was a time in the autumn when she came out of her shell. She seemed much more relaxed. I thought she was in love; there was that dreaminess about her. I asked her. I said she looked lovely, in love . . ."

A boy ran past them, rubber soles squealing against the marble. He took the steps two at a time.

"What did she answer?"

"She said she was. She seemed happy."

"And then?"

"It didn't last. I imagined it had ended, her affair. She looked sad. She didn't pay as much attention to her appearance as before."

Laura remembered Britta in the café at NK, pale face, how her nails had been bitten short. She felt a sting of sorrow. Perhaps she was wrong. Perhaps this was about an ex-lover.

"When did you think it had ended?"

The student pursed her lips. "Before Christmas. I remember thinking what a shame, she wouldn't have the holidays together with him, whoever he was."

"Do you know if Britta had any German friends?"

"German?" She raised her eyebrows. "No. Well, I wouldn't know."

"Did you see her with any businessmen or . . . ?" Laura prompted.

"I never saw her outside the *nachspiele*. She didn't go out."

"She didn't go out?"

Laura couldn't believe her ears. Britta partied all the time. She couldn't bear being at home.

"No. She never came to the parties, or the bars."

On a sudden hunch, Laura asked, "The students at the *nachspiele*, do you . . ." *Do everything together? Spend every waking minute in each other's company?* "Are you close?"

The student shrugged. "We do projects together."

Then Professor Lindahl had changed, Laura thought. If the professor no longer ensured that they fell in love with one another as much as they were infatuated with him, then he had changed, indeed.

LAURA HAD DECIDED to spend the night at the Gillet Hotel. The evening air was bitter. The late afternoon sky a crisp dark blue. She took the detour by Ekermanska's House and stood for a while outside. The square was empty. She tried again to imagine a person carrying Britta's dead body across it, fumbling to unlock the door, but she couldn't see it.

A young man came down the slope from the main university building. On seeing her, he paused.

"You shouldn't be here," he said.

"Why?" she asked.

"Haven't you heard about the murder? It happened right here, on an evening just like this one. You shouldn't be walking around on your own."

"Who do they say did it?" she asked.

"The Germans."

"The Germans?" Her ears pricked up.

He shrugged. "Who else would it be?" He took a step closer to her and lowered his voice. "There are German divisions hiding in Sweden, you know, getting ready for the Allies on our soil." He nodded. "They are preparing to take over the protection of the Swedish mines."

Rumors. God, sometimes it felt like this nation was only held together by shreds. She knew it wasn't true and yet it scared her. The image of German soldiers hiding out in the north of Sweden. "I'll be fine," she told him. "You go on. I won't be long."

He nodded and, after hesitating briefly, left. It was as if he had decided that her fate was in her own hands.

The river outside the hotel was rippling black. Twilight was darkening the shadows, graying the fronts of university buildings and the hotel. Walking up the stairs to her room, she glanced into the bright dining room. The small tables were full of students, chatting, screaming, laughing. They were beautiful, she thought. No sign of wariness or fear here. They looked . . . clean. Untouched. Us, she thought. Us not long ago.

How sad it was, she thought when she was lying in bed, the way the professor had sent her off. She had disappointed him. But then, he'd always questioned her commitment, so perhaps it hadn't come as a surprise. He had a way, the professor, of finding their weakest spot and putting his finger right on it, prodding, asking questions, having them turn themselves inside out under his scrutinizing gaze to find answers they didn't know they had. He did throw out hooks with bait for them to bite. But it was done to help them improve themselves. The questions he asked them individually had them pondering for weeks, questioning themselves, moving boundaries they'd previously thought were set in stone.

"That's how you live, isn't it?" he'd asked her once, when they were out for a walk, which is how he preferred to conduct his teacher-student meetings; walking along the river, or in one of the parks. Him, smoking; the student adapting their pace to his, pointing out obstacles, looking out for him. "Without ever committing to anything."

"No," she'd protested and then hesitated: was it? "I like to keep my options open," she'd said.

"I wonder why? You're passionate about things; you have convictions. Why wouldn't you act on them?"

"Committing is foolish." The vehemence in her voice had surprised her. "It's ideological. We move. We adapt. We stay opportunistic."

"'We,'" he'd remarked. "Who was it in your life that didn't commit, Laura?"

A flickering image before her: a woman, a ghost, looking much like herself.

Professor Lindahl nodded. "Your mother," he said.

She could barely stop herself from gasping. How on earth did he guess? There was no room for family or friends in Professor Lindahl's company—only him and their fellow students.

"No," she'd lied.

She hadn't told the others about Professor Lindahl's line of inquiry. It was too much. Too close.

II.

JENS

Daniel Jonsson was waiting for Jens to arrive. Before Jens had put down his briefcase, Daniel was closing the office door silently behind them.

"It's gone."

"What?"

"The copy of the register that showed the calls between Günther and the Danish and Norwegian foreign ministers is gone from my office. I've searched everywhere. I called my friend at the registrar. The calls are missing from the Security Services register, too. He refuses to confirm what was on record previously. Says he cannot remember."

"Perhaps you were mistaken."

The archivist shook his head. "I would never have approached you if I didn't have the proof in my hand. And there's more . . ."

There was a clanking sound by the door. Both fell silent, waited, but it remained closed. Jens exhaled, realizing that he'd been holding his breath.

"I called my counterpart in Denmark again," Daniel said, in a quieter voice. "He no longer wanted to talk about it. He said he'd been mistaken. There had been no calls."

"Mistaken?"

Daniel nodded. Jens paused.

"You realize what you're implying?" Jens asked.

Daniel looked pained. "I do."

Voices in the corridor now. They both stared at the door again, but the voices continued past.

"How would a person get phone calls removed from the logs of the Security Services?" Jens asked.

Daniel pushed his glasses higher up on his nose. "He's the minister, isn't he?"

He was, but how did it work? The registers were serious business. Suspected spies, extreme views, communist tendencies. All details were known and kept for the eventuality of war. It seemed unlikely Günther would have that power over them.

"Don't tell anyone about this," Jens said.

"I don't like it."

"Neither do I."

"What will you do?"

Jens shook his head. "I have to think about it. Don't tell anyone," he repeated.

Daniel nodded and slipped out through the door.

Jens let his breath out. What on earth would make the minister take such action? What was so special about these contacts that they had to remain secret? There were communications between countries all the time. What could they have talked about? The fate of the Jews? No, Günther normally discussed that even with Jens. They drew up plans and communications together. A military operation, then? No. Sweden was neutral; Denmark and Norway, occupied. A military intervention or support would have to pass through the government and Parliament. Jens felt cold. What was he going to do?

Jens had no friends in the ministry. He picked up the phone and called Sven.

Jens and Sven had met at university, studying economics in the same year, and had stayed close ever since. The first time he saw Sven in class, with his sensitive face, tweed suit combined with a crisp shirt, soft-spoken, he had written him off. Jens's normal friends were brasher, louder. But then the two of them ended up working on a project together. Jens had found he enjoyed the other man's company, and he came to value his opinions. Jens was ambitious. He hadn't thought Sven had those aspirations. He'd been surprised when Sven ended up working for Möller, the minister of social affairs, in the same capacity as Jens worked for Christian Günther. "I didn't tell you I was applying," Sven had said. "I didn't think I would get it." Jens had thought the minister of social affairs was the lucky one, to have Sven working for him.

"Sven Feldt."

"It's me, Jens."

"Hi." Sven sounded happy. Jens couldn't remember when they'd last spoken. They'd both been busy.

"I was hoping for dinner," Jens said. "Tonight, perhaps?"

"That would be great, but it has to be a late one. The fallout from the riot in Uppsala is keeping us busy."

They agreed to meet at the restaurant Norma in Old Town.

"Everything alright?" Sven asked.

"Absolutely." Jens thought about the typist listening in and recording his response right now. "You?"

"Same," Sven said cheerily.

The war was making everyone sound positive.

Jens sat down at his desk. Perhaps, like Kristina told him, the minister knew best, and he ought to leave well enough alone. But to doctor records . . . Jens felt someone ought to be told. Günther could hardly be planning a military operation on his own. But he remembered a rumor . . . Günther encouraging Germany to support an overthrow of the government in Sweden, to put Sweden on Germany's side.

It was early morning, and already he'd had it. He picked up his briefcase, opened it and swore. He'd left his notebook at home. He swore again.

Well, he needed it. He and Kristina had slept at his small flat in Old Town last night. He could be back before anybody noticed. He took his jacket and left everything else the way it was.

He crossed Norrbro Bridge, the soft sounds of moving water underneath him eerie in the silence. He missed the hum from the cars. Early on, he'd enjoyed the peace. Now, he felt Stockholm was but a shell of a city without the traffic pumping through its veins. He continued past the Three Crowns castle, past the Stockholm Cathedral with its sculpture of Sankt Göran and the dragon and into the small streets of Old Town.

He didn't know what to do about the archivist's missing registers, but he'd talk to Sven about it. Sven would give advice.

He followed Österlånggatan, peeking into the dark side alleys that led down to the water, many of them now blocked off with heaps of firewood. These streets used to contain trade of all sorts, but the whole of Old Town was being renovated. Vendors were no longer welcome.

Farther along, the door to his apartment building opened and a man exited. Jens stopped abruptly. Karl Schnurre? There was no mistaking the corpulent figure. What had he been doing in Jens's building?

Schnurre began walking in his direction. Jens jumped back into a side street and pressed himself against the wall. Schnurre passed on the pavement so close to him that had he looked his way, he would have seen him.

Jens tried to think who else lived in his apartment building and couldn't see who Schnurre would possibly have been visiting. Not Mr. Bellman on the main floor. He was a hundred years old. The ladies on the second floor were both retired, living alone. One of them had been a schoolteacher, the other a shopkeeper. Neither of them had any German connections, as far as he knew. There was only his flat remaining, and the one opposite him, which was usually empty. The owner, a Mr. Enander, Jens had never met. Occasionally, he had heard sounds from the apartment late at night. It was said that Enander was a traveling businessman who used his flat mainly as a pied-à-terre.

When Schurre had disappeared around a corner, Jens walked to his building, unlocked the door and ran up his stairs, hoping that he'd be wrong and that Kristina would be long gone. But when he opened the door to his apartment, she was still there.

"Jens?" she said. She came out from the kitchen wearing an apron and holding a kitchen towel in her hands. "What are you doing here?"

"I forgot my notebook," he said.

She laughed but didn't let go of him with her eyes. "Oh, you are funny. Don't move, I'll get it for you!" She walked to pick up his notebook from his desk and put it in his hands. "Here you go." She stood so that she blocked the entrance to the kitchen. Should he say what he'd seen? Ask her if she knew what Schnurre could have been doing in Jens's building?

There was a knock on the front door. "Miss Bolander?"

"Oh, that must be the dry-cleaning service I ordered." She

passed him to open the door. Quickly, Jens glanced into the kitchen. On his kitchen counter, newly washed, were two coffee cups with plates.

He looked at her straight back as she counted coins for the boy.

"Well, I'm off," he said finally. "I'll see you later."

"See you tonight," she said and kissed his cheek.

JENS DIDN'T LIKE this. Not one bit. Kristina didn't know Schnurre, did she? Apart from that one dinner—when Barbro had asked to bring the man—he didn't think they'd met.

He walked back to work, troubled. Kristina would never meet with the man on her own. He was a German senior official. She couldn't. That would be immensely dangerous in all sorts of ways. And why? What reason would they have to meet?

He exited Old Town by the statue of Sankt Göran.

Three gentlemen in hats and long dark coats were now standing on Norrbro bridge: his own minister, Christian Günther; the minister of social affairs, Möller; and Prime Minister Hansson. The Swedish government, basically, on a Stockholm bridge at midday. What on earth were they doing out here?

Günther was the first one to see him. He frowned. Hansson's bushy eyebrows shot up.

"Gentlemen." Jens nodded.

"A good day for bumping into old friends," Günther said.

"Yes," Jens smiled. "Indeed."

He walked past them. There was no way the three of them had "bumped into" each other. Their agendas were full. And there was no meeting scheduled between them.

Whatever they are discussing, he thought, it's urgent and they don't want to be overheard. He couldn't remember them ever having taken similar precautions before and his mouth felt dry. He hoped it wasn't about another turn of the war. Whatever it is, he thought, it's important.

12.

Blackåsen Mountain

Taneli woke up in the middle of the night, panting. A dream, he thought. Just a dream. But the smell in his nostrils was so strong, his stomach heaved. He thought he might vomit.

On the other side of the tent lay his mother and father; their puffing rhythmic, heavy. Above him, through the hole in the cloth, he glimpsed a blue sky, the burnt tinge showing him it was still night. The thrush that had to move its nest on their arrival from a tree beside and which had been singing nightly ever since, was crooning its dull *tjyh-tjyh-tjyh*.

Taneli crawled toward the opening of the tent and went outside. He inhaled the fresh air as if he could drink it. His pulse was still beating rapidly in his neck. Raija came bounding over. She danced around him, nipped his hand, looped his legs and almost tripped him up. He patted her head and then walked to the river, Raija skipping at his heels.

It wasn't a normal dream, he thought as he squatted down by the chilly water, cupped his hands and drank. In fact, it wasn't a dream at all. Just a scent. The odour on your hand after touching a fire pot, or red rock in the ground. Cool, humid. Tangy. *Iron.* That's what it was. Iron. Not usually a bad smell, but this time it had been overpowering. In his dream, he had gagged. And there had been such fear: his heart had been pounding, his eyes tearing up and then this all-consuming reek that ate itself into his head, down his throat, into his tummy . . .

He stood up and tried to shake the feeling off. He was scared. At the fire pit, he sat down next to the charred ground. He bent forward, put his arms on his knees. Raija flopped down beside him and her warm body pressed into his. He closed his eyes. He was still tired. Perhaps he could sleep, he thought. But each time his body relaxed, the memory of the dream jolted him back. Raija didn't move. She was a solid lump by his side.

As always, Nihkko woke up first. His tent opening was pushed aside and he crawled out. He was agile even though his hair was white, his face a wrinkly brown and his walk bowlegged as if his center was being pulled toward the earth.

Nihkko approached Taneli and began building a fire. Soon, there were orange flickers among the dry twigs. Taneli sat up. Now, he realized how cold he was. He couldn't wait for the flames to grow stronger. Nihkko disappeared, waddling down to the river with the pot, then returned and hung it on the stand to boil. Then he sat down cross-legged and waited.

"I couldn't sleep," Taneli said.

Nihkko poked in the fire with a stick, adjusting the branches. He was easy to talk to. Some of the older ones were. They took the time and had the wisdom to remain quiet when people stumbled, trying to express what they were feeling. Not all of the old ones were quiet, though. Nihkko's wife, for example, never stopped talking. Taneli didn't know how Nihkko could put up with it. It would drive him mad to have a woman babbling in his ear all the time.

He told Nihkko about his dream. He tried to describe the scent—how powerful it was, how violent.

For a long time, Nihkko said nothing. He just sat. Taneli waited.

"Your sister," he said at last.

At first, Taneli didn't understand, then he did.

"Yes."

"Do you still believe she is alive?"

Taneli nodded.

"Has she ever tried to . . . contact you?"

Taneli frowned. Not exactly. He just knew she wasn't dead.

Nihkko sighed. "How old are you now, Taneli?"

"Nine."

"You are young," Nihkko said, "but growing older. As you grow, there will be new abilities, new skills. New *sensitivities*." He stressed the last word. "The two of you are connected, that much is clear. Perhaps she is sending you the scent."

"A clue," Taneli said. At first, he felt ecstatic. Then he got worried. "Will there be more?" he asked.

"I don't think she will stop now, do you?"

Taneli shook his head.

"I want you to be attentive and careful," Nihkko said. "Don't let her take over your head. Don't, under any circumstances, let her lead you. The dead may mean well, but death can change them. They no longer know what is right or wrong. They become very selfish."

Taneli shook his head again: she was not dead.

Nihkko raised a finger. We disagree on this, yes, he seemed to say. "She is not the only one who has vanished," he said then. "There have been many."

Many? Who? Taneli drew in his breath sharply.

"Many of our kind." The elder nodded. "You remember Ámmon?"

Taneli nodded.

"He was one of them."

Taneli had thought Ámmon had died of natural causes. How come he didn't know about this? How come it wasn't discussed?

Taneli knew why. In their traditions, it was believed that if you put words on things, you made them real. A person was not sick, just tired. The herd was not scared, only alert.

One after another, the tent openings moved. People were coming out, yawning, stretching.

"Nihkko?" The sharp voice of his wife.

Nihkko seemed to shrink. Then he lifted his hand and waved to her.

"Be very careful," he repeated to Taneli in a low voice.

"I was thinking about the herd . . ." His wife began talking before she'd reached him. Taneli rose.

THE ENTIRE DAY, Taneli waited for his father to come home from the mine. When he came, he went straight to the river to wash and Taneli followed him. Taneli sat down on the shore and watched as his father rinsed himself: one arm, then the other, his chest, his armpits, his stomach—his leather trousers getting dark from the water. He scooped liquid in both hands and doused his face, over and over and over, as if there was more to wash off than just the dirt and soot. The water must be freezing cold, but his father didn't care. He's washing it off, Taneli thought. The mountain.

Taneli's cousin Olet and some of the other boys his age were angry with the men working for the mining company. "Our land in the first place," they said with hard eyes. "The settlers should never have been allowed here. We should have fought them."

Nihkko wouldn't tolerate such language. "The Sami are not fighters." He'd shut them down.

But Olet and his friends were still talking. They'd gather in the forest close to the mine and debate. Their voices were angry and carried far.

But Taneli could see there had been no choice for his father and the others.

When his father was done washing, he came to sit beside his son.

Taneli glanced at him. His face was sinking in on itself, his head balding, his skin a gray shade from the dirt of the mine that could never be washed away. In time, his father would become like one of these rocks, Taneli thought. No one would be able to tell the difference.

"I wanted to ask you something," Taneli said.

The rock beside him blinked his eyes as if the mere thought of Taneli asking questions was painful.

"Could you tell me the history of Blackåsen?" he asked.

Taneli could feel his father stiffen, but he didn't immediately say no.

"What do you want to know?" he asked.

"All of it," Taneli said.

His father remained silent. Taneli wasn't sure if he was going to answer, but then his father took a deep breath and began. "Our people used to say Blackåsen Mountain had the most powerful spirit of all. A spirit strong enough to challenge the Christian God. Its spirit was fickle, unfair in punishment, quick to anger, difficult to please. In olden days, our tribe used to cross Blackåsen twice each year: on our way to and from the winter pastures—that was when we spent the summers on the other side, before they said we were not allowed. Each passage was followed by rituals. We sacrificed; we took great care not to take anything from the mountain without asking. And it allowed us passage. The mountain haunted those who settled near it, but never us. Then the settlers found the iron. When they started drawing it out, I feared the worst. I kept waiting for the mountain to respond, to punish them, slaughter them. But nothing happened. Nothing. Look at it now; they've halved its size, flattened it into this unremarkable hill"—he snorted—"and still no response. But wait . . ."

Taneli held his breath.

"They say there's more iron *beneath* the mountain than in the mountain itself. That the ore continues downward, all the way to the middle of the earth. As if there is more of it down there than on the surface. That's when it will happen."

His father had lowered his voice and Taneli shivered.

"Once they've reached flat ground and start rooting into its depths, going deeper, that is when the spirit will rise up and crush them all. Its revenge will be on a scale unheard of and it would be better for us all if we were as far away as possible."

He sounded as if he were talking about the end of the world.

"I wish I didn't have anything to do with this, but . . ." He shrugged. "And I have been punished." He nodded. "Severely punished."

Javanna, Taneli thought.

"Does anything . . ." Taneli said hesitantly, "live on the mountain?"

His father pulled back and looked at him. "What do you mean?" He shook his head. "Not now. Once upon a time, the wildlife was everywhere. All the animals and birds wanted to make their home there. But now, with the explosions and the machines . . . nothing can stay there."

And yet . . . , Taneli thought. A smell of iron strong enough to make him vomit. Javanna was telling him something about the mountain.

13.

LAURA

Laura lay watching the faint gray glow entering through the curtain until her room was light enough to see. She had slept poorly, woken up repeatedly, tossed and turned. The decor hadn't changed. Once, she had come here to the Gillet Hotel with a lover. He'd been a student, his confidence drawn from the fact of his father being an influential politician. But what had been love at first sight had dissipated with dawn. She had lain there in this same light, looking at the boy beside her, watching his thin, ash-blond hair, the light stubble on his cheeks, the mouth that looked vulnerable as he slept. Her father wouldn't like him. He was not a "good friend," despite his influential family, she remembered thinking, even though, of course, she didn't care about what her father thought. Before he woke up, she'd gotten dressed and left.

Britta, too, had once stayed at this hotel. They'd compared notes on how the bedrooms had been furnished. "Though it never occurred to me it could have been love," Britta said, and Laura exploded in laughter.

She'd assumed that the reason Britta hadn't wanted to fall in love was so she could remain free, not get tied down. But then she *had* fallen in love. Laura wished she knew with whom.

She ate breakfast at the hotel restaurant and didn't recognize any of the waiters, although she used to know them all. Perhaps the familiar ones had left. Perhaps it was because normally, she'd be an evening guest, not a morning guest. Whatever it was, it made her feel old.

INSPECTOR ACKERMAN WAS at the police station, at his desk, smoking. The room was small and cold, white walls aging yellow from cigarette smoke.

He looked up, moved the cigarette to the other hand, then stood to greet her. She realized he resembled Humphrey Bogart. The thought made her smile. Britta would have loved that. Britta would have noticed it even if her best friend had just been killed. Humphrey Bogart is investigating your murder, she thought, and immediately felt her mouth twitch into something like a sob.

Inspector Ackerman was studying her face. The column of ash on his cigarette was long and fell onto the table. He brushed it off his papers with a flick, pulled the ashtray closer and put the cigarette out.

"I understand that when you studied here, a group of you were close." He launched straight into it and pointed at a chair for her to sit.

"Yes?" She drew up the wooden chair to his desk and sat down.

"Other students say you behaved like a secret society."

This surprised her. They hadn't been interested in the other students and it felt strange that other students would remark about them.

"There seems to have been a lot of resentment against your group," he said.

"I had no idea," she said. "It's true we were close. Perhaps a 'secret society' is how it appeared to others."

"You lived together?"

"No. We had our own accommodations. But we studied in my apartment."

"From what people have told us, Britta didn't make new friends after you left."

"It might have been difficult for her to . . . join in, after we left. I know it would have been for me."

Though if anyone could have, it would have been Britta. Britta had chosen not to.

"And yet you haven't stayed in touch with one another since leaving. Don't you think that's strange?"

Laura shrugged.

"The war, of course," he said. "But I wonder if something happened that made you not want to stay in touch?"

Laura tightened. It was all flooding back: Matti's frightened eyes; Karl-Henrik reeling off the same things over and over, like someone obsessed; Erik throwing a glass at the wall.

"No," she said. She could tell him, she thought. It was irrelevant. But the whole thing had lodged in her memory as reprehensible. She was ashamed of own her part in it.

He was looking at his papers. "Don't you think there is something you should have told me when you saw Britta's body?"

She shook her head. "What?"

"Her eye was gouged out."

"Yes."

"Only one," the policeman said.

"Yes?" Her chest squeezed together.

He banged the table with his palm. She jumped.

"Don't act as if I'm stupid!" he snapped. "People we spoke to say your group were obsessed with the old Norse tales. If I'm not mistaken, Odin lost one eye. When you saw her, you must have thought of it."

But nobody knew about their interest in the Norse tales. Nobody could know this. There had only ever been the five of them. They hadn't spoken to anyone else about what they did together. They had no other friends. And then she realized where he was heading.

"You think it was one of us."

"I am exploring all avenues."

She shook her head. Couldn't believe it.

"This has nothing to do with us," she said.

He didn't respond.

"And in that case, it could only have been me or Erik," she continued. "The others are gone."

The policeman looked down at his papers. "Matti Karppinen works for the Ministry of Information in Finland. He has followed the Finnish foreign minister to Sweden on numerous occasions. Karl-Henrik Rogstad was injured in a bomb attack in Oslo in early January. Since then, he has been recovering in an apartment in Stockholm. The night Britta was killed, you were all in Stockholm. It could have been any one of you."

The others were in Stockholm? She had no idea.

"Someone said your group fell out with each other."

Who was it? Who?

"Who?"

"Are you saying it's true?"

"No." She found herself avoiding his gaze. "I just wonder who would think they knew us that well. We kept to ourselves."

"Was there anyone among you who had a reason to want her dead?"

"No." This was absurd.

"Britta died the night before you found her. Where were you the day she was killed?"

She shook her head. But his gaze didn't waver. She cleared her throat.

"I was at work for the trade delegation." She paused to think. "That day, we had a lot of translation to do. I worked late. I finished around ten. Then I walked home. The next morning, Andreas called."

"Did anyone see you later that night?"

"I live on my own."

"So no," he said, writing notes.

"Are you going to interview the others?"

"Of course."

"I spoke to a fellow student who said she thought Britta might have been in love," she said.

He frowned. He didn't like her asking the questions. "We heard that, too, but nobody seems to know who he was."

"When I was in her room looking for her, her brown leather satchel was missing. Did you find it?"

"No?"

"She used to have her notebooks in it, all her school work."

"We didn't find a bag."

"She might have noted something down. Her wallet might have been in it, too."

"We'll keep it in mind," he said.

He didn't care, she thought, but he was the kind who did. She got an image in her head, the outline of a shadow, the killer, tall, dark, throwing the bag in the river.

There was one more thing she had to know. "Have you come across any . . . Germans in your investigation?"

"Germans?" He scoffed. "Miss Dahlgren, this is not a spy novel. Why would there be Germans?"

"I just thought," she mumbled, "with the war and so on."

The inspector shook his head. "We have come across no Germans during our inquiries." He pushed back his chair, made to stand up.

"Andreas Lundius has disappeared," she said quickly.

"What do you mean?"

"A boy at his dorm says he left bringing a big bag."

He raised his eyebrows.

"Did you not know this?" she asked.

He shook his head. "On the contrary, we asked him to stay put."

"He seemed frightened, too. Did he tell you anything of value when you interviewed him?"

"Nothing."

"But . . ."

"Stop." He raised a hand. "Are you going around asking questions?"

Her lack of answer was answer enough.

"That ends right now," he said. "If there are developments, I will let you know. Meanwhile, you can go back home, Miss Dahlgren. Rest assured we will speak again."

"Just one last question," she begged.

He paused, frowning.

"Have you spoken to Professor Lindahl?"

His behaviour nagged at her. He had cared too little about the death of a woman who had been his student for eight years. But perhaps he kept more distance from them than she had thought. Or perhaps she just hadn't liked the way he sent her off without helping.

"Of course," he said.

She nodded. *Alright*. "Do you need help in packing up her things? I'd like to do it."

He hesitated.

"Her family might want them back."

"We've gone through her room already . . . Yes, you can pack them up."

As she stood up, her knees were weak. She had sweated through her shirt. She walked down the stairs and thought about him knowing about Odin. That had surprised her. She wouldn't have taken him for the kind who knew about Norse history. Why? Because he was a policeman? How prejudiced she was.

He suspected them. That was unbelievable. None of them could have harmed Britta. She'd been the center of everything, the heart of all of them.

LAURA PUT DOWN the boxes she had gotten from the student dorm administration and sat down on Britta's bed. The room now smelled sour, like old cigarettes. The bed linen was soft under her hands, not washed for a while. She allowed herself the tears, felt herself melt.

There was a knock on the door. Laura quickly wiped her cheeks. She opened the door. There was a policeman outside. He was in uniform. His face looked pasty and grim.

"Inspector Ackerman asked me to help."

Of course. He wouldn't leave her alone in here. Silently, she swore to herself.

"Wonderful," she said. "I've started with her desk. Do you mind folding up her clothes?"

The policeman tore through the wardrobe. Laura would have wanted to take her time, to touch the garments, remember when she last saw them. And shouldn't he feel in the pockets? But perhaps they had already done that.

She turned to the desk, working fast now so that he wouldn't come to help. She threw the bottles and dried flowers into a garbage bag. The photo of her and Britta, she put aside. She would take that one herself. With the postcards, she hesitated. Would Britta's parents want them, to see that their daughter had been popular, loved, or would it open old wounds? She read the cards. On one postcard, there was no text, but a large heart drawn with blue ink. She turned it around. The postcard showed the House of Parliament, windows lit, people walking on the bridge, a car driving across, the photo taken before the war. *Greetings from Stockholm*, it said in white type. It was a tourist card that you could buy anywhere. The postmark said Stockholm. It had been sent last November. Had he sent this? Her lover? House of Parliament? And what kind of a person sends just a heart? An individual who is certain the recipient will know who it is from. Someone who is not one for many words. She looked over to the back of the policeman, folded it and put it in her pocket.

There was a scribbled note, on a page torn from a notebook: *Worst is that evil which could be normal.* Britta had crossed out *normal* and replaced it with *good.*

"Did you find anything?"

She startled. "A lot of garbage."

"Is this box done?" He pointed to the one by the desk.

She nodded. As he walked out, she put the note in her pocket with the postcard.

The room was bare and looked small without its things. Another student will live here, she thought and felt a sting of pain. Another student with dreams, hopes, loves and heartbreaks.

"Are you ready?" the policeman asked.

As much as she'd ever be, yes.

14.

JENS

What did he know about Kristina?

Jens stared at the blank paper before him on his desk.

He knew her, his mind protested, while another, smaller, voice told him that if he was honest with himself, he didn't know her that well. They'd met at a foreign affairs department party a while before Jens had been appointed Günther's secretary, flying high, self-assured smile on his face, knowing the recruitment was his for the taking. Another smile, mischievous, her eyes on his a fraction too long. *You think you're special?* Kristina was shrewd, spirited, long dark hair and blue eyes, her slim figure encased in an emerald green dress. The two of them had met again a couple of days later—this time on their own—and ended up at her flat. They'd gotten engaged two months after that.

Kristina worked for her father. Managing her father's assets in Stockholm, passing messages, writing letters, accounts . . . Secretarial work. That was how he'd thought of it.

He hadn't met her parents. Kristina's father was a diplomat, stationed in South America—Rio? Mexico City? They hadn't been back to Sweden since Jens and Kristina met. Jens had felt he ought to have obtained her father's permission before asking her to marry him, but Kristina had made him understand that, in view of the circumstances, her father wouldn't mind and they could go ahead and make plans. Jens had introduced Kristina to his father, of course. It was an awkward meeting. Both Kristina and his father had seemed uncomfortable but did their best to hide it. "I always trusted your decisions," his father had said later.

It struck Jens now what a nice thing that was—for a parent to trust their child's decisions—even though he was quite certain that Kristina was not what his father had imagined as a daughter-in-law.

Why?

His father was a schoolteacher. It was obvious that they would have different views on what a "good wife" was. He hadn't spoken to his father for a couple of weeks. I must remember to call him, he thought.

No, he didn't know Kristina's parents and she didn't have siblings. But he had met her godfather, Artur, many times. Artur wouldn't stand for anything untoward with the Germans.

Or would he?

You couldn't be sure, that was the thing. Many Swedes would have welcomed a Nazi occupation. Hitler was hailed as the savior of Europe; the organizer of an unruly patch of geography. It hadn't just been the dread of Russia. It had been . . . adulation.

Even if Kristina had met with Schnurre, that didn't mean she was pro-German. She might be working for Sweden. He had entertained the idea the other night that Barbro Cassel was a swallow for the C-Bureau. Perhaps Kristina was, too?

The idea was ludicrous. It made him scoff out loud. His girlfriend, a spy? He would have noticed!

There was certainly a perfectly reasonable explanation. He should have asked at once, instead of sitting here, making up stories.

I'm scared, he thought. I'm letting my work-related insecurities flow out into other areas of my life.

Well, that was a sobering thought. One he didn't like one bit.

Instead, he tried to remember what Kristina had told him about her relationship with Barbro Cassel after the dinner with Schnurre. They had gone to school together. And now one of them was working for the German trade delegation and was friendly with Karl Schnurre. That was all he knew.

Kristina didn't have many friends. She knew everyone, but at the same time no one. There wasn't a close girlfriend who called all hours of the day, or with whom Kristina went to have coffees. There was no one he'd been introduced to as her "best friend." Instead, she was always available to him and he had to confess that he rather liked it that way. Available, but not clingy. Supportive, but independent. Yes, he liked it.

That's it, he decided. He knew Kristina. He'd asked her to become his wife. To love and to hold . . . Kristina was as upset about the war as he was, and there was no way she was on the side of the Germans or was a spy.

When he got home, he would ask her about it. He wouldn't make a big deal out of it. "Oh, by the way, you have no idea who came out of my building this morning . . ."

He tapped his pen on the paper before him again. He was trying to draft a memorandum for the minister with suggestions about how to get more Jews safely to Sweden, but his thoughts were scattered.

He wondered again about those phone calls between the Nordic ministers.

He threw his pen down and rose then walked down the corridor to the archivist's office. He knocked and opened the door. When he saw the woman at the desk, he momentarily thought he was in the wrong room. "I'm sorry . . ." he began.

She looked up at him. She was in her fifties, with graying hair and pink lipstick, and she was sitting at Daniel Jonsson's desk. The room was different from the last time he'd been here; tidy, organized. The numerous coffee cups were gone. There was a potted plant on the desk and a couple of photo frames with pictures of two smiling children, the woman herself, looking two decades younger. And a new carpet?

"Jens Regnell, secretary to Christian Günther," he said.

She rose and curtsied.

"I was looking for Daniel Jonsson."

"Who is he?" she asked.

"An archivist. He normally sits here."

She looked surprised at that.

"Where is he?"

"I don't know. I was asked to come in."

"But is he sick, or . . .?" Jens tried.

"I don't know," she said again.

"Do you know how long you're here for? Is it temporary?"

"No, I work here now, that's what they said. They called last night."

Who called? he wanted to ask, but most likely it was the personnel department.

"Welcome," he said instead.

"Thank you. Can I help you with anything?" she asked.

"No, you get settled in. It's nothing urgent."

He stopped by the administration office instead and sat down on the edge of the desk of one of the young women. She stopped typing and looked up at him: keen blue eyes, a smiling face.

"Yes, Mr. Regnell?"

He could feel the eyes of the other women on his back.

"I wonder if you could help me?" He lowered his voice. "Daniel Jonsson, the archivist, is not at his desk and there is a new woman there instead. Could you please find out where he's gone and how to reach him?"

"Of course, Mr. Regnell."

"He has a book of mine that I'd like to get back," Jens said. "He probably forgot. No need to make a big thing of it—it would embarrass him—but if you could find out, that would be great."

"Of course."

"Oh, and if you could find out who the new woman is, that would be great, too. She told me her name, but I've forgotten it already."

She smiled, and he smiled back. He rose and walked back to his office.

He sat back down at his desk. Where on earth had Daniel gone? He was certain that if the archivist had known he wasn't coming back, he would have told Jens and said goodbye. What had happened to him? A transfer, perhaps?

He sighed, opened his drawer to get a letter opener and saw that thesis again. *Nordic Relations Through the Ages—Denmark, Norway and Sweden on a New Path.* By a Britta Hallberg. Why on earth had he kept it? It wasn't as if he'd ever get the time to read it. He picked it up and threw it in the garbage bin.

Things would feel better after seeing Sven tonight. Sven had a knack for seeing things clearly, making things simple.

15.

BLACKÅSEN MOUNTAIN

"This bloody place," Abraham said. He threw a stone into the creek. "I'll never take a job in that hellhole. Fuck no." He spat at the ground beside him.

Gunnar was silent. His friend was grieving. The mountain had just taken Abraham's father, Georg. Gunnar knew what it felt like; he himself had lost a sister. All their fathers worked in the mine, came home broken. Meanwhile, without ever mentioning it, all the wives and children constantly worried, knew that there were worse destinies than being broken. It was a weight on their lives. Would something happen today? Or tomorrow?

Gunnar didn't want to work in the mine, either. But it paid the most. And there was always work. Abraham was a year older; he had already turned thirteen with only one year left to graduation. And now, with his father dead, he'd have to make his mind up very soon as to what to do. Gunnar felt guilty. His father was the mine foreman. Not that his father decided anything or had it much easier than the others. But he knew from experience that his father was a hard man.

It was recess. Gunnar and Abraham were behind the school building by the creek. Gunnar's father had told him about

Abraham's father yesterday morning. Gunnar had already known something had happened as the mine was quiet. Without the normal racket, he'd heard birdsong, the whistle of the wind. And then anxiety wrapped around him like ropes. He'd been relieved when he saw his father; it wasn't him. Only for it to prove to be Abraham's.

Gunnar was sitting on the grass. Abraham still stood watching the water. Behind them, the grinder was chugging. Every now and then there was a screeching.

"No, as soon as I've finished school, I'm leaving," Abraham said. His voice sounded choked.

"Where will you go?" Gunnar asked.

"Anywhere." Abraham spat again. "South."

South. Closer to the war, Gunnar thought. Not that Sweden was really involved, but still. He would go too, he decided. But his sister had gone to Uppsala to get away, and she had died anyway. He'd been proud of her: she'd managed, he'd thought. She had done it. Found a way out. All the fights with their father. She'd proven him wrong. *University.* Not that Gunnar had doubted. His sister had been smart. And then, in the end, it had all been for nothing.

There was the crack of a stick breaking and the boys turned.

It was Mr. Notholm, the owner of the hotel, the Winter Palace. His blond hair was greasy, and he had combed it back.

Gunnar didn't like him. His father had told him how Mr. Notholm had arrived once the hotel was already built and forced Mr. Olsson, the original owner, to sell to him.

"Forced?" Gunnar had asked his father.

His father frowned, as if he felt he had said too much. "Rumor has it he knew something about Mr. Olsson," he said, "That Mr. Olsson didn't want widely known."

Most people here had something in their background, Gunnar was certain. Otherwise why come in the first place? He had looked at his father; wondered why he was here and who knew what things about him.

"What are you boys doing?" Notholm said.

"Nothing," Abraham said.

"I would have thought you weren't allowed to leave the schoolyard during recess."

Abraham shrugged. "A man's got to do what a man's got to do," he said pluckily.

Gunnar looked at him. "A man?"

Notholm laughed. "I like that," he said. "I could use the help of a few young . . . men. Young men who aren't afraid of doing things that might be breaking a few rules. I need help in tracking something down. I'll pay you."

Abraham straightened. "We're not afraid."

The skin on Gunnar's back tingled, and he shivered. As if someone had just walked over his grave, his mother always said. He wanted to say that he didn't want to work—not for Notholm. But then it would sound as if he were afraid.

"Good," Notholm said. "I'll call on you soon."

"Abraham? Gunnar?" It was their teacher. She was young, on her first assignment. They all had a crush on her.

"We should go," Abraham said uncertainly. "Otherwise, they'll wonder."

Notholm smiled. Mocking? "Of course," he said then, exaggeratedly serious. "We don't want them to wonder."

16.

LAURA

Laura met Erik at the Grand Hotel again in the late afternoon. As she saw him at the bar, she felt a jolt, reminding her what it felt like to be in love.

She shook her head at herself, smiling at her thoughts. Erik was not her type, nor was she his. Seeing him promised an evening full of drinking and laughter, that's all. Since the war had begun, she hadn't gone out and had fun. She and her friends had been at university and overnight, they'd had to grow up. A part of her must have decided that side of life was gone for ever; she was an adult now, with responsibilities. But with Erik, she felt young; how pathetic was that?

Beside him at the bar, a group of German soldiers were drinking. They were wearing the black uniforms of the SS. *The audacity.* It had happened more often at the beginning of the war—German soldiers passing through Sweden on a break. Nowadays, you rarely saw them in uniform. They knew public opinion had changed. She was amazed these ones dared.

Erik had already ordered her a drink and she sat on the leather barstool beside him.

"It's good to see you." He looked into her eyes over the rim of his glass, his brown eyes seeming black in his pale face, and she felt the same jolt again. Not her type, she repeated to herself.

"You too," she said and lifted her glass. *Thank you.*

The soldiers behind him laughed loudly and she felt a stab of worry. Erik had been known to pick a fight. But it only seemed to amuse him. Pigs, he mimed. He leaned into her. "There was no other free space," he explained. "Now, I'm thinking perhaps we would have been better off standing."

Laura smiled.

"So, did you go to Uppsala?"

She nodded.

He shook his head, at the idea of her going, or of Britta's fate, or both.

"I saw the policeman," she said. "Has he been in contact with you?"

"No. Will he be?"

"He says he wants to speak with all of us."

Erik took a sip from his drink.

She turned her glass around, looked at the drops of condensation making their way down toward the liquid. "He told me all of us are in Stockholm now."

"What do you mean, 'all of us'?"

"Matti, Karl-Henrik, you, me . . ." She shrugged. "Did you know they were here?"

"Not at all."

"I can't believe they haven't gotten in touch."

"We did leave one another rather abruptly." He avoided her gaze, perhaps remembering his own role.

They had.

"You said something back then," she said.

"When?"

"Back at university. You said we were being watched."

"Did I?"

"Yes. You said Loki was following us."

Loki, the sly trickster god, scheming, caring only for himself. The flaw in the otherwise perfect world of the Norse gods.

He scoffed. "Was I drunk?"

"Probably," she admitted. But, as she said it, she thought about Inspector Ackerman. Someone knew things about their group and their interest in the Norse legends. She had a vision of this shadow following them, a shape-shifter: Loki.

"The war breaking out." Erik cleared his throat. "We all felt it, didn't we? Things spinning out of control. Ties being made and unmade. People you knew, advocating a different side. Not knowing who to trust. It was easy to feel paranoid."

"The policeman knew we had fallen out. Someone had told him"

"Well then, it was most likely Matti or Karl-Henrik, as they're both here."

"What if there was a Loki? What if he's the one who killed Britta?"

Erik shook his head. "Nobody got that close to us, Laura. We kept to ourselves."

"A secret society." The words rang in her ears.

"So," he said, "were there any German connections? Links to your secret project?"

He was making fun of her.

"She'd changed," she said.

"Who?"

"Britta."

"In what way?"

"She kept apart."

He took a sip of his drink. "We've all changed."

"It's like she no longer had any friends. I couldn't find out anything. Apart from one thing—a student said Britta had been in love. A relationship that went wrong and left her heartbroken."

Erik bent his head.

"Were you in love with her?" she asked him.

"With Britta?" He smiled.

She nodded and remembered his face whenever he looked at Britta. The only time his eyes softened.

"Weren't we all?"

In her mind's eye, she saw Britta's face again. Laughing, raising her glass in a toast. Laura sighed.

"But just a bit." Erik had leaned closer to her, his arm warm against hers. There was a glint in his eyes. "A teeny tiny bit."

Before she could react, the bartender was in front of them.

"Mr. Anker?"

Erik scowled.

"There's a phone call for you. In the lobby."

Erik walked through the bar and out into the adjacent lobby, the lean frame, the focused gait. A policeman on the hunt, Laura thought to herself again. Her drink was making her mind fuzzy. When Erik came back, she'd suggest they have dinner.

She saw Erik in the lobby, speaking on the wall-mounted phone close to the reception desk. He was gesticulating as if angry. Tense times.

They were playing American jazz; Billie Holiday's *I Cried for You*. The bar was full. Stockholm was a small town in many ways. There weren't that many restaurants or hotels. People ended up in the same places. The hotel was home to the international press headquarters, and it was always buzzing with news and with rumors. In the bar, there were people she recognized, people who she knew by reputation, or who had been pointed out to her: representatives of the British intelligence services, of the Gestapo; Finns and Norwegians in exile; Swedes from the Security Services; Italian fascists; Eastern-European "travellers"; "businessmen"; everybody spying on everybody else. She had been warned about them, shown photos, told they would try to befriend her, get her to talk, and then use her to get to Wallenberg and the negotiations . . . She avoided meeting anyone's gaze, as many of them would know who she was and have been shown photos, too.

"A neutral, green island in an otherwise dark, German Europe," one of the British diplomats had described Sweden.

She was done. She'd tell Wallenberg she had found no proof of any German links, or links to them. She'd listen to the policeman who had told her not to ask questions, let him do his job.

Through the crowd, she spotted Erik again, hanging up the receiver with such a force it was as if he were trying to hammer the phone itself down from the wall. He leaned his forehead against it, then spun around and headed back to her. She felt that same jolt again. She didn't want to like him. She *didn't* like him—not in that way. It was just that right now, he represented *before*.

"Dinner?" he asked.

"LET'S ENJOY THE spring night," he'd said as they left the restaurant, though Stockholm was in total darkness apart from the occasional dimmed lights of a cab or a tram rattling past. It wasn't that late, but there was a chill in the air, and they were both shivering by the time they reached her house.

Then he was adamant that they should have one more drink at the small bar in the building opposite hers.

"A nightcap," he said.

She could have invited him up to hers, but she was worried about what that would entail. She wasn't stupid; Britta's death had rendered her fragile. Him, too, most likely.

"You haven't told me yet what you're working on now," she said as they sat down at a small table by the window. The bar was warm. It smelled of cooked food. She lifted the edge of the blackout curtain stretched over the window and peeked out. On his side, Erik did the same. She half expected the waiter to scold them. Outside, it had begun to rain. Spring weather, unpredictable.

Across the street, the door to her apartment building opened, a brief square of light. A man, hands in pockets, head down, walked out into the rain without looking around. Laura let go of the curtain at the same time as Erik.

"This and that," Erik said. "I write articles about the occupation in Denmark, try to get people engaged."

"How is your family doing?"

He shrugged. "Last I heard, alright. We don't speak often. Dad's a policeman. Sabotage has been increasing—small acts of resistance—and the Germans want those caught to be severely punished. He struggles with that. The Germans are bloody brutes."

In the beginning, the Danish government had been trying to predict German directives, implementing them before they were issued. But rumor had it that the resistance was finally getting itself organized.

They sat, quiet, both lost in thought.

"It was as if Professor Lindahl didn't care that she was dead," she said.

"What?"

"When I saw him. It was as if he didn't care that Britta had died."

"He has a lot of students, Laura."

"But didn't you think we were . . . special to him?"

"No, I can't say I did. I mean, I enjoyed studying under him, but he was just a teacher."

She couldn't believe her ears: Erik had been infatuated with Professor Lindahl. They all had been—but he, the most.

"You always want these guarantees, Laura. That we'll all be together forever. That we're the best ones ever. The most loved ones, the most brilliant. Life isn't like that. Things change. People turn out to be just average."

She bent her head. His words stung. But it was true: things did change. And people moved on more quickly than she did.

Erik fingered his glass, then yawned.

It made her yawn, too.

"Time to leave," she said, although it wasn't yet nine according to the clock behind the bar.

"Let's have one more," he said, even though his glass was half-full.

"We should go."

"We could go dancing. Or to the China variety show?"

She hesitated. It was tempting, but she was exhausted, so she shook her head.

"Come on, Miss Dahlgren. For old time's sake."

"Another time. I'm tired."

She stood up.

As they stepped out, rain, driving in vertical bands, hit her on the top of the head and began running under her hair. Erik raised the collar of his jacket and grabbed her hand, and they ran across the street. At her door, she dawdled, couldn't find her keys. Erik pushed the door. It was open.

The hallway was lit, but it felt different.

Erik walked in behind her, as if he felt her hesitation.

"I don't know . . ." she said and began walking up the stairs to her apartment on the second floor.

Nothing had changed, and yet . . .

The door to her flat stood wide open, the dark room behind it resembling a gaping hole.

She inhaled sharply.

Erik put out his arm to hold her back. "They might still be in there. Let's leave, Laura. Come on!"

She ducked under his arm, walked to her door, reached her hand inside and flicked the switch. The hallway light was bright yellow. Her chair lay overturned. Its seat had been slashed. Her father had given her that chair. It used to stand in their hallway at home. "You can sit on it and remember your old father and grandfather and all that they've given you," he'd joked.

The drawers in her dresser had all been emptied onto the floor, her clothes pulled out from the entryway closet. Who would do such a thing? She continued walking into the flat and each room was the same. All her belongings. All her things were scattered on the floor: photos, books, jewelry, clothes . . . She tried not to step on them, watching where she put her feet. There was a smell. A bitter smell. Plastic burning?

She needed to call the police, but in the living room, her phone had been ripped out from the wall, the contact hanging loose.

The smell was getting stronger. Sulfur?

Rapid footsteps behind her. Erik, eyes wide.

"Get out of here! Now!"

He grabbed her arm and pulled her through the hallway. She stumbled as she followed. They ran down the stairs, jumped the last steps. At the bottom, he threw himself against her and they fell as her apartment exploded, shaking the building, and sending a white puff of dust down the stairs.

A moment of silence. Then panic. Doors opened as her neighbors fled, running down the stairs, screaming as they passed the damage on the second floor.

Sirens. The police were on their way.

LAURA WAS STANDING with a blanket over her shoulders that a policeman had put there. The rain had stopped. The street was a stretch of blank wetness. The sky was dark blue. On the other side of the road, the windows of her apartment had been blown out, gaping holes in the night. There had been a brief, violent fire that the firemen had extinguished, but the sides of her windows were charred black, flames reaching out to grab at the bricks outside. There wouldn't be much left inside. It all felt unreal. If Erik hadn't pulled her out . . .

"The man," she said to Erik.

"What?"

"While we were having a drink, a man came out of my apartment building."

"I didn't see." He touched her cheek with a finger. "You're bleeding."

She shook her head. "How did you know? How did you know we had to leave?"

"I walked into your kitchen. The bomb was there, on the floor by the stove."

"A bomb?" A policeman had come up to them.

"Yes," Erik said. "At least I think so."

"What did it look like?"

"A piece of pipe. There were wires going to an alarm clock. I thought . . ." He shrugged. "It looked like an explosive device to me."

"There was a smell, too," Laura said. "Sulfur."

"A pipe bomb, perhaps," the policeman said.

"My apartment had been burgled."

"Anything missing?"

Laura thought about the jewelry on the floor, the television in the corner. All her belongings pulled out of drawers and cupboards.

"I don't know. It looked more as if they'd been searching for something."

"What would that be?" the policeman asked.

"I have no idea. I work for the trade committee that negotiates with the Germans, but I never take work home."

She had to call Wallenberg. She had to let him know.

"A man came out of our building, perhaps fifteen minutes before we went in," she told the policeman.

"What did he look like?"

"I couldn't really tell. He had his head down."

"We will need to talk to you again," the policeman said. "Later tonight, or tomorrow. The forensics team is here now. Where will you go?"

"To my father's house." She gave him the address.

"It might not be us who come to see you."

No, she thought. This was a bomb. It would be the *Hestapo* who came—she used the nickname for Sweden's Security Services.

"Miss Dahlgren. Miss Dahlgren!"

A man in a trench coat and hat was waving to her from outside the cordoned-off area. Emil Persson, a journalist at *Svenska Dagbladet*, or *The English Daily*, as the Germans called it. Emil had done a piece on her father not long ago: "The Central Banker Who Keeps Sweden Steady." Her father had liked the article. "You're so vain," she'd teased him. He had just laughed.

"What happened?" he asked when she reached him.

"I don't know," she said.

"A bomb? Was it in your flat?"

"She won't answer questions." The policeman had followed her. "Right now, Miss Dahlgren will go home. We'll inform you when we have anything to reveal."

Laura nodded to Emil Persson. *Another time.*

"But why your flat, Laura?" he shouted after her as she left. "Does it have to do with your father, or with Wallenberg?"

They got a lift in a police car. Erik insisted on coming with her and dropping her off.

"That was close," he said as they sat together in the backseat. He'd taken her hand, or she, his. The skin was warm, the hand strong.

"It has to do with Britta," she said.

He shook his head. "This probably has to do with your work. A bomb . . . A lot of people don't like the stance Sweden has taken with the Germans."

Collaborators, not neutral, prolonging the war; she'd heard all the comments. The Finns and the Norwegians felt that Sweden had sold out. In many ways, they had.

"And now there will be others who don't appreciate that Sweden is turning pro-Allied."

She was surprised he knew this. Perhaps it was just plain obvious to everyone.

"Then they wouldn't start with me," she said. "I'm just a low-level administrator."

And not like this, she thought. There would have been a contact, a warning, an attempt to get her to cooperate. No, this was different.

"You travel with Wallenberg. People say you're his right hand."

Did they? Was she? It was true, he liked having her in the room. He said she gave him a different insight into the negotiations.

They were coming up to her father's villa and she saw it as Erik must see it: the avenue of elm trees, the majestic white mansion; from what she knew, he had grown up in very different conditions. But he didn't seem to notice.

"It's too much of a coincidence," she muttered. "First Britta and now this."

"Whatever it is, I don't like it," Erik said. "Tonight was a close call. You do realize that, don't you?"

She did. But none of it made sense.

SHE CALLED JACOB Wallenberg on the number he had provided for emergencies.

He interrupted her. "Where are you?"

"At my father's house."

"I'll be there in half an hour." He hung up.

Laura and her father waited in his study. Her father kept walking around, turning to stare at her, then sitting down again.

"Why wouldn't you tell me she had died?"

"I just didn't," she said. "I guess I was still shocked."

"And then you went back there?" He raked his hands through his hair, then stood up again. "Why, Laura? Why?"

"Why are you angry with me?" she asked.

"I'm not angry with you. But this had nothing to do with you. You should have known to leave well enough alone."

She thought of Professor Lindahl saying one had to be "careful about these things."

But what had she done? Asked a few questions? She had found out nothing, but the two events being linked seemed incontestable to her. She remembered her overturned apartment. They had been looking for something, she thought again. What if it was never about what she might have shared with Britta, only what Britta might have shared with her? But why blow the apartment up? To kill her? And in case whatever they were looking for was there, even if they hadn't found it—did they want to destroy it?

When Wallenberg arrived, the two men shook hands, then both turned to look at Laura, their foreheads wrinkled. They looked so similar that on another occasion she would have laughed.

Laura stood up and went to pour herself a whiskey, thinking she might need it. She took a sip. It burned in her chest.

"Tell me all of it," Wallenberg said and sat down on the settee beside her father's desk.

When she had finished, he pursed his lips and tapped the frame of his glasses against his chin. Laura could feel the room bristling from the energy between the two men.

"I asked Laura to make sure the death of her friend didn't have something to do with us," Wallenberg said to her father.

"How could you?" her father exploded. "A murder, and you send her to ask questions?"

Laura cringed; it was as if this was between the two of them and she wasn't even there.

Wallenberg sighed. "You're her father. I do understand how it must seem."

"So, this is about your work then?"

Wallenberg shook his head. "I don't think so. Our group have received no threats, apart from the usual ones. The negotiations are tricky. We're caught between Germany and the Allies." Wallenberg and her father exchanged a glance—they were both well aware of the gravity of the situation. "But if this was about us, I can't imagine they would have tried to blow Laura up. It would be far more likely that they would have tried to get her to talk—like they apparently did with her friend."

Laura agreed with him.

"Unless other things have happened that you're not telling me?" Wallenberg said to Laura.

"No." Laura shook her head. "No!" she insisted when they both kept staring at her.

"The Security Services will come and see you tomorrow," Wallenberg said. "Whatever you tell them will go to Germany—the political side of Germany."

He was meaning the Gestapo and the SS, she thought. The Security Services were still awfully close to them. Acting almost like a fifth column. The country was leaking like a sieve.

"You mustn't lie, and you must tell all of it. But I want you to know it doesn't stay with them."

Her father sighed.

"My phone calls are listened to," Wallenberg said. "My phone has been tapped since the beginning of the war. I am certain the same is true for you. How do you feel?"

How did she feel? Confused. Not as much scared or sad as empty. She'd been proud of that flat. It had been her home for the last five years.

"Alright," she said.

"I don't want you to come into work," he said.

"I can work!" Laura protested. "I'm fine."

"Perhaps," he said, "but I cannot have you there until we know what this is."

He wasn't thinking about her, he was protecting the negotiations. Their negotiations.

She exhaled. "But you asked me to ask questions."

"I did. But now I think you were right: this has nothing to do with us. It has everything to do with you. And your friend."

She felt sullied, although she had done nothing wrong.

Her father didn't seem surprised. He'd known Wallenberg would do this. He'd expected it. That was what happened when you were a woman, she thought. If something happened involving you, regardless of whether it was your fault, you were dropped, as if you were contagious.

"Well then," her father concluded the conversation, "you are home now. You'll be safe."

And as simply as that, she had lost her job, too.

17.

JENS

The administrative assistant came to find Jens as he was about to leave.

"It was hard," she said, lifting thin eyebrows as if it had surprised her. "The personnel department claims they cannot give out details."

"I guess they have their rules," he said.

"Usually, it's not this difficult."

He waited.

"Daniel Jonsson is off sick. The lady who has taken his place is called Emilia Svensson. She used to work for the Ministry of Defense and she'll be here until further notice."

"Ah," he said, "thank you. Sick with what?"

She shook her head. "They don't seem to think he's coming back."

It hadn't taken them more than a night to find a replacement. Normally, if an employee was unwell, their position would remain unfilled until it was certain that the person wasn't returning. Perhaps there had been an accident?

"I did manage to find his address, though," the woman said and handed him a piece of paper. "You know, if you need to pick up your book."

JENS WAITED FOR Sven inside the Norma restaurant, but as it became clear his friend would be later than agreed, he ordered his food. He sat at the wooden table and read the day's papers again. The waitress behind the glass counter was dark-haired and green-eyed. She was wearing a checkered dress and a cap. She had a thin, triangular-shaped face with sharp features and angles, the skin blue-white and so vulnerable looking where her chin met her ear. She caught his stare, looked away, but then met his gaze again and smiled.

This time, Jens broke away. He had Kristina now. Though Kristina had no vulnerable areas by her chin. He frowned at the thought of having to confront her about Schnurre's visit. He sighed. *Oh, by the way, you have no idea who I saw* . . .

Jens waited for over an hour, but Sven didn't show. As he put his hand in his pocket to grab his wallet, his fingers brushed the note from the administrative assistant containing Daniel Jonsson's address. Perhaps he was only putting off talking to Kristina about Schnurre.

DANIEL JONSSON LIVED in an apartment on Folkungagatan in Södermalm, walking distance from Old Town. As Jens crossed the waters over to Södermalm, he stopped and looked back, thrown by the views, as always. There was no other city as beautiful as Stockholm. The sea winding itself through the town, the bridges, the pastel-colored houses, the many church spires. He could not live anywhere else. But the city was shifting so much that he sometimes had the impression he could hear the stretched fabric ripping: the industrialization and the population increase had brought with them massive changes. There was the new upper class; people coming from the trades and industry. And parliamentary democracy was just over twenty years old. People expected a lot from something that was still forming. It had to become more equal, rights for everyone, and Jens wanted to be a part of that.

The windows of the building where Daniel lived were dark, like all the other Stockholm windows. The air smelled warm, of greenery and dust.

He rang Daniel's doorbell, but nobody answered. He tried a couple of times and stepped back, but the windows remained dark. As he was about to leave, a man opened the street door from the inside, hat pushed low. Jens took the door from him and entered. Daniel Jonsson lived on the third floor. He took the steps two at a time.

He knocked on the door. No response. Could Daniel be so sick he'd ended up in hospital? He knocked again, then bent down to look through the mail slot. The apartment lay dark and still and yet . . . Jens had the feeling someone was there. Holding their breath, standing motionless.

"Daniel?" he called into the darkness.

There was no response.

"Daniel." He was whispering now, though he wasn't sure why. "This is Jens, from the ministry. I need to talk to you."

No response. Jens stood up, took his notebook from his bag and tore out a page. On it, he wrote his name and home phone number. He thought for a minute, then added his address. *Please get in touch*, he wrote. *I believe you.*

As he got home, his own flat, too, lay in darkness. On the kitchen table was a note from Kristina: *My father called. I have to work tonight and so I will sleep at home. See you tomorrow?*

———

IT WAS A busy morning. The Germans had lifted their ban on ships bringing imported goods to Sweden. They'd have coffee and fish again, Jens thought. And new shoes. Sweden had also been invited to attend formal trade negotiations with the United Kingdom and the United States. Günther had asked Jens to do some preparatory work.

Jens: "Do you think the Allies actually might bomb us if the negotiations don't go well?"

Günther, face grim: "I think they could."

There was a knock on the door and Sven entered, wearing his usual tweed suit and with his hair combed back. His face, normally fragile-looking with its large, downturned eyes, curved nose and thin lips, looked even more so.

"I'm sorry about standing you up last night," he said in his soft voice.

Jens shook his head. "Don't worry."

"We got delayed working on the budget." Sven pulled a face. "And then, later in the evening, there was an explosion in an apartment in central Stockholm. The police called the minister as we were leaving."

"An explosion? I didn't hear about it."

"The woman who owns the apartment works for Wallenberg in the committee that trades with the Germans. They are treating it as a terrorist attack." Sven shrugged. "Nothing will be said officially or released to the papers."

"She works for Wallenberg? We would have met, then. Who is it?"

"Her name is Laura Dahlgren."

They had met once, here at the ministry. Jens remembered a young woman with blond shoulder-length hair and big gray eyes. Beautiful, yet slightly detached and aloof. Smart. Intense.

Her eyes hadn't left him, never blinked, as he had talked about the ministry's role in the negotiations. She felt superior, he'd thought. Entitled.

"Are there many such things we don't hear about?" Jens prompted.

Sven shrugged. "Not many."

"But?" Jens asked.

"Recently, there have been two: the bomb and a murder."

"A murder?"

Sven nodded. "Here's the thing," he said, lowering his voice and glancing at the door. "The woman who was murdered and the woman whose apartment blew up were friends. They went to university together. What are the chances of that?

"Rumor has it that the murdered one was a swallow."

Jens thought about Barbro Cassel and Karl Schnurre. What a life these young women were condemning themselves to. Kristina's face slithered through his mind, but he closed that thought down, wouldn't go there. He couldn't see Laura Dahlgren being a secret agent, however. She was too intense. Who would want to go out with her?

"What is the C-Bureau doing about the murder of their agent?" he asked.

Sven scoffed. Unlike his father, he had little respect for the C-Bureau. He thought them brutes who should not have been allowed in the first place. "Probably trying to stay as far away from it as possible, covering up any tracks leading to them, and throwing out a few leading the wrong way."

"But the Security Services have gotten themselves involved, so there must be a threatening scenario of some sort."

Jens wondered if Sven had told his minister about the C-Bureau. An impossible situation: torn between two loyalties;

one to his father, who'd helped set up the C-Bureau, and the other to his boss, who ultimately headed up the rival agency.

"Who was she?"

"A student. A party girl. A nobody. But clever and well liked. A good source for the Bureau, too, from what I have been told."

Well liked, Jens thought. She would have had lots of "clients." He thought about Barbro Cassel, though the woman obviously hadn't been her, as Barbro had been to their dinner the other night.

"What was her name?" he asked, just to make certain.

"Britta Hallberg."

Not Barbro. Though the name sounded familiar.

"You need to find out more," Jens said. "This doesn't sound right."

Sven shrugged. "It's being managed by the Security Services."

"Which come under your boss. Surely he'd want to know more? This is about activities on Swedish land. If it has to do with foreign forces, then Günther needs to know as well."

Sven looked away.

"Sorry," Jens said. *Too much.* He raised his hand. "I'm pre-occupied with my own issues. A few days ago, an archivist here asked me to find out why Günther had spoken to the foreign ministers of Denmark and Norway, in order to log the conversations. I spoke with the minister and he claimed the conversations had never taken place. Not only did he deny it, but I think he threatened me. Or, my job, rather. I went back to the archivist, whose paperwork has now gone missing, as have the records in the registrar. And now the archivist himself is 'off sick.'" He marked the quotation marks in the air with his fingers. "This is why I wanted to see you yesterday. I wanted to ask for your advice."

"Do you trust the archivist more than Günther?" Sven asked.

They were whispering now.

"The archivist is known to be diligent and conscientious."

Sven nodded. Answer enough. He too had heard the rumors about the foreign minister.

"How would one go about getting the records changed?" Jens asked.

"I have no idea. Möller would have to approve it, I guess. Günther couldn't just waltz in and ask to have them changed. And if my minister knew, I think I would, too."

"Perhaps he knows someone," Jens said.

"Who knows someone. Perhaps."

"I'm not sure what to do about it."

Sven pursed his lips. "Leave it. It's just some phone calls."

"It doesn't feel right. If they weren't important, they wouldn't have been deleted."

Sven shrugged. "You need to trust your minister."

Easy for him to say. Sven was Möller's right hand. He genuinely believed in his minister.

"There's more," Jens said. He told Sven about Karl Schnurre at dinner and then at his apartment.

Sven bit his lip. Jens reckoned he was taking care not to say something that could be taken as a criticism of Kristina. The two had met, but, like his father, Sven had seemingly not taken to Kristina, nor she to him.

"Be wary," he said at last. "Schnurre is dangerous. Both for the connections he has abroad and those here in Stockholm."

"I'm sure it's nothing. I'll ask Kristina about it."

Sven frowned. "Or perhaps not?" he suggested.

That would mean a relationship built on a lie. A life filled with monitoring the person you lived with, looking for inconsistencies, suspecting . . .

Sven shrugged. "I only mean, this is the one you're going to marry, and it could come across as a serious accusation. You don't know anything for sure."

Sven didn't trust Kristina, Jens thought. Did he? God, he no longer knew.

Jens realized what had been bugging him earlier. "What was her name again, the young woman who died?"

"Britta Hallberg."

Britta Hallberg. But that was the person who . . .

He pushed back his chair and looked in the garbage bin he knew would be empty. Silently, he cursed. He rose. "I have to go."

"Are you okay?" Sven asked. "You don't look good."

"I'm fine," Jens said, not trusting his own voice. "A meeting I forgot."

JENS RAN DOWN the corridor and glanced into each office on the way, but he couldn't see the cleaners. He hurried down the stairs and caught up with a member of the cleaning staff in the lobby.

He grabbed the woman by her sleeve. "I threw a document away yesterday by mistake."

She looked at his hand and he let go; he raised his hands in an apology, smiled. "I threw it in my garbage bin. Is there any chance I can recover it?"

She shook her head. "Garbage is burned each evening," she said, and he knew it was, but he had hoped.

Jesus Christ.

He went back to his room, the walk now feeling unbearably long. Sven had left. Jens sank down behind his desk.

So a woman, a swallow, is murdered in such a way that the

Security Services get themselves involved, but before she dies she sends him, Jens, a thesis?

Sven said she was a student.

But why send it to him?

Jens had been invited to speak in Uppsala. A Professor Lindahl had asked him to come to a *nachspiel*, to talk about Sweden's foreign policy to a small group of students. The professor had a reputation for being extraordinarily intelligent—the government used him all the time—but he had made Jens feel uncomfortable. He was one of these androgynous characters. Face of a poet. Thought himself a genius. Jens tried to remember the women in the room. The only one who stood out was a blonde, with a northern accent, who was beautiful in a slightly vulgar way. Please don't let it be her—he thought—she'd been so full of life, of zest, but of course it would be. He was certain. She had asked questions, he remembered now; intelligent questions about history and truth, about how much was known at any one time and how much of that which was known was later lost, hidden or *reshaped*. He had told her that everyone interpreted events according to what they saw and heard, each man with filters shaped by his own past—he was referring to the philosopher Immanuel Kant's green sunglasses. But, he had argued, there was such a thing as a universal truth, an accurate history, and a good man would try to get as close to it as possible, trying to notice his own filters, and look beyond the same.

"A good man . . ." Yes, that was what he had said. And then she had sent him a document before dying.

18.

BLACKÅSEN MOUNTAIN

Director Sandler paced his living room. Restless. It was a small town. At times, it felt way too small. He had the impression the forest was leaning in on them, gradually advancing to swallow them up. He had been to see Georg Ek's widow and found the conversation hard to let go. It was always difficult to evict a family and, rather than support him, the foreman had contradicted him. There was no way the boy would make the cut. He was too young, too skinny. He hadn't even grown facial hair yet.

"The boy . . ." he'd said to Hallberg afterward.

"Yes?" The foreman jutted his chin out.

"He isn't ready."

"We look after our own. The others will carry him until he is."

"We can't carry people. This is a business."

Hallberg's eyes narrowed. "I don't think you have any reason to complain of the work so far, do you? Our workers slave for you night and day for minimal wages."

Sandler had backed down, even raised his hands as if in surrender. Didn't want to get into a discussion about wages. But now he was troubled. He wasn't in charge of the mine. It was clear. Things were running well enough without him and he didn't like it.

SANDLER SADDLED HIS HORSE. There was nothing like a riding trip in the forest to clear your mind and he needed his mind cleared.

He grabbed the reins in his left hand, put his foot in the stirrup and swung himself up. The horse jogged a couple of steps to the side, then settled under his weight. Sandler squeezed with his thighs, feeling the warm muscles of the horse shift.

He steered the stallion out of the garden. It twitched. This animal loved to gallop; needed it as much as he did. It was just waiting for his command. Once on the road, he kicked his heels into the horse's sides again. And they were off.

They galloped down Blackåsen's main road. People stepped aside. His horse. His land. His people. *Here goes the director again. A crazy man on a crazy horse.* So be it, he thought. This was his outlet.

He needed a foreman he could trust. He would replace Hallberg. The foreman's second-in-command wasn't yet up to the job, but there had to be someone else.

At the end of the town, horse and rider left the road and took a trail into the forest. The trail was finally free of snow. The stallion lengthened its strides, and Sandler rose in the stirrups and crouched over its neck.

Faster, he willed it. Faster.

The world became a blur, but he trusted his mount. It knew what it was doing. He could feel its muscles move underneath his hands. He could feel his own anxiety pouring off him and away.

He rode like one possessed, down the trail and into the forest.

It wasn't until they reached the large river that he slowed down. The horse was breathing heavily, just like he was. Sandler inhaled, felt his lungs ache.

They stopped by the water and the animal bent its head to drink. The forest was silent. He'd gone far enough to not hear the constant clamor coming from the mine. Peace, he thought.

He closed his eyes, listened to the trickling of water.

The stallion shook its head as if it knew how he was feeling. Then it tensed and turned. A noise. Sandler heard it, too. Someone else coming—also on a horse . . . No, more than one horse. At least two.

He didn't want to see anyone. He slid off his mount and led it into the forest behind him. He stood underneath its neck, held the bit close to his own face, willed it to be silent.

Just a moment later, two horses emerged. Notholm. The sight of him made Sandler cringe. And with him, Dr. Öhrnberg. This surprised him. Öhrnberg was a respected man in the community. A scientist. He was a quiet, thoughtful man. He'd always struck Sandler as very cultured; wise, even. He had never seen the two men together before and he couldn't imagine what business they could possibly have with each other.

Their horses drank from the river, just as his had done moments earlier. Beside him, his stallion shifted. Perhaps at the sight of other animals. Director Sandler stroked its neck.

"It shall all be done," Notholm said.

"I never doubted it." Öhrnberg looked out over the river.

Notholm nodded. "One thing, though."

"Yes?"

"One of them—a particular one—is for me."

"For you?" Öhrnberg turned to look at his companion.

Notholm shrugged. "Just for me."

Öhrnberg sighed. "That is not what this is about. It's not what we want."

"That is my condition: this one has to be for me."

"Fine," Öhrnberg said. "Just no mess."

"No mess."

The two men sat up taller and directed their horses onto the path. Sandler waited until he was certain they were gone. They were up to something, he thought. It's none of your business he told himself. But it had to do with Notholm. And even though he'd been told to leave well enough alone, Notholm *was* his business.

19.

LAURA

Laura was still in bed. She was in her childhood bedroom in her father's house and nobody would care if she stayed there all day. She couldn't remember the last time she had slept in. She didn't like oversleeping. It was such a waste: a whole day ahead of you, reduced. She much preferred to be tired than to sleep for longer. Britta had loved sleeping till late in the morning.

Her father had left early that morning. He had wanted to stay and attend the police interview. She had said absolutely not. She was an adult. Even if he and Wallenberg didn't treat her as such. Grumpily, he'd accepted.

"You are home now," he'd said last night. "You'll be safe."

She could think of nothing worse. Returned to where she was eight years ago, before starting university. A child in the house of her father. Everything she had fought for, gone. Her independence, vanished. She had always planned a way out: if she hadn't enjoyed history at university, she would have changed to economics—she had made sure she knew the professor. If the negotiations with the Germans came to an end, she would continue working with Wallenberg in a different capacity. But not once had it occurred to her that Wallenberg might drop her. He liked her.

Once, during a business trip to Germany, the two of them had remained at the bar when the others had retired.

"You see patterns where others see nothing," he'd said. "You don't realize it yourself, but in the negotiations, you make huge leaps to draw conclusions and you're always right. A gaze, a phrasing, a face . . . You immediately seem to know what it means. Intuition . . . intellect, I don't know what it is but it's quite remarkable."

She hadn't known what to say.

"I can't wait to see what will happen the day you dare start acting on these impulses rather than just telling others about them," he said. "That day, you will begin to trust yourself."

He was right about her not believing in herself, but she hadn't thought it was obvious to others.

"Intelligent, like your father," Wallenberg had said.

She knew what high praise that was; knew the admiration men held for her father.

"I'm thinking you might even be better than your father," Wallenberg had said.

And now, she had become a liability, a security risk, and he had dropped her. Another reason he was good at his job: he did not mix personal feelings with whatever work was at hand.

Someone had destroyed her life. She'd lost her best friend, her flat and her job. Her eyes burned and she closed them. There was nothing left. They had killed her friend and then tried to take her life, too. She might have died, had not . . . had not Erik asked for a nightcap?

No, she thought. She knew Erik.

"It has to do with you. And your friend," Wallenberg had said. Did it?

It was strange, she had to admit. The missing eye, the body at the Historical Society. It could be seen as a message to them. But why? Nothing in their history together merited a murder . . . And a bomb.

She sat up, swung her legs over the side of the bed and stood up. I shall carry on, she said to herself. That was what her two male role models had taught her: to carry on. *Something will come up.*

After she'd dressed, there was a soft knock on the door.

"There is a phone call for you," the maid said.

She walked downstairs and took the receiver.

"Hello?"

"Hi, Laura. It's Emil Persson from *Svenska Dagbladet*. How are you?"

"I have nothing to tell you," she said. "Really."

"Was it your flat?"

"It was."

"But why?"

"I have no idea."

"Mind if I dig around?"

"Be my guest." She hesitated. "Let me know if you find anything."

Her grandfather was standing in the doorway: "Laura, the police are here to talk to you."

THERE WERE TWO of them. Her grandfather asked if she wanted him to stay, but she shook her head. One of the policemen was older, her father's age, silver-haired, but with the bumpy face of a boxer. The other one was younger, close to her own age.

He was dark-haired, and his face was open. Wallenberg had told her to tell them everything and so she did. All of it, starting with Britta's death.

"Have you been threatened in any way?" the older policeman asked.

She shook her head.

"What about the work you're doing for Wallenberg—have there been threats there?"

"Not aimed at me. I think this has to do with Britta's death."

The older one lowered his head. "You said you were best friends," he asked. "If she was frightened, surely she would have told you?"

Their visit at NK flashed through her mind.

"I imagine she would have if we had met more often," she said, with effort. "But we rarely saw each other after I left Uppsala."

"I thought girlfriends told each other everything," he insisted. "Are you sure she didn't hint at anything?"

She shrugged. It was her fault that Britta hadn't told her what she was frightened of, that time she came to Stockholm, but, with Britta, she had never known everything. She had understood there had been affairs, men, dates, but she had rarely known who those men were. She didn't think Britta was hiding things: it was more that the details didn't matter much to her. Laura also knew very little about Britta's past. Britta had not spoken about her family, or her upbringing—possibly for the same reason.

Had Laura told Britta everything? Yes, she thought; she had. Not always willingly, but whatever she hadn't said, Britta had seemingly understood anyway.

"Again," she said, "I think she would have, had I been there. Haven't you found out anything yet?"

The older policeman frowned. "The explosion only happened last night."

"Yes, but the other policeman in Uppsala, he's been on the case since Britta was killed."

"Ah . . ." The older policeman looked at his papers. "Inspector Ackerman . . . We don't know that the two are linked yet. At the moment, we are treating it as two separate incidents, as well as two linked events. The murder might have been connected to Britta's personal life."

The older policeman closed his book. The younger one stood up. "May I use your washroom before we leave?"

"Yes," she said. "It's in the hallway."

He left the room. The older policeman was still watching her.

"If I were you, I'd lie low for now," he said.

She nodded. *Yes, yes.*

He leaned forward. The red bumps on his forehead were flaking. His eyes were small, his gaze hard.

"No." He shook his head. "I would lie really, really low. I wouldn't talk to anyone or see anyone. Heck, I'd probably not leave the house."

The hair on her arms was standing up even though they were the police and she was supposed to feel safe with them.

The door opened in the hallway: the younger one, coming out of the washroom.

The older policeman stood up. "We'll see ourselves out."

HER GRANDFATHER WAS sitting in an armchair in the living room. He didn't rise like he usually did when she came in, just lifted his hand in greeting. He looked small.

"Everything alright?" he asked.

"Yes," she said. "Are you cold? Do you want me to make up a fire?"

"It's spring. There's no need for fires."

"If you're cold, you're cold."

"No, no." The steely military resolve was still there. "No need."

She fetched a blanket and put it over his knees, though he scoffed. She sat down in the chair beside him, mind buzzing.

The older policeman had sought to scare her. Why? People had tried to kill her and now the police were attempting to scare her.

Wait. She slowed herself down. Had they tried to kill her?

The bomb was set on a timer. She thought about the man exiting the apartment building. That had been perhaps fifteen minutes before the bomb went off. Enough time for him to disappear. They had no idea when she would return and she had come home early, for her. If they wanted to be certain to murder her, surely the bomb would have had a mechanism that was triggered by movement, so it would go off when she came in?

No, they had executed Britta but had tried to scare Laura off—and potentially destroy anything compromising that Britta might have given her.

"What are you thinking about?" her grandfather asked.

"About all of this," she confessed. "My friend, my flat . . . It's a lot to take in."

"It would be a lot for anyone." He had clasped his bony white fingers in his lap on top of the blanket. Now, he unfolded them and pinched at the wool. "So what will you do?"

She sighed. "Regroup. I need to find a new job, a new place to live . . ."

He nodded, but his fingers had fallen still again in his lap.

She realized he'd asked what she would do about Britta. But I will do nothing, she thought, confused. The police were on it, the Security Services . . . She wondered how Britta's family had taken the death of their daughter. But she no longer had a brief to investigate.

But it occurred to her that her grandfather was disappointed.

20.

Jens left messages with Professor Lindahl at Uppsala University, but he didn't hear back from him. He wrote down the table of contents of the thesis from memory, repeated it to himself over and over, but it told him nothing. He was certain there hadn't been a note stuck into the thesis; after all, he had flipped through it. Thus, the dissertation itself was the message. A message he hadn't read.

He leaned his head in his hands. It's not my problem, he thought. There were the unregistered phone calls the minister had made, there was Kristina potentially meeting with Schnurre, there was the missing archivist . . . There was his normal work!

But a young woman had been killed. Another one had barely escaped the same fate. How could he possibly leave it alone?

It seemed likely that the first had been murdered for her involvement with the C-Bureau, but, if so, why had she sent him the thesis? And if there was something in her paper that was related to her death, why send it to him and not to her handler at the Bureau?

Laura Dahlgren was alive, however. He decided to try to talk to her. He called Wallenberg, who told him that in view of what had happened, she was on leave and could be found at her father's house in Djursholm. Jens heard something in Wallenberg's tone. Displeasure? Christian Günther was at an all-day meeting at Parliament. Jens took the tram out to the address in Djursholm.

The Dahlgren home was a white villa next to the glittering sea. A wide avenue of elm trees led up to the dwelling, which was designed in national romantic style, two floors, wood paneled with a plated roof. The middle section of the house protruded to face the water, with a tower on top. He could just imagine what it would be like to sit in that section; you'd feel right next to the water. No wonder Laura had such an air of entitlement. Looking at the old trees in the garden, now abounding with white flowers, he'd bet anything that they'd be full of apples in summer. He rang the bell.

It was Laura herself who opened the door. She frowned when she saw him, recognizing him but perhaps not able to place him. Her wide gray eyes were still. Her nose was narrow and ended with a tiny bump. Detached beauty, he concluded again.

"My name is Jens Regnell," he said. "I work at the Ministry of Foreign Affairs. I'm secretary to Christian Günther. We've met at the ministry."

There was a crease between her eyebrows. "I know."

"I wonder if I could have a moment of your time?"

She turned and waved him to follow her into the living room. It was just like he'd thought it would be. If he looked out the windows, the water was right there. You had the impression of sitting on a dock. She sat down and nodded to an armchair.

"This is going to sound strange—" he said.

"Did they send you?" she said, interrupting. "The Security Services?"

"No. Nobody knows I'm here . . . In fact, perhaps we'd better keep it that way."

Laura said nothing. Her face was stern . . . or suspicious?

"A couple of days ago, I received a package," he said. "It contained a thesis."

Now, she leaned forward, mouth open. "No."

"I threw it away," he confessed, quickly.

"Was it Britta's? Britta Hallberg?"

He nodded.

"Did you read it?"

He shook his head.

"Oh God," she said.

Irritation rose within him. "It was sent to me cold, without a note," he said tartly. "I had no idea what it was. I do have other things to do apart from reading students' dissertations." He took a breath, forced himself to calm down. "It was only when I was told she had been murdered that I realized . . ."

"You threw it away," she said. "I can't believe it!"

She was stubborn, he could see it now. The type that never lets things go, never forgives.

They fell silent.

"I heard about what happened to you," he said, after a while, "and that the two of you were close. I thought I'd come and see you . . . ask what's going on."

She shook her head. "I don't know. I was the one who found her . . . body. Wallenberg asked me to see if there were any links to our negotiations, and then there was a bomb in my flat . . . I knew her thesis was missing. The answer must have been in it—don't you think? Why would she have sent it to you otherwise?" She wrinkled her forehead. "And why would she send it to you, anyway?"

He shook his head. "I don't know. I gave a speech at a dinner hosted by her professor, but otherwise, I have no idea." He hesitated. "She asked about history and about truth . . ."

"Asked what?"

He shrugged.

"Do try to remember," she said.

He swallowed down his irritation. "Well, it was as if she was trying to gauge how easy it was to hide the past . . . discover if you could reshape history after the fact."

"We used to talk about that. Debate how much of history was written by the decision makers in the way they wanted . . . Were you having an affair with her?"

"God, no!" Jens threw his hands out. "That was the only time I ever met her."

"At the *nachspiel*," Laura clarified.

Jens cleared his throat. He hesitated. But this woman was trusted by Wallenberg himself. She was on the negotiating committee with Germany. She had been vetted. "What I tell you now is confidential," he said. "Under no circumstances must you tell anyone else." He waited for her to nod before continuing. "There is a second intelligence agency here in Sweden called the C-Bureau. They have several young women working for them. They call them swallows. Women who get to know people of interest—and report back. They party with them, accompany them, and take note of what they hear and see. Only a handful of people know of the Bureau's existence. I'm told she was one of them."

"A spy?"

He shrugged. More or less.

"Britta," she mumbled. She closed her eyes then opened them again. "Britta would have been brilliant at it. Nobody would have suspected her to be anything but a party girl. But she could hold her liquor and she was smart. And she would have loved doing something for Sweden.

"Her fellow students said she had stopped going out in Uppsala, but perhaps she had only changed venues . . . Do you think she found something out that got her killed?"

"I don't know, but if so, the killer must think you know the same thing."

"I haven't seen her for months. If it had to do with her being a . . . swallow, and she found something out, then this could be linked to Germany after all."

"Or the Allies." He shrugged. "But then, why the thesis?"

Laura bit her lip. "Do you remember the title of it?"

He nodded. "*Nordic Relations Through the Ages—Denmark, Norway and Sweden on a New Path.*"

"Not Finland?"

"I guess not."

"No Germany?"

He shook his head again.

She exhaled and seemed relieved.

He continued, "The table of contents was as follows:

i.   *Introduction*
ii. *Objectives and Demarcations*
1.   *History: The Scandinavian Unions*
2.   *The Reich*
3.   *The 1800s: A New Way*
4.   *The 1900s: A New Threat*
5.   *Behind the Scenes of the Three Kings' Meeting in 1914*
6.   *Outcome from the Three Kings' Meeting in 1939"*

"Wait!" She rose to get a piece of paper and a pen from the desk.

He recited the table of contents again from memory.

"You remember it all?"

"Yes."

She was looking at him suspiciously.

"I have a good memory."

"Pity you didn't read the thesis," she muttered.

He sighed.

"She must have sent it to you for a reason. Her murder could have had to do with the bureau you told me about. She'd been in love. She'd changed. She'd stopped going out with friends. I know she was scared. But the fact that she sent you her paper must mean that there was something in there she thought you needed to know."

"I thought the same," he admitted.

"Do you know what happened at those meetings?"

"Yes . . . but not if anything happened 'behind the scenes.'"

"She starts with the history of the Scandinavian Unions . . . Do you think they were planning a new one?"

"Not that I know. The meetings were only held to reaffirm the neutrality of the three countries, in case of war."

Jens didn't tell her that the Finland's President Ryti had approached Günther recently with the idea of a union between Finland and Sweden. Günther had rejected it straight out; Finland had allied itself with Germany. There would be no union.

"What will you do?" she asked.

He shook his head. "The police are investigating . . ." He thought about Sven. The investigation was under his boss. "I'll tell them about the thesis, of course."

She frowned.

"The police . . ." she said.

He waited.

"It's strange, but the Security Services were here yesterday, asking questions about the bomb. I felt like . . . they wanted to scare me."

There was a weakness by her mouth now, a faint vertical line on her cupid's bow—a scar he hadn't noticed before. She had just survived a bomb attack. He felt bad about forgetting that.

"They're probably just worried," he said carefully. "It's an attack on Swedish soil. They are looking after you, making sure you won't get hurt." Or killed, he thought.

She didn't respond.

He rose. "Thank you for taking the time to see me."

As Jens approached his apartment building that evening, a person stepped out from the shadows. Jens called out and took a step back.

"*Shh.* It's only me."

"Sven? You scared me," Jens said.

"Sorry." Sven's face was in the shadows. "I didn't mean to."

"What's going on?" Jens took a step closer to his friend.

"You know what I told you yesterday? About the murder and the explosion?"

"Of course."

Sven shook his head. "I made it sound like a state matter, and it turned out to be something completely different."

Jens hesitated. "What do you mean?"

"It was personal. The police have proof that the woman in Uppsala was killed by a jealous ex-lover."

"Are you sure?"

"Oh, absolutely." Sven nodded. "They know who he is."

"And the bomb?"

"They think it was put there by the same man. He was apparently obsessed with Miss Hallberg. Perhaps he thought Miss Dahlgren had encouraged her friend to leave him."

Laura said Britta had been in love. She said Britta had stopped going out, stopped seeing her friends. That she was scared. Which could be consistent with having an obsessive lover. And Jens could see that Laura would have gotten herself involved if ever a friend was in peril. She would have gotten in the man's face. But then there was the thesis . . .

"What about Britta Hallberg being a swallow?"

Sven shrugged. "I guess these women are ideal for that because they're good at parties, good at building relationships, but then there's that risk of their personal lives coming back to haunt them."

"Before dying, she sent me her thesis."

"Really?" Sven's teeth gleamed white in the faint light. "And?"

"I didn't read it. I threw it out."

A door opened farther down the street and they both looked toward the sound.

"Perhaps she hoped you'd offer her a job." Sven shrugged. "Only this month, I received two such documents."

There had been no letter introducing herself or asking for a job, Jens thought. But perhaps there had been one. He remembered how carelessly the envelope had been taped back together. A botch job, he had thought at the time. It could have fallen out, or the censor could have forgotten to put it back inside.

"I spoke with the policeman in charge on behalf of Möller," Sven said. "They are just about to arrest this guy." His lip curled, showing his distaste. "Apparently he has a history of abuse . . . I'm sorry I made it sound like a security risk."

"No worries," Jens said. "This is good news, though sad for Britta."

Sven nodded. "I also took the liberty of looking into the phone calls you mentioned."

"You did?"

"They were top secret. They were calls about the Jews in Norway and Denmark and how to secretly organize their passage to Sweden. That's why they were removed from the ledgers. Our leaders don't want Germany to find out."

"Oh." Jens exhaled. He could totally see why. It was one thing to grant passage to Jews who came to your borders or inquire about those with Swedish links. It was totally different to try to extricate Jews from territories occupied by Germany. That might be deemed a declaration of war.

"So there's no need to be concerned. Günther is doing the right thing even if he doesn't tell you about it."

"Yes. Thanks."

"*And* I asked around about your archivist."

"Really?"

"I know you. You worry about things and I wanted to make sure . . . He is off sick, Jens. Rumor has it he's become delusional. Imagining things, thinking he's being followed, that kind of stuff."

Daniel had seemed perfectly lucid to Jens. But then, what do we know about anyone? Perhaps the man's contacting Jens about the phone calls had been part of it—delusions, paranoia . . .

A strange thing to discuss in the street, Jens thought. "Do you want to come up?" he asked.

Sven shook his head. "Some other time."

"Thank you, Sven," Jens said. "The whole thing was beginning to weigh on me."

"No worries at all, my friend." Sven patted him on the shoulder. "Let's have that dinner soon."

21.

BLACKÅSEN MOUNTAIN

Taneli was at the foot of Blackåsen Mountain. There was a cluster of trees from where you had a view over the mountain and the railway. He tried to see it as it must once have been, tall and proud, forest-clad, lush, singing with life, but now it was nothing but a black lump. It had been important to the others in his tribe, but it hadn't played any part in his life. The mound was full of men, ants on an anthill. There were a lot of Swedish soldiers marching on the platform. Their gray shapes lined the open pit beneath the mountain, too, and the tunnels where men were working. A train approached. The gigantic black machine puffed and rolled into the station. Onboard, other soldiers, Germans hung out the windows and smoked. Suddenly, a man ran onto the platform. He came from between the station house and the railway hotel. He was screaming: "For Norway!"

A swift movement through the air. The man threw something. There was a bang. Some smoke. But nothing happened to the train. The German men in the windows laughed as Swedish soldiers wrestled the perpetrator to the ground. They lifted him away by his arms. His head hung low and his feet trailed behind him. The Swedish soldiers couldn't feel good about protecting the trains. But trains filled with Germans heading west was what the government had agreed to. "A small price to pay," they'd said, "for peace."

The sky above them all was a thin blue, more water than sky.

Behind Taneli, a branch broke and he was startled. It was a man he didn't know, thin, wiry, black-haired, with distinctive features. A Sami, that was for certain.

"So Taneli Turi is visiting us today," he said and nodded. "Coming here looking for answers."

Taneli stiffened. "How do you know my name?"

"I know a lot of things," the man said, smiling broadly. His eyes were large. The whites of them showed. Crazy, Taneli thought. Beside him, Raija responded and growled.

"Now, now," the man said. He looked at the dog and Raija immediately fell silent and lay down. She lay flat on the ground, eyes lowered. She normally only listened to Taneli.

"Who are you?" Taneli demanded.

"I am Áslat," he said and leaned in close to Taneli. "Your guide," he added.

"I don't need a guide."

"Oh, but I think you do. You need to find someone. I know where to find someone."

"How?" he asked. How did he know this?

"I know things."

"But do you know who I need to find?" Taneli asked.

"Your sister," he said. "Maybe the others, too."

Taneli's heart thundered in his ears. "Tell me," he said, and his voice sounded hoarse.

"It will cost you."

At this, Taneli's heart sank. He should have known this man

was a swindler. Nobody could possibly charge money to help another person.

"Two hundred Swedish crowns," Áslat said.

"I don't think so," Taneli said.

He might be a child, but he wasn't stupid.

"She chose your name," the man said.

Nobody knew this. Nobody apart from Taneli, his sister and his mother. "Don't tell your father," his mother had always said. "He wanted a different name for you. Don't tell him I let your sister choose."

Taneli flew at the man, pounded at his chest, tried to get his hands around his neck. "You have her! It's you!"

Áslat simply held him at bay. He laughed at first. Black teeth, sour breath. Then he grabbed Taneli by the shoulders and whispered, "Not me, silly boy. But I know who does."

Taneli stilled. Áslat let go of him.

"Where would I possibly get that kind of money?"

"That's your problem," Áslat said. "I'll tell you what you need to know. Tomorrow night, Taneli. We meet back here tomorrow night."

He walked away.

Two hundred crowns. That was an impossible amount of money. Even if they sold their reindeer, they wouldn't raise that amount. Not that the others would ever agree to it.

He was too young. Taneli felt this in every fiber of his body. He was a child. He didn't know how to handle this.

His cousin Olet had once said, "Only ever follow people you trust into the forest." And this Áslat could not be trusted. There was a reason for his willingness to help Taneli: a reason, and a price to pay. There was also the matter of how Raija had obeyed him. When Taneli gave her commands, the dog's eyes were happy, her whole body ready to spring into action. When Áslat spoke to her, she lay down as if she'd given up. As if she were dead.

But he had to find a way!

The knowledge tore at him. Here was a man who *actually* knew something. Javanna was alive! The man had said someone was holding her.

As Taneli walked home, he took the long way, circling the town. He was in no rush to get back. He didn't walk along the streets, but behind them, on the forest tracks. He passed the workers' houses, the school the Sami were not to attend, the parks. He came to the mining director's villa, large and proud. This house had no role in the world but to be pretty. And large. Its small, decorative windows sparkled in the sun. Taneli didn't have any money. But the man who managed the mine did.

TANELI WAITED OUTSIDE the director's villa all day, peering through the windows. When Sandler came home, his horse lathered with sweat after their ride, the stable hand took the animal away. The housekeeper walked through the rooms, sweeping things with what looked like bird feathers, wiping surfaces with a cloth. She served him dinner and then she left. The house grew quiet. Sandler didn't seem to have a family. Taneli sat beneath a window, one facing the back. It must be hot inside, for a window had been left open. The director had a dog. Taneli had already fed him dried meat and now they were friends. It was a fierce dog but a very hungry one.

He thought of Raija, left tied up in the forest. He'd had to bind her; otherwise she would have come after him. She cried when he left. He worried in case someone found her and untied her and she came running to find him. He didn't think his new canine friend would appreciate this.

There was a smell of smoke. Taneli half rose. The muscles in his thighs quivered. The director was smoking a pipe, sitting in an armchair by his bookshelf, an open book in his lap. Where would a man like this keep his money? Hopefully not on him. When he fell asleep, Taneli would enter the house and look. But the man didn't seem to have any intention of going to bed. Taneli understood him. After the dark winter, once spring came, you wanted to enjoy every minute of light. It was evening now. The sky had taken on a gloomier tone. The birds were singing, but their tweeting was more mellow. If you weren't born here, you'd probably never notice the difference.

Sandler yawned and covered his mouth with one hand. Finally, Taneli thought.

Then there was a knock and the front door opened. Taneli sat down, but then he couldn't hear. He waited one beat and rose again. It was a man, the one who had come to measure their skulls. Not the one who had done the measuring, but the other one, the one taking notes. The one with the empty eyes. The one who had kicked his dog.

"Rent again?" the director said. He didn't sound pleased. Taneli saw that he was a head taller than his guest.

"Yes," the man said, admonishingly. "Rent."

"The problem is, I don't know what the rent is for," Sandler said.

"Best keep it that way," the man snarled. He handed him a package.

What was it?

The director turned it around in his hand and flipped through it with a thumb. The paper wad was dirt colored with printing on it. Money!

"Don't underestimate me," Sandler said. "I warn you. Don't think we're done."

The man laughed. "Like all of us, you just do as you're told."

The man bowed, but it wasn't an honest gesture. More mocking than sincere. He walked out and closed the door behind him. Taneli was astounded. How dare that man talk to the mining director like that? He was the most important person here! What nerve!

Sandler stood for a while without moving, then he walked to the chest in the far corner of the room. He touched its side, and there was a small click. A tray popped out and he threw the wad in there and closed it. He turned off the lamp by his chair and walked out. He didn't bother to close the window, or he'd just forgotten about it. The stairway creaked and soon another window opened above Taneli.

Taneli waited. He waited some more. Not taking any chances, he gave his new dog friend some extra dried meat to occupy him and then he entered the house. It was easy. He just lifted himself up on his hands, put a foot on the windowsill and jumped down inside. He stood and listened, but the house was quiet. Taneli was light, but the wooden planks squeaked as he walked, as wood did, but hopefully the director was fast asleep by now. He couldn't imagine the punishment if he was caught: beaten, jail. Worse. The rejection of his people.

By the chest, he paused. He begged forgiveness of the tall man who slept on the floor above, perhaps the spirits, too, and his tribe. I am no thief, he thought. It is for something good, he added, even though at this point he was uncertain. Then he ran his hand over the piece of furniture. He found a dimple in the wood and pressed it. There it was, the click. He put his hand in the tray and took out the money. There was a lot. All the bills bore the number 100. He wouldn't take more than he needed. Just two bills. He put the rest back and closed the tray.

Then he turned and he was there: the director. Taneli hadn't heard him coming. He gasped. Sandler was watching him, blue eyes steady above the beard. Run, Taneli! a voice screamed inside him. Leave the money and run! But he couldn't move. He had become stone. The director was still watching him. For the briefest of moments, Taneli saw himself through the man's eyes: a small boy, short, slight, with weak shoulders, and large, scared eyes, unmistakably Sami with the blue *kolt* and the hat, and the black hair. A Sami boy whose skull shape was more Swedish than Sami, money clutched in his hand.

"I came to shut the window. Because of the bugs," the director said slowly, as if it were he who must explain himself, and then he turned and left . . . left Taneli there, in his house, stolen money and all. The stairs squeaked again as the director went back upstairs.

22.

LAURA

When Jens Regnell left, Laura had to sit down. Britta had sent her thesis to him. Why? After a speech at a *nachspiel*?

She remembered the first time she had seen Jens at a dinner she'd attended with her father. It wasn't long ago. Christian Günther had given a speech, which was followed by a question and answer session. Journalists had been invited. At the end, one of the journalists had asked the foreign affairs minister if they might hear a few words from his new secretary. Günther had left the podium—reluctantly? And then this young man had stood up. A boyish smile, an earnest face, relaxed and unfazed. He'd introduced himself and said what an honor it was to work for the minister. A reporter had asked him what he wanted to accomplish, and he had responded that his job was to ensure the foreign affairs policy was executed successfully. But what about him, personally? Then he'd said what an exciting period it was to be in politics—foreign affairs or not: "Perhaps for the first time, we have a real chance to ensure that each Swede has the right to good housing, good healthcare, a good education and—in our old age—safety and comfort. I am delighted to be able to be a part of this. To wage a war for these rights, which, to me, seems the only good reason for waging a war."

As he continued talking about the vision he had for Sweden, she remembered the room growing still. They were witnessing something extraordinary. He's the next one, she'd thought. Social Democrat, obviously. She'd vote for him regardless. She gauged her father's reaction, as always, and, sitting beside her, his face reflected the same feelings she was experiencing herself. Jens Regnell was special.

She'd met Jens in person a couple of months later, with Wallenberg. Then, he had already seemed weighed down with the burdens of ministerial office. He'd been stressed, focused. There had been none of the passion she'd seen at the podium. She'd left feeling disappointed. But how many men managed to keep their visions alive as reality hit them?

Britta had sent her thesis to him. Even though she didn't know him, she had thought he might pursue it.

Britta hadn't sent it to Laura. Britta had not trusted her enough. Just like the coffee conversation at the NK. Britta had chosen not to confide in her.

Who was it in your life that didn't commit, Laura? Professor Lindahl's voice in her head. Her heart thudded hard.

She had to admit to a feeling of relief when she heard the topic of Britta's thesis: *Nordic Relations Through the Ages— Denmark, Norway and Sweden on a New Path*. When Jens first told her about the thesis, she'd felt a rush of fear, thinking that perhaps Britta had continued the project they had been working on during their university years—the one that ultimately drove them apart—and that her murder did have something to do with the five of them, after all. But Britta's thesis contained nothing about Asatru, the Norse faith.

PROFESSOR LINDAHL HAD invited the archbishop to one of the *nachspiele*. He'd been talking about church and state, their links and the role of the church in the new Sweden.

"Incredible," Erik had stated, once the archbishop had left.

"What?" Karl-Henrik had asked.

"The man—the archbishop, I mean—seems lucid. A rather intelligent man. Educated. And then there is this mystic belief in this all-seeing, all-knowing chap above, steering things according to his liking. *Praying* to someone you cannot see; believing in something you cannot possibly know."

"Millions of people all over the world believe in similar things," Karl-Henrik said.

"But most of them are not educated," Erik argued.

Was that true? Most people were not schooled; that was correct. But whether most religious people were or not, she didn't know. Wasn't religion, in some ways, for the educated ones only?

"A wonderful way of keeping people subdued, in line."

The professor leaned forward to tap his cigarette in the ashtray. He seemed to be smiling to himself.

"What about Asatru—the Norse faith—that you bore us with all the time?" Matti asked.

"But that's just sagas, legends. It's our heritage. Not something to *believe in*."

"What did I miss?" Britta came back from the washroom.

"Erik is thinking about becoming religious," Laura said.

Erik grunted. "Very funny. I was just saying that it's totally implausible for an intelligent man to believe in . . ."

"Well, this class is all about expanding our boundaries and

dealing with the implausible," Professor Lindahl said. "And so I, in my role as your guide, see it as my duty to promptly challenge you, Mr. Anker, to find yourself a faith."

Britta burst out laughing.

Erik turned to her, glowering.

"I'm just trying to imagine it!" She wiped her eyes.

"I'm an atheist!"

The professor rose. "Not anymore, you're not, Mr. Anker. Find yourself something to believe in. In fact," he paused, "I extend the challenge to all of you. What would it take for you to become passionate speakers for a faith, like the archbishop? What thing would sway you?

"Now it's time for me to go home, my dears. You may, of course, stay as long as you want."

And with that he walked out.

They waited until the big wooden door at the front slammed shut.

"Jesus bloody Christ!" Erik swore.

"Walked right into that one," Laura said. "And took us right with you."

Erik swore again: a long tirade.

"Actually, it's a really interesting question," Karl-Henrik said. "What *would* it take?"

"I already believe in God," Matti said. His eyes were glowing. Teasing, Laura thought.

"No, you fucking don't," Erik said.

Matti laughed out loud.

"The whole thing is ridiculous," Erik muttered.

"We see it all the time," Karl-Henrik said, "perfectly rational people with a faith. What convinces them?"

"Perhaps he didn't mean it?" Erik said, hopefully. "Perhaps it wasn't a proper assignment?"

"Oh no, I think it was," Britta said.

THAT NIGHT, MATTI had stayed as he sometimes did, and they found themselves making love. Laura was surprised at herself but thought she knew the reason why; it wasn't serious between them and had no chance of becoming so.

After, Matti kissed her shoulder. "What are you thinking about?"

"Erik," she said.

He poked a finger in her side, hard. "I've just made love to you and you're thinking about Erik."

She laughed. "Actually, I was thinking about the professor's question to Erik and all of us," she clarified.

"It's not exactly history . . ."

"But there is a lesson there. Otherwise, the professor would never have asked. What subject does he prod you about?"

Matti turned to grab his cigarettes. "I'm not telling," he said. "You?"

"Not telling."

No, some things were better kept to yourself.

Matti lit a cigarette, pulled on it and then handed it to her.

"But he got it wrong with me," Matti said. "The thing he prods me on."

"Really?"

Matti shook his head, serious now. "He's not always right, you know."

Yes, the professor was human too, she thought, but didn't feel it.

She was woken by the sound of the front door opening. Karl-Henrik, she thought. There were soft footsteps, past her bedroom door and into the reading room. The library door shut quietly with a click. She glanced at Matti—didn't want him to wake up and wonder. Nor did she want Karl-Henrik to know Matti slept over.

But Matti was breathing soundlessly and Laura could feel herself twitch. He looked peaceful, like a child. It made her smile. She crept closer to him, put her head just beside his, began breathing at the same pace. When she next woke up, Karl-Henrik was long gone and Matti was getting dressed.

IN HER ENTIRE life, Laura had not committed to anything. Not really. She had never put herself at risk. But her thoughts of Britta would not leave her alone until she found out what had happened.

Enough! This was not who she was going to be.

She rose.

WALLENBERG MADE HER wait. He had never, ever made her wait before. Her father could have given her what she was about to ask Wallenberg, but she didn't think he would have complied. He was too worried about her. *You're home now*—his voice echoed in her ears. She stood in the hallway at work and her former colleagues avoided meeting her gaze—as if she had done something wrong! What excuse had Wallenberg given for her absence? Her cheeks burned. She refused to look at her desk in case another person was already sitting there. She held her head high and looked out of one of the windows. The sky outside was a high blue. And the rejection didn't break her. On the contrary, she let it fuel her, make her stronger.

"I thought I'd made myself clear," Wallenberg said, when he finally received her.

The face that normally softened when he spoke with her was bland. Cold, even.

They'd worked together for three years and he had dropped her like a stone.

"You did," she agreed and forced herself to smile. She put her hands on his desk and leaned closer to him, standing her ground. "For three years, I worked for you. I gave you everything I had. Now, I think you owe me," she said. "And this is what I want . . ."

23.

JENS

Hi."

Kristina came out into the hallway to greet him. She smiled, wrapped her arms around his neck and kissed him on the mouth. She was in a marine-blue dress, her hair in a high ponytail. She wasn't wearing much makeup. She'd adopted the girl-next-door-look, he thought, and promptly felt ashamed of himself.

"I've missed you," she said.

"I've missed you, too." He had.

"I've made dinner. I thought it might be nice if we ate in tonight."

"That sounds great."

Jens threw his briefcase on the chair by the door and hung up his suit jacket. His stomach gave a twinge at the aroma of food cooking. As he walked into the kitchen, he loosened his tie and folded up his shirtsleeves. He went to the window and lifted the blackout curtain to look into the small, dark street below. Not a dock on the water, but his home, nevertheless.

"How was work?" Kristina asked.

Jens thought of his hasty meeting with Sven outside. "Good," he said. "Actually, very good. Some things have been on my mind, but they all reached closure today."

Yes, his fears had been in vain. Only now did he realize how worried he had been. He'd thought the worst—an intrigue involving the foreign minister and the ministry—only to—thank goodness—be proved wrong. He'd have to go to see Laura again. Make sure she knew. Though the police would most likely tell her themselves, when they'd arrested the perpetrator.

"Drink?" Kristina asked.

"Yes, please." He sat down at the table and she poured him a glass of red wine. He took a sip, felt his mouth grow warm. He stretched out his legs and leaned back in the chair. "How was your day?" he asked.

"Good." She placed a casserole on the table. "I carried out some business for my father: made phone calls, wrote letters . . ." She pulled off her oven mitts, then untied her apron, took it off and hung it over the back of her chair before sitting down facing him. "Nothing important," she said as she served him stew. "Not like you."

"Everyone's day is important."

He took a bite of the food. Chicken, creamy and mild. "This is good, Kristina," he said.

"I'm glad you like it."

She bent her head as she ate and her ponytail fell over one shoulder, dipping beneath her collarbone.

"You know what?" he said. "The other day, when I forgot my notebook and I came back for it, I saw Karl Schnurre leaving the building. Was he with you?"

"No." She frowned. "Of course not." Then her face lit up. "Oh, I know what that must be," she said eagerly. "I'm not allowed to tell you, but I will anyway. I bet you Schnurre paid a visit to the gentleman in the flat opposite you."

"To Mr. Enander? But he's never here."

"Well, he must be here every now and then. Apparently, he travels back and forth to Germany. Sometimes, he brings things for Schnurre."

"Wow," Jens said.

"I know, right?"

"How on earth do you know this?"

"Ah. Here comes what you're not supposed to know: Barbro has more than one boss, if you see what I mean. She said that we might notice a surveillance team, and if we do, it has to do with Mr. Enander."

So he had guessed correctly about Barbro.

"I'm really surprised you know this. About her double role, I mean."

"I'm sure she wouldn't have told me if I hadn't figured it out. We've known each other for a long time. After a while, it became obvious. I asked her."

Kristina stood up to gather their plates from the table. She turned on the tap to let water pour into the sink, ponytail swaying down her back. She pulled the apron over her head and tied it around her narrow waist. "What was the business that came to a close today?" she asked, as she put the plates in the water and started to wash them. "If you can tell me, I mean."

He didn't see why not. It wasn't classified, after all. "A woman was killed last week in Uppsala and then, a few days later, there was a bomb in her friend's flat here in Stockholm. Before she was murdered, she had sent me her thesis and I was worried that it had to do with me or the ministry in some way. But apparently it was a personal matter. A jilted lover."

"How did you find out?" she asked.

"Sven came to tell me."

Kristina turned to face him. There was a wrinkle between her eyebrows. She wiped her hands on the apron. "Don't take this the wrong way, Jens, but why do you think Sven is telling you things?"

"What do you mean?"

"I know you're friends, but do you really trust him?"

Jens couldn't believe his ears. "I've known him for years. Yes, I trust him."

She nodded. "Okay. It's just that I find him a little bit too keen to give you information. I wonder if he's doing it to make sure you see things the same way he does."

She walked up beside him, put her hand on his shoulder and kissed the top of his head. "I'm only trying to look after you."

"I know," he said and put his arm around her waist.

He didn't want to admit it, but there was something about the way Sven had come to find him tonight, to tell him not only about the ex-lover, but also about the missing phone calls and about the archivist's illness, that jarred him. Why stand outside his door until he came home? Why not wait until tomorrow? It hadn't been that urgent, had it? And why had he gone so far as to find out what had happened to Daniel Jonsson? It did seem over the top.

But his friend was thorough. Sven would have felt awful about telling Jens something that wasn't a hundred percent correct. He would have wanted to ensure he made it up to him.

As he lay with Kristina in his arms that night, he found it hard to sleep. Daniel Jonsson had suffered from delusions, and he wished he had known, though he wasn't sure what he could have done about it. The archivist had seemed a lonely figure—odd—but never delusional.

He yawned. His arm was falling asleep and, carefully, he pulled it out from underneath Kristina's neck. She stirred and twisted away from him onto her side. He turned to lie on his back and closed his eyes. There was something else he was supposed to remember, but he didn't know what it was.

24.

BLACKÅSEN MOUNTAIN

The boys had agreed to meet with Notholm by the large river. Gunnar told his mother that he would stay at school and do his homework. Now, he regretted it. It would have been better if he had lied and said his mother needed him at home. But he had been scared Mr. Notholm would just come and find him. He shrugged to himself: Mr. Notholm was just a man—a respectable man, too. Owner of the town's hotel. That thought didn't make him feel any calmer, though. But Abraham's cheeks were red. He really wanted this. And he was the oldest.

There was the clop of hooves and Notholm entered the glade on a black horse.

"There you are," he said and smiled, but he didn't get off his horse. "I have a mission for you."

Abraham raised his chin higher. His eyes gleamed.

"I want you to catch me a hare," Notholm said.

"Bah!" Abraham answered. "Catching a hare isn't hard."

"That's true," Notholm said. "All you need is the right bait."

Catching a hare was actually quite difficult, Gunnar thought. Hares could run as fast as a horse. But there were tricks. Though he was certain Mr. Notholm knew them himself.

"I'll come by this evening," Notholm said. "Catch me a hare and you'll get paid." He turned his horse, as if to take off, then changed his mind and reined it in. "Oh, and I want it alive."

Alive. That was more problematic.

The two boys discussed it after Notholm had left. They needed a trap that wouldn't kill the animal.

"A snare," Gunnar said.

"But we need to be able to set it off," Abraham said. "To try to catch it by the legs, rather than the neck."

Abraham had some wire. Hares had habits; they knew this. There was still enough snow to find tracks. It took them a good hour before Abraham shouted that he'd found some.

They followed the animal's trail until they came to a kind of tunnel in the undergrowth. A couple of sticks and a few rocks created a channel that the animal had already passed through several times. That was where they set their snare, using buds and berries for bait.

Then they waited. They took turns lying near the snare. The other stayed in the glade, so as not to disturb the process. Waiting grew tiresome, but they tried to stay vigilant. To hear it come. To pull the wire just at the right time.

"We'll never make it," Abraham said in the late afternoon as they swapped places yet again.

Gunnar shrugged. You couldn't force these things; you had to be patient.

"What if we try to find its den?" Abraham suggested.

"Won't work," Gunnar said. "It'll hear us long before we find it."

Abraham kicked a stone.

Gunnar went to lie down. It was warm. The sun was still standing high and he could see the remaining snow melting,

194

becoming a translucent blue. Sometimes larger pieces fell from the overhead branches with a faint *scrunching*.

He could feel himself doze off and shook his head to stay awake.

Then he saw it. The hare. It came jumping on the path, just as they had imagined. A wiry white animal with long legs and long ears. A meter away it stopped, its nose quivering. Perhaps it had sensed him. Come on, he willed it. Come on.

The hare hesitated but then continued forward, leisurely jumping. Gunnar held his breath. One jump. Two. Three . . .

He pulled the snare.

"Yes! I got it!"

Abraham came running. The hare was on the ground, its hind legs caught in the metal snare. It was struggling to get free. Gunnar put a foot on its neck to hold it down. The wire had cut through its skin and there was blood on the white fur, but its legs were unbroken.

"Good job," Abraham said.

Gunnar felt himself beam.

They relaxed. Having tied up the hare, they sat down in the glade again, chatting and mucking about as usual.

It was early evening when the clop of a horse's hooves approached again. They rose and got ready.

When Notholm entered the glade, Abraham held the hare up—like an offering, Gunnar thought. He held its front legs in his left hand, back legs in his right. The animal was bouncing its body, trying to get loose.

"You did it," Notholm said. "Well done. Alive, too. Now, can you kill it?"

"Of course." In one swift movement, Abraham laid the animal down, grabbed the stick he had prepared and placed it over the hare's neck. He stepped on one side of the stick, and then the other, pulling the hare's body upward by the hind legs.

There would be a small pop, Gunnar knew. You would be able to feel the neck bones give in your hand. But it was quick, relatively pain-free for the animal and didn't damage the fur. Their parents had taught them.

The animal was shuddering. It was already dead; this was just the body moving.

They looked up and found Notholm frowning.

"Now, where was the fun in that?" he said.

Beside Gunnar, Abraham's mouth was half-open.

"No," Notholm said. "*This* is how it's done."

He turned on his horse and opened his satchel. Inside it was another hare, its legs also bound—but alive. Still alive.

Gunnar held his breath. His stomach clenched.

Notholm took out his knife. He held the animal up and slit its side. A small cut, the ripping of tearing cloth. The animal began to bleed. Notholm held it up in the air. Blood was leaching down his bare arm, dripping onto the ground. The hare was writhing in pain. Thrashing. Notholm laughed. Then he brought the animal back down and, holding its face with one hand, he cut off the hare's nose.

Gunnar's knees softened. He was going to faint.

And the animal screamed. Its shriek was piercing; as loud and as human as that of a baby. Gunnar wanted to cover his ears. He couldn't stand it. He'd never known hares could scream.

25.

LAURA

There were three addresses on the paper Wallenberg had given Laura. She had them and the police report in her hand.

"I'll do the most difficult one first," she promised herself. But they were all difficult. "I'll do the most revolting one first," she decided.

Sven Olov Lindholm, the head of the SSS, could, at the moment, be found in an apartment on Fleminggatan in Stockholm, Wallenberg had said.

Since Jens's visit, she'd been trying to puzzle it together. If Britta had been a swallow, seeing Sven Olov Lindholm could have been part of the work she did for the C-Bureau. Laura liked the idea that Britta had been spying on him. Perhaps trying to find out more about their plans for the Easter meetup. Perhaps Sven Olov had found out. Perhaps he was the one who'd killed her.

The thought went through her head that she ought to leave this to those who knew how to investigate. But then she thought about the visit from the Security Services and about commitment.

She found the house, an older apartment building, and rang the doorbell.

"Yes?" A woman's voice.

"I'd like to speak with Sven Olov Lindholm," Laura said.

"Who's asking?"

"Britta Hallberg," Laura said.

The door clicked open. Laura's heart sank. She would far rather they had asked, "Who?" She walked up the stairs and an apartment door opened on a floor above her.

"Up here," a man said.

She turned the corner. Sven Olov; blond hair, blue eyes. Very Aryan. She scoffed. He could have been good-looking if it weren't for his nose leaning slightly one way and his mouth slightly the other. And if it wasn't for the arrogance, which was all over his lifted chin, the curved eyebrows and in the way he leaned with one arm raised against the doorframe. He did not seem like a person who'd just heard an acquaintance had come back from the dead.

"You're not Britta," he said.

"No. Britta is dead."

He stirred. "Dead?"

She nodded.

"How?"

"She was murdered."

Sven Olov stood tall. He looked behind her as if he thought she might be followed. "I have nothing to say to you," he muttered and turned away.

"I'm Laura Dahlgren. I work with Wallenberg." She raised her voice. "I negotiate with Germany. I have good connections with the same people you do."

He had stopped. "How did you find me?"

"Wallenberg himself gave me the address."

Sven Olov pursed his lips.

"Nobody else knows. And anything you tell me stays with me," she said.

THEY SAT DOWN in the kitchen. The room looked tired; the laminated cupboard doors had once been a bright green, but bumps and dents had made the paint crack. The walls were brown stone. The lampshade hanging from the ceiling was knitted with tassels. It must have been white in the beginning, but now it was a light gray. He put out an ashtray and they both lit cigarettes. She could hear low voices from inside the apartment. The woman. Other people, too.

"Why are you here?" he asked.

"She was my best friend. Someone said you had coffee together not long before she died."

"Who?"

"Britta had told another good friend of hers she was meeting you." She tried smiling, thought of Andreas and how he had gone missing.

He was frowning. "How did she die?"

Did he already know? She didn't think so. His reaction in the stairwell had seemed genuine.

"She was shot," Laura said.

He exhaled; a slow long breath.

"Communists," he said then. In contrast to his first reaction, this one didn't sound genuine. He was looking past her as he spoke.

"Why would you say that?"

"Uppsala is totally infested with them. Them, Jews and Norwegian criminals."

His lips curled, and even though she tried not to react, her stomach clenched.

"Why did you two meet up?"

He turned to look at her. He was weighing up whether to tell her or not, she guessed. But the Wallenberg name had opened doors. "It was quite an interesting conversation," he said. "This is why I remember her. Otherwise, it's hard, as I meet a lot of young women."

She forced another smile.

"She wanted to know what our links were with the State Institute for Racial Biology in Uppsala. If we ever did any work together."

This was the last thing Laura would have expected.

"Work?" she asked. "What kind of work?"

"That's what I asked. I know, of course, about the racial studies they do—you know, the skull measurements and so on. She asked if we took an active involvement in that, or any similar project, and I said no. Our battle is the political one. The science is already clear."

"What did she say?"

"She insisted. She said that there was an organization that was working with the State Institute and how could I not be aware of it if I was the head of the Nazi party?" He scoffed at the memory.

"And then what?"

"Nothing." He shrugged, but his eyes wavered.

"You set her off on a trail, didn't you?"

He remained silent.

"She was tortured before she died," Laura said. "Whatever you know, you need to tell me."

He leaned forward. "You have no idea what you are getting yourself into," he said quietly.

"Tell me," she insisted. "No one will ever know it came from you."

"I want you to leave now." He rose.

"But . . ."

"Leave!" he yelled. There were footsteps from the bedroom and another man showed up.

"Please show her the door," Sven Olov said.

"My name is Laura Dahlgren," she shouted as she was pushed out of the apartment. "You can find me. When you're ready to talk!"

SHE NEEDED TO think. She walked down Fleminggatan and sat down at the first café she found and ordered a tea. Another woman sat alone at a table, too, and their eyes met briefly; a small sensation of recognition. Not many women went to cafés on their own.

The State Institute for Racial Biology. Why would Britta have asked about that? And what kind of "work" was she asking about? This did not sound like spying on Germany—this was a Swedish institution.

She thought more about Sven Olov Lindholm. Once, the Nazi parties had been taken seriously. Racial biology was the way forward. A strong people, a powerful nation, eugenic experiments . . . Freud, Nietzsche, Darwin, their own Carl von Linné had all had thoughts on the matter.

Her group of friends had been seduced, too. She remembered a *nachspiel* discussing "the elite." At the time, they had all agreed that it was the right and responsibility of better placed people to lead; most people were ignorant, and ability was not distributed equably. Though they had disagreed on what "better placed" meant. It had gotten heated. She remembered both Erik and Matti shouting; Erik completely refusing the notion that ancestry had any bearing on it and Matti screaming that a lineage ensured high intellect and special skills.

"Better people, better ideas," Professor Lindahl had said. "What about nations?"

And they'd been right back at the subject of race, Laura thought.

"Why would it matter where you were born?" Britta asked.

"Isn't that what you're arguing, though; that it does matter where and to whom you're born? That everyone is not equal?"

Yes, they had been seduced.

Then stories began to emerge from Germany about what was going on with the Jews. *Svenska Dagbladet* had published several reports about missing Jews, thousands of them: Emil Persson himself had authored a few. The Swedish government had kept quiet, but the right-wing upswing had stopped in its tracks. The Swedish Nazi parties were shown in their true colors: a bunch of petty lawbreakers who bullied and tried to provoke fights.

Sven Olov Lindholm had told Britta something. Britta would have charmed him. She would have managed to get answers out of him. Now he was scared.

Their kind only understood one language, she thought. Like most groups. The Germans with whom they negotiated, for one. They understood the language of power. If you were weak, you were trampled over, but if you were strong, you had a chance. Early on, one of the Germans in their negotiating committee had been interested in her on a personal level. He had tried to get her to have dinner with him and grew more and more annoyed with her refusals. He'd begun to wait for her outside the meeting rooms, Wallenberg raising a warning eyebrow. Then, one night, the German had been outside her hotel room. He'd grabbed her, tried to have his way with her.

She'd been prepared. The room key was in her hand, and she had jabbed him in the eye. She wasn't a military man's granddaughter for nothing. She left him in the corridor, bent over, bleeding. The next day, he wasn't part of the negotiations. Nothing was ever said, but there was a new air of respect toward her from his countrymen involved in the negotiations. The man himself never came back.

HEAR SWEDEN'S LEADING NAZI SPEAK, it said on the posters outside Hotel Carlton. Laura walked in. The meeting room was filled with young men in army shirts and riding trousers. There were plenty of young women, too. She'd heard the party had been successful in recruiting them. Not that they were believed to have political views, but they were helpful—in distributing those flyers, carrying the flags and so on.

Laura walked to the front. She sat down in the first row, crossed her legs and waited. She was the first thing Sven Olov saw when he came on stage. His mouth half opened then closed. She smiled. I will stalk you, she thought, until you tell me all that you know. I will bring the thing that you are scared of with me and stalk you until you see me as a risk to yourself. I will stalk you and stalk you and stalk you . . .

26.

JENS

It was a beautiful morning. The sun was out. Jens paused briefly on the doorstep to feel the warmth on his face. The weekend had been wonderful. He and Kristina had walked around Stockholm and met up with friends. The first few warm days of spring. The first proper weekend off in a long time. Farther away, in one of the doorways on his street, a man in a gray suit wearing a dark fedora was standing smoking a cigarette. As Jens looked his way, he took out the newspaper that was folded under his arm, unfolded it and began to read. He was probably one of the policemen watching Mr. Enander, Jens thought. They'd have to do better than that if they wanted to evade notice.

As he got into work, one of the administrative staff popped her head through the door to say that Günther had called a meeting of all personnel straight away.

Jens grabbed his notebook and a pen and followed her into one of the meeting rooms.

Günther was already standing at the front. People streamed into the room until it was full. As the last people to arrive found seats and fell quiet, he began to speak.

"Daniel Jonsson died last night."

Died?

"Most of you know him as an archivist who's been working here at the ministry for a decade. What you most likely don't know is that for some time, Daniel had suffered from a weak mind which, ultimately, led to a difficulty in separating reality from fiction. Last week, he was put on indefinite leave. Last night, regrettably, he took his own life."

The floor dropped underneath Jens. His ears began to buzz. He had to look down to steady himself. When he glanced up, Christian Günther was staring straight at him.

"We grieve for Daniel Jonsson," the foreign minister continued, "but his death has also left us with a problem. Through his position, Daniel had access to all kinds of sensitive material. In view of the delusions he was suffering, we don't know if he shared information. We don't know if he instigated something that is now running without him."

Jens's hand flew up to touch his tie. He shivered; felt cold, sick. The note, he thought. He'd pushed that note through Daniel's door slot when Daniel first disappeared. What had he written? *Please get in touch*, and *I believe you*. He cursed himself. Why had he added that last sentence? How incredibly stupid. He had formed a mental picture of Daniel—on leave, on his own, depressed. He was always trying to be nice—that was his problem, just like Kristina and Sven kept pointing out.

"The Security Services will manage this situation," Günther said. "And while they are in the process, you might find yourself being interviewed."

Only now did Jens see the men in dark suits at the back of the room. Three of them, arms crossed.

"Any questions?" Günther was looking out over the audience.

"How did it . . . he kill himself?" someone ventured.

"He hanged himself in his flat. His sister found him this morning."

The room fell silent.

"I wanted to let you know myself," Günther said. "The funeral will be next week, but his family are looking after that. We have offered our condolences, of course. Feel free to take a moment, should you need it."

People rose. There was a mumbling of concerned voices as they walked out.

JENS RETURNED TO his office and sat down heavily in his chair. Daniel was dead. And Jens's note was in the apartment. Had they already found it?

Daniel had been delusional. He might well have given information out to people who should not have it; like the phone calls he had told Jens about. How many other "suspicious things" had he seen and passed on to other people? Oh, why had Jens not been more careful?

Günther had already warned him, told him to leave well enough alone. And only now that Jens knew what the phone calls had been about, did he understand why. Jens should have listened to Günther, trusted him, rather than thinking he knew better. And now there was that note he had left for Daniel: *I believe you.* The fact that he had written this note after Günther had already warned him would not go down well.

He sighed and tried to calm himself down. Justice would prevail. He believed this. He knew this. He would explain what had happened and he would be heard.

The phone rang. He answered: "Jens Regnell."

"Sven here. I have something of yours."

"Something of mine? What?"

"Just some papers. You forgot them at my apartment when you last came over."

They hadn't met at Sven's apartment for months.

"But . . ."

"I know you need them," Sven said. "I'll wait for you by the statue of St. Göran and the dragon at Köpmantorget in ten minutes."

SVEN WAS STANDING by the bronze statue, the thorny green dragon bristling above his head. He had his hands stuck in his coat pockets even though the weather was warm.

"What's up?" Jens asked, irritated. He'd had to show up at short notice and his day was already not going well. But he'd concluded on the way over that perhaps Sven needed his help. Otherwise, why the rush?

"I think I should ask you that," Sven said and pulled his hand out of his pocket. In it was Jens's note to Daniel Jonsson.

Jens exhaled. "How on earth do you have this?"

"Möller, my minister, sent me to Daniel's home when we heard what had happened. The police were there, but they hadn't begun their search."

Jens was still looking at the note in Sven's hand.

"The note was on his desk, Jens. For anyone to see."

"You took it?"

"Of course I did."

"You shouldn't have."

"You know it was necessary."

"No," Jens shook his head. "No, I don't. It's illegal."

There was a sneer on Sven's face. It vanished as quickly as it had appeared.

"You're too naive, Jens. Plenty of people are just waiting for the opportunity to bring you down."

Jens shrugged. "This note is innocent. I can explain it. I know you have my best interests in mind, my friend. But to take this away from a scene the police are about to search . . . That's just plain wrong."

"Jens, listen to me. You could go far, really far. We both know you could go all the way. It would mean something if you did: you would change things. And to be incriminated by a small thing like this . . ."

Sven offered the note to him. Jens took a step back. "No," he said and held up his hands. "I won't take it. You shouldn't have done it."

BACK AT THE office, he wondered what his friend would do with the note: try putting it back or throw it out? Sven had faith in him. Sven looked out for him . . . They'd looked out for each other. But this, this amazed him. Sven knew what was right and wrong.

It would have been easy, a small voice inside him said. You could have taken the note. Nobody would ever have known. The whole thing would have gone away . . .

No! *He* would have known. This was the mindset he was fighting against: complacency, entitlement, lies. He would have none of that. He had never taken the easy route—he wasn't going to start now.

Across the hall, the foreign minister's door was closed. Jens sighed.

27.

BLACKÅSEN MOUNTAIN

Sandler was tired; he hadn't been able to sleep. He'd been robbed. By a kid. A *Sami* kid. He grumbled at the thought. On seeing the boy, black hair falling over eyes as scared as a rabbit's, two things had gone through his head: first, if this boy had dared to come, he must really need the money; second, the director had realized he didn't know who to call upon. I'm being robbed by a . . . child? He couldn't see himself do it. He should have, of course. He could only hope that this wouldn't unleash a whole series of robberies, with people saying that stealing from the director was like taking candy from a baby.

And then there was his overarching worry about Notholm's visit and the sheer insolence of the man when he came with his payment. The director bristled at the thought. Notholm was up to something; Sandler could feel it in every fiber of his being. And, regardless of what his superior said, he could not leave it be. He was in charge. If something happened, it would be his neck on the line.

He swung his legs over the edge of the bed and rose. He pulled on his trousers and put his head in his shirt, buttoning it as he trotted downstairs. His office was empty. He noticed that the boy had pushed the window shut upon leaving.

The director opened it and shouted out, "Saddle my horse!"

The stable boy undid the door to the stables and waved.

"Breakfast, sir?" the housekeeper asked.

"Not today."

He walked out. His dog was sitting by the stairs, wagging its tail.

"You worthless piece of . . ." he mumbled then relented and patted the beast on its head. "I couldn't be mean to him, either," he admitted to the animal.

HE FOUND THE foreman in his office. Hallberg wrinkled his forehead upon seeing him but nodded to the chair opposite his.

"How are things?" the director asked.

The foreman raised his brows. He tapped a finger on the file in front of him. Not one for small talk.

"There's something I've been wondering about," Sandler said.

"Yes?"

"Notholm . . . He rents land from us—land on the mountain itself. What do you know about it?"

Hallberg clasped his fingers and leaned back in his chair. His hands were large and calloused, the rims of the nails black.

"The land's been rented out for a long time," he said. "Maybe fifteen years."

"But Notholm hasn't been here that long?" The director remembered hearing he came a few years ago and took over the hotel.

"Before him there was someone called Ivarsson."

Somebody else? What kind of project could be handed over? Did this Ivarsson sell the project to Notholm?

"Who is with Notholm in this?"

"I don't know."

"What do they need the land for?"

The foreman puckered his lips. "I don't know."

"You don't know?"

"No, I don't." They had raised their voices. Then they fell silent, staring at each other. Sandler took a deep breath, trying to calm himself. He just couldn't get through to this pigheaded, small-minded . . .

"It's none of our business," the foreman concluded.

The director scoffed. "It's on the mountain itself. Imagine if something goes wrong. Just imagine."

"We've been told to leave them to it. It doesn't interfere with operations. Their location has been designated such."

"Who told us to leave them to it?"

The foreman shrugged. "The government."

Both men paused.

"How about we go and find out what they're doing?" Sandler suggested.

"You mean actually approach their site?"

"Aren't you at all curious?"

Hallberg stood up. "No, I have to say, I'm not. You know how busy we are. I don't have time for a pointless little excursion."

"Well," the director said, also rising, "I don't think it's pointless."

SANDLER TOOK THE longer route riding back home, through the forest. He had hoped he'd find a way to reach Hallberg, but it was not to be. He should have known he couldn't discuss things with that man. He was like a stone wall. Everything just ran into him and fell to the ground. Sandler determined he would find out what the men on the mountain were doing. Even if he had to do it himself. By the river, behind the school, he saw Notholm. The director halted his stallion. Notholm seemed to be waiting for someone. Sandler tied his horse to a sapling and approached under the cover of the trees.

A boy came out of the school, one of the older ones, blond, hair cut so short you could see his scalp. The director had seen this one not long ago . . .

Ah, yes. Georg's boy. The one to whom the foreman had offered employment in the mine.

"Where is the other one?" Notholm asked. "Your friend?"

The boy shrugged and kicked his foot on the ground. His cheeks looked red.

"Too much for him, was it?" Notholm laughed. "Well, most people are feeble. I'm glad to see that you're not fazed."

The boy looked up at the man before him.

Somehow, the director thought, Notholm had become this boy's master.

"We have the bait," Notholm said to the boy, "and I've set the trap. It will happen where I told you. Tonight. I want you there."

The boy nodded. "Of course."

Sandler watched as the two nodded their goodbyes. Tonight.

28.

LAURA

Wallenberg had warned her about the leg. "A sabotage gone wrong," he'd said. "The bomb went off before the passengers could leave the train. Had it not been for a doctor traveling on the train, your friend wouldn't have survived. His colleagues transported him to Sweden, but unfortunately, his leg got infected and they had to remove it."

Yes, she was prepared for the leg. She wasn't prepared for the face.

She had to steel herself not to react. "Hi," she said.

Karl-Henrik stared at her. Most of his jaw was missing. His neck was scrunched up on one side and his head leaned. Could he even speak? He was leaning on his crutches in the doorway to his apartment and one trouser leg was pinned up. She swallowed. Karl-Henrik used to be good-looking. Reserved, strict. Good-looking.

"Hi," he said, at last. He spoke through the side of his mouth. His voice had taken on a metallic quality.

Britta would have reacted loudly, with an explosion of love and tears that nobody would have been able to resist. Britta would have hugged Karl-Henrik, caressed his damaged face, and told him it didn't matter one damn bit. He was still gorgeous, still him. Laura was not Britta.

"I didn't know you were in Stockholm until now," Laura said meekly. "I'm so sorry about what happened."

There was an awkward pause. Then Karl-Henrik said, "Don't be sorry about that. Be sorry about Sweden's role in all this."

Did he know she'd been working with Wallenberg? That she had negotiated with the Germans to provide them with the iron people said was prolonging the war? She lowered her gaze.

The hardest part wasn't his face, she thought when they sat down, but his eyes. They were naked; bare. She had a feeling she was looking into his soul. Karl-Henrik had always kept his distance from other people. She imagined that now he had to depend on others to help him. She could understand how awful that would be for him. It would be an affront to his pride and his independence.

"You heard about Britta?" she asked.

"He came," he said. "The policeman."

"I wanted to ask you to meet with us."

"What do you mean by 'us'?"

"Erik, me, Matti . . . We need to talk about this. We need to try to understand what happened to her."

He shook his head. *Absolutely not.*

"Please. I need you, Karl-Henrik. We need you. She was our friend. Before she died, she sent her dissertation to someone. It's gone, but I was thinking that together, we could figure out what was scaring her . . . *Who* was scaring her."

"I don't think I can do it," he said. "I don't think I can focus on the suffering of one single person when I know what's going on in the world at large . . . When I know what's going on in my own country."

"But perhaps we can understand the suffering of one person.

214

We can't do it for everyone. Please . . . She was your friend. And you were the best critical thinker among us."

An image of Karl-Henrik popped into her head, surrounded by books, furiously taking notes, eyes gleaming. "Look here, Laura. Come! See this . . ." His enthusiasm had been infectious.

Still he said nothing.

"We used to be good at thinking together, remember?"

"Fat lot of good that did us," he muttered. He sighed.

"For Britta," she pleaded.

"Alright then. I'll meet up with you just once."

"We'll come here," she said without thinking. Perhaps he'd be offended. "To make it easier," she added lamely and made it worse.

SHE FOUND MATTI in the Grand Hotel, the one out by Saltsjöbaden, where he was visiting with a delegation from Finland. The Finns had rejected the Soviet terms for peace again and again. It wouldn't be long before Stalin lost his patience. It wouldn't be long before he stood at the doorstep of Sweden.

She waited for Matti in the lobby. When he arrived, he no longer looked like a sprite but a businessman. He was dressed in a dark suit; his face had grown serious and his old mischievousness had been replaced by sternness. She didn't know this new Matti. She remembered a whisper in her ear, his hot mouth on her own, teasing. "Always observing. Never taking part." I'm taking part now, she thought.

"Laura," he said.

He took her arm and led her away toward the terrace. He didn't want to be seen with her, she realized. Before, if anything, it had been the other way around. When they were outside, he let go of her and smiled. Some of the old Matti was in that smile.

"It's been a long time," he said.

She smiled back. It had been.

"I'm here because of Britta."

He turned serious again.

"I wanted us to get together to talk about it."

Matti raised his hand. "I was told about it. I thought you might come, but it's out of the question."

"Why?"

"For many reasons."

Because of what happened, she thought. Please forgive us.

"I'm here on behalf of my country," he continued. "Finland is at war and it's a critical time for us. I have neither the time nor the mental space to get involved."

"But . . ."

"If Finland loses, Laura, Russia's western border will be the Baltic Sea. Think about that."

"She was your friend. A friend who was tortured and then shot."

Matti smiled—a smirk. Contempt? "I have many such friends nowadays, Laura. It's a no." He squeezed her arm again. "But it was good to see you," he said, in a gentler voice, nodded and with that, he was gone.

"ABSOLUTELY NOT," ERIK said, when she had mentioned the purpose of her errand.

"Seriously?" She might have expected it from the others but not from Erik.

"I will not get dragged into this."

"But why not? It's Britta we're talking about."

"Laura, Britta is dead. Your flat was bombed. I don't know

what you're trying to do here, but the police should be doing this work, not you, or me, or any other layman."

And no matter what she said, it was to no avail.

LAURA WAS DISAPPOINTED. She had honestly thought she would be able to convince them. She felt bad for Karl-Henrik. She didn't want to tell him the others had said no. Well, she wasn't going to let it go.

Last errand of the day: Sven Olov Lindholm. This time, he was speaking on Södermalm in a café. She sat down at a table and had the pleasure of seeing him looking for her as he stood up to speak, his face turning white when his gaze landed on her. She smiled and winked. Still here, she mouthed. For as long as it takes, she thought.

His speech was the same: Communists and Norwegians. Blah-blah. Jews. He made her feel sick. A small man, she thought to herself, trying to seem bigger.

Afterward, on the street, she was accosted by a man, bald and thickset. "Sven Olov wants to see you," he said. She followed him back in, to a room at the end of the café, and there was Sven Olov, drinking a glass of water.

"I will tell you what I told your friend," he said, "but then I do not want to see you again."

He put his glass down with a clink. As if to make the point.

She nodded. That was all she needed.

His face was harsh, pale. "I told her that there are whispers. Rumors. The State Institute for Racial Biology is working on a project, yes, but the organization that supports them in this is much more powerful than a mere political party."

"Who?" she asked.

He shook his head. "I don't know. I only know the project is deemed critical for Sweden's future."

"Why did she come to you?"

He shrugged. "Race being the common denominator, I guess."

"How did she find out about this project?"

"That I don't know."

What had come first? Had Britta begun working on the thesis and discovered something through her research? Or had she been told something and then started researching it?

Sven Olov Lindholm leaned forward. "Whoever is behind this will stop at nothing. Look at what they did to your friend. If I were you, I would run as far as I could in the opposite direction."

"So what have you been up to today?" her father asked at dinnertime.

They were having steak and a French red wine. The war felt a million miles away from Villa Dahlgren.

"Not much," she said, curtly.

Her father could have changed Wallenberg's mind, had he wanted to. He should have stood up for her, she thought. She remembered a conversation she'd had with Britta after the war had begun when it had become clear what Hitler was like. They'd discussed how people would react if a leader like that appeared in Sweden; whether someone—someone strong, well placed and persuasive—would be able to get people to listen and oppose events. "Your father could," Britta had said. "Right? He's powerful enough. He could if he decided to." She'd waited for Laura to nod, as if it was important to her that Laura's father would intervene in the fate of their nation.

Laura had agreed. Her father could.

It struck her now that her father might be happy about her having lost her job.

"Just looking up a few old friends."

"Friends of Britta's or friends of yours?" He put a forkful of meat into his mouth.

She shrugged. "Friends of both of us."

"Why?"

Her father had stopped eating and was watching her over the frames of his glasses, a frown-wrinkle between his eyebrows.

"I haven't seen these people for years as I didn't have the time, but now I do."

"I don't think it's a good idea," her father said and shook his head. "You need to stay away from Britta's fate and the past. These things . . ."

"Can drag you down with them?" she filled in, using Professor Lindahl's words.

"They can," her father said. "Believe me, Laura. Whatever this was, you're better off as far away from it as possible. These people obviously don't shy away from anything. Leave it in the hands of the police."

"Will you try and find a new job?" her grandfather asked.

"There's an opportunity at the bank," her father said. "I think you'd be perfect. The supervisor would be happy to see you any time. Tomorrow, perhaps?"

"I just thought I'd take some time off before getting into something new. It's been hectic these last few years."

Her father was still watching her. "Don't push it," he said. "You were incredibly lucky to survive, make no mistake. Don't give anyone a reason to change that."

29.

JENS

Jens Regnell?"

The woman reminded him of someone. She had dark curly hair and thick glasses. Her features were thick, the nose round, the chin protruding. She'd approached him outside the ministry as he headed home. Despite the warm weather, she was dressed in a large and bulky coat.

"Yes?"

"My name is Annika Jonsson. I am . . . was . . . Daniel Jonsson's sister." Her eyes blinked behind the glasses. Now he saw the likeness.

"I need to talk to you about his death."

Reflex: Jens's head turned to see if anyone was watching.

"Pretend we know each other." He put his arm under hers and smiled broadly. She stiffened but then let him lead her. "Something to drink?" he asked. She nodded.

He took her to a coffee shop on the bank. It was late afternoon and, apart from one other couple, the café was empty. There was no coffee either, only coffee substitute, the kind made of chicory. You got used to it.

"How did you find me?" he asked.

"Daniel was so happy to get your note. He told me you worked with him. I thought perhaps you could help."

"Help with what?"

"Daniel wouldn't have killed himself."

"His state of mind . . ."

"His state of mind was just fine!"

The other couple turned to look at them.

"Sorry," she whispered, eyes large. "Daniel was scared but not insane. He was a Catholic. He believed taking your own life was a sin. Someone did this to him."

"Why was he scared?"

"I don't know. It began when he was made to go on leave. That's what he said happened: he was forced to take a period of leave."

"Who? Who forced him?"

"His boss."

The head of Administration.

"He began saying that he was being followed." She caught Jens's look and she shook her head. "No, I actually think he was. Once, through the window, I saw Daniel coming home. There was this other man walking behind him. Daniel stopped a couple of times, to tie a shoelace and to look out over the water, and when he did, this man stopped, too."

"Did Daniel say anything else?"

"I asked him what was going on and all he said was that he'd discovered something in the archives that he wasn't supposed to know about and that knowing that information was dangerous."

Jens thought about the phone calls and the plans for arranging passage to Sweden for Norwegian and Danish Jews.

"Did he talk about Jews?" he asked.

She pushed her glasses up her nose with one finger. Jens winced. Daniel used to do that.

"No. He talked about the legacy of history, and how, depending on who's in charge, history will be remembered differently. 'They'll tailor it, Annika,' he said, 'for the supposed good of the nation.' He got annoyed when I didn't believe him. History is history, right?"

Jens thought of Britta and her questions at the *nachspiel*. Bizarre. Daniel's thoughts echoed hers.

"He didn't happen to mention the three kings' meetings, did he?" he asked, thinking about Britta's thesis. "You know, when the Kings of Denmark, Sweden and Norway met to declare our countries' neutrality?"

"Actually, he did." She looked surprised. "How did you know?"

Jens's heart sank. "A wild guess," he said, grimly. "Tell me."

"He didn't talk about the meeting itself, and not to me, but I overheard him speaking on the phone. He was trying to locate a person who oversaw guest relations at the hotel where the attendees had been staying."

"Do you remember the name?"

"No . . . I'm not sure I ever heard it." She lowered her head and when she raised it again, her eyes glistened. "I was staying with him this past week. I felt he needed the company. But yesterday, I had to go home to my own apartment to water my plants and when I came back this morning . . ."

Her shoulders fell and she sobbed. "I think they waited for me to leave. He wouldn't kill himself for me to find him."

=====

WHO WOULD HAVE participated in the three kings' meeting in 1914? Jens thought after he left Annika. Or, rather, who would know what had taken place behind the scenes?

The three kings were alive, but there was no way of asking them. Their advisers, some still in place, would be loyal to their monarchs.

The foreign ministers from all three countries had also taken part, Jens remembered, but they had all changed since then. Even at the 1939 meeting, Günther had not yet been appointed—not that he would ask him. In fact, since 1914, there had been no fewer than fifteen Swedish foreign ministers—each with their own secretary. Each government had been short-lived, one reason why people were arguing that democracy was not viable.

But how did this fit with the phone calls and the attempt to create safe passage to Sweden for the Jews?

He wondered . . . Annika thought Daniel had been killed, but you would hardly kill someone if you were trying to save others. But something was off.

Jens walked back to the ministry. He half jogged up the stairs to the archives. He hadn't seen Emilia Svensson, Daniel Jonsson's replacement, since the day of her arrival. The homey atmosphere in the archives had continued. In addition to the potted flowers and the photo frames he'd seen, there was now a large cookie jar and a picture of roses on the wall. She was settling down. There was an aroma of cinnamon. He was glad to see she hadn't yet left for the day.

"I need help," he said.

Emilia grabbed a pen. Her mouth seemed to tremble slightly—nervous? Or had she been warned about him, been asked to pass on the requests he might make?

"The three kings' meetings in 1914 and in 1939. I'd like to see what we have regarding those: who attended, minutes, bulletins, any other details. Can you help me?"

"Of course. Is it urgent?"

He hesitated. "Yes. And I'd like you to keep this request quiet."

He was putting himself out there now. Hoping she would listen.

"Of course," she repeated.

"I'll wait in my office."

When Jens got back to his office, there was a folded piece of paper on his desk that hadn't been there when he left. He opened it. There were two names written on it in black marker. *Harald Lagerheim* and *Jim Beckman*. In parentheses, after the name Harald Lagerheim, was *Ask about Rebecka*. He turned it over. There was nothing else. How strange. He didn't know who these men were. Who would have put the note on his desk? It could have been anyone in the ministry, he thought. They didn't lock their doors.

HE CALLED KRISTINA to tell her he'd be late.

"How late?" she asked.

She normally didn't care. "I'm not sure," he said.

"I just want to see you."

"I'll try to be quick," he promised.

The door opened. The foreign minister. Jens cut his call with Kristina, hung up the phone and half rose, heart in his mouth. It's about the note, he thought.

"Good," Günther said. "You're still here."

Jens looked behind him. Any minute now, Emilia would come with the box. He winced. What if she said what was in it? What if Günther asked?

"I had some work to finish," he said. "What can I do for you?"

"I'm giving a speech tomorrow at Parliament."

"Do you want me to read it?"

"No, no, there's no need. Staffan has already read it. But I need someone in the administrative department to come with me to take notes and they've all gone home."

"No worries. I'll arrange for one to come with you tomorrow."

"For ten o'clock."

"Absolutely."

Still he didn't leave, just stayed leaning against the doorframe. Normally, this would be Jens's dream. Currently, it was his nightmare. Please, he thought. Please, Emilia, take your time. Don't come now. Whatever you do.

"Is everything alright with you, Jens?"

"Yes." Jens tried to smile.

"This thing with Daniel not affecting you too badly?"

"No. I mean, it's terrible. I didn't know he was ill."

"Not many did. You're looking pale. Not getting a cold, are you?"

"Not at all."

Günther nodded and stood up straight. "Right, then," he said. "See you tomorrow."

He closed the door behind him, and Jens sank down onto his chair, legs trembling. Jesus, he thought. That was close.

A few minutes later, there was a knock and Emilia Svensson came in with a box containing the papers he'd requested.

"Thank you," he said. "I'll return it myself when I'm done."

He put the box on the floor so anyone entering wouldn't see it, still feeling shaky at almost getting caught.

The material was surprisingly slight. There was an agenda: in 1914, the Kings of Sweden, Norway and Denmark had spent a day and a half together. They had met on the Friday before noon and, after lunch, took part in various public engagements. At dinner, their foreign ministers had joined them. Saturday, the royals had attended a church service and then visited two schools. Meanwhile, the foreign ministers and their aides had been working and had reached unity regarding a communiqué. The announcement from the first meeting established the three countries' neutrality. The one sent out after the second kings' meeting repeated that message and ascertained that the three countries were determined to ensure their rights to maintain traditional trade relationships with all states—including the warfaring ones—to provide for their people. In World War I, Sweden had not traded with those deemed "in the wrong," and the population had suffered from starvation. Sweden had sworn not to repeat that mistake. Thus, during World War II the iron deliveries to Germany had continued. An image of Laura flashed through his mind. This was her domain.

There seemed to have been no real outcome of the meetings apart from the symbolic value. On Saturday night, the royals departed.

At the bottom of the folder lay a note as to the sleeping arrangements: King Christian had stayed at bank director Carl Herslow's place, King Haakon at the house of Louise Kockum, the widow of a local industrialist, and the Swedish King had stayed at the residency of the county governor.

It seemed unlikely to him that the monarchs would be able to do much behind the scenes. Each would have his entourage; each would be continually in the public eye. They had slept at different locations guarded by soldiers.

But the foreign ministers had all stayed at the Hotel Kramer in Malmö. That gave him an idea.

KRISTINA'S GODFATHER, ARTUR, answered on the second ring.

"Artur Helsing."

"Hi, Artur. It's Jens."

"Hi." Artur sounded surprised. "Everything alright?"

"Yes, yes. I am calling you with a question . . . for work."

"Oh!" Artur chuckled. "Well, if I can help your ministry, we're in trouble."

"When you were in business, I think you said you used to stay at the Hotel Kramer in Malmö?"

"That's correct. Who wouldn't have? It's a French castle in the middle of a Swedish town."

"I'm sitting here with the old notes from the three kings' meeting in 1914. It's a long time ago, but you wouldn't happen to remember anyone who worked at the hotel back then, would you?"

"Actually, I do. I remember it well because he says it was the pinnacle of his career when the foreign ministers all stayed there, and everything went well. Harald Lagerheim. He was in charge of guest relations at the hotel."

Jens unfolded the note that was on his desk. *Harald Lagerheim. Jim Becker.* Who on earth had put it there?

"Would you know of a Jim Becker?" he asked.

"I do know one Jim Becker, yes."

"Who is he?"

"Former Security Services. He was let go a couple of years back. It's a sad story . . . He used to be an expert on explosives. Then his daughter died in a car accident, if I remember correctly. He was never the same after that."

"And what about the name Rebecka?"

Artur laughed. "There are many Rebeckas, Jens."

"Is Harald Lagerheim still alive?"

"Yes, he lives here in Stockholm. He moved here after his retirement. We play bridge together."

"Could you please introduce me? Send me with your warmest recommendations?"

"Not a problem at all."

"Ask him if I can come tonight."

30.

BLACKÅSEN MOUNTAIN

The foreman sat for a long time after the director's visit. He'd always been of the view that whatever happened on the mountain stayed on the mountain. There was very little the people in Stockholm needed to know. They got their iron. They didn't need to get involved. Never needed to know about the conflicts, the technical difficulties, the worker issues . . . He had never ratted on anyone: not even when they had that alcoholic director. It was like a code of honor. *His* code of honor.

But he had made a promise.

He rose to look out the window. Men walking, carrying, lifting, their clothes black and faces sooty. He knew the sound to be deafening but he was so used to it now, he didn't seem to hear it any longer.

Blackåsen mine. His mine.

Sandler wasn't the worst director Hallberg had seen—many had come and gone. He was young. Young and ambitious. In his mind, the foreman likened the directors to peacocks. He had seen one in the royal park once, parading about, flaunting its tail feathers. These young men were well educated; quickly promoted. They knew all the right words. They could talk about the work as if they knew it firsthand. But they'd never actually worked the mine, didn't know how she breathed, what she responded to, how to make her give up her riches, when she'd turn on you and defend herself. They had no clue. For them it was all calculations on paper. For him and his men, it was life and death. If you didn't listen to the mine, made one wrong decision—that was that.

He walked back to the desk and sat down heavily. He pulled out one of the drawers and rummaged through it until he found what he was looking for at the far back. A once white card with a phone number.

Of course, he, too, had wondered what those men were up to on the other side of the mountain. Like he'd told the director, it had been going on for over a decade. Finally, a few years back, his curiosity won out. They had built another corridor into the mountain—he'd been to see it from a distance. He'd seen them carry boxes inside. He guessed it had to do with weapons. He thought they were experimenting, trying out something new.

When they'd found Georg's body, he'd wondered if, for some reason, the man had gone that way. Gone too far.

But these people didn't kill.

"If anyone ever asks too many questions," the man from Stockholm had told him, "you call this number and let us know. If anyone persists and won't let it be . . ."

He'd taken the card, this very card. He still remembered it looking small and crisp white in his hand—he'd been worried he'd soil it when the man was looking. The man had been dressed in a black suit with a white shirt—so white as if the grime from the mine couldn't touch him.

He'd nodded.

"No matter if it happens twenty or thirty years from now, you call."

He had nodded again.

"It's vital for Sweden."

He had sworn he would.

And he felt they had paid him back. He had held on to his job all this time. And when his daughter had proven to have a good head, they had offered her a university education. The former director had made out that the money came from him, but the foreman had known—had felt—that it came from this man—or men—in their black suits and white shirts in Stockholm. They were rewarding him for his loyalty.

He looked at the card again and felt his chest tighten. What happened on the mountain stayed on the mountain. But he had sworn . . .

He lifted the telephone receiver and dialed the number.

"My name is Hallberg," he said. "I am the foreman at the Blackåsen iron mine . . ."

When he hung up, he felt sick. He had set something in motion. Something that couldn't be stopped.

31.

LAURA

She had agreed to meet Karl-Henrik at his apartment. Laura had not told him the others weren't coming. Up to the last minute, she had hoped Erik would call and say he had changed his mind, but he didn't. She couldn't believe he didn't want to get involved.

She knocked on the door. She waited a while and then Karl-Henrik opened it.

"Welcome," he said with his new voice and used his crutches to move backward in the small hallway. He moved slowly down the corridor, and she followed him.

In the living room were a quiet Erik and an equally quiet Matti. She stopped abruptly, hardly believing her eyes.

Matti rose. "Red or white?" he asked.

Laura was reeling. They were here! They had come through for Britta. She could feel her eyes prickle.

"Red," Erik said. "She was always red."

"Actually, to be precise, she was always whiskey," Matti said.

Erik's face tightened. Had he ever said sorry to Matti for what happened? She didn't think so.

"Red is fine," she said quickly. Matti poured her a glass.

"Our Finnish friend here is in a hurry," Erik said. "He has to go back to support the German war effort, so we'd better get down to business straight away."

If only he could just shut up, Laura thought. There was no need to make things worse. But that was Erik's default position when he felt uncomfortable: attack.

Matti raised his chin. "Finland is fighting a separate war. We're defending ourselves against Russian aggression. We have no political commitments to Germany."

"You're fighting with them!" Erik banged the table in front of him with his fist. "Side by side. You're collaborating with the fucking Nazis."

"I'm not sure the Danes were any better," Matti said. "How long did you resist the invasion? Oh yes, you didn't. I saw the film."

There had been a newsreel: Danish policemen greeting the Germans, handing over their weapons, smiling, chatting. Laura, too, had seen it, during a lunch break.

"We're just taking back what was stolen from us," Matti said.

Laura glanced at Karl-Henrik. He was the one who had lost the most. His face was blank, revealing nothing.

"Matti . . . Erik . . ." Laura's voice sounded frail to her own ears. "Please, not the war. We won't agree on anything related to it. Can we not talk about it? For Britta's sake?"

"You're asking the impossible," Erik said. "The war is omnipresent."

Matti nodded. On this, they were of the same mind.

"Please?" she said.

There was a pause then Matti asked, "So what do you have?"

"Her autopsy report." Laura took out the document Wallenberg had given her. "The table of contents of her thesis,

which she sent to a person in Foreign Affairs. A conversation
. . ." She told them what Sven Olov Lindholm had said—that
the State Institute for Racial Biology was undertaking a project.
She told them about asking her questions and about the subse-
quent bomb in her flat.

"Who did she send her thesis to?" Erik asked.

"The foreign minister's secretary," Laura said. "He'd been
invited to a *nachspiel*: that's how they met."

The *nachspiele*. They fell silent. The best of times, Laura
thought.

"Andreas was with you when you found her?" Matti was flip-
ping through the autopsy report. He made a face, and Laura had
to look away at the sight of the photos. She nodded.

"He was the one who alerted me that she was missing. He
disappeared soon afterward. I think he was frightened."

Matti held out the autopsy report to Erik. Erik shook his head.

"And the table of contents of her thesis?"

Laura took out the paper she had brought with her. "The
title of Britta's thesis was *Nordic Relations Through the Ages:
Denmark, Norway and Sweden on a New Path*. And here are the
headings." She passed the paper to Erik.

"Bah," Erik snorted. "Anything can be lurking behind a chapter title. We know that. Why didn't she send him the whole thing?"

"She did. Unfortunately, he threw it out."

"What a jerk."

Laura could feel herself bristling. "It was sent to him cold,
without a note. He had no idea why and threw it out. That's not
strange, is it?"

Was she defending Jens? She surprised herself.

Laura cleared her throat. "I'm assuming Britta didn't have
time to finish it. There's no conclusion . . ."

"Well," Karl-Henrik said, "the first chapter must have been about the various constellations our countries have lived through throughout the years: the Kalmar Union where Denmark, Norway and Sweden found themselves under one king; Norway's union with Denmark, then Norway's with Sweden . . ."

"Scandinavia only," Matti said. "Finland is nowhere in her thesis, even though Finland was in a union with Sweden longer than anyone else. And at the meeting in 1939, it wasn't just the three Scandinavian kings—Finland participated, too, if only to have our request for support against the Soviet Union rejected by the rest of you."

Matti's face looked ugly with bitterness. Laura understood. It was personal. Their project as students, and what happened after, and the refusal of Sweden to help when Finland had been threatened by the Soviet Union. A month later, the Soviet Union bombed Helsinki and began the Winter War.

"A New Way," Karl-Henrik continued. "That could be about anything. So much changed during the 1800s."

"But mustn't it be linked to the unions?" Matti said.

"Perhaps only by its impact on them." Karl-Henrik shrugged.

"What if they were planning to reunite?" Laura asked.

Karl-Henrik shrugged again. "We don't know this."

"A New Threat," Laura said. "Hitler?"

"Could be." Matti shrugged. "Or it could be a threat to this "New Way"—whatever that is—mentioned in the previous chapter."

"Why on earth does she have a section on the Reich in there?" Laura asked.

"Well, Hitler is in charge of two of the three countries currently," Karl-Henrik said.

"Some would say all three," Matti muttered.

"And why so early in the thesis, ahead of 'A New Way'? Ahead of 'A New Threat'?"

They fell silent, staring at the headings before them.

"It's pointless," Erik said. "We're just guessing."

He was right.

"I wonder," said Laura, giving voice to what she had thought when she met Sven Olov Lindholm, "if she came upon this—whatever it was—during her research and then wrote about it? Or whether someone told her something and she started researching after the fact? Jens, the foreign ministry's secretary, said Britta was a swallow."

"What's that?"

"Basically, a spy. A young woman who involves herself with foreigners in Sweden—important people—to gather information."

The room fell silent.

"Would she have done that?" Erik asked.

"She hated the Germans," Karl-Henrik said. His eyes glistened. "She would have done anything to fight them."

She had hated them. Or, rather, what they did.

"Then it's likely that this has to do with something she found out through that work," Erik said.

"Can we retrace her steps?" Matti asked.

"Or we could begin with what Lindholm told you," Karl-Henrik said, "and approach the State Institute for Racial Biology. Perhaps it *is* all about race."

"What project about race would merit killing Britta?" Erik asked. "Racial projects are no secret. They're approved by the government: just look at the sterilization of the feebleminded."

Laura shrugged. "Lindholm said the project was deemed crucial for Sweden's future, and that rumor had it that the people involved would stop at nothing."

They fell silent.

Karl-Henrik was frowning.

"What are you thinking?" Laura asked.

"I can't see Britta writing a thesis about the unions with-out including the Sami," Karl-Henrik said. "She was passionate about their rights."

"The Sami . . . Andreas is Sami," Laura said.

Karl-Henrik shrugged. They fell silent.

"What about our project?" Laura said.

"Oh, don't go there," Erik scoffed.

"But what if it has something to do with Britta's death? Ultimately, they both dealt with race."

"It's the concern of the times," Erik said. "It was only natural that we would pick that domain for our project. But you can clearly see that hers is totally different."

Matti rose. "I'm pressed for time. We're leaving tonight, but we'll be back here in Sweden in two weeks. I can meet you then."

Erik's face was scornful.

"Who would know about a race project involving the highest levels of society?" Matti asked, as he pulled on his gloves.

Laura thought of Jens. "I might know someone who could find out."

"Who would know more about her work as a swallow?"

"Perhaps the same person," Laura said.

"We should look into what organizations the State Institute for Racial Biology has links with," Karl-Henrik suggested. "I can do that. I have time."

"I'll help you," Erik said.

"I need to leave," Matti said. "But I'll be in touch. If it is like Lindholm says, we're all putting ourselves at risk."

His face was serious. He looked old. The war beat it out of you, Laura thought. All that mischief and jokes, all gone.

Erik rose. "I'm leaving too. Laura?"

"In a minute," she said.

He nodded, and they said goodbye.

"How did you get them here?" she asked Karl-Henrik, once they were gone.

Karl-Henrik smiled and even though his face twisted sideways, his eyes were the same gentle eyes. "I thought they might refuse. It's harder to say no to a victim."

She smiled. She wanted to put her hand on his cheek but wasn't sure he'd let her. She wanted to say something kind.

"I remember when you used to come at night to the apartment," she said. "I never told you, but I felt good knowing you were there in the library."

Karl-Henrik frowned. "I never came to your apartment at night."

Laura felt a rush of fear. "It wasn't you?"

"Of course not."

"Then who was it?"

"I have no idea."

She thought of the nightly footsteps, the full ashtrays, the empty whiskey glasses. She felt scared, even though it was a long time ago.

"Why would you think it was me?" he asked.

Yes, why would she? What on earth had possessed her to believe she knew what Karl-Henrik needed and then not speak to him about it?

Someone, perhaps a stranger, had been in her home at night a few times every week and she had no idea who.

32.

JENS

Harald Lagerheim proved to be Artur's opposite in many ways. Whereas Artur was a large, jovial man, Harald was bony and hunched over. Artur was friendly and generous. Harald seemed wary, his eyes narrow, his mouth a thin line.

"I'm Jens Regnell."

"Yes, Artur called. He told me you would come."

"May I come in?" Jens asked when Harald made no sign of inviting him.

Harald moved backward, and Jens followed. In the kitchen, Harald pointed to a chair and Jens sat. The apartment was small and painted brown. The kitchen seemed unused; perhaps Harald didn't cook. Jens would have expected the home of someone in guest relations to look more cared for, with greater attention to detail. The other man remained standing, leaning against the kitchen counter with his arms crossed.

"I work for Foreign Affairs." Jens leaned forward, hands open, trying to make a connection.

"Artur said."

"We're updating our files from the three kings' meeting that took place at the Hotel Kramer in Malmö in 1914. You were the manager of guest relations then?"

Harald didn't respond.

"Do you remember it?"

"Of course I remember it."

"This is going to sound strange, but do you know if there were any other discussions between the foreign ministers in addition to them drafting the announcement?"

"How would I know that?" Harald sounded affronted. "Their meeting was held in the utmost secrecy. None of my staff was privy to it or would have tried to guess what was going on. The Hotel Kramer is a respectable institution."

Jens hesitated.

"Sometimes things are just known: people overhear things, notice things . . .'"

Harald scoffed. "Other places, perhaps. Not at the Hotel Kramer." He pushed off from the kitchen counter. The meeting was over. Jens rose.

"So how many of you are going to come?" Harald asked in the hallway.

"What do you mean?"

"You're the second one to ask me these questions. How many of you will there be?"

"What did he look like, the first one who came?"

"Gray, unruly hair." Harald wrinkled his nose. "Glasses . . . Unkempt. He kept pushing his glasses up his nose with a finger, as if they were too big. Corpulent. Filled up my whole kitchen, he did."

Daniel Jonsson, Jens thought. Daniel had been here. This man knew something. He could feel it. Taste it in his mouth. He hesitated. "I also want to ask about Rebecka," he said.

Harald blanched. He looked as if he might faint. When he spoke again, he sounded choked. "You," he spat out, "are of the worst, worst kind. There was nothing untoward between me and that young woman. I was cleared of all wrongdoing."

Jens realized he'd hit upon the other man's life secret. With this information, he was now forcing the other man to tell him what he did not want to reveal.

"I'm sorry," he said.

A red flush had spread over Harald's cheeks and neck.

"I didn't . . ." Jens began.

"I'll tell you what I know and then I want you to leave and never come back," Harald said. "You can tell Artur, too; I never want to see him again. The foreign ministers were working on a matter so secret that we were not allowed to serve them coffee or lunch in the room—they sent their own staff to pick up the food. But I did overhear something. A conversation in the corridor between a minister and his aide. I didn't try to listen in. I didn't want to hear what they said, but they were right outside my office. They were talking about setting up an organization for studying eugenics. "It will be the vehicle," one of them said. "The government needs to approve it," the other one said. And then the first one responded with something like, "We are the government." So, I wasn't surprised when the State Institute for Racial Biology was set up in Sweden a few years later."

"The vehicle for what?"

"I have no idea. And I know nothing more. This was the only thing. Now, I want you to leave. Don't you ever come back."

Jens turned in the doorway. "I'm sorry."

The breath had left the other man. His shoulders were hunched. "She was just a very good maid," he said, faintly. "I wanted to give her a break. People read other things into it. She was easily influenced, went along with them and accused me. One act of kindness and look where it got me."

JENS FOUND JIM Becker outside his house in the south of Stockholm. The night was lighter and softer than it had been in months. Summer was coming. The man was looking at a flowering tree in his garden; pondering it, with his hands clasped behind his back. Emilia Svensson had found Jens the address— she was proving quite useful. Jens still felt awful about the conversation with Harald Lagerheim. Whoever had left him the note on his desk knew things about people. *Bad* things. If he ever got a second note, he would not use whatever information it provided him with. He was not like that. No matter what.

Jim was in his seventies. His face was wrinkled, and a pair of steel-rimmed square glasses perched on the end of his blunt nose.

"Yes?" he said when Jens opened the gate to his garden.

"Jim Becker?"

"Yes?"

"Jens Regnell, Ministry of Foreign Affairs."

"Oh."

He wasn't surprised to see him, Jens thought. It was more as if he'd known that, sooner or later, Jens would come. Perhaps he, too, had had a visit from Daniel Jonsson.

Jens walked over to stand next to him by the tree with its pink flowers. There was a bittersweet scent in the air. It reminded him of crushed almonds. "A beautiful tree," he said. "Apple?"

"Cherry," Jim replied. "I'm thinking I might have to cut off one of the larger branches. The tree is getting old. Carrying all that weight becomes hard."

"What a shame."

"It's life. So, what can I do for you, Jens Regnell?"

Jens hesitated. This man had been part of the Security Services. Jens wouldn't lie to him.

"I'm following a trail," he said. "It's come to my attention that more might have happened during the three kings' meetings in 1914 and 1939 than was previously known. I'm trying to find out what."

"And how did you get my name?"

"Someone left a note on my desk."

"Anonymously?"

"Yes."

"That should tell you something."

Yes . . . but what?

"Someone wants this known," Jim said. "I wonder who? You see, most people do not want this known at any price."

"You know what happened then. Please tell me."

"No. I got involved once and that was a mistake. I won't make that same mistake again."

"It's important."

Jim looked him in the eyes. His eyes were kind and calm. He seemed sad. "Yes," he nodded. "Yes, it is."

"A woman has died for this already," Jens said. "And a man." As he said it, he knew it was true. This was why Britta and Daniel had died. No ex-lover. No mental problems. This. What Sven had told him had not been true. Whoever had given Sven the information had lied to him.

"More than two," Jim said.

He nodded goodbye and walked to his door. Jens remained standing under the tree and watched the door close.

===

HE GOT HOME after midnight. He tried to shut the door quietly.

"Jens?"

He exhaled and walked out into the living room. Kristina was sitting on one of the sofas in a morning gown, a magazine in her hand. "You're still awake?" he asked.

"I did say I wanted to see you."

"I'm sorry." He kissed the top of her head. "It's been a long day."

"Sit down," she said.

He didn't feel like relaxing but complied and sat down beside her. She wrapped her arms around him.

"Günther is working you too hard," she said. "I'll have a word with him next time I see him."

Jens tried to turn to see her face.

"I'm only joking," she said. "You're very diligent. That's a good thing."

"Yes," he said and put his feet up on the coffee table, tried to relax. But the restlessness inside was clawing at him, making him twitch. He was so close to answers, he could feel it, and yet so far away. Kristina hugged him tightly. He felt he couldn't breathe.

LAURA DAHLGREN WAS waiting in Jens's office when he arrived the next morning. She was sitting on his desk, swinging her legs. He startled.

"How did you get in?" he asked.

Normally, visitors were seated in the waiting room and then they were announced and accompanied to the office of the person they wished to meet.

"I'm very resourceful," she said. She stretched her legs out in front of her, then slid off the desk.

She was wearing a white jumpsuit and her blond hair was ruffled at the back as if she hadn't had time to comb it properly. Her gray eyes were large and serious.

"I need your help," she said.

"With what?"

"The same thing we discussed last time we met."

She shouldn't be here. It was getting dangerous.

"Who knows that you're here?"

She shook her head. "No one."

Apart then from the guards at the door, the secretaries . . .

"No one," she repeated.

"Our archivist died a few nights ago," Jens said. "They called it suicide. But he'd been asking questions about the 1914 meeting of the three kings. Something happened there."

She took a step closer to him, standing so close that he could see the tiny white scar on her mouth.

"Before she died, Britta met up with Sven Olov Lindholm, head of the SSS. He told her that the State Institute for Racial Biology was working on a project supported by the highest levels of society. He said that the project was crucial for Sweden's future, and that rumor had it the people involved would stop at nothing." She was speaking rapidly, in a low voice.

"At that meeting, the foreign ministers were working on something secret. They discussed establishing an organization for studying eugenics," Jens told her. "'It will be the vehicle,' they said."

"Vehicle for what?"

"I don't know . . ."

Laura took a paper from her pocket and unfolded it. "We discussed the chapter titles of Britta's thesis; it could be about some sort of a union . . ."

"I just think that if there were a union in the making, I would know," Jens said.

"Whatever it was, she must have had a source. Perhaps someone she met as a swallow."

"Or something she found during her researches. Who's 'we,' by the way?"

"Former fellow students of Britta's." She noticed his gaze. "You don't have to worry. They have even more to lose by looking into this than you do."

"More to lose than their lives?"

She fell silent. "I guess you're right. Ultimately, that's what's at stake. These friends are reliable; that's what I meant."

"I was told Britta was killed by an ex-lover," he said. "And that this ex-lover also planted the bomb in your flat. They think you encouraged Britta to leave him."

"If she had a lover, I didn't know him."

"Who's in charge of the investigation into her murder?" Jens asked.

"Inspector Ackerman in Uppsala," Laura said. "We'll investigate the links the State Institute for Racial Biology has with other organizations and we'll try to find Andreas. He was a close friend of Britta's who disappeared after she was killed. Could you see what you could find out about a race project involving 'the highest levels of society'?"

"Not just our society then," he remarked.

"What do you mean?"

"Well, she mentions Denmark, Norway and Sweden."

She paused. "Yes," she said. "You might be right." Her face was pale.

Jens thought about the missing phone calls between the three countries and the foreign minister's reaction when he'd

246

asked about them. It was impossible. Sven had said it was about the Jews. But then Sven had also said Britta's murder was personal.

Laura was still looking at him, frowning. A lock of hair had fallen over one eye and he was gripped with the impulse to brush it to the side.

"Yes," he said. "I will see what I can do."

"Can you find out who Britta met up with?"

"I don't know anyone . . ." Then he thought of Sven's father. "I can try."

"Be careful," she said.

He nodded.

"If you need to reach me, you can either call my home with a bogus question—I'll ask them to let me know if you call—or you can come to this address." She stuck a piece of paper in his hand and folded his fingers around it. "A friend of mine lives there. He can get in touch with me. Just make sure you aren't followed."

"What if you need to reach me?"

She smiled and her face brightened. "I'll just show up."

"You'll have to sign in," he said. "You'll be noticed."

"Good luck, Jens. Speak soon. Be careful." And with that, she was gone.

Jens waited for a while, and then he walked down to reception.

"May I look at our guest register?" he asked the secretary, leaning on her desk and smiling his best smile.

She returned his smile. "Of course." She pushed the book over to him.

Laura Dahlgren had not been signed in.

He went back to his office and called the police station in Uppsala and asked to speak to Inspector Ackerman.

"Jens Regnell, Ministry of Foreign Affairs," he said when the other man came to the phone. "I want to inquire if you've arrested the person responsible for the murder of Britta Hallberg?"

"Who did you say you were?"

"Jens Regnell. I am the secretary to the minister of foreign affairs."

"No, we haven't," the policeman said.

"I was told an arrest was imminent."

"Then you know more than me. This investigation has proven a real pain. It's as if we're being blocked every step of the way. We still have no idea what this was about."

33.

BLACKÅSEN MOUNTAIN

All day, Taneli felt sick with fear. Any footstep, any snap of a broken branch became that of the mine director arriving at their camp, together with the police. The director had seen him up close. He wouldn't be hard to find.

When Sandler had left Taneli standing in his living room, Taneli had considered putting the money back. If he didn't keep it, perhaps the man would let him off. Though why would he? Surely intent was as bad as the act. Taneli was in his house! And then he thought about Áslat and about his sister. In the end, Taneli had stuffed the bills into his shirt, climbed out the window and run. Now, he agonized. The money was tormenting him and he didn't know where to put it to keep it safe. If he put it in their *kåta*, their dwelling, his mother would surely find it and drag him in front of the elders. If he hid it, and someone else found it, they'd claim the bills were a gift from the spirits. In the end, Taneli carried the cash on him, terrified that the notes would fall out if he bent down, or get destroyed if he sweated. He moved like a stick through their camp, unwilling to engage in anything, continuously glancing toward the path leading to town.

"What's wrong with you?" Olet, asked, frowning.

"Nothing," Taneli mumbled.

Taneli and Olet were supposed to mend the fence around the reindeer enclosure. The animals were far away, up in the high mountains with some of the men. At this time of year, they'd be calving. The summer camp would be lovely: cool and insect-free. But they were still here, in the heat and with the bugs, because Taneli's father, along with others, was forced to work in the mine. They couldn't just leave these men behind and so their group had split in two. The animals would be back here late summer, before winter began; by then the enclosure must be ready.

"You're not helping," Olet complained.

There was this girl, Sire, and Taneli noticed how Olet ended up by her side whenever there was a chance. If Olet wasn't so much older than Taneli, and if Taneli wasn't so worried about other things, he'd tease him.

Taneli bent down to pick up the hammer. The money chafed against his stomach. He swung at one of the slats and his body broke out in a sweat. He couldn't keep the bills inside his shirt. It wasn't going to work. He turned away from Olet, took them out and put them in his hat, which he folded on the ground.

"You'll burn your head," Olet said. "The spring sun is strong."

Taneli muttered something about Olet minding his own business. Olet frowned but let it pass.

They worked the whole morning, replacing the old, rotted slats, reattaching those that had loosened.

"Lunchtime," Olet said finally, after a glance at the sky.

Taneli wiped his forehead. It was getting hot.

Before he could stop him, Olet bent down to pick up his hat.

"No!" Taneli said.

Olet paused mid-movement but not because of Taneli's order.

"What is this?" he said and took out the money.

"It's mine!" Taneli tried to snatch the notes out of his hand, but Olet pulled away.

"What *is* this, Taneli?" he asked, his voice angry now. "Two hundred crowns? Where did you get these?"

"Olet." Taneli tried to sound reasonable. "It's mine. I need it. You can't take it."

He took a step forward, but Olet ducked and lifted the money over his head. He was five years taller than Taneli.

"You have to tell me."

"I stole it from the mine director," Taneli blurted out and had the brief satisfaction of seeing Olet drop the money on the ground as if he'd burned himself. Taneli bent down and grabbed it.

"Have you gone mad?" Olet asked, his cheeks red. He had balled his fists as if ready for a fight. "Do you realize what you've done? What do you think they'll do to Nihkko?"

To Nihkko?

"I had to do it," Taneli said.

Olet's face was tight.

"I had to," Taneli repeated. "There's this man. He has information about Javanna, but I need to pay him."

Olet stepped away. "Have I taught you nothing then?" he muttered.

Taneli raised his voice. "He says she's still alive. He knows where she is. I have to know. I have to *try*."

"Taneli." He shook his head. "Nobody knows where your sister is. He's lying to you."

"Olet, *please*," Taneli pleaded.

"What are you going to do when they come for you?"

"I don't know."

"You won't be able to pay them back if you've given the money away."

Taneli hung his head.

"They'll put you in the stocks. Or in jail."

"But what if I find her, Olet? What if?"

Olet sighed, but his face softened. The knots of muscles around his mouth dissolved.

"You're on your own in this," he said.

At least that meant he wouldn't be telling Nihkko.

WHEN EVENING FELL, Taneli was waiting by the clump of trees where he'd first met Áslat. Blackåsen Mountain was nothing but a mute, dark block. The sky was a mixture of light blue and light pink, with orange clouds and streaks close to the hovering sun. The train platform was full of soldiers. Another German train was probably approaching. Taneli wished Áslat would hurry up.

A branch snapped.

Áslat.

Taneli turned to the sound, relieved.

But the man coming to meet him on the path wasn't Áslat. It was the man who had come to measure the boys: the one with the empty, light blue eyes. He was on a horse, and his eyes were fixed on Taneli.

Hello, he mouthed.

A trap!

Taneli turned and began to run. Not toward the platform; the soldiers would take him immediately. Not in the direction of Blackåsen town, as he'd be stopped by the inhabitants. The forest. The only place where he'd be able to hide.

Olet had been right, he thought.

He found the path and ran faster.

Behind him, the thrumming of horse's hooves. If he stayed on the path, the horse would run him down.

There was a smaller trail, a funnel into the trees.

He took it.

Next thing, he was lying on the ground facedown and someone was sitting on him, his arms pressed to his side by the person's legs.

"I've got him!"

A boy's voice. Jubilant. Taneli tried to turn, to fight, but he was caught.

"Good work," the man said.

It was over. It was all over.

The boy turned Taneli over and hoisted him up. Holding his arms behind his back, he forced Taneli to face the man with the empty eyes. Taneli was wriggling, but it was to no avail.

The man was smiling. "You're mine now."

Then another man's voice. "Let him go."

On the path behind the man with the empty eyes, also on a horse, was the director.

The man with the empty eyes seemed to growl. "Director." He pulled out a weapon: a revolver? But he couldn't . . .

There was a shot, and Sandler fell heavily off his horse. It sounded like a sack of grain falling to the ground. His mount neighed and ran down the path headed for the town.

He had killed him!

Taneli wanted to scream but nothing came out. He had killed the mine director!

The boy had loosened his grasp on Taneli's arms as if he, too, was shocked at what had just happened.

The man turned to face them. He was still smiling. "The director made himself a target," he said.

A target? He was the director!

Then, suddenly, the man's horse let out a high-pitched neigh and reared up, its front legs kicking the air. The rider wasn't expecting it and fell backward. The horse set off down the path, galloping, dragging the empty-eyed man behind it, his foot caught in the stirrup.

The boy behind Taneli let go of him and set off running down the narrow path, leaving behind Taneli, Sandler, and Olet, who appeared out of the bush, bow and arrow in hand.

"You shot his horse," Taneli whispered. He felt feverish.

Olet was bending over Sandler.

"He's alive," he said, "but he needs help."

The boys carried the director through the forest. He was very heavy. They had to stop often, rest his body on the ground, and then lift him up again. There was a wound in his chest. There was a lot of blood. A spreading scarlet patch on his shirt.

"We'll take him to his house," Olet said. "They can call for the doctor."

"You saved me," Taneli said. "You saved *us*."

Olet didn't respond.

They struggled on with their burden. Sandler's legs were slipping out of Taneli's grip. His lower back hurt. "I need to rest," he said. They lay the body down again. "I just wanted it to be true," Taneli said.

"I know," Olet said.

"But he knew things about Javanna. Things he couldn't have known unless she told him."

The man who shot the director, Taneli thought. He is the one who told Áslat these things. He is the one who has Javanna.

At Sandler's villa, they knocked. The housekeeper opened the door. She screamed when she saw the director's body on the steps.

"We found him in the forest," Olet said. "He needs a doctor."

They made to leave just as the director came to. His hand shot out and grabbed Taneli's arm.

The stable hand had arrived, standing at the foot of the stairs. He and the housekeeper were both looking at Taneli.

The director's hand was still clutching Taneli's arm.

Olet was backing out through the garden, shaking his head.

34.

LAURA

How would you go about creating a religion that you yourself could believe in?

Their whole last year at university, 1939, had been spent debating this. What would it take for them to become passionate believers in something?

Laura was on the train to Uppsala, remembering. What had seemed impossible in the beginning had become easier.

"So, we just . . . invent a God?" Erik had asked, early on.

It had been a bitter January. Rain followed by more rain. Nobody wanted to go out and they spent the evenings in Laura's apartment. On the radio, Hitler was giving a speech. The man's voice was intimate and yet strong. They all spoke German and it was fascinating to listen to him.

"Any better idea?" Laura grumbled. Erik had landed them in this spot in the first place.

"The obvious elements," Karl-Henrik said. "A common belief system; stories and myths supporting those beliefs; rituals . . . Religion has to be organized to survive . . ."

"A creation story, a quest for salvation, the end of times," Erik reeled off. "All religions are basically the same."

"This feels bizarre," Britta said.

"All gods were made up," Karl-Henrik pointed out.

Interesting, Laura thought. They all claimed to be atheists, yet to think that God in the Bible had been made up felt sacrilegious.

"How about we don't invent anything new, but we take Asatru and see what would be needed for us to buy into it?" Karl-Henrik said. "After all, that was the question: What would it take for you to believe?"

"Why Asatru?" Britta asked.

"Why not? We know it pretty well by now."

"I'll never believe," Erik muttered.

Behind him, Hitler's voice on the radio was building: "It was nearly two thousand years before the scattered Germanic tribes emerged as one people; before the countless lands and states forged one Reich.

"We may now consider this process of the formation of the German nation as having reached its conclusion. The creation of the Greater German Reich represents the culmination of our Volk's thousand-year struggle for existence."

They had all fallen still, listening.

"Regardless of how you feel about him, admit it—he is hugely inspiring," Britta said.

"But why?" Karl-Henrik said. "What about him do people find inspiring? Why do we?"

"National pride . . . There's this sense they could achieve anything."

"Superiority," Britta said. "Of Germany, of their race. Patriotism. You want to be a part of it."

"It's all feelings. No ideology," Erik muttered.

"It works," Matti said. "He's playing strongly both into the past and the future for the German people—it has to work."

"He's rewriting history," Britta said.

"Indeed," Matti said. "And they believe him."

"I think that's it," Karl-Henrik said slowly.

"What?"

"What if, in Asatru, the element of race was stronger? The Nordic race and the superiority of the same."

"Nah, wouldn't do it for me." Erik said.

"Sure, it would," Karl-Henrik said. "What if Asatru was better at defining a community and got believers to swear complete allegiance to one another, their territory and to Asatru? Don't you think that could get you going?"

"You, too, could become a Viking?"

"Something like that."

"That could be interesting," Laura said, hesitating. "But it's not enough. People need a quest. A calling."

"Yes! You build up the elements around the chosen ones, their intrinsic superiority, and . . ."

"And?"

"Their inherent right to rule."

"And then whip up enough emotion to get them to act," Britta said, thoughtfully. "A glorious, firebrand leader."

"Manipulation," Erik said.

"All religion is manipulation," Karl-Henrik pointed out.

"You'll need a threat."

"Easy. Whatever threatens the superior race."

Matti had a strange look on his face. "What?" Laura asked.

"Do you think that's what he's doing?"

"Who?"

"Hitler. Creating a religion."

"Of course it is," Karl-Henrik said. "He already has. You just have to listen to the broadcast."

"Fucking clown," Erik said.

LAURA'S VISIT TO the student administration office came up empty. While she knew Andreas came from Blackåsen, the administrator had no address or details for his next of kin.

"Don't they live in . . . groups?" one of the office staff asked.

"And they travel, don't they?" her colleague added. "They don't have homes."

Laura didn't know. But Andreas's studies had been sponsored by the church. She remembered Britta talking about a priest up north. "Not my type, but he did do some good," she'd said.

She was mighty lucky, the housekeeper at the vicarage told her. The archbishop was in town. Laura walked across the cobblestone square to the cathedral. The sun was hot, and she took off her cardigan, folded it over her arm. She glanced at the Historical Society as she passed it and shuddered.

Her shoes made tapping sounds on the stone floor. She remembered an occasion during their university days, when she was looking for Erik; another student had told her he was inside the cathedral, and she had found him in the nave, standing gazing up at the arched ceiling by von Linné's grave.

"What are you doing?" she'd asked.

"Worshipping," he'd said, turning to face her, his glassy eyes widening as if surprised. He'd reeked of beer.

It seemed funny now. At the time, though, she'd felt she had to get him out of there as soon as possible.

It was cool in the church and Laura put her cardigan back on.

The archbishop had a tiny smile on his face. He was dressed in a black robe and wore a large silver cross on his chest. His hands were large and looked soft. "You would like to know the whereabouts of a Sami student?"

Their voices sounded strange in the cathedral: muted and echoey at the same time.

She didn't think he recognized her from the *nachspiel*. But then, years had passed. She wondered how he would feel if he knew that his talk at the *nachspiel* had inspired them all to become pagans?

"He was sponsored by the local church to study here. He is a friend. I think he might be in trouble. He might have traveled home. I'd like to offer him my help."

It's a fine balance, she thought. Honest, but not too honest.

"He's a friend? Of yours?" He raised his brows.

She nodded and looked down on her shoes.

"Well then," he said. "We can call the local priest, if you like. After all, caring for the smallest among us is a Christian duty."

She waited while he spoke with the operator and got connected. Someone on the other end answered and the two exchanged pleasantries. It must be a shock to a local priest when the archbishop called, she thought.

He covered the receiver with his hand. "What was the name of your friend?"

"Andreas Lundius Lappo."

The archbishop repeated the name. He had a soft, black leather book that he wrote in while the priest spoke. When they were finished, they said goodbye.

"He knows the boy well," he told Laura. "He said he's bright. He comes from one of the local groups. They spend the summers up in the high mountains and then come closer to Blackåsen during the wintertime. But he says the boy hasn't returned home. He hasn't come to visit the church."

It didn't mean much, Laura thought. Andreas might not have wanted to be seen in town.

"I appreciate you trying," she said.

"I hope you manage to locate him," the archbishop said.

She had never given Andreas the time of day. But I will find him, she thought, and then I will.

JUST LIKE LAST time, she found Inspector Ackerman in his office at his desk. He seemed surprised to see her. Surprised—and something else.

"What are you doing here?" he asked.

"My friend, Britta . . ."

He rose and closed the door behind her. "I've been taken off the case. The Security Services are managing it now."

She thought of the two men who had come to her home. "What happened?"

"Yesterday, some jerk from the foreign ministry called and asked if I had arrested the killer. Next thing I know, these two men show up and say I'm no longer working on the case. They didn't want to know the details . . . didn't ask if I had found anything out. I tried to tell them about her Sami friend, Andreas, who disappeared after her murder and who is a person of interest. I don't think they even listened. They just took my papers, told me my involvement was over and left."

"They blew up my flat," she said, uncertain who "they" were. Shadows, she thought.

He scrunched up his mouth. "I've also been accused of fraud. An anonymous letter."

"Fraud?"

He shrugged. "I have a feeling that you cannot be involved with this matter and get away unscathed." He looked at her, his forehead lifted into a hundred wrinkles and a tiny smile played at the corners of his mouth. "Don't worry. It's not the first time I've been in trouble."

KARL-HENRIK'S LIVING ROOM was full of paper. Handwritten notes on the sofa, on the table, on the floor. Just like old times.

"I see you've started," Laura said. She smiled.

"I got lucky," Karl-Henrik said. "I found a Norwegian who used to work for the State Institute for Racial Biology in administration. He's seen the correspondence the institute undertakes, the meeting logs . . . He's a gold mine, though he doesn't know it. I ask questions and he says he has no idea, and then he still answers." Karl-Henrik laughed, a rasping sound.

"And he's willing to spend time with you, answering questions?"

"They feel guilty," Karl-Henrik said, lightly.

Seeing Karl-Henrik's wounds must crush those who'd fled, she thought. It must remind them of what others had sacrificed.

"It's amazing, Laura," Karl-Henrik said and held out a paper with circles and lines on it for her to see. "This institute has its arms going everywhere. Everywhere! The more I look, the more there is. There are anthropology committees, the Institute for Legal Genetics . . . but then there are links to the universities, to the museums, to hospitals—even the Royal Academy of Fine Arts! And then you look at the individuals who are connected to it. They are all prominent: businessmen, politicians. I know race is a widespread concern of the times. I just didn't know how . . . *organized* it would feel."

She thought of the archbishop's black book.

"The church?" she asked.

"Oh, yes," he responded and pointed to a black circle on his paper.

Them, too.

"Erik was here," Karl-Henrik said.

"Yes?"

"I sent him off to look into the Danish side of things. The Danes have also been pretty active."

Where would Erik get his information? Most likely from the Danes hiding out in Stockholm.

"Did you have any luck in finding out where Andreas has gone?" Karl-Henrik asked.

Laura shook her head. "He hasn't been seen up north. Perhaps he doesn't want to be seen. Perhaps he's hiding."

"So what will you do?"

"I'm going to go there," she said, the idea becoming reality as she spoke the words. "I want to find Andreas and speak to Britta's family."

There was a glow about Karl-Henrik amid all his papers. He loved this. Digging into a mystery, following a trail. Then she remembered Erik, back at university, saying that Loki, the trickster god, was following them. She thought about her night visitor in her Uppsala apartment.

"Be careful," she said to Karl-Henrik. "If you feel you're being watched, let me know."

Not that she knew what she'd do about it.

"I've been saying that I'm working on a project for Professor Lindahl." Karl-Henrik smiled. "That seems to go down well with everyone."

═══

WHEN SHE CAME home, Emil Persson called. "Funny business," he said.

"What?"

"The bomb in your apartment. Nobody wants to admit it happened. And your friend died, too."

"Yes. Yes, she did."

Laura hesitated. Such a big leap of faith. But Emil had proven himself to be just. He had not chosen the comfortable path in his journalism; you only had to read his articles about the missing Jews to know this.

"Emil, you haven't heard about the State Institute for Racial Biology being involved in a new project, have you?"

"No. Has it got do with this?"

"Maybe."

"I'll put feelers out."

35.

JENS

There was a cocktail party at one of the ministries. To "raise morale," the foreign minister had stated with a smirk. Jens wasn't certain whether he had been joking or not. Kristina was with him, glass in her right hand, left hand under his arm. She was wearing a simple black dress, with her hair swept back from her face. She was smiling and greeting other guests; appearing to know more people than he did. The room was decorated with crystal chandeliers and flower arrangements. The buffet tables were laden with food. It was hard to think that just across the water, the world was at war and people were starving to death.

Jens was troubled: he had found something on his desk again today. He'd been away for not more than ten minutes, talking to one of the administrative assistants about a travel schedule, and when he came back, it was there. Whoever was leaving him things must be watching him. It was a drawing this time. It was an overview of a mine: a diagram of the mine galleries and shafts. A single word was written beneath: Blackåsen. He had no idea why it had been left in his office. He did know he wasn't supposed to have it. He worried about how bad it was that he did have it . . . if it could be considered spying. And why? Why give it to him? He didn't understand what the plan of the mine had to do with anything. "Someone wants this known," Jim had said. But what? Who?

"Nice to see you again, Miss Bolander."

Christian Günther. Jens could feel himself straighten.

"Likewise," Kristina purred.

"He doesn't let us see you, now that you're an item."

"I'll make sure to change that." Kristina touched the minister's arm.

Günther then turned to Jens and lowered his voice. "Sad thing, this business with Daniel Jonsson."

Jens nodded.

"Have they spoken to you yet? The Security Services?"

Jens tensed. He tried to smile, but his jaw felt stiff. "Not yet. Will they?"

"It's likely. They'll talk to whoever had interactions with the archives."

Jens nodded. Then the minister didn't know about the note. At least, not yet.

"You know that thing you asked me about a while ago?" Günther said.

The phone calls? "Yes?" Jens said.

"I think it would be better if you didn't mention it . . . To anyone."

Really? Before Jens could ask anything more, the foreign minister gestured to a corpulent man in a gray suit, standing farther away. "Mr. Richter!" he called and with that, he was gone.

"He's amazing," Kristina said, following him with her eyes.

"What do you mean?"

"Now, don't get jealous!" She smiled and tucked her hand

back under his arm. "I just find him bright, that's all. This is only the second time I've met him, and still he remembers my name. We should try to have him over. Throw a big party."

She was ambitious, Jens thought. For him, for them . . . "Most Swedes don't like him," he pointed out.

"Most Swedes haven't met him."

THEY WERE HALFWAY through the evening—many conversations later, many invitations made and received—when Jens noticed Jim Becker by the buffet table. Jim was the last person he had expected to see there.

"I'll go and get more food," he said in Kristina's ear and left her with the group.

He picked up a plate and put a sandwich on it from the buffet, slowly approaching the place where Jim stood.

"What a coincidence," he said, in a low voice.

"From now on, Jens Regnell, nothing is a coincidence," Jim said, his gaze focused on the platter of cheese as he picked up a piece. "Meet me outside in ten minutes." He turned and said something to the woman on his other side.

Jens found Jim standing in the shadows alongside the house, hands in his pocket, coat collar up.

"I'm surprised you're here," he said.

Jim nodded. "Hiding in plain view can work quite well. Let's walk."

The evening was warm. A pleasant wind swept over the bridge. Farther down the bank, a man was laughing, then a woman followed suit.

"There was a lot more to the kings' meeting in 1914 than was let on," Jim said. "They said the foreign ministers spent that

Saturday working on the neutrality declaration, but the truth is, they were working on something else."

"What?" Jens asked.

"For quite a while now, some people in Sweden, Norway and Denmark have talked about a Scandinavian Reich under one strong leader. The foreign ministers' meeting that day was the culmination of months of work on developing a program that, over time, was supposed to take the three countries there."

"Impossible."

"Why? There've been unions before."

"And how does Germany fit into this?"

"It didn't at the time. But when Hitler later emerged as the German leader, and it became clear he would wage war, the committee decided that the three countries should remain neutral. The plan was to wait for Germany to destroy itself in war. They thought that a Scandinavian union could then win over Germany and expand its territory to what it was like during the reign of Karl XII to include the whole Baltic region and, perhaps, beyond."

Jens whistled. The Reich, he thought. Britta's thesis hadn't been talking about the German Reich at all.

"There's more. There are two spines to the program. One is a Scandinavian union under one leader and the other is a continual improving of the Scandinavian race."

Jens shook his head. "Meaning?"

"Scandinavia is thought to be one of the few places that has never been overwhelmed by foreign conquest and in which there has been but a single racial type from the beginning—a race supreme to all the others—one that needs to be safeguarded."

"And how do they propose to do that?"

Jim shrugged. "The usual: breed from the best; prevent further mixing . . . Remove what is not pure Scandinavian. Remove, but also draw knowledge from, for the sake of science."

Jens's mouth was dry. He swallowed. "Drawing knowledge from . . . ?"

"Human experimentation," Jim said. "And this was where some of us could no longer sit by and watch."

This couldn't be happening. Not in his own country. "Look in your own cupboards," Schnurre had said. Was he aware that this was going on?

"So what happened?" he asked. "What's happening now?"

"At the meeting in 1939, the decision was made to abandon the program. There was new leadership in all three countries, new ideas. The program was deemed the product of the past, a fleeting madness, embarrassing. Hitler had begun his journey with similar ideas and people found him not necessarily wrong but crude. It was abandoned, shut down."

Jens nodded.

"Only it wasn't," Jim said. "It's being kept alive."

Impossible. "By whom?"

"Bureaucrats, the fanatics . . . Those who still want this at any price. Those who hate what's different. The governments know it's continuing, but they have lost control."

"Who's involved?"

"We no longer know. The State Institute for Racial Biology certainly has a central role; members of the three countries' Security Services, too, but it has taken on a magnitude that is unbelievable."

"Is Christian Günther in on it?" Jens thought of the phone calls.

"I don't know."

"Are you . . . Are you working against this?"

Jim shook his head. "At one point, I was. But . . ." He looked away. "One of my team members got killed: shot. A mugging gone wrong, they said. And then my daughter died in a car accident, but, by then, there was no doubt in my mind what had happened. I don't think anything can stop the program now. It's taken on a life of its own. The people involved are much too powerful. I'm only meeting you because . . . because, if you're willing to risk it, I owe it to those who have died to give you something to work with. My daughter was headstrong. She was a strong believer in right and wrong. Were she alive today, she would never have let me stop—regardless of the consequences."

"I'm so sorry," Jens said.

Jim nodded.

"Is Blackåsen mine involved in this?" Jens asked, thinking of the drawing on his desk.

"There were rumors that the human experimentation took place up north."

"I wonder why . . ." It was isolated, yes, but far away.

"The Sami," Jim said coldly. "They are not deemed pure Scandinavian."

Jens exhaled. *Oh God.*

"This is so big, Jens," Jim said. "You'll find yourself hunted. You'll put your loved ones in danger. You'd better be certain before you go any further."

"I don't see what choice there is."

Jim shrugged. "Have it your own way. What concerns me though, Jens, is this note you told me of, the one that gave you my name. Someone wants you to know about this. Who are those people working in the shadows and what do they want?"

"They want to help me," Jens said.

"Not necessarily," Jim said. "There are other reasons for making something known."

"Where did you go?" Kristina asked, when he came back.

He wished intensely that he could share his findings with her, with anyone.

"I just got caught speaking to someone," he said. "But I'm back now."

36.

BLACKÅSEN MOUNTAIN

Around midnight, there was a faint knock. Gunnar opened his eyes. There it was again. It came from the window. A small tapping sound. Gunnar's father stirred. His mother sighed deeply. His brothers were snoring. Gunnar sat up. Slowly, he tiptoed to the door. He pushed the handle down, waited, but the bedroom was silent.

Outside, at the bottom of the steps, was Abraham, his face white in the moonlight. Abraham had met with Notholm again. Gunnar had refused after what he'd done to the hare. Abraham had called him a coward. But Gunnar still had nightmares about the animal. He'd been scared of saying no, though, worried about what Notholm might do.

He took the steps down to his friend. Closer to, he could see that his friend had been crying. His eyes were red, his cheeks dirty.

"What happened?"

Abraham just shook his head.

Gunnar shivered and wrapped his arms around himself. A cold wind trawled up his bare feet and legs. "Abraham, what happened?"

"Mr. Notholm had a gun."

"What?"

"He shot the director. He killed him!"

Gunnar couldn't believe what he was hearing. It was impossible.

"Where is the director now? Where is Mr. Notholm?"

"I don't know. I need to leave," Abraham said. "Before anyone realizes. I just wanted . . ." His voice broke. "He said the director had made himself a target," he said.

Gunnar felt cold. People were not prey.

"Just tell my mother that it wasn't me who did it," Abraham said.

Abraham's mother. She'd just lost her husband.

"I'm sure we can work it out," Gunnar said, even though he wasn't at all sure.

Abraham was shaking his head. "Not this."

"But how will you manage?"

Abraham shrugged. "I'll manage. Promise you'll tell my mother."

"I promise."

Abraham walked away. Gunnar watched until he turned the corner of a house and was gone.

ALL MORNING, GUNNAR waited for activity at the mine to come to a halt. The director's death would be an enormous event in their town—especially if he had been murdered. Gunnar could not imagine what kind of a response would follow. But there was nothing. Abraham's desk remained empty. In the morning, the teacher had asked if anyone knew where he was, but Gunnar had said nothing.

Perhaps Notholm had hidden the director's body, he thought. But surely they would soon discover he was missing?

But the explosions from the dynamite and the droning of the sorting band continued without end.

37.

LAURA

Laura was packing a bag. She didn't know what to expect from Lapland. It was spring, but she assumed that up there, it would still be cold. Perhaps there would even be snow?

There was a knock on her door.

"Your grandfather said you were planning a journey." Her father was standing in the doorway. He must have just come in from work as he was still wearing a tie. He was frowning.

"I'm going north."

"Why?"

She stopped packing. The single word had sounded accusing, as if her father was admonishing a young child.

"I want to find out what happened to Andreas, Britta's friend."

"Still on Britta." He shook his head.

"Yes," she said heatedly. And again, more calmly: "Yes."

"You've lost your job, and your apartment, and you're still pursuing this?"

"She was my best friend."

"But it's not sensible, Laura."

"Perhaps I'm not sensible." There was an edge in her voice she didn't recognize.

"You're being immature," her father said, "and I would have expected more from you. Britta lived the life of a loose woman and that brought on an ugly end."

She tried to ignore the way he spoke about her. "Someone told Britta that the State Institute for Racial Biology was working on a project crucial for Sweden's future, and that rumor had it that the people involved would stop at nothing. She was on the trail. She wrote about it in her dissertation."

"The State Institute?" Her father scoffed. "Really, Laura? Schoolwork doesn't get people killed."

"But—"

"No but. Think for a while. Think!"

"If it was about her personal life, then why the bomb in my apartment?"

"I don't want you to go," he said and turned toward the door. "In fact, I'm telling you not to."

"I don't see how you can do that," she said, but he had already left and closed the door behind him.

WHILE WAITING FOR her train on the platform, she found herself looking in the direction of the station house. She kept imagining her father coming out of it, coat flapping around his legs, long, determined steps coming toward her, grabbing her, dragging her out of there by her neck. Ridiculous. But there was something in the back of her mind, a memory. She'd been a child. Disobedient or . . . ? Had something like that happened?

No, she was letting her mind run away with her. Her father was the most measured man she knew. Opinionated, clearly. Forceful, certainly. But on her side. He was worried about her, she thought. His only child, putting herself in danger.

A man exited the station house, coat flapping in the wind, and her chest tightened. Then she saw who it was: Jens Regnell.

He walked up to her. "I made it," he said when he reached her.

"How did you know where I was?"

"I'm resourceful," he said, then smiled. "I got your grandfather on the telephone. He told me."

Jens didn't look well. His face was pale and there were black shadows under his eyes. He looked as if he hadn't slept for days. And yet, she couldn't help feeling drawn to him. He was handsome, but that wasn't why. The earnest eyes, perhaps. The open face.

"I have some information," he said. "And it's awful. I'm not even sure I should tell you."

"Tell me," she demanded.

He locked eyes with her, then nodded. "In 1914, the foreign ministers were asked to explore what it would take to put together a Scandinavian Reich under one strong leader. They did this based on the supposed supremacy of the Nordic race."

In her head, Laura could hear Karl-Henrik's voice, way back when: *You build up the elements around the chosen ones, their intrinsic superiority, and . . . Their inherent right to rule.*

"They set up a committee to work toward this aim," Jens continued.

Her train was coming into the station. Jens began speaking faster. He leaned forward speaking directly into her ear. "There was more to the program, though. They needed to maintain the purity of the Scandinavian race: breed from the best but also eliminate the worst."

People descended from the train. They came carrying bags and holding children by the hand.

"In 1939, at the second meeting, they decided to abandon

the program, only they haven't managed to shut it down. It's ongoing, managed by those who want this. It's a whole network, Laura. They kill whoever gets in the way."

Laura thought of what Karl-Henrik had said: that the institute had arms going everywhere.

"They conduct human experiments, Laura. And apparently this happens in the north. On the Sami."

His voice in her ear was too loud. She couldn't stand that, or what the voice was telling her. She tilted her head away.

"Are you sure?" she asked, and her voice sounded hoarse. This would explain why Andreas had left. If he knew . . . And if Britta died for this . . . He had fled. She felt sick.

He nodded. "As sure as I can be. The person who told me is ex-Security Services. Someone left a diagram of Blackåsen mine on my desk . . . It might be taking place there, in the mine."

"How?"

"I don't know. Perhaps in a shut-down section of the mine . . . I don't know."

The train attendant came down the platform. "All aboard!" he called.

Laura began walking toward the train, Jens beside her.

"I'll ask questions," she said.

"Please don't. Can you imagine what they would do to you if this is true?"

"So what are we going to do?"

He shook his head. "I don't know. We need evidence."

"And if we had evidence?"

"We'd expose it," Jens said. "If everyone were to find out, it would be impossible for them to continue. We're a neutral country. People are beginning to react to what Hitler is doing in Germany and beyond. The reaction would be fierce."

Laura thought again of Karl-Henrik's diagram. There were so many people involved.

"Wouldn't they just go into hiding?"

"But it would stop and, at the end of the day, isn't that the most important thing? More important than the perpetrators getting punished."

She carried on walking.

Jens took her arm and turned her to face him. "Don't try and get evidence on your own. Please be smart. I'm worried that we're just pawns in this terrible thing. Some people want it hidden at all costs. Others want it known. We're caught in the middle."

"Are you coming or not?" The train attendant had reached them.

"Yes," she said, hastily. She put her hand on Jens's cheek but couldn't find the words. He took her hand and squeezed it. She just nodded.

THE TRAIN ROLLED north. At first, Laura had the impression she was sitting on needles. She kept swallowing and wiping her mouth. She kept repeating to herself what Jens had told her, her mind bouncing from one thing to another. It was unbelievable. It was horrific. It was sick. It couldn't be true. And then again, it probably was. What if it took place in the mine? She was on her way there. She thought of Britta's father: the foreman of the mine. Did he know? Was this how Britta had found out? Through the father, who had thought her a tart?

She leaned back, looked out the window without seeing, let the landscape outside still her as evening approached. The gray sky stretched out and the bands of spruce trees that framed the moving train on both sides were black. This is the way the iron travels, she thought. She couldn't believe she hadn't already gone to see it.

A Scandinavian Reich based on the supposed supremacy of the Nordic race.

It wasn't hard to believe.

After all, it was what had happened to them; they had started to believe in it.

She knew who had noticed it: Matti, of course. A Finn, not a Scandinavian.

For months, they had studied the Scandinavian race for the project on faith, looking for proof points as to why the race was superior. They'd written them down as arguments: Denmark, Sweden and Norway never having been overwhelmed by foreign conquest, thus one pure single racial type from the beginning: taller, blonder—Matti had stuck out his tongue at them. They listed the conquests of the Vikings and, later, took a particular interest in the victories made by Karl XII. Their people were conquerors. They formulated the quest of their new version of Asatru, the Norse faith, as one for land: to regain the territories lost by Karl XII. The symbols and myths of their pursuit became the gods themselves and the tales found in the *Prose Edda*.

It was interesting, Laura had thought. The five of them had been caught up in this high-energy feeling. The more they researched, the more committed they became. The more *plausible* it seemed. Important, even. She could see a leader using the arguments they were creating to whip up emotion and instill action. She could see it.

And then, one day, they'd been debating something so trivial that she couldn't even remember what it was. They'd all been of the same opinion, apart from Matti, who had disagreed with them.

"You're wrong," Britta had said.

"I don't think so." Matti's voice had been light. She remembered this, remembered getting disproportionately annoyed at his lightness. He didn't understand how important it was, she'd thought. He just didn't understand.

"Four against one," Karl-Henrik said.

"I still don't think so."

The room fell quiet and still. It wasn't a good stillness. Matti had noticed it now, too. His face had become serious.

"Come on, Matti," Erik said. "Just go with it, alright."

"No."

Then Karl-Henrik had muttered something along the lines that obviously Matti wouldn't understand . . . couldn't understand. And she recalled it because it came from Karl-Henrik. It was something she would have expected from Erik, who was the hotheaded one. And also, because she had agreed with him: Matti wouldn't understand. He was different. I slept with him, she'd thought to herself and felt shame.

"You're incredible," Matti had said, moving his eyes from one person to the next, looking as if he was actually seeing them for the first time. Laura had lowered her gaze when her eyes had met his. "You actually believe this shit."

38.

JENS

Sven's father was in the military. He looked like an impatient, aggressive version of his son. He moved with force and one facial expression quickly replaced another, as if all life stayed with the father and the son had been given an economical version. Did Magnus Feldt know that his son was homosexual? Jens hoped he did and that he accepted it.

A drunken evening, in the corridor outside the washroom: a young, slender man squeezing Sven's arm, then his hand moving across to linger on Sven's crotch—Sven himself smiling with a delight Jens had not seen on his face before or since—until he noticed Jens, that was.

Yes, Jens knew that Sven was homosexual even though they'd not spoken about it. Homosexuality was still illegal, still considered a mental derangement. It had never bothered Jens one bit.

"I'm glad you could see me at such short notice," Jens said.

"Anytime," Magnus said. "My son's best friend . . . And the secretary to the foreign minister, too."

They sat down in the living room, though Magnus was quickly up on his feet again. "A drink, perhaps?"

"Sure," Jens said. "Whatever you're having."

Magnus poured a beer and handed it to him. "So, what can I do for you?" He took a sip of his own drink, smacked his lips and showed his teeth.

"It's delicate," Jens said.

Magnus laughed. "There's a war on our borders. Everything's delicate."

"It's about the swallows."

Magnus's mouth opened and then closed. "Sven told you."

"No, no . . . This came from somewhere else. It's more that I was hoping that you knew something about it," Jens said carefully, the way he had planned, so as not to land Sven in any trouble. "With your position in the military, I was thinking that it would be strange if you didn't."

"I might do," Magnus admitted.

"I'm wondering about a particular young woman . . . Her name was Britta Hallberg. She was supposedly in the program, but she was killed a month ago."

"Yes, I heard something about that."

"Do you have any idea who she was seeing? Professionally, I mean . . . As I work for Christian Günther, I'd just like to be aware."

"Of swallows and where they nest? I'm not involved in the actual running of the program."

"Is there any chance you could find out for me?"

"I probably can."

"Please don't tell anyone . . . It's delicate . . ."

Magnus smiled. "More so for me than for you."

IT WAS A warm, pleasant evening. In Kungsträdgården park, the cherry trees had exploded in pink clouds. He sat down on one

of the benches underneath. This beautiful city, his city, evil running just underneath their feet. It was as if their whole society
was built on a lie. He thought about Laura up north. Perhaps he
should have gone with her. It had all happened so quickly, he
hadn't had time to think. But she was smart. She'd know to be
careful. He hoped so, anyway. He wished he could contact her,
but he'd have to wait until she came back. If I don't hear from
her within a week, he promised himself, I'll go and look for her.

They knew what it was now, but not who was involved or
how to try to stop it. Laura had told him her friends were trying
to map the relationships between the State Institute for Racial
Biology and other organizations, but even so—what were they
going to do about it?

We need proof, he thought. At the moment, it's just hearsay.

He leaned his head back on the bench. Above him, a roof of
rosy white blossoms. They were going to come for him. He knew
too much. Was he ready for that? No, he wasn't. He might lose
his life for this. But it was impossible to know about it and remain
standing on the sidelines. Though Kristina might be at risk . . .

He sat up. With Jim, they had killed the ones close to him,
not Jim himself.

He needed to hurry.

As HE OPENED the door to his apartment, he could hear women
laughing. He exhaled, a long, slow breath.

"Jens?" Kristina came out in the hallway, followed by Barbro
Cassel. "We were just saying goodbye."

The cheeks of both women were glowing. Jens put his arm
around Kristina's waist. He buried his face in her hair. She was
fine. Everything was fine.

"Oh," she said, "I think someone's missed me."

"I did," Jens said. He let go of her. "Don't leave on my behalf," he said to Barbro.

"No," Barbro said. "I have to. I was just on my way."

She turned to hug Kristina goodbye and smiled at Jens. "Hopefully, next time I'll see more of you."

"How was your day?" Kristina asked, as she sauntered into the living room.

"Interesting," he said and hung up his jacket.

"Oh no," she said.

"What?"

She came out into the hallway with a yellow scarf. "Barbro forgot it."

"I'll run after her," Jens offered.

He took the scarf, ran down the stairs and caught up with her outside the front door.

"You forgot this," he said.

"Ah, thank you. It's my favorite."

Farther away in one of the doorways he could see the man with the fedora, smoking.

"You need to tell them that this is too obvious," Jens said, nodding in the direction of the man.

"What?" Barbro looked up at him.

"The surveillance on Mr. Enander. Kristina told me. She shouldn't have," he added.

There was a strange look on Barbro's face. "I really don't understand what you're talking about, Jens."

Before he could answer, the door opened behind him and Kristina came out. "And you forgot these as well," she said and handed Barbro a pair of gloves. "They were on the hat shelf."

"My goodness!" Barbro said. "I don't know where my head is today."

Jens walked up the stairs behind Kristina. The front door shut with a bang behind them and it startled him. He felt light-headed. Barbro had acted as if she really didn't know what he was saying. But if she hadn't told Kristina about Mr. Enander, then who had? And he remembered the two coffee cups in the sink the day that Schnurre had come out of his house.

39.

BLACKÅSEN MOUNTAIN

Sandler had never known such pain before. The right side of his body was burning. Every breath squeezed itself in and out of his chest. But he would live. Dr. Ingemarsson had said so. "Your lung collapsed," he'd said when Sandler woke up. "I've expanded it with oxygen; the tube needs to remain in for a couple of days and then we'll close the wound."

He eyed the doctor's handiwork on his chest. A plastic tube ran from his body into a bottle of water on the floor, the water bubbling as he breathed. Where the tube entered his chest were several large black sutures. "To seal the skin," the doctor said when he pointed to it.

"What about the bullet?"

"I don't think we'll ever find it, but we don't need to."

Sandler tried to imagine living with a bullet inside him for the rest of his life.

The doctor wanted to report the event to the police, but Sandler had refused, said absolutely not. His superior had told him to leave well enough alone, not to rock the boat. Telling the police would most definitely be rocking the boat. He'd said their access to Blackåsen Mountain had been granted from the highest levels. No, whatever was going on, this was something he had to solve on his own. But the man had shot him. Actually shot him.

"We can't have a murderer running amok in our town," the doctor said, packing up his bag.

"We won't," Sandler said. "I'll deal with it."

"Perhaps he'll shoot someone else."

"I said I'll deal with it!"

The director had raised his voice. His heart was beating rapidly. He oversaw this town. It was his right to decide. The doctor met his gaze from behind steel-rimmed glasses. "Fine," he said. The director was still in charge.

"Don't tell anyone what has happened."

"What do you want us to do with the boy?" the housekeeper asked, wringing her hands, once the doctor had left.

He needed to ask the boy what Notholm wanted with him. "Give him a room," Sandler said.

"It's highly unusual," she tried.

"Give him a room." He raised his voice for the second time and lost his breath. His chest wheezed and he gulped for air.

Bloody hell, he thought when she left. He was still in charge but only just. People were questioning his decisions left and right.

He closed his eyes as the pain tore at him. The doctor had wanted to give him morphine, but that, too, he had refused. He needed to stay clearheaded.

Why had Notholm tried to capture the boy? At least the boy was safe in his house.

He opened his eyes. The man had actually shot him. Cold-bloodedly, without any fear for the consequences. What kind of support did Notholm have?

Director Sandler tried to sit up and failed, pain cutting through his side as if he were being knifed.

"Get me the boy," he called. "Get me the boy!"

The housekeeper opened his door. "Director!" she exclaimed, seeing him trying to lift himself up. "You should be resting!"

"I want to talk to the Sami boy," he said. "And I want the stable hand to bring me my gun."

Her mouth opened.

"Now!" he commanded.

Her mouth shut again.

If only he understood what was going on, he thought, it would make it easier to decide on the right action to take.

He tried to breathe slowly and focus to lessen the pain.

The Sami boy opened the door. He didn't reach very far above the door handle. Sandler tried to gesture for him to come in but found he couldn't raise his arm.

"Enter," he said. "Sit down." He nodded to the chair by the end of the bed.

The boy sat down, touched the shaped armrests with his fingers, broke off in his movement and put the hands in his lap.

"What is your name?" asked the director.

"Taneli," the boy answered.

Sandler nodded. "So what was this all about?"

Taneli hesitated. He didn't know if he should tell the whole story. But if the director was a part of it, he wouldn't have tried to save Taneli, would he? The director had taken a bullet for him.

"You owe it to me to tell me," Sandler said.

Yes, Taneli figured, he did.

"I think they are stealing people," he said.

"Stealing people? What do you mean?"

"My sister disappeared," Taneli said. "There have been others, too. Other Sami. There was this man . . . he said that if I paid him two hundred crowns, he would tell me where they kept her. When I came, he wasn't there. This other man was. I think it was a trap."

That was why he took the money, Sandler thought. To save his sister. But stealing people? Sami people. That made no sense. What did they need them for?

Taneli pulled out the bills from inside his shirt and held them out to the director. "I'm sorry," he said, his gaze firm.

"It's fine," Sandler said. "Well, not thieving, of course." He tried to make a stern face. "That's not fine, but I understand . . . Why would Mr. Notholm want you?"

"Mr. Notholm?"

"That was the man who tried to take you last night."

"I think it was because I said I didn't want to have a Swedish skull," Taneli said.

"Why would Mr. Notholm care if you didn't want to have a Swedish skull?" Sandler asked, perplexed.

Then he thought about Dr. Öhrnberg's dealings with Notholm. Öhrnberg was a scientist specializing in eugenics and was in charge of the local arm of the State Institute for Racial Biology.

"He was there when they measured us. I said I didn't want one. I think he got upset." The boy shrugged.

Could Notholm be petty enough for that to vex him? Sandler already knew the answer.

"The man I thought I was meeting . . . Áslat. He knew things about my sister that only she could have told him. If this was set up by Mr. Notholm, then he must have told Áslat. It must mean that Mr. Notholm has her."

There was a knock on the door and the stable hand entered with Sandler's revolver. He handed it to him, frowning as if worried. Sandler ignored his look, checked that the weapon was loaded and put it on his bedside table.

"I suggest you sleep in here," he said to Taneli when the stable hand had left. He was sleepy now and speaking took a great effort. Notholm and Öhrnberg . . . He needed to think this through. He would deal with it but not now. "I don't know how wide a grip Mr. Notholm has on this town, that's all. I want you to be safe."

Leave if you want, he thought. He was now so tired, he couldn't be bothered. He closed his eyes, then remembered the loaded revolver by his side. What if the boy shot him?

Never mind, he thought. Never mind. The worst had already happened.

SANDLER SLEPT FOR a long time, only waking up for brief moments. He wasn't certain how much time had passed. The Sami boy, Taneli, was sleeping by the window on the floor. He was just a kid, the director thought. The light threw shadows on his face; his eyelashes looked like thick feathers.

The boy opened his eyes.

"Good morning," Sandler said.

"Good morning."

"I'm sorry we didn't get you a bed."

The boy smiled. "We don't use them," he said.

No. He guessed they didn't.

The housekeeper entered with breakfast. She helped him sit up, puffed his pillows and then lifted the tray into his lap.

"Please bring breakfast for the boy, too," he said.

Her mouth compressed, but she nodded.

"How long have I been asleep?"

"Two days," she said. "The doctor has been looking in on you regularly. He said he expected you to sleep a lot."

She straightened his covers.

"There's a rumor going around," she said, before leaving.

"What kind of a rumor?"

"That you're dead, sir."

Well, he couldn't have that.

"Get Dr. Ingemarsson to come here," he said. "Tell him he needs to remove the tube."

THE DOCTOR REMOVED the tube and restitched the hole. "Complete rest," he said, "for a week or more."

Taneli was watching them. If the doctor was surprised at seeing Taneli there, he didn't say.

"I need to go for a walk," the director said. He tried to move. Goddamn, it hurt.

"One week," the doctor reiterated and didn't help him.

As soon as the doctor left, Sandler turned to the boy. "You need to help me," he said. "To get up."

"The doctor . . ."

"Dr. Ingemarsson has no idea what we're up against here. It can't look like I'm losing control. I don't know what that would unleash. Will you help me?"

The boy helped him rise and then get dressed. "Goddamn, bloody, almighty," Sandler muttered to himself. "Jesus Christ!" The pain was so severe it made him feel faint. But he had to get out there: just show himself. Who knew what they'd do otherwise?

THEY WALKED DOWN the main street: the director and the boy. Not far down, they met Hallberg with a group of men. Sandler was exhausted. It was too early. His left side was screaming with pain, but he forced himself onward, knowing people were watching. He wanted to lean on the boy but didn't. As if Taneli sensed what was going on, he moved closer. *Reaching distance.*

"You're here," the foreman said.

"Of course. Where else would I be?"

"I heard you were ill . . ."

Ill. At least not dead.

"Rubbish," Sandler said. He felt clammy and wanted to wipe his forehead but didn't.

Another man was approaching on the road. Notholm! Taneli stiffened. Sandler also felt himself tense up. But Notholm wouldn't dare trying anything here. Would he?

The foreman was also looking at Notholm. "My God," he said. "What happened to you?"

The right side of Notholm's face was one big sore, his right eye swollen shut. He walked with a limp and held one arm tight to his side.

"Fell off my horse," he answered, looking at Sandler.

"That must have been some fall," the foreman said.

"It was."

Hallberg turned to Sandler. "Well, we have things to go through, whenever you have time."

"Good. I'll come by."

As the foreman and his team walked away, Sandler and Notholm locked eyes.

"All you had to do was to leave well enough alone."

"You shot me. You'll pay for this."

This was war.

"We'll come for you again. If it isn't me, it will be another." Notholm looked pointedly at the boy. "And then one day . . ."

Sandler put his hand on Taneli's shoulder.

"I wouldn't be so sure about that."

40.

LAURA

She woke up and had no idea what time it was. Falling asleep
had been difficult. She didn't know when the sun had finally
gone down—if it ever had. It had remained daylight as she
lay there hour after hour, tossing and turning. The noise from
Blackåsen mine was relentless: grinding, booming, thrashing.
How on earth could people live here? The Winter Palace hotel
was decent, but its curtains were useless. The hotel was walking
distance from the railway station. As the train had arrived last
night, she'd seen the armed soldiers standing on the platform,
watching the trains, protecting them.

She found her watch. Eight o'clock. Perfect. She had called
ahead and arranged to meet the mine director this morning at
his home: Rolf Sandler.

She wasn't certain how to play it. She needed to find
Andreas, but she didn't want to put him at risk. Then there
was the schematic of the mine on Jens's desk; the possibility
of human experimentation being conducted in the mine. The
director had to know about this—it was his mine!

"Start from the top and work down," someone had taught
her. *Wallenberg?* Most likely. It would be easier for her to ask

questions of others once she could say she'd already spoken to the man in charge.

She had to admit to being scared, though.

On the steps outside the hotel, she found the air surprisingly cool. "Just a bit farther down," the receptionist had said and pointed. On the other side of the road lay Blackåsen Mountain. On her arrival last night, seeing it from afar, it hadn't seemed like much; a blunt, black shape, its surface cut into terraces. But then, as the train had drawn closer she could see the magnitude of it and the open pit at its base. You beast, she'd thought.

Her father would have loved to see this, she thought, then frowned. She would have to tell him what was going on when she returned. He'd be just as shocked. He would be able to help.

She began walking to the director's house. It was cold, but her hands were sweaty. She tried not to think about the impending conversation. Instead, she tried to imagine her friend sashaying down the street; short skirt, long blond hair. She couldn't see it. Perhaps Britta had changed when she moved to Uppsala? But on the other hand, she could never imagine Britta pretending to be something other than what she was.

The town wouldn't be here if it wasn't for the mine. What a life, she thought. Brought here by the mine. Living off it. Dependent on it. Britta, with her lively, questioning nature, must have hated everything about it. She must have felt shut in, constrained. Though it was a green town with nice houses. Actually, it was much more pleasant than she had expected.

She reached the house and knocked on the door.

"Miss Dahlgren?"

A tall, dark man came toward her through the garden. He was limping. It was his leg, she thought. But he also held his arm tight to his side, so perhaps it was his ribs. "I'm sorry," he

296

said. "I had to pay a quick visit to the mine. I'm the director, Rolf Sandler. Please come in."

Laura thought he was a beautiful man. In all likelihood, the most beautiful man she had ever seen. His dark beard was neat, his hair thick. His skin had a warm tone to it and his eyes were clear blue. Something was worrying him, though, she thought. Why would she think that? The wrinkles on his forehead, perhaps. The weariness of his eyes. But then, being the head of the mine would be a job with a lot of responsibilities.

He knows, she thought. It's his mine. He must know.

Sandler opened the door to his study and invited her in.

"We'll take coffee," he called over his shoulder to a woman farther down the hallway. "What a pleasure," he continued, this time to Laura. "Of course, I've seen your name on letters and other documents, but to meet in person is a nice surprise."

He took her hand.

"It's kind of you to receive me at such short notice," she said and removed her hand.

He pointed to a sofa and they sat down. The housekeeper came in with a coffee tray.

"So, what brings you to us?" he asked.

"I'm looking for a friend of a friend," she said. "A Sami man who has gone missing."

He inhaled. It was such a small sound that she couldn't be certain, but it sounded like a gasp.

She hesitated. "He's a student in theology at Uppsala University. But he's from Blackåsen."

Sandler shook his head, his face bland now. "I wouldn't know him. I haven't been here long . . . I had assumed your visit had to do with the mine."

She shook her head. "Not this time."

"Why are you looking for him? If you don't mind me asking . . ."

"He was a close friend of a friend."

"*Was?*" The director suddenly had a frown line between his eyes.

She hesitated. "My friend died."

"Died, as in . . .?"

"She was murdered."

"And this had to do with this young man? Do you think he did it?"

"*No!* No, I don't. It's just that he disappeared afterward. I was hoping he might know something about it."

"Disappeared?" Sandler sighed and his frown line grew deeper.

She nodded, changed tack. "The State Institute for Racial Biology is active here, isn't it?"

"With the Sami populations, yes," he said, slowly.

"What are they working on?"

"The usual things: measurements, studies and so on."

Laura nodded. She couldn't say any more.

The director was looking at her as if evaluating her.

"Is . . . *this* linked to your friend's death?" he asked, finally.

She ought to lie. She ought to. But he looked so *honest.* How do you know who you can trust?

Nobody, she answered herself. You can trust nobody. But she had always trusted her instincts.

"I think so," she admitted.

He exhaled, rising with effort, pushing himself off the sofa with his hand. He walked to the door opposite the one they had come in and opened it. "Taneli?" he called into the room.

A young boy came out. His hair was black, his eyes dark. The clothes told her he was Sami.

"We've had some . . . incidents here," Sandler said. "Could you tell us your story, please, from the beginning?"

She hesitated.

The man's eyes were a piercing blue. "Trust me, I understand the risk you feel you are taking." He unbuttoned his shirt and showed her a large bandage around his chest. "Even though I don't understand what's going on, I'm pretty sure I was shot for it."

She could see it now, the pain showing on his face: the shiny forehead, the blank eyes.

She had to risk it. And so she told them both all of it, about Britta, her death, the meetings of the three kings, the aim for a Scandinavian Reich, and—she hesitated, a child being in the room, after all, but the director nodded to her to continue—human experimentation, perhaps in the mine.

When she had finished, Sandler had covered his mouth with his fist. He let his hand fall to his knee. "This explains everything."

The child had bent his head. The man put his hand on the boy's shoulder. "Sami people have gone missing. His sister was one of them."

Laura was so sorry. She wished she could offer comfort but found none.

"There is an area in the mine," Sandler continued. "I've been forced to rent it out—to the owner of the Winter Palace hotel. I think it's them. Is there no one who could intervene? The government? The Security Services?"

She shook her head. "They're in on it—or at least factions of them are. We need evidence to be able to denounce them publicly. We don't see any other way."

"Who's in on it here?"

She shook her head. "The Institute, obviously. Otherwise, I don't know."

"They'll need staff," he mumbled and frowned. "And this . . . missing Sami man?"

"We were hoping he knew who they were. Britta died and he disappeared immediately afterward."

"What's his name?" the boy asked.

"Andreas Lundius."

"I know him," the boy said. "Andreas Lappo. Or, I know his family. They're not far from here. I can take you there."

"Really?" she asked.

He nodded.

"How will you take me there?"

He looked at her shoes. "We have to walk," he said, hesitant now. "Through the forest."

"I can walk," she said.

"It's about two days."

"I can do it."

"I can't come with you," Sandler said. "I'm worried what will happen if I leave town. Things here feel vulnerable. Also," he grimaced and pressed his side, "I'm not sure I would be of much help as things stand."

"Tomorrow morning," the boy said. "We leave early."

She nodded. She'd be ready.

"I was going to see Britta's family . . ." she said to the director before leaving, asking for his advice.

"Who are they?"

"Her father is the foreman of the mine. Hallberg."

"Hallberg? She was his daughter?" Sandler frowned and then shook his head. "I wouldn't go see them," he said. "I see him every day. He never mentioned that his daughter died. I tried to talk to him about this area in the mine at one point; suggested we go see it. He blankly refused. I guess, right now, we just don't know who's in or not."

And that was the crux. They didn't.

41.

JENS

I'm sorry to call so late."

Jens had picked up the phone, not quite knowing he'd done it. It was the middle of the night. A woman's voice.

"Who is this?" he asked.

"It's Julie, your father's neighbor. It's your father, my dear. He's in hospital."

"Why? Is he alright?"

"I found him on his porch. Maybe a heart attack. He's been taken to the Karolinska Hospital. They don't think he's going to make it."

HE CURSED HIMSELF the whole way to the hospital. They got him, he thought. There was nothing wrong with his father's heart. In fact, for his age, he was remarkably healthy. Jens had been worried about Kristina, but he'd never imagined that they would attack his father. If his father died . . . Oh, he couldn't think about it.

Jens's mother had died of cancer ten years earlier. Since then, it had just been Jens and his father. His mother had been sick for so long that, in fact, it had almost always been just the two of them. He could see the gray-haired man before him now, stooping slightly, preparing sandwiches of soft bread and a thick slice of cheese with his clumsy fingers.

Without him, I'll be an orphan, he thought, and the pain was so clear, so sharp, it cut through him and made him wince. Not his father. Anyone but his father!

He ran in the main entrance of the redbrick building and found the way to the ER. The hospital smelled of disinfectant. The lights were bright, the corridors clean. At the reception desk, a nurse was standing.

"I'm looking for my father," he said. "He was admitted earlier tonight. Henrik Regnell."

She looked at her register. Flipped a page over. "I have no one here with that name," she said.

"Look again," he demanded.

She lifted her book, ran her finger down the lines of names. "No," she said. "No one called Henrik Regnell has been brought in. In fact, no one has come in at all tonight. Our last patient was admitted early in the evening."

"But they called!"

"Who called?"

"His neighbor."

"Could he have been taken to a different hospital?"

"I don't know. Perhaps. She did say Karolinska."

The nurse shook his head.

There was a pay phone on the wall. Gripped by a sudden thought, Jens approached it and dialed his father's number.

One ring, two, three . . . then his father's sleepy voice: "Henrik Regnell."

"Dad?" Jens's voice broke. He leaned his forehead against the cold metal of the telephone.

"Jens? What's wrong?"

"Nothing, Dad." Jens squinted hard to try to stop the tears from coming. "I had a minute . . . thought I'd check in on you."

His dad chuckled. "Nothing wrong here, Jens. Apart from someone calling and waking me up at two in the morning."

"Sorry." Jens sniffled.

"I'm joking. It's always good to hear your voice. Are you alright?"

"Yes. Dad, do you have a neighbor called Julie?"

"No, there are just old men out here, you know that."

Three of them, with weather-beaten skin. Coffees by the boats each morning and each afternoon since retirement, not saying much, spending their time together looking out over the sea. He did know that.

"I forgot."

"Strange question for the middle of the night."

"Yes. Yes, I guess it is."

"Come and visit, Jens."

"I'll come soon, Dad. Until then . . . please be careful."

"I'm always careful, Jens. I'm old."

As Jens hung up, the nurse was watching him. "False alarm," he said.

"That's stressful," she answered.

"Yes. Very."

"How did that happen?"

"I'm not quite sure."

He walked down the corridor back to the main entrance. This had been a warning. No doubt about that. *You can never keep the ones you love safe. If you continue . . .* The woman who called it could have been anyone. This is how it begins, he thought. And it won't stop until it's over. One way or another.

Sven was at his apartment when Jens came to find him many hours later. Jens hadn't gone home after the hospital. He'd found an all-night café and had nursed his one beer until morning came. Kristina would find an empty bed beside her when she woke up. Who would they take from him first? He ought to stop. Stop the questions, stop looking, go back to his work and do his best for Christian Günther. Who was he to take this on? What did he ever think he could accomplish? But how could he ignore it? If he stopped, then this . . . thing would continue. If everyone stopped, where would it end? And how could you possibly stop, knowing what was going on, what was being done to people?

"Jens," Sven said when he opened the door, "you look awful. Everything alright between you and Kristina?"

"Yes, but everything else is wrong."

"Come in."

Sven prepared him a cup of coffee. He was dressed in slacks and a light blue shirt open at the neck. Saturday morning. Jens sat down at his kitchen table.

"They lied to you," Jens said. "Whoever told you about Britta being killed by a former lover, about Daniel committing suicide, about those phone calls being about the safe passage of Jews. They lied to you."

"I doubt that very much," Sven said.

Jens told Sven all of it from beginning to end. Halfway through, Sven sat down opposite him.

"Jens, God, I don't know," Sven said when he had finished. "A mega conspiracy, human experimentation, racially motivated murders? I can't believe it's true!"

"It is."

Sven was still shaking his head.

Jens frowned. "It's true," he repeated, "starting with Britta dying and the bomb in Laura's flat."

"That was an ex-lover . . ."

"I called him, Sven. I called the policeman. He said he had no idea what I was talking about."

"If you call again, you'll find that the policeman you spoke to has been removed from his post. I heard it yesterday. He's a gambler, apparently, who neglected his job. And he's under investigation for fraud. The policeman now in charge will tell you that it was an ex-lover, I'm sure. They have arrested him."

"What's his name?"

"I can't remember, Jens. I can find out . . . But call and you'll see I'm right."

"What about the man who lost a daughter? What about the phone call about my father?"

"The woman rang you by mistake. She never mentioned your father's name, did she?"

Jens thought back at the call and had to admit Sven was right: she hadn't. But there was no doubt in his mind. It was them. It had been a threat. Not someone calling the wrong number.

"And as for the man who lost his daughter, when we're grieving, we see what we want to see, Jens. Sometimes it's easier to blame somebody else for our misfortune rather than accept it was a meaningless accident."

"Daniel was being followed before he died. His sister . . ."

"Daniel was sick, Jens."

Jens paused. Sven was leaning forward, elbows on his knees, the open blue eyes, the expression on his face one of intense concentration. "Why are you trying to invalidate everything I say?" he asked.

Sven leaned back and lifted his hands as if to placate him. "I'm not. I just don't think you're right."

Sven didn't believe any of it. Or was there something else? Why was Sven not willing to entertain the thought, not even hear him out? Jens hesitated.

Sven sighed. "There isn't one scrap of proof for what you've told me. It can all be explained away." His face changed to one of concern. "I worry about you, my friend. You've been under stress lately. Perhaps . . ."

Jens stood up. "There's nothing wrong with me. I would have thought you, of all people, would believe me."

Sven shook his head slowly. "Oh, Jens, I wish I could. Listen, my friend, it's the weekend. You need to relax."

Jens walked out, slamming the door behind him. Outside on the pavement, he stopped and took a deep breath. It didn't bring relief. He couldn't relax. It was all wrong, he thought. All wrong.

42.

BLACKÅSEN MOUNTAIN

The woman from the south, Laura, was staying at the Winter Palace. Taneli couldn't imagine a worse place to stay, now that they knew about Mr. Notholm. But the director had said that if Laura changed her lodging that would raise questions, and she had agreed. Taneli wondered if she'd been able to sleep last night.

He sat waiting for her on a large rock in the forest behind the hotel. It was early. "First thing in the morning" could mean something different to Laura, of course. He should have contacted his parents, he thought. He wondered if they were worried and what Olet had told them. It was a small town: they'd know one way or another where he was. Though they wouldn't know why. Olet would also be looking after Raija, he knew. All of a sudden he missed his home so much his chest twisted. He'd go home once they were back, he decided. Laura came around the building. Her blond hair shone silvery gray in the morning light. She was tall, he realized. She was wearing trousers and a jacket and she'd changed her shoes for a pair of heavy boots.

"Good," Taneli said and pointed to her footwear.

"They're men's boots," she said. She lifted a foot off the ground. "They must start young in the mine."

Taneli shrugged. He didn't know.

"I was wondering," she said as they set off. "You said it was a two-day walk. Where will we sleep?"

"In the forest," Taneli said.

"What will we eat?"

"We'll find something," he answered.

She looked back at the hotel—as if she might change her mind—but then she didn't say anything more. As they left, Taneli glanced over his shoulder. He got a feeling the black, clipped mountain was watching them. Brooding. He thought about what might be kept inside it and about his father telling him that the mountain's spirit was fickle, unfair in punishment, quick to anger, difficult to please. But to hold captured people . . . How could you? he thought and felt the mountain lean on his back. He walked more quickly, eager to be gone.

They walked the whole day. At the start, they were silent. Both of them had things to think about. Later, they began to talk, first about small things: the weather, the region. Taneli pointed out animal tracks to her. He showed her flowers and roots you could eat. Whenever they found a rivulet, he told her they had to drink until they weren't thirsty any longer. The woman's face was serious. Her speech, too. Did she ever laugh? She was the kind of person you wanted to make laugh. There were stars in her gray eyes around her pupils. Taneli thought it might be a sign. Stars leading the way.

Midafternoon, Taneli began to worry that something was following them. But there were no sounds or sights; more like a feeling. Perhaps it was the woman's past, hovering. He wondered what it was trying to tell her.

Late afternoon, Laura began to tire. She stumbled, her pace slowed and she kept waving her hands at the mosquitoes. Taneli announced that it was time to stop. He built a fire and lit it. Not for the cold, but for the comfort of light and the smoke. Before them, the river was bouncing blue with snowmelt and the sound of life relaxed everything around it. The ground was bumpy with stones and new grass. There was a cluster of birch trees on the top of the hill behind them. They were young and reedy. Their leaves were pushing to get out of their shells, small, shimmering green tops on each bud.

"Sit in the smoke," he told her. "It will hurt your eyes, but the bugs will stay away."

He had to build her a shelter for the night, he thought. Close to the fire, so that the smoke would continue to ease things for her.

"I'll find us something to eat," he said.

She'd taken off her boots and was rubbing her feet, grimacing.

It took him a while, but he found them a grouse. When he came back with it, her eyes widened. She watched as he removed the feathers and the innards. He put it on a stick and placed it over the fire. Soon, their glade smelled of roasting meat. When it was ready, he handed her some on a stick. She took a bite.

"It's good," she said, eyebrows raised as if surprised. Taneli nodded and they ate.

"When did your sister disappear?" she asked when their stomachs were full.

"In winter," Taneli said. "But she is still alive."

It was strange to talk about it with a stranger. He fell silent for a while, thought of his family again.

"How do you know your sister isn't dead?" Her voice had turned gentle.

"I just know," he said. "My sister is special to our people. Perhaps that is why they haven't killed her."

"And why are you with the director?"

"He saved me," Taneli said. "And then we saved him."

That's how it was and now they were bound together, the man and the boy. He found he didn't mind. He liked the tall man, who had proven kind beneath his sternness.

They couldn't sleep where they had eaten. The leftovers would attract other, bigger, animals. He put the innards in the river. He put out the fire, tidied up and then gestured for her to follow.

They crossed the river and he found them another glade; made a new fire. Then he built her a shelter of spruce branches.

She lay down but her gray eyes were open wide.

"Sleep," he said. "I'll keep watch."

She smiled for the first time. "Thank you, Taneli," she said.

43.

LAURA

Laura had thought she'd never manage to sleep out in the open with a fire close by and mosquitoes wailing in her ear, but she must have done; at first, she didn't know where she was, and then she saw the boy, still sitting up, watching her. He must have been awake all night. She felt bad. He was just a child. She was the adult: she should have stayed up. But he smiled.

"Good morning," he said.

"Good morning."

She'd been lucky. Taneli was a good guide. At least, that's what it seemed like. On the other hand, she was deep in the forest, so who could tell?

"How far away are they?" she asked.

"Not far. Half a day's journey that way." He nodded.

They walked. Today, the sun was bright, and she could feel her scalp getting warm. They were climbing uphill now. She had to lean forward and push her feet down to get a good grip. The forest was pine and spruce. It smelled nice: fresh, green. She hadn't known a forest could smell like this.

Taneli stopped suddenly.

"What?" she asked.

He put a finger over his lips. His forehead wrinkled.

"What?" she whispered.

"I hear someone," he whispered back. "Someone also walking this way."

A pulse began to tick in her throat. "Are they following us?"

His face was serious. "Perhaps."

He took her hand and led her along a side trail until they came to a river.

"We will walk in the water," he said. "Take off your shoes."

She took them off and followed him down into the ice-cold water. The riverbed was full of sharp stones and she winced. They came to a passage where the stones were larger and slippery. Taneli turned around and took her hand and she supported herself on this little boy who seemed to be able to walk on anything, while she could barely move forward.

She could no longer feel her feet because of the cold water.

After half an hour, he nodded. "That should be enough," he said.

They got out and put their shoes back on.

They were walking faster now. Every now and then Taneli would stop and listen, then nod, indicating that they were alright.

And then, midafternoon, just like Taneli had said, they came out of the forest above the tree line and onto the bare mountain. Clinging to the mountainside were dwellings: wooden structures in the shape of tents. The next gulley was full of people and reindeer. She stood for a while watching the animals and people move in patterns that were unfamiliar to her.

"Here," Taneli said.

She followed him. A man came to meet them. A Sami, wearing leather trousers and a woven hat with a big, colorful tassel on top.

"We're looking for Andreas Lappo Lundius," she said.

He eyed her suspiciously and then frowned at Taneli, most likely for bringing her here.

"It's important," the boy said. "We wouldn't have come otherwise."

"He's with the animals," the man finally said, nodding in the direction of the fenced area in the valley.

"The reindeer are calving," Taneli said.

Now she saw it. A reindeer that had just given birth. The reindeer was lying down and her tiny black calf was trying to stand beside her. The miracle of life, she thought, and felt moved.

There was a commotion in the fenced area. The children and women were helping the animals. It was a while before she noticed him, Andreas. He was sitting on a log, farther away, among the men.

A silence spread amid the disorder as they approached. Men, women and children, all with their eyes on her. Then Andreas stood up. He raised his hand as if to say it was alright and walked to meet them.

He was dressed in leather trousers that were bloody at the thigh. His hands were bloody, too, and one held a knife. He was a different man here, in his element. A man, not a boy. Tall, calm. Britta would have seen him like this, Laura thought. No wonder she'd seen something in Andreas that the rest of them hadn't.

"You," he said.

She nodded. "You left suddenly."

He looked out over his tribe and the animals giving birth. It was everyday life to him but exotic to anybody else.

"I know what's going on," she said. "Well, I think I do. But I don't know who. Or where." Or what to do next, she thought.

Andreas didn't speak.

"How did you and Britta find out?" she asked.

Still he remained silent.

"*Please*, Andreas," she said.

"I'm surprised you care," he said and turned his black eyes on her.

"I'm here," she said.

He sighed, looked out over his people and seemed to make up his mind. "It started many years ago," he said. "Perhaps as many as ten. Sami people would vanish, never to come back. We thought perhaps wild animals . . . We thought perhaps it was something even more dreadful. Then, sometimes, we found bodies."

She waited.

"Their bodies had been . . . cut," he said, frowning as if he couldn't understand it. "In the most awful ways. Their innards," he pointed to his own chest, "could be missing. Parts of them, like hearts or lungs, gone. Their heads could be opened and emptied."

"Didn't you tell the police?"

"They did nothing. We told the mining company, too. Here, they're the law."

She thought about the director. But he was new to his post. "And?"

"And nothing. For them, as long as there are enough of us for the work to go on . . ."

"How many?" she asked, tasting bile.

"Here in our lands, I've counted over one hundred," he said. "But then we heard the same was happening in Norway. People missing. Bodies found.

"I told Britta," Andreas said. "She was my friend. I felt there wasn't much to be done about it." He shrugged. "But then, last autumn, she met someone who knew more."

Someone she met in Uppsala, or perhaps in Stockholm. Perhaps Sven Olov Lindholm, Laura thought. But he hadn't seemed to know much.

"He told her about what was happening to the Sami. Later, just before she died, he gave her proof."

"What kind of proof?"

Andreas shrugged. "She said photographs. Names of people involved."

"Where is it now?"

He shook his head. "It was with Britta. She went to Stockholm to show it to someone she said had the power to make a difference."

Someone who had the power to make a difference . . . Who? Jens Regnell? But if they had met, he would have said.

"The only person she mentioned who was in on it was her professor," Andreas said.

Laura couldn't help but gasp. "Professor Lindahl?"

"That's right."

That was awful. It couldn't be true. Or could it? A number of things suddenly made sense. They had trusted him. Her heart ached.

"This person who gave her evidence," she asked, "do you have any idea who it was?"

"No. She called him her 'uneasy friend.'"

The first person who came to Laura's mind was Erik. She had no idea why.

Britta had been a swallow. It must have been a friend she made in that role. Someone working for the Security Services?

"Do you know what she wanted to do with the evidence?"

"She said we were going to expose them. This person who she said could make a difference was going to help her."

Same reaction as us, Laura thought. And then the person she reached out to must have been in on it. Britta had been trapped.

Andreas had turned his gaze to look past her at the dense forest beneath them at a lower elevation. His eyes narrowed. He opened his mouth. He looked surprised, naked.

"Why did you bring him here?" he asked.

"What?"

Taneli's hand on her arm.

Andreas was still staring at the forest. She turned but couldn't see anything. Nothing but shadows and trees.

Then Andreas swirled around, as if to run. And as he did, his head snapped to the side, and there was the crack of a bullet. He fell to the ground, his neck at an angle, his face missing.

Everything was happening in a haze—Taneli, his mouth moving, screaming something to her. Behind him, the animals in their fenced area were panicking, running round and round. The Sami women swept up the children and ran, the men dropped their equipment, let everything go. There was nowhere to hide on the bare mountainside.

Then Taneli pulled her hair. The pain brought her back to her senses. Now, the sounds were unbearable: horrible bleating, thundering hooves, people screaming. Taneli dragged her with him toward the fence and forced her down on the ground behind the animals.

"They shot him," she mumbled, shocked, not knowing who she meant. Who had Andreas seen? She rubbed her face and her hand came away red and wet with Andreas's blood.

"He saw something . . ." And then, with horrifying insight: "It was us. Me. We led them here! I did!"

Taneli was looking at the forest below. "We need to leave."

Laura's body was shivering, shaking. Andreas was dead, and this was her fault.

"Now," he said. "Now!"

They began to run back to the tree line from where they'd come.

It had to have been a sniper, she thought. While she and Taneli had walked uphill and come to the camp from the side, whoever followed them had walked through the valley and reached the camp from below.

She and Taneli continued to run into the forest. When she thought she couldn't run any longer, Taneli slowed down and stopped.

"Are they following us?" she asked.

He listened for a long time, then shook his head. "No," he said.

Why wouldn't they? Laura thought. Why wouldn't they follow her and kill her, too? She was the one looking for answers. Why hadn't there been more shots?

A wail burst from her lips. I did this, she thought.

"It wasn't your fault," the boy said.

"I led them here," Laura said. Her head was hurting. She couldn't think straight. "They didn't know where he was until we found him, and now he's dead."

She put her head in her hands then straightened. "The director," she said. "He knew we were coming out here. He was the only one who knew."

The boy shook his head. "It wasn't him," he said.

He put his hand on her arm, a child's hand with grubby nails, and she wished he'd remove it. She didn't want his comfort; she didn't deserve it.

"We couldn't have known," he said.

They walked in silence until night fell, and they made another camp. Once again, the boy found food, but Laura couldn't eat. Andreas was dead. She lay down and, just as he had done the previous night, the boy sat by the fire. But she couldn't sleep. Perhaps she would never sleep again. For the first time, in a very long while, she yearned for her mother. She turned away from the fire and the boy so that he wouldn't see her face.

44.

Two Security Services agents were waiting for him in his office when he arrived. Jens wondered how long they had been there and if they had already gone through his things. He felt violated. And scared. Very scared. Did they know about his involvement? Were they here because of Daniel or because of what Jens had found out?

"What can I do for you?" he asked and threw his briefcase onto his desk in what he hoped was a confident manner.

The older of the men, silver-haired, with a large, swollen nose, said, "We'd like to talk to you about your colleague."

"Daniel Jonsson," the other one added. He was younger, dark-haired, honest-looking.

"Tragic affair," Jens said. "I didn't know he was sick."

The older one nodded. "Very sick. Delusional. Conspiracy theories . . . you know the drill." He curled his lips. "I'm surprised you didn't notice. I'm told you worked closely with him."

"I saw him as diligent. He didn't give me any reason for concern."

"People can get . . . contaminated, when they work with someone like that. They, too, begin to see things that aren't there."

"I don't," Jens said.

"Are you certain?"

"I'm quite certain I only see what's there."

The older man had paused. Now he chuckled. "If that's how you want to play it."

Want to play it? Jens didn't want to play anything. But what choice was there? It won't happen here, he thought. This is the ministry. Nothing will happen to me here.

When they left his office, he stood up and walked to his door. The men walked farther down the corridor and across to the foreign minister's office. When they knocked, Günther let them in. Jens waited for a long time, but the agents didn't come out while he was watching.

IT HAD BEEN a long day. It was late when Jens finally left. They got him as he walked home. He didn't know at what point he became aware of being followed, but by the time he entered Old Town he was certain. The street was empty. He should have taken another road. He'd known they would come for him sooner rather than later, so he ought to have been more careful. He lengthened his steps. One of the followers laughed. The laughter echoed in the empty street.

Should he run? He glanced over his shoulder. Three of them. Young, fluid in their movements. Confident. Walking fast. Not policemen—they were much too smart for that—these were hired thugs. Jens wouldn't be able to outrun them. Not the three of them.

He kept his head down and walked faster. Every now and then he glanced up, hoping to see other people—but the street lay as deserted as when he had entered it.

He had to try. He set off at a fast run.

The men yelled, and their feet thudded on the pavement as they came for him.

Jens ran as fast as he could, but they were faster. They were approaching, and there was no way out.

When they were right behind him, he swung around, hitting out with his briefcase. The first man screamed and bent over, holding his nose.

Jens backed away, but the first punch landed on his cheek and it was as if his face had exploded. I won't give up, he thought. Not this easily. He leaped forward and grabbed the man who had hit him. They stumbled together for a moment before the man's partner hit Jens on the head from behind with something heavy. Jens dropped to his knees. His vision was going in and out of focus. The man in front of him grabbed his head in his hands and brought up his knee to hit his nose. There was a crack—a dull, deep snap that seemed to run all the way to the back of Jens's head.

He was bleeding now. There was blood on his hands. The kicks were raining over him pitilessly, hitting all the weak spots on his stomach and back. Jens was on all fours, then on his side, trying to curl up and protect his head.

Before he slipped out of consciousness, which by now seemed merciful, one of the attackers leaned over him.

"Final warning, secretary," he whispered. "Final warning."

WHEN JENS WOKE up, he didn't know where he was. Then he realized he was lying in one of the side alleys behind a heap of firewood. The windows above him were all dark. Gingerly, he sat up. His stomach heaved and his head reeled, but everything stayed in one place. He touched his face and winced. His ribs were killing him. And his lower back, his buttocks. There was an empty bottle of vodka beside him. By the smell of him, they'd poured it over him before leaving. He got to his knees and, using the wall for support, stood up. He thought he was going to vomit and squeezed his eyes shut and waited until the nausea passed. Good grief, he thought. But he'd live. He'd just suffered a massive beating.

He began to walk home. It wasn't far, but in the state he was in, it might as well have been the other side of town.

He lurched and had to steady himself using the houses beside him to walk. To anyone looking, he would have appeared drunk.

He staggered up the stairs to his apartment. Inside, it was dark. There was a note on the hallway table: *Sleeping at home tonight. Working. Kristina xxx*

He laughed and didn't know why. It was just so typical.

He caught a glimpse of himself in the mirror above the table: both eyes swollen, his nose and one of his eyebrows bleeding, blood all down the side of his face, blood on his teeth. Sores on his cheeks and forehead. He probably needed a doctor.

Jens limped into his living room. He grabbed a bottle of whiskey, sank down in the armchair and pulled the cork. He took a swig and then leaned his head back.

Normally, he would have called Sven, but not this time. He didn't want to hear this, too, being explained away. Kristina, he thought. Why was he not even considering calling her?

45.

BLACKÅSEN MOUNTAIN

They'd been gone for four days. Sandler had expected it and yet he feared something had gone wrong. He was also always watching his surroundings. Every sound startled him. Notholm had shot him and said they would try again. He hadn't seen Notholm since that day. Perhaps he'd followed Laura and Taneli. If they don't come back, he thought, I will . . .

And that was where his plan ended. What on earth could he do? There were others who were on their side—that was what Laura Dahlgren had said—but she hadn't given him any names. "Let's not," she'd said. "The less each one of us knows the better."

He agreed. Only, if she didn't come back, he had no idea where to turn next.

His superior within the industry had also been like a mentor to him for a long time. But when Sandler had raised the issue of Notholm renting land, he had refused to discuss it. Did he know what was going on? Was he onboard? Or was he, too, only following orders without knowing what they implied?

The magnitude of what they were up against struck him in waves. He looked up at the black lump of stone and his chest squeezed together imagining what was happening inside.

He was standing at the foot of the mountain with Hallberg, discussing breaking a new tunnel. It was hard to concentrate. The air was cool, but he felt hot. Feverish. He shivered. Things had to continue as usual. If he didn't keep the facade up, people would wonder. The foreman was pointing to something on a map he had brought, but Sandler had stopped listening. Had this man just lost a daughter? He found himself studying him until the foreman stopped talking and frowned.

"What?" Hallberg said.

"I heard a rumor about your daughter."

The foreman touched the sides of his mouth with black fingers. "Yes," he said finally.

"I'm sorry. I didn't know."

"She had it coming," Hallberg said, without taking his eyes off the mountain.

Sandler couldn't believe his ears. "I beg your pardon?"

"She had problems," the foreman said. "Too smart for her own good. She thought herself better than . . . this." He continued looking up the mountain. "The previous director decided she should study." He shrugged, as if her studies had been the problem.

And therein lies the whole issue, Sandler thought. He assumed the foreman would have been happier if his daughter had been daft; if she had had no prospects but to stay here with them.

Perhaps the men in the mine were all working together to cover something up . . . keep the secret. Even if it meant sacrificing daughters.

No. It couldn't be. But some people must be working for Notholm and Öhrnberg; helping them run things. The question was who.

He was sweating now. He could feel a drop running down his back.

"We don't always know what is truly in somebody else's heart," he said. "My condolences."

Then a stab of pain in his chest made him bend forward. His pulse rate was rising, his heart pounding in his ears. The foreman put his arm under his, helping him to straighten.

"Are you alright?" he asked. "Director?"

"Of course," Sandler said with effort. "A muscle spasm. It happens sometimes."

He removed his arm from Hallberg's grip.

Without looking, he knew his wound had begun bleeding. He pulled his jacket closer, making sure it was covered.

WHEN HE RETURNED to his house, they were back. He could sense it. He found them in his office, Miss Dahlgren standing up as he entered, Taneli already on his feet.

They were both pale and their clothes were dirty. Laura had tied her hair back.

"What's happened?" He eased himself into a chair, groaning with the effort.

"They shot him," she said. Her hands were clasped in front of her as if she needed to hold onto something.

"Who?"

"Andreas. It's my fault. They must have followed us."

"Who shot him?"

She shook her head. "I don't know. He only had the time to confirm what we knew."

"God," the director said.

Her eyes were large. "They'll stop at nothing," she said. "It's my fault he's dead."

Sandler shook his head. That wasn't true, but it would take time for her to see it.

"You're both still alive," he said.

"I know." She nodded and looked at him. Why? she seemed to ask him. Why am I still alive?

Yes, indeed, why?

"So what will you do?"

She exhaled. "I'll go back to Stockholm tonight," she said. "On the train."

"But you can't leave us," the boy said. "They've still got them. They've got my sister."

Sandler and Laura's eyes met. Neither of them believed the girl was still alive.

"I need to leave in order to help," Laura said. "I can't see any other way to stop this than to make sure the world knows. Britta thought the same. That would force them to stop. But we need evidence. At this point, this is but a tale. We need more than that. Will you ask someone to investigate Andreas's murder?"

"I don't know," Sandler said, truthfully. "Normally the Sami manage themselves. I'll have to talk to our police constable and see."

They both fell silent.

"What will you do when you get back?"

"We have to somehow enter the State Institute's building in Uppsala. Surely there would be something there. Meanwhile . . ."

He waited.

"I don't know," she admitted.

"Meanwhile, we'll hold the fort," he decided.

46.

LAURA

Her grandfather was up when she got home. She was tired after the train ride and stricken with guilt and loss.

"Your father is very unhappy with you."

She paused. "I know," she said then. At the moment, everyone's unhappy with me, she thought. Including myself, first and foremost. She hung her jacket in the wardrobe and picked up her bag.

"He is *angry*, Laura."

"I know. He's worried about me. But he's overreacting."

Her grandfather remained in the hallway. Laura paused. He hesitated, seemed to be weighing his words. "I think you need to be more careful around your father, Laura."

"*Careful?*" She frowned, didn't understand.

Her grandfather had clasped his hands and now he looked down at them. Laura put her bag down again.

"Your father is a very strong man. In fact, I cannot think of a single time when he hasn't gotten his own way. I never know what he's up to—of course—but, for some reason, lately, I've worried."

"Worried? Why?"

"Your father can be merciless with those who get in his way. The older he gets, the stronger this trait seems to get."

She wasn't certain what her grandfather was telling her. He knew how close they were. "Not with me," she said.

"Laura." Her grandfather touched his heart with his hand and for a moment she thought he might falter. "You are special to him, that's true. So far you have been shielded from his anger. But you don't know what he's capable of." He shook his head. "I wouldn't disappoint him if I were you, Laura."

She hesitated, then patted him on the shoulder, picked up her bag again and walked toward the stairs.

HER FATHER WAS still in the kitchen reading the paper when she came down for breakfast the next morning.

"Good morning," she said.

Her father didn't respond.

He'd done this before when they had argued. The silent treatment. She would bring him round. She poured herself a cup of coffee. She sat down to face him.

"I disobeyed you," she admitted. "And there was danger. But we found things out. It's big, Father."

He folded the newspaper shut and glared at her.

"Britta was onto something," Laura said. "The three kings' meeting in 1914 set up a committee to work on establishing a Scandinavian Reich under one strong leader. They did this based on the supposed supremacy of the Nordic race."

Her father was still there. Frowning but still listening. That was good.

"There was more to the program, though. They were work-ing to maintain the purity of the race by breeding from the best, but they were also eliminating the worst. It's still happen-ing today.

"I went there. To the north. To see Andreas, Britta's friend. He knew what they were doing and they shot him for talking to me." Her voice broke. "This is why Britta died. She trusted the wrong person. Whoever she told was in on it."

Her father's face was blank; she couldn't tell what he was thinking.

"It's true," she repeated, frowning, trying not to cry.

"Do you have any evidence?" her father said.

"I was there. He was shot in front of me."

Her father shook his head. "Something that will hold up in a court of law."

"No," she admitted. "Britta had. But it's gone. But you could help." She leaned forward and looked into his eyes. "With your contacts—"

"Laura." Her father interrupted her. "I am the governor of the Swedish Central Bank. What do you think would happen if I began to inquire into some potentially dubious racial practi-ces in our own country? What do you think would ensue if that became known?"

"People are dying. They are being *experimented* on."

"How can you be so naive?" Her father's face was white. "We are in the midst of a war. *A World War!* You *know* how close a Soviet invasion could be. Or an Allied one. It's all hanging by a thread. What do you think these powers would do if they heard what you've just told me? All they're waiting for is some excuse. They would tear us apart. As a nation. As a people."

"But . . ."

"*No*. You have a responsibility, Laura. And that responsibility lies with your country, goddammit. *Your country!* Your fellow citizens. Not to Britta. Not to some friends. And definitely not to the Sami people."

47.

JENS.

Jens looked like a boxer. The face was swollen, his nose bent. He touched his face and winced. At least his eyebrow had stopped bleeding. Well, he couldn't go to work looking like this.

He called the foreign minister, half hoping he wouldn't answer and that he could just leave a message with the administrative staff.

"Günther."

"Hi," Jens said. "I'm sick." He coughed. "A terrible flu."

"You haven't seemed well for a while," the minister said. "Perhaps you're overdoing it."

Do you know? Jens wondered. Do you already know what happened to me?

"I might be off for a few days," Jens said. He caught a glimpse of himself in the hallway mirror again. "Perhaps as much as a week."

"Take your time," Günther said. "These things can be contagious."

═

HE CALLED KRISTINA'S apartment as he didn't want her to come over and get a shock at the sight of him, but there was no response.

Instead, he lay down on the sofa. He had to lower himself, slowly. Every bone in his body screamed. So this is what it's like to be beaten up, he thought. He'd always been able to talk himself out of anything: it had never happened to him before.

Cathartic, in some way, he thought and then he had to laugh.

Ouch, his ribs hurt. He put his hand on his side, then closed his eyes. Would he continue the quest?

How could he not?

I won't think about it, he thought. Right now, that was a problem for tomorrow.

The apartment was warm, and a dim light came through the windows. He could feel himself relax, twitch . . .

The doorbell rang. Jens rose and walked gingerly to the door.

What if it were them, ready to finish the job? He gripped the umbrella that was standing beside the clothes rack.

"Who's there?" he called.

"It's Sven."

Jens opened the door.

Sven saw his face. "My God," he said, shocked. Then he saw the umbrella in Jens's hand. "Are you heading out?"

"No. Just . . ." Jens put the umbrella back.

"I heard you were sick," Sven said. "They said it was the flu. I thought I'd pop by."

"Well, now you know," Jens said.

Sven shook his head. "I can't believe it. Can I come in?"

Jens hesitated.

"I just want to talk to you. About what you said last weekend."

Jens didn't want to hear himself be explained away again.

"I was wrong not to hear you out," Sven said. "I'm sorry. I . . ." Sven rubbed his forehead with his knuckle. "I guess I'm scared, too, Jens."

Scared? He ushered Sven in and closed the door behind him.

"With my leanings, I'm an easy target. I always feel I have to be careful not to give people any reason to come after me."

The knot in Jens's chest was dissolving.

"I'm rather an easy target for blackmail." Sven gave a false chuckle.

"I understand," Jens said, and his voice sounded muffled to his own ears. "Thanks for telling me. I . . ."

They both bent their heads. Jens felt like he might cry. They had never talked about Sven's homosexuality before.

"Thanks for telling me," he repeated.

Sven cleared his throat and raised his head. "But I have reconsidered," he said. "My best friend needs my help and that's worth the risk. So please tell me the whole story again."

They went into the living room and Jens told him everything, from the beginning up to what had happened last night.

"Who do you think is involved in all this?" Sven asked when he had finished.

Jens shook his head. "I don't know. Who told you what the phone calls were about and that Britta's killer had been caught?"

"A fellow in the Security Services. He's Möller's contact."

"You see, they're everywhere."

"So what will you do now?"

"Recover," Jens said. "Regroup. I don't know," he admitted.

"What can I do?"

"Keep your ears and eyes open? Try to see who might be in on this? I honestly don't know, Sven. Just be careful, please.

As you can tell by now, whoever they are, they're not messing around. What you told me today . . . They wouldn't hesitate to use that."

"Can I do anything for you now? Do you need anything?"

"Just rest, I think. I'm not up for anything else."

Sven nodded and rose. "Look after yourself, my friend. We'll speak soon."

48.

BLACKÅSEN MOUNTAIN

Abraham's mother. She was sitting in the kitchen with Gunnar's mother as he opened the door. Gunnar turned on his heel to leave again.

"Son?"

His father was there even though it was a working day? This was serious.

"Yes, Dad." Gunnar turned back to the adults in the kitchen.

Abraham's mother's face was white, her eyes red. She'd become skin and bone since he last saw her. When she stared at him, he found he couldn't meet her gaze. Instead, he bent his head. His shoes were scuffed, dirty.

"Frida has come to see us," Gunnar's mother said. "Abraham has been missing for a week. Do you know something about it?"

"No," he mumbled.

He lifted his head. His father narrowed his eyes at him. You didn't want to end up on the wrong side of him. His sister and his father had never seen eye to eye. The fights they'd had . . .

"Gunnar?" his father prompted.

Gunnar sighed. "Abraham said something happened when he was out with Mr. Notholm."

336

The adults exchanged gazes. He could feel their confusion.

"Why would he be out with him?" his father asked.

"Mr. Notholm asked us to do some work for him . . . Only Abraham agreed. I don't know what happened, but Abraham said Mr. Notholm killed Director Sandler."

Gunnar's mother covered her mouth. Abraham's mother wailed and Gunnar's mother turned to her and put her hand on her shoulder.

"Abraham wanted to make sure I'd tell you that he had nothing to do with that," Gunnar said and had to clear his throat. "With the killing."

"But the director is alive," his father said, forehead wrinkled.

Yes. Gunnar nodded.

"But where did he go?" Abraham's mother cried.

"He said he was going south. He said he'd be fine." His words sounded lame even to his own ears.

"*He'll* be fine." She laughed and shook her head. She began scratching at the raw skin of her hands. Gunnar couldn't bear it. She drew blood as she raked, and it was spreading in long red streaks, getting under her nails. He felt queasy. He wished his mother would tell her to stop. Abraham's mother put her face in her hands, rocking back and forth.

"I wasn't there. I don't know what happened," Gunnar said.

"I saw the director," Gunnar's father said in a low voice to Gunnar's mother. "It was clear he was in pain. And Mr. Notholm, too, was injured."

"Mr. Notholm had said the director had made himself a target," Gunnar said.

His mother gasped. "But the director is in charge of the town." She had leaned forward and put her hand on her husband's arm. "He could have Mr. Notholm jailed if he wanted to," she whispered. "Doesn't even need a reason."

"Perhaps for some reason he can't this time," Gunnar's father said.

Gunnar was shocked when he saw his face. His father looked sick.

49.

LAURA

The historians and Jens Regnell were sitting in silence in Karl-Henrik's living room. Laura and Jens had been talking at length; Jens, with his swollen, bruised face, a reminder of what they were up against.

"A Scandinavian Reich," Karl-Henrik said, at last. He shook his head and his voice sounded full of something like admiration. "The thing that struck me when I was trying to map out the relationships the Institute has with other organizations is the breadth of it. I've found links to seemingly every domain: business, academia, politics, the military . . . There's no end to it."

He had pinned up his notes on the wall, a giant spiderweb of names. Matti was standing in front of it, reading, his fingers following the lines, mumbling as he recognized some.

"Technically, based on this chart, we don't really know who's at the center of the struggle for a Scandinavian Reich," Karl-Henrik said. "These are the people and institutions with links to the Institute. Some of them won't know. Others might be seduced by the vision of power . . ." He shrugged.

"Professor Lindahl is right in the middle," Laura said. She was standing by the window and could feel a faint draft coming from outside. She wrapped her arms around herself. "How do we find out who else is involved?"

"I'm not sure we should try," Erik said.

Matti turned around to look at Erik. Laura paused, uncertain she had heard correctly.

"How can you say that?" she asked.

"You heard what they told him." Erik nodded in Jens's direction. "It's too big. There's nothing we can do."

Was Erik afraid? His body was tensed up, as if ready for them to attack him. Laura had never seen him frightened. Erik feared nothing. Feared no one.

"There's always something you can do," Laura said. "At least we have to try."

"And get yourself killed in the process? Your flat has already been bombed and you've been shot at. What will it take for you to stop?"

The bells from the church next to Karl-Henrik's apartment began to ring as if to accentuate his words. Laura turned to look out at the people exiting the building. A funeral. Everyone dressed in black. She could see the priest standing on the steps, shaking hands, offering consolation.

"Actually, that was one of the things that was strange," she said and turned back to the room. "They didn't shoot at me."

"They didn't?" Matti asked.

"There was only one shot—the one that killed Andreas. And yet, they could easily have killed me and Taneli, the boy I was with."

"And the other thing?" Matti asked.

"What?"

"You said that was one of the things that was strange."

"Oh yes. The other thing was what Andreas said before he

died. 'Why did you bring him here?' It was as if he saw his killer in the forest and recognized him."

"The mining director or the hotel owner?" Erik shrugged.

"Could be," Laura said. "But it was definitely someone he recognized."

"Why didn't they try to shoot you?" Karl-Henrik repeated.

"Perhaps that would've turned it into a bigger thing? Something they couldn't keep local?" Jens shook his head.

"I don't know," Laura said. "But what do we do now? How do we stop this? What if they still have people imprisoned up north?"

"We have to cut off the organization's head," Jens said.

Matti sat down. "Don't you think that would be just like the Hydra? For every head we cut off, two will emerge? Besides, how would we cut off a head? I am assuming you mean figuratively."

Jens sighed. Laura understood. She, too, wanted the perpetrators punished for what they had done. She wanted them brought to justice. She looked at her friends, their suits, their groomed appearances. None of them had any real power. Not power like this. They weren't strong enough.

"We need photographs, or something tangible," Matti said. "And we need a newspaper willing to publish it."

"I know a journalist," Laura said and thought of Emil Persson. "He works for one of the big newspapers. He'd do it."

"Despite the risk to himself?"

She nodded: he would.

"Who is he?" Erik asked.

"You don't know him."

"And the proof?" Jens asked.

"For that, we must go to the Hydra's den," Laura said.

═══

ERIK WAS WAITING for her on the pavement when she got out of Karl-Henrik's flat. Tomorrow night, they'd agreed. They were going to pay a visit to the Institute.

"What's up?" he asked.

She didn't want to tell him. She revered her father. She had never said anything negative about him. Even thinking it, felt disloyal.

She sighed. "I told my father," she said. "I'd hoped he would help us."

"But no?"

She shook her head. "He said it was irresponsible to continue: that if this became known, we were putting Sweden as a nation at risk."

His face showed what he was thinking.

"You agree," she said.

He shrugged.

She lowered her head: what if they were right? What if this put Sweden in danger?

"But people have died. Our best friend did. She thought it was worth fighting for."

"She wouldn't have wanted us to put ourselves at risk," he said.

Laura didn't say anything.

"Especially not you. She loved you."

There was something sheepish about him: his hands deep in his pockets, not meeting her gaze. It suddenly dawned on her.

"It was you," she said. "You were the one she was having a relationship with."

He looked away.

"Why didn't you tell me?"

"It was long over."

"Why did it end?"

342

He sighed. "I had wanted it for so long. And then, one day, out of the blue, she called me. I guess, when it finally happened, reality didn't match up to the dream. We tried, but pretty soon we both agreed that there was nothing there." His voice sounded thick. "It just wasn't meant to be."

"Why?" Laura had asked Britta at one point. They were sitting on a park bench by the river. "Why wouldn't you date Erik?"

Britta's eyes were fixed on the other side of the water. She'd seemed absent. "No." She'd shaken her head.

"But why?" Laura had insisted.

"There's something in him," Britta had said. "A kind of darkness. Something in his past."

"We all have dark things in our past," Laura had said. "You, me, Karl-Henrik, Matti . . . All of us are messed up. It doesn't mean there can't be light in the future."

"But Erik has a ruthlessness about him," Britta had said.

"Ruthless" was too strong a word. Erik was insensitive, rash. He could be hugely irritating. But ruthless? No.

"He's had a lot to cope with," Britta said.

But she changed her mind, Laura thought, and gave it a try. Britta rarely changed her mind. She must have been so lonely, so desperate, that she was willing to try what she had previously thought wouldn't work for her.

Her eyes filled, and she pushed her fingers into her eyelids to make it stop.

50.

JENS

The doorbell rang. A woman was in the hallway. She had turned to look out the window. Black hair bouncing on her shoulders, a twinset and a woollen skirt. She heard the door open and glanced over her shoulder, hip tilted. Barbro Cassel. Then her mouth and eyes widened: "My God, Jens. What happened to you?"

"Wrong place, wrong time," he said.

She walked close to him and touched his cheek with her finger. "This is bad. Are you alright?"

"I've been better," he said. "What can I do for you?"

She bit her lip. "I wasn't certain I should come. I called your work. They said you were off sick."

Jens waited.

"You asked me about a Mr. . . . . Enander? Said Kristina had told you something about me even though she shouldn't have?"

"Yes."

"I have no idea what she's talking about and I thought it might be important that you know that."

Jens's heart sank. He didn't want it to be true. "Kristina told me you spy on the Germans . . . Schnurre in particular. She

344

told me Schnurre had gotten a package from Mr. Enander in my house and so he was being watched by the Security Services."

Barbro shook her head. She seemed sad. "It's not true, Jens. I'm not a spy. I don't know Mr. Enander. And, I'm so sorry, but I know quite well who Schnurre sees and doesn't see, and the only person he is acquainted with in your building is Kristina."

Inside the building, someone was hammering. *Bang. Bang. Bang.* Jens focused on the sound . . . didn't want to hear what else was coming.

"In fact, Kristina was the one who got me the job with Schnurre. Said she was acquainted with him through her father's business."

Jens bent his head. It was worse than he had thought. Kristina was working for Schnurre, he felt certain now. And Jens was the secretary to the foreign minister. What might he have told her during their courtship? How could she have done this, and why?

Whether we like it or not, they might win this war and we might have to learn to get on with them. Her voice in his head.

Kristina was ambitious. And she had hedged her bets.

He found Barbro watching him.

"Alright," he said. "Thank you."

She nodded and started walking to the door.

"Why are you telling me this?" he asked. "She's your friend."

She turned back to face him. "I'm not a spy, Jens, and I won't be accused of being one. Could you imagine what would happen to me if Schnurre were to hear that?" She shook her head. "I'd be dead within the day."

SVEN HAD BEEN right not to trust Kristina, Jens thought, as he walked with long strides to Kristina's apartment. And she had tried to drive a wedge between them. Somewhere deep inside, he, too, had known what she was about. How could he have been so stupid to not trust his own intuition? He had known. It occurred to him that he ought to call the Security Services to tell them about what he'd just found out, but then he didn't exactly trust them at the moment either.

"Jens?" Kristina's voice sounded happy as she came out to greet him. "What a lovely surprise . . . My God, what happened to you!" Just like Barbro, she reached up to touch his cheek and he took a step backward.

"How could you?" he said, in a low voice.

"What?" Kristina looked surprised. How many times had he then witnessed her interacting with people they met? Enchanted, intelligent, concerned, she could do them all. It was all flooding back now: Kristina meeting the foreign minister, at her dinners, always hard at work. Acting. People believing in her. Envying him for her and for her social skills.

"I know," Jens said. "You work for Schnurre."

"For Schnurre . . . the German Schnurre?" Kristina paused, then burst out laughing. It was a hearty laugh. As if what he'd said was truly amusing. Her eyes glittered.

Jens remained silent.

"Jens?" Her mouth was still in a half smile. Willing him to laugh with her, willing him to tell her it had been a joke.

"Schnurre did not come to see Mr. Enander. He came to see you."

"No!"

Jens held up his hands. *Stop.* "That day, when I came home and saw Schnurre leaving my building, there were two coffee cups in the sink. *Two.* But only you were home."

She shook her head, serious now. "I know you've been under

a lot of pressure lately but this . . . This is crazy talk, Jens. Me working for the Germans? Of course not!"

"Then who visited?"

"A friend," she said.

"Who?"

"You don't know her."

"You have no friends." He was being cruel now, wanting to inflict some of the hurt that he was feeling. He had trusted her. She had fooled him. Worse: she had used him.

Kristina shook her head. "I don't know who's been telling you stories, and perhaps you're right: perhaps, as it proves out, I have no friends. But to accuse me of working for Germany . . . We're engaged to be married, Jens. You need to have faith in me. Whatever I've done, I've done for you . . ." She raised a finger to stop him before he spoke. "And no, that does not go as far as jumping into bed with the Germans. I do have boundaries, you know."

If she was telling the truth, then Barbro Cassel had been lying. Why would she have done that? He could see no reason.

Kristina seemed so honest. He wanted to trust her. But he realized he hadn't trusted her for a long time, perhaps never. He wasn't certain she had boundaries—that was the long and short of it. And he did.

"I don't know what to think," he said, truthfully.

She exhaled, a slow, long breath. "Well." Her voice caught. "Then I think all has been said." She stretched out her trembling left hand in front of her, pulled off the gold ring that sat there and handed it to him.

He took it.

"I loved you, Jens," she said. "I really did. I still do."

He wanted to say that he had loved her, too, but found he couldn't do it.

51.

BLACKÅSEN MOUNTAIN

A target." The foreman felt sick. He should never have called. What on earth had he been thinking?

He had to stop this before it was too late. He would make amends; lie if he had to.

He found the little white card and dialed the same numbers. "This is Hallberg at Blackåsen mine," he said.

It was a woman who answered this time; last time it had been a man.

"I'm guessing you have the wrong number," she laughed. "This is a dressmaker in Stockholm? Unless you're ordering for someone?"

He apologized, hung up and dialed the number again. The same woman answered. This time he tried.

"I need to speak with the people about Blackåsen mine," he said.

"My dear sir," she said, "nobody here knows anything about a mine. We make dresses."

He felt sweat break out on his forehead. "I insist," he said. "You tell them to stop whatever has been put in play."

"I can't tell anyone anything." She lowered her voice. "But

it's my experience that once things have begun, they don't stop, do they? They have to run their course?"

The foreman banged down the phone and swore to himself.

What had he done? His phone call would get the director killed. "A target." He exhaled slowly. His hands were trembling.

No. Not like this.

He rose, pushing back his chair so forcefully it fell behind him. He walked to the door and yelled: "Manfred!"

A man approached hat in hand.

"I want a man watching the train station," Hallberg said. "I want to know if someone arrives and plans to stay in town. Second, I want a couple of men watching the director. *Guarding him.* I think he might be in danger."

He stopped himself, waiting for the questions that would surely follow.

"Does this have to do with Georg's death?" Manfred asked.

That startled him. He hadn't expected that question. "I think it does," he said, finally. "Yes, I do. Tell your men not to let the director out of their sight."

He sat down when Manfred left. He'd have to talk to the director and he wasn't looking forward to it. "I'm the man who got you shot," he said out loud.

IT DIDN'T TAKE more than a couple of hours for Manfred to return. "Four men," he said, "on the train from Stockholm. Suits. Hats. They're staying at the Winter Palace hotel."

"Four . . . And the director?"

Manfred nodded. "Harald, Egon and Ivar are outside his house."

"Don't let him out of your sight," the foreman repeated.

"And if they come for him?"

"Stop them; no matter what."

Manfred hesitated. "There's a boy staying with him."

"A boy?"

"Sami."

That was strange. What would a Sami boy be doing with the director?

The foreman shrugged. "Doesn't change anything," he said.

52.

LAURA

In the midst of all the misery, she was happy. Happy that they had found one another again—she and Erik, Matti and Karl-Henrik. For they had, hadn't they? It was just like the old days. Though Britta, of course, was missing. So it wasn't like the old days, really.

At university, things had gotten so bad; she had to admit that she'd never thought they would speak again.

After that first fight, they'd seen Matti in class but avoided each other. He walked past them, not sparing them a glance.

He should have known better, Laura had thought.

Known better than what, though?

It wasn't logical, their rage. For that was what it was, rage. They were totally furious with Matti for having held an opposing view, for being different, for being Finnish. For being.

Yes. For being.

And rather than things quietening down, they got worse. She could see it in the way Erik's gaze followed Matti when he walked in. She could feel it in the way Karl-Henrik avoided getting close to him. She could sense it in herself.

Then one morning, Matti came to school with one eye swollen shut, his cheek bruised and his lip torn. Laura bumped into him in the hallway. "What happened to you?"

"Well, you should know," he muttered and moved to walk past her.

"Wait." She reached for him. "What?"

He looked at her, studied her. There was a solemnity to him that she hadn't seen before.

"You know who did this," he stated.

"No." She shook her head, then realized what he meant. "Us? No."

He said nothing.

"Erik?" she asked. "Karl-Henrik?"

"With a band of others."

She couldn't believe it, but his eyes were scared.

"I'm so sorry," she whispered, but he was already off.

That night, Laura was woken by someone getting into bed with her. She sat up, gasped.

"It's only little me," Britta said, her voice full of laughter. "Either you need to get better at having people jump in and out of your bed, or you shouldn't leave the door open at night."

"Oh God! You scared me." Laura flopped down on the pillow again, her heart still pounding in her chest.

Britta put her head on Laura's shoulder. She had been off school for a couple of days. A migraine, she'd called it. Laura figured she'd spent the time with someone.

"I saw Matti today," Laura said.

"Mm-hm?"

"He'd been beaten up. He said Erik and Karl-Henrik did it."

Britta propped herself up on her elbow.

"They couldn't have," Britta said. "Could they?"

She wanted to say no. "They might," Laura admitted.

Britta was already standing up. "Get dressed."

"Now?"

"Yes, now." Britta began marching up and down her room. "What the hell do they think they're doing?" she muttered. "They've taken this way too far."

When Laura was dressed, Britta grabbed her by the hand and dragged her out.

"They were still at the club, when I left," she said.

They found Erik and Karl-Henrik on Main Street. Erik was in the bar, surrounded by a group of young men, doing all the talking. Karl-Henrik was over by the far wall, drink in his hand, observing.

"What the fuck did you do?" Britta said, after pushing through the crowd around him.

Erik stopped talking. "What?"

"Come with me. You, too," she ordered Karl-Henrik.

They were on the street outside the club. "What did you do to Matti?" Britta asked.

"Nothing," Erik protested. He'd brought his beer outside and now took a sip.

"Don't give me that." She glared at Erik and then at Karl-Henrik.

"He was being rather difficult," Karl-Henrik mumbled.

Britta's mouth opened, then shut. "No, he wasn't. We've had differences of opinion before, a thousand times. It's never mattered one bit. In fact, we like it when we can debate things. Be honest, this was different."

"What do you mean?" Erik said.

"We've taken on the values of the project. We now judge Matti differently because he's Finnish and not Scandinavian. It has to stop."

"Our job is to protect the project!" Erik was raising his voice.

"What the fuck is wrong with you?" Britta screamed. On the other side of the pavement, a couple hurried past, throwing glances their way. "We got angry with a friend because he wasn't the right kind?"

"We know about the superiority of the Scandinavian race. Only someone from the Scandinavian race can partake in this new world."

"We made that up. We invented it! It's not true." Britta's cheeks were red. "It's a bloody superhero B-movie!"

Erik had turned white. "You'd better shut your mouth."

"Or what?" Britta said in a low voice. "Or you'll beat me up, too?"

They stared at each other.

"Oh, and your precious project . . ." Britta said. "Just so you know. I burned our notes before coming here."

Erik threw his glass at the wall of the building and it exploded in a million shards.

"Tell me you weren't in on this," Britta asked Karl-Henrik when Erik had stalked off.

"I didn't think it was for real," he mumbled. "I didn't think they'd actually do it. I didn't think they would actually hurt him. I didn't think . . ."

Back at home, Britta did burn the notes from the project. All of them. All their writing: a mighty bonfire. Laura handed her the pages, one after the other. Britta cried the whole time.

The next day, Germany invaded Denmark and Norway and they didn't get a chance to sort it out.

It had been good of Matti not to bring it up again when they met. How did Erik and Karl-Henrik feel about it now? Probably like her, ashamed.

For a brief while, they'd let insanity take over. It was the times. Luckily, they'd come to their senses. Clearly, not everyone had.

53.

JENS

Jens, Laura, Matti and Erik were on the same late evening train to Uppsala, but they didn't sit together, as they thought four people traveling in a group would attract more attention than separate individuals. Jens sat across from Laura, a few rows away. He was reading a paper, but he hadn't turned the pages once. His body still hurt, a dull throb. Laura sat on the other side looking out the window. She looked cool and unruffled, as if she were on her way to a lecture, rather than a break-in. How on earth did she manage it? Erik was in the next car and he assumed Matti was in the one after that. Jens hadn't been certain Erik would join them. But, at the agreed time, he'd been on the platform and Jens had had to stop himself from nodding to him.

These people were so different from one another, he thought. Unlikely friends. Erik was hotheaded, a fool in many ways, in Jens's opinion. Matti seemed sober, totally focused on his job for Finland. Karl-Henrik was, in many ways, the biggest brain; the analyst. And then Laura . . .

They were unlikely friends and yet it was clear how intimate they were. Something had come between them at some point, he was pretty certain. They seemed to think they were no longer close, but they were wrong. Rarely had he seen people respond to each other like they did. They seemed to know what each of them needed before it was said out loud. Matti would sometimes walk close to Laura, as if to support her without saying a word. Karl-Henrik would just need to look at Erik for him to quieten down. Erik could make the serious three laugh with abandon. Laura chose who spoke. With her gaze, she gave them the word. He wondered what role Britta had played.

They got off the train in Uppsala. Most of the other passengers were young, likely students. Jens glanced around. It was impossible to tell if they were being followed. There was a cold headwind and he took the street leading to Fyrisån. They had decided that each would bide their time until midnight, when they would meet outside the cathedral.

Farther down Bangårdsgatan, he entered one of the bars and ordered a beer. The waitress took an extra-long look at his face but said nothing.

He tried not to think, for he had nothing good to say to himself. Instead, he watched the people in the bar, so young, so carefree. If they only knew! He wished he didn't. You didn't know how you would react when faced with something like this. You just didn't. Erik had advocated doing nothing. And wasn't that what was happening in the world at large? If you weren't directly involved, you looked the other way.

Before midnight, he rose and stepped out into the cold. Through the window, he saw that somebody had already taken his table. It was just as if he'd never been there.

═══

THE SQUARE LAY empty and the cathedral seemed to tower over him as he entered the area. God is watching, he thought, even though he didn't believe much in God.

He met the others by the side of the church. Erik took Laura's hand and squeezed it. Jens felt a sting but didn't understand why.

"Are you sure about this?" Erik asked. "Once we break in, there's no going back. We can still walk away."

"But we can't," Laura said. "We can't know and do nothing."

"Perhaps there's another way . . ."

She shook her head. "We've discussed it. This is the only way left."

"No going back," he repeated. "So far, you've been lucky. After this, all bets are off."

"I'm sure," she said.

Matti nodded. Jens, too.

"You don't have to come," Laura said.

Erik shook his head. "If you go, I'll go."

They approached the building from the side and followed its stone foundations to the back. It used to be a school, he remembered hearing. It was Matti who was eyeing all the low windows, pressing on them, as if trying them. They were in luck; one of the windows was slightly open. Matti put his hands under the sash and lifted it. Then he sank down and offered his knee. One after the other, they climbed in through the window. When it was his turn, he lifted himself up on the window frame.

They were in what looked like an office. Desks and chairs. The walls were lined with bookshelves, crammed with books. There was a skull on one of the desks. A fake one, he hoped.

"It's a big place," Matti whispered. "Four floors. I suggest we split up and take one floor each."

"What are we looking for?" Erik whispered.

"Photographs, or reports, or similar," Matti said. "Something we can bring with us. I'll take the top floor."

"I'll take the one beneath you," Laura said. "You can go beneath me," she said to Erik.

Jens nodded. "I'll do the ground floor."

The rest walked toward the door, opened it, waited, but the building lay quiet.

Jens turned on one of the desk lamps and began by looking on each desk but found nothing of obvious value. He pulled out a drawer. It was full of paper. This was going to take forever. Above him, somewhere, a door opened. Erik.

The person at this desk appeared to be working on skull measurements. The drawers contained papers with long lines of data: jaw, forehead, circumference. There was an instrument on top of the desk. Tongs with numbers? Some sort of a measuring tool. It was cold to the touch.

The second desk contained pretty much the same things. This was taking too much time.

There was a scraping sound from the floor above him.

On the wall, between two bookshelves, was a door. A storage room? He tried the handle, but it was locked. Randomly, he opened the top drawers of the desks closest to it. In one, there was a key.

Holding his breath, he put the key in the lock. It turned. He opened the door and found a light switch inside. He turned it on and in front of him was a spiral staircase leading into a basement. His heart began to pound faster. He walked downstairs but kept turning and eyeing the door above him, expecting it to slam shut, the lock to slide home. He knew it was his mind playing games with him, but the feeling was so strong, it was like a premonition.

Downstairs was a table that resembled a surgical table from a hospital and a lone desk. The shelves were full of jars. Jens walked closer and wished he hadn't. Organs in liquid: livers, brains. He cringed and turned away.

The desk was covered in photos. He couldn't help but gasp out loud. Those photos . . . He'd never be able to get the images out of his mind. Bodies with gaping wounds, or crudely sewn together; bodies blackened from burns or perhaps from poison. Bodies missing limbs, missing organs. The faces were emaciated and distorted with pain.

He forced himself to see all of it, lift all the papers, look in the books. Then he went to get the others. Don't close the door. Don't shut me in here with this, he prayed, as he ran up the last few steps.

Erik's expression hardened when he arrived.

"I found something," Jens said.

The others followed him down the spiral staircase into the basement. Their reactions at seeing the photos were much like his own. Matti turned away, groaning. Laura looked ashen. Erik leaned heavily on the desk with one hand.

"This isn't proof," Erik said after a while. "It could be argued away."

"But this is," Jens said. He held up a book he had found before going upstairs. His hands were trembling.

"Subject five," he read, "faints when cut open without anesthesia, dies from hemorrhaging after ten minutes." He flipped a page. "Subject thirty-three, dies of starvation after one week. Subject thirty-four, fed water, dies after four weeks. There are photos of each one." His voice sounded thick. "And I found this." He lifted another book. "Names," he said, "and money. I think this might be the list of people involved."

"And look here," Matti said and pulled down a file from the bookshelf above the desk. The label on the front read *Our Manifesto*. Matti read out loud: "The Scandinavian race has long been neglected, made to live like all other races with the same problems . . ."

Laura covered her mouth with her hand. "But that comes from our project. We burned all of it. How did it end up here?"

"We don't have much time," Matti said.

"Let's take all of it," Jens said, "or as much as we can, so we don't miss anything. When are we seeing the journalist?"

"Tomorrow afternoon," Laura said. "Well, later today. We're meeting him at Karl-Henrik's."

Laura cried as they packed the documents in the bags they'd brought with them; silent tears running down her face and dropping onto her hands. Jens couldn't bear seeing her tears, but there was nothing he could say in comfort. People were doing this to other people. It was unthinkable.

When they left the building, they made sure to lock the door to the basement.

"It might buy us an hour or two," Matti said, "before they realize."

They left the same way they'd come and closed the window behind them. As they walked to the train station, Jens felt tainted with the vileness from the Institute's basement. He'd seen the face of evil there, and the knowledge of what was being done by human beings to other human beings would take root inside him.

It was dawn before they arrived at Karl-Henrik's apartment. They handed him the bags containing the photos, the books and the folders.

He met Jens's gaze.

"It's awful," Jens said. But there were no words that could do justice to what they had with them. He just shook his head and handed him the bag he was carrying.

"Go home," Karl-Henrik said. "Get some sleep. Come back later."

54.

BLACKÅSEN MOUNTAIN

Another dream. Taneli sat up abruptly. In the bed, the director's shape, a slight wheezing as he breathed. It had been Javanna again. Voices, barely human, both men and women. Moans, screams, whispers. The moaning was full of fear. The screaming must have been going on for a long time for the voices were so hoarse, they cracked and ended up in nothing. The whispers had been the worst. They came when there was nothing else left. Sighs wrung out of deep and empty pits, out of that which was forever broken. And then, cutting through it all, Javanna's voice: *Not much time left now.*

"What do you mean?" he had asked.

Hurry, little brother. Hurry.

"What do you mean? What do you mean!"

But all was silent. And then he woke up. Why wasn't there time? And hurry how?

Taneli had clenched his teeth so hard it hurt when he relaxed his mouth. He stood up, careful not to wake the director. Taneli didn't like his raspy breathing. He sounded sick. But the doctor had said he would be fine.

Taneli snuck through the house. Some of the floorboards creaked, but the director wouldn't hear anything tonight.

He opened the front door slowly and just enough to sneak out.

The night sky over Blackåsen Mountain was as light as day. Soon there would be no night at all. Taneli missed the camp. It didn't feel right to sleep inside, so far away from everything alive. Especially now, in spring.

He hesitated. Something was wrong with the picture before him. It took a while, but then he spotted them. Three men. Miners. Were they watching the director's house? It looked like it. They hadn't yet seen him. Not very good watchers, he thought.

He crouched and hurried down the steps and alongside the house. At the corner, he stopped, looked back. No, they hadn't noticed.

He walked through the town, worried that someone would see him. Mr. Notholm, perhaps. He took the forest path instead and felt the springiness under his feet. He inhaled the scent of pine and resin and dry leaves.

He hadn't planned where he was going but soon realized that there was only one destination: the land the director had said Mr. Notholm rented from him.

ON THE SIDE of the mountain there was an entry wound. Standing nearby were men and a line of horses.

Taneli squatted down behind a large pine to watch them.

Sami people carried boxes out of the hole in the mountain's side, down the slope and then added them to sacks hanging over the backs of the animals. Sami people. But not like any Sami he had ever seen before. These ones were skin and bones. They walked gingerly, knees buckling under the weight. They looked ancient. They were the missing people, he was certain.

Taneli rose. He needed to see Javanna. But there were no children. No women. Only men.

A man on a horse, a whip slicing through the air. "Faster!" he yelled.

Mr. Notholm!

Notholm turned to another man also on a horse. "I can't believe you're forcing us to move," he muttered.

The other man was dressed in a black suit. He was sitting leaning on the horse's neck, arms crossed. "What did you expect?" he said, unmoved. "People are getting too close."

"We could just have shut him up," Notholm said.

"He's not the only one," the other man said. "Enough now."

"There are so many things to pack up," Notholm complained.

"Better get a move on then."

They were moving. That was what Javanna had meant! Once they had moved, he'd never find them.

Taneli retraced his footsteps, slowly at first. Then he began to run. He needed to wake the director.

"HE JUST LEFT," the housekeeper said, mouth tight. She still didn't like him. "Went to see the foreman."

Taneli whirled around, pushed open the door and ran after him.

He saw the director farther down the road, approaching the mine. The foreman was standing waiting for him and the director reached out to shake his hand.

Then, suddenly, he went down on his knees, as if to pray.

"Help!" the foreman yelled as he bent down and tried to keep him upright.

Taneli stopped.

Men came running.

Taneli began to run again. Soon he was beside the director and put his hand on his. It was burning hot. He felt the foreman look at him, but he didn't say anything. Someone got a stretcher. Gingerly, they lifted the director onto it.

"His skin is on fire," Taneli said.

"You!" the foreman shouted to one of the younger men. "Get Dr. Ingemarsson. Ask him to come to the director's house."

"Faster," he yelled at the men carrying the stretcher. They half ran toward the villa. The director lay absolutely still. He might be dead, Taneli thought.

The housekeeper met them in the hallway. She silently followed the men up to the director's bedroom.

The director's skin was flushed. He had sweated through the front of his shirt.

The foreman and Taneli's eyes met.

The doctor came running up the stairs, his coat flapping behind him.

"Everyone out," he said.

55.

LAURA

Laura couldn't sleep. She was lying in her childhood room. The safest place on earth, though it didn't feel like it any longer. The house was quiet. Nobody had been up when she came home, but she would have avoided her father anyway. She didn't understand how he could overlook the fact that people were dying. *Dying*. And being *tortured*. Surely it had to be exposed. This was the man who had always been there for her. Who had taught her everything she knew. Who had raised her. Who had all the right answers. She had always trusted his opinion.

Sleep, she told herself. You need it. Just a few hours. Sleep.

Those photos . . . Her stomach clenched. She turned on her back as if to avoid the images, then ended up covering her face with her hands. *Subject thirty-three* . . . She still couldn't fathom it. She wanted to go through the names register line by line, wanted to know exactly who was involved. And their project for Professor Lindahl was quoted in the manifesto. She had read it on the train back and many paragraphs came directly from their work. She remembered writing the words. She would make them pay for what they had done. Professor Lindahl, the most. He had betrayed them. On the train, Erik had flipped through the list of names, but she had been too scared to take out the other papers in public. She would go through them all with Emil today. He would help them. Hang them out for society to deal with. They would pay. And then her father would understand.

Traveling back, Matti had sat beside her. "It was my Finnish heritage," he'd said. "That's what Professor Lindahl always prodded me about. He insinuated I was worth less than the rest of you and that I'd end up dragging you down. He kept asking why I couldn't see it. Or if I just wouldn't admit it. He always asked as if he was genuinely interested. I ended up feeling I wasn't in your league."

She felt a sting of sorrow for the young man she'd known. And then his friends had gone down the same road. How awful.

"Why didn't you tell us?"

"Would you have listened?"

She had to admit they wouldn't have.

"Funny, though," Matti said. "When we had that fight, I left feeling it was my fault and that I had dragged you down after all." Then he had paused and she hadn't known what to say.

"We're losing the war, Laura," he said. "Sweden will end up having the Soviet Union for its neighbor and of Finland there will be no trace."

"Are you certain?" she whispered.

"Oh yes." His face was gray. "This war will end up taking everything."

"Yet still you are here, tonight, with us," she said.

"If I'm learning anything from this," he said, "it's how important every single battle is. If you don't fight whatever comes your way, how can you live with yourself?"

═══

"Laura!" Jens was coming toward her on the pavement outside Karl-Henrik's apartment. He looked like she probably did herself: tired and pale, his bruises still livid on his face. His blond hair was standing straight up, as if he, too, had tossed and turned without being able to fall asleep.

"You came," she said. He had said he was going back to work.

He nodded. "Couldn't leave it," he admitted. "At work, they think I have the flu," he added sheepishly. "How are you?"

"I've been better," she said, meeting his gaze. "You?"

He just shook his head.

She sighed. "I guess we should go up. Emil will arrive in an hour. I'd like to see the list of names before he comes."

They walked up the stairs and rang the doorbell.

"He's got space to publish tomorrow," she said.

"Does he know yet what it is?"

"I've only told him it's huge and risky and that it will bring the sky down. He seemed to like that idea," she said dryly.

"Some people are like that," Jens said.

Yes. Not long ago, she herself had been like that.

Laura rang the doorbell again.

"Has Emil done something similar before?" he asked. He then seemed to shake his head at himself. Nothing could be similar.

"He's done articles on the fate of the Jews in Germany, which caused a quite a stir. He is young, hugely ambitious. He won't be doing this for the same reasons as we are."

She frowned. "Why isn't he answering the door?"

Jens shrugged. "Perhaps he's ill?"

He could have fallen. On his crutches, all on his own. He could be hurt. Laura pressed the door handle. The door was unlocked.

"Karl-Henrik?" Laura called into the apartment.

No response. They exchanged a glance. Laura licked her lips. Something was wrong.

Jens walked in ahead of her. "Karl-Henrik?" he called.

Nothing. Jens walked down the hallway. As he peeked into the living room, he turned as if to stop Laura from entering, but it was too late. She was already beside him, taking it all in.

The living room was destroyed. The sofa and armchairs had been cut up, the padding pulled out. The books had been ripped out from the bookcase and seemingly thrown across the room. And there was blood. A huge pool of it, followed by a red path leading into the kitchen.

Laura couldn't breathe.

Jens stepped over the bloody path. She followed him. In the kitchen, they found Karl-Henrik lying facedown. He bent down to feel for Karl-Henrik's pulse. He shook his head and raised his eyes to meet Laura's. They were too late.

Jens reached for her, perhaps to take her in his arms, but she pushed him away. Instead, she sank down, leaning against the wall and sat staring at her former friend. He wouldn't have stood a chance. So much blood. She covered her face with her hands. Not Karl-Henrik!

She squinted her eyes as hard as she could. Her chest caved in with the pain. Karl-Henrik was gone. They should never have left him alone. They should never have . . .

The documents . . .

She forced herself together and opened her eyes. Forced her gaze away from her friend on the floor. Karl-Henrik's shelves were empty. His notes had all been removed. She rose and walked on shaky legs through the living room, searching for the bags they had brought this morning—nothing. She looked into the bedroom—they weren't there, either. All the material they had gathered was gone. *Fuck.*

She exhaled. *Fuck, fuck, fuck.* There were no notes, no files, no photographs. They'd taken them. Her friend was dead and all the proof was gone.

She walked back into the living room. Jens seemed to have come to the same conclusion. He met her gaze and shook his head.

They had killed Karl-Henrik right there in the middle of the room. His crutches were lying at the far end. The plaster on the wall above was cracked. They must have thrown the crutches against the wall. The wrecked room, the murdered man; the neighbors must have heard something. They had dropped the bags off with Karl-Henrik at seven that morning. The blood was dried brown. She knew nothing about crime scenes, but it occurred to her that the killing must have happened shortly after they had left. Perhaps someone had seen the perpetrators.

How did they know? she thought. Who had told them? Why oh why did they have to kill him . . .

She could visualize Karl-Henrik pulling himself along with the help of his arms and had to close her eyes briefly. It broke her heart imagining the scene.

"We have to go," Jens said. "If the police come now while we're still here, we'll be the prime suspects."

She squatted down by Karl-Henrik and put her hand on his back. I should have told you, she thought. How much you mattered.

"Come on," Jens said. "I'm surprised they're not here already. With all the noise, someone ought to have called them."

She straightened.

"How did they know?" Laura asked as they ran down the stairs.

Sirens! They were coming. Jens dragged Laura by the hand. They exited the building and hurried past it to a nearby café. They snuck in and sat down at one of the tables. Laura's heart was pounding. She was shivering, cold with shock.

"Tea?" the waitress asked.

"Yes," Jens said. "Two."

Through the window, they could see the arrival of the police: two squad cars, a bunch of officers running in and out of the building.

"It's like sorcery," Jens said. He shook his head. "It's as if they know how to be one step ahead of us at all times. I don't understand . . ."

"Emil!" Laura said.

They had forgotten all about the journalist. Then, on the other side of the pavement, they saw the young man. Trench coat and hat—briefcase under his arm. Jens half rose but Laura grabbed his hand and he sat down again. Emil spotted the police cars and slowed his gait. He put his head down and walked on, past the police, past the house.

"Clever man," Jens mumbled.

"I told him to keep away from the police."

The waitress came with their drinks. Laura's hands were shaking. Jens put his hand on hers. They must have looked like any young couple meeting for afternoon tea, perhaps upset after hearing some bad news: problems at work, maybe, or a death in the family. She took a breath and blew the air out slowly.

"It's all gone," he said. "What do we do now?"

56.

JENS

Only we knew," Laura said. "Only us. Unless one of you told someone else."

Matti and Erik shook their heads. Jens did the same. He had told no one. Of course not. They were in Jens's apartment in Old Town. It was overcast outside, dark clouds covering the sky.

"He died," Laura said, and her voice broke.

Jens wanted to put his hand on her shoulder, but it was Matti who moved closer to her.

"Perhaps the journalist . . ." Erik began.

"Oh, don't be daft!" Laura exploded. "It was the scoop of a lifetime!"

"We could have been followed," Matti said. "They could have had someone watching the Institute; someone we never noticed."

"Two of our friends have died," Laura said. "And it's all been in vain. We have nothing!"

She shut her eyes, then opened them again. "Yet we're still alive. Why?"

"Perhaps because of him," Erik muttered and nodded toward Jens.

"What do you mean?" Jens asked.

"He works for the Ministry of Foreign Affairs. How do we know he's not involved in this?"

Jens could feel himself bristle. No. He wouldn't get dragged into a war of words with this joker.

"I am not, but it's true, you can't know. Just like we can't know with you." He turned to Laura: "Or even you. But the four of us are all that is left. We have to trust each other."

"If they know, why don't they come for us?" Laura said. "Why are we protected?"

"We aren't," Matti said, slowly. "Look at what happened to Karl-Henrik."

"I think that's . . . new," Laura said.

"They don't have to come for us," Jens said. Even to himself, he sounded tired. "If you told people at this stage—who would believe you? I'm certain that if we manage to get fresh proof and hold onto it, they wouldn't hesitate, but at this stage," he shrugged, "the sad reality is that they don't have to."

"All our leads are gone," Laura said.

"There's still your professor . . . What was his name?"

"Professor Lindahl."

He nodded just as she shook her head.

"We'd never get to him," she said. "When we studied under him, I always had this impression that he was one step ahead of us."

"Then I guess we need to be two or three steps ahead of that," Jens said.

The sun broke through the clouds, daylight in all its glory. Laura, Erik and Matti looked white with tiredness. He imagined he looked just the same. Dead. They all looked dead.

═══

THAT AFTERNOON, JENS passed by the office to say he was no longer sick, and he'd be back the following day. On his desk were two messages: Sven's father, Magnus Feldt, had tried to contact him. Jens was so tired that he felt he could sleep standing up, but he called Magnus anyway.

Magnus cleared his throat. Speaking over the phone was not ideal, especially if the subject matter was politically dangerous. Jens could imagine him standing up, moving about, full of restless energy.

"Aha," he said. "Well, I called you regarding our friend."

Keeping it vague, Jens thought. "I thought that might have been it."

"I thought you would like to come with me to meet someone."

The fat man in the oil painting on Jens's office wall was staring at him, as always. Sneering.

"I'd love to," Jens said.

"Valhallavägen 132. I'll meet you outside in half an hour?"

The stomach swelled underneath the painted man's gold chain. *Not enough. Not enough.*

They finished the call. Jens took two steps and lifted the painting down, turning it to face the wall.

Behind him, someone cleared their throat. *Christian Günther.*

"So you're back," he said, looking at the painting on the floor. "Flu all gone?"

"All gone," Jens said.

His face had mostly healed, but he still had dark shadows under his eyes. Günther moved closer to study him now, as if he were looking for that very same thing.

"Very good. Schnurre was asking for you when I met with him yesterday."

Jens felt cold. "Asking for me? Why?"

"I don't know," Günther said. "He said he had something for you. Do you know what that might be?"

"I have absolutely no idea," Jens said.

"Well, I suggest you look him up. These Germans, when they don't get what they want . . . And then I want to know what it was all about."

Jens thought of Barbro. And of Britta, who was now dead.

"Yes," he said.

"Jens . . ." Günther started.

"Yes?"

Günther looked away. "Nothing," he said. "I'll see you tomorrow."

JENS WALKED THROUGH the small busy streets of Norrmalm, past the beautiful Östermalm Market Hall with its towers and glass ceiling. Past Humlegården Park and the Royal Library. Beautiful, glorious, and yet he would never look upon anything the same way again.

When he reached the gray, insignificant building on Valhallavägen, Magnus Feldt was already waiting for him outside.

"Come," he said and pushed open the door.

The office was in a normal flat, with two secretaries in the hallway. Magnus Feldt bypassed them with a nod and walked into a room that proved to be an office.

"Jens," he said, "this is Major Ternberg of the C-Bureau."

Major Ternberg was a middle-aged man; his hair was short, his eyes deeply set. His face was expressionless. He shook Jens's hand.

"Major Ternberg is managing the undercover operations concerning Germany," Magnus said.

Ternberg frowned. Magnus had said too much.

"Well, I'll wait in the hallway," Magnus said.

"I'm only meeting you because of Magnus," Ternberg said. "I assume I don't have to tell you that this meeting never happened. We don't exist."

Jens nodded. "You don't exist," he repeated.

"So you want to know about Miss Hallberg."

Jens nodded again.

"Britta was an unusual recruit. We prefer them to be employed: secretaries, translators . . . They tend to be more effective. She was also the first one we took on with a higher education."

Jens cringed. He could see it: naive young women, drawn in by some promise, spying on men older and shrewder than themselves, then unable to get out. And this man was not going to help them.

"But then there's Karl Schnurre," Major Ternberg said. "And he supports no fools."

Schnurre. Again.

"Britta was recruited with the one task of getting close to Karl Schnurre."

"And did it work?"

"Ah, yes. It did. We had her sit next to him at a dinner. That's all we had to do. Herr Schnurre liked her very much. He enjoyed sparring with her."

"And then what?"

"Then nothing," Ternberg said. "Britta died. We lost our source." He shrugged.

Jens felt his lips compress. Her death meant nothing to this man. "Do you think he killed her?" Jens asked.

"We know for a fact he didn't. He wasn't in Sweden the day when it happened."

"He could have hired someone."

Ternberg shrugged. "Naturally. But we won't look into that. We're trying to find someone else for him, someone equally effective. That will be more valuable to us than trying to frame him for some woman's death."

Jens was lost for words.

"I can see what you're thinking," Ternberg continued. "And yet, without us, Sweden would not have access to what the Great Powers are thinking and planning. And at the end of the day, at this stage of the war, for a small country like ours, knowledge is everything. Stop asking questions about Miss Hallberg. In the large scheme of things, her death is a very small matter."

Jens thought of Kristina, but he wouldn't ask about her. He wouldn't want to land anyone in this man's grip.

"I am not a spy," Barbro had said. "I won't be accused of being one. Could you imagine what would happen to me if Schnurre heard that? I'd be dead within the day."

Britta had been friendly with Schnurre. Now she was dead. They knew why she was dead, but it was still a hell of a coincidence.

57.

BLACKÅSEN MOUNTAIN

The boy was pacing the living room, wringing his hands.

"He'll be alright," the foreman said, though he had no idea.

"He has to be. He must!"

The doctor didn't come down. This was going to take some time, Hallberg thought.

"What are you doing here, anyway?" Hallberg asked. "Why aren't you with your people?"

"It's a long story," the boy said.

"We have time."

"I'm not sure I should tell you," the boy said. "What if you're one of *them*?"

It's the funniest thing, the foreman thought. This Sami boy, here in the director's house, so small and so dramatic! Then he thought of "them" and felt himself harden.

"Well," he sat down. "There's only one way to find out."

The boy bit his lip. The foreman could see his doubts. He tried to make his face gentler, more relaxed. *You can tell me.*

"Do you know Mr. Notholm?" the boy asked.

"Hate his guts," the foreman said.

This answer seemed to please the boy. "Me too," he said. "My sister disappeared in winter, but it began before that."

WHEN THE BOY had finished talking, Hallberg felt sick to his stomach. His daughter . . . This was why she'd died? He'd always assumed it had to do with a partner of some sort. "We don't always know what is truly in somebody else's heart," the director had said. Perhaps he was right.

He'd adored his only daughter when she was little. He couldn't wait to get back from the mine to see her toddling toward him on those fat white legs, the grin on her face when he lifted her up and how she buried her face in his neck. He had loved her so much it hurt.

Then she became a ten-year-old know-it-all; a sassy teen-ager—still a know-it-all. When she looked at him, her father, her siblings, her surroundings, it was on her face, as clear as if she'd said it out loud: she was better than this; better than them. She *resented* them.

She had been altogether different to them, almost like a changeling. Bright, for sure, but too selfish to use that intelligence for anything good.

But this . . . She had pursued an injustice, and that's what had gotten her killed.

Contrary to what most people assumed, the foreman had a lot of respect for the Sami. He was horrified by what the boy had just told him.

And it appeared his daughter had reacted just like him. His heart swelled. If he'd been on his own, he would have put his face in his hands and cried. For her, for himself, for the loss.

He cleared his throat.

The boy was still looking at him, his face worried.

"Here's what I want you to do . . ." the foreman said.

58.

LAURA

She wanted to come home, nurse her wounds, sleep a little, but her chest tightened with anxiety as she approached their house. The villa that normally lay in full splendour in the lush landscape, by the glittering sea, seemed unusually quiet. Though it was still day, the blackout curtains were drawn.

She opened the door. Instead of calling out "I'm home!" as she usually did, she paused inside the entrance and listened.

Nobody's home, she thought and exhaled.

She began walking down the corridor. She peeked into the kitchen and there he was: her father.

"Well, look who's here," he said.

She waited.

"I think that you're still not listening to me," he said.

She hung her head . . . thought about Karl-Henrik lying on the floor in his own blood.

Her father frowned. "Have I ever given you bad advice?"

"No." *Never.*

"Then why won't you listen to me on this?"

"Because it's about people," she said. "This is real. Another friend of mine died this morning."

"Then stop! For God's sake, Laura. Stop!"

"How could I? How can you know and not help?"

"You'll harm your country in ways you cannot begin to imagine. I have never asked you for anything, but I am asking you this: let it be."

She shook her head.

"Laura." Her father inhaled deeply. He seemed to be trying to calm down. "You owe me this. All I've done for you? Who got you into university?"

She hesitated. "I got in on my grades . . ."

"Ah." He nodded. "You think that was enough? A 'donation' to the university, that's what it took. Who made sure Professor Lindahl involved you in his little group? And the job with Wallenberg—who got you that?"

She was staggered. Had it all been her father? Had she achieved nothing on her own?

"You've sailed through life on my bank account, on my reputation, on my name. By yourself, you're nothing. And now I'm asking you, you stupid girl, for just one thing: leave this alone. Before it's too late and real harm is done."

"Merciless," her grandfather had called him.

"Is this what you did to my mother?" she asked, in a quiet voice.

He exhaled, a hard puff of air.

"This is how you drove her away when she wouldn't comply with your wishes? Pushing, threatening, *belittling* . . ."

"You are just like her," he said.

She clenched her fists by her sides.

"What did you do to make her leave?" she asked.

Her father rose from his chair. "I didn't make her leave!" he yelled. "One morning she was just gone. She didn't think to take

383

you with her, did she? I raised you instead. I gave you everything. I made it all happen for you . . . But I didn't raise you to this . . ."

"To what?" She was yelling, too.

"To disgust me!"

And that was it: nothing more needed to be said. Laura walked backward out of the kitchen, shaking her head.

59.

JENS

Jens was walking back to his apartment in Old Town, but as he reached the water, he stopped. He had to know what Schnurre had for him. The German trade delegation was housed not far from the foreign ministry. Walking distance, in case of a takeover. As he entered the building with the red Nazi flag flying high, he felt sick. Inside, he asked for Mr. Schnurre, hoping he'd be there, yet at the same time hoping that he wouldn't be.

"Jens," Schnurre said, as he was shown into his office, "you look absolutely dreadful."

"Yes," he said. Yes, he probably did.

"Coffee!" Schnurre shouted.

Jens startled.

They sat in silence until, a few moments later, a woman entered with a tray and served them each a cup.

"So, to what do I owe the pleasure?" The large man leaned back in his chair, resting his hands on his desk with the fingertips touching.

"You were asking for me."

"Aaah. That's right. I did." Schnurre did not elaborate further.

"And I wanted to ask you a question," Jens said. He tried to sound calm, though his heart was beating hard. If he was wrong, he'd cause immeasurable damage. If he was right, that seemed no better.

"Yes?"

"Do you remember the dinner party at my . . . at Kristina Bolander's house?"

"Of course."

"As you were leaving, you asked me if I thought we Swedes were clean. 'You should have a look in your own cupboards,' you said."

"Ah, that," Schnurre said and waved his hands as if it was nothing, just meaningless conversation, but there was a new look in his small eyes. Watchful. Calculating. Jens could see why Schnurre was Hitler's envoy in Stockholm. He felt cold.

"I'd like to know what you meant," Jens said.

Schnurre sipped his coffee, but his eyes did not leave Jens.

"I think I know some of it," Jens continued, "but I need to know who's involved."

"Who?" Schnurre shook his head. "Perhaps this is rather a question of who isn't'.

"You know," Jens said. "You know the details."

Jim Becker had said that the program had taken on an unbelievable magnitude. Was Christian Günther involved? His other colleagues? Friends?

Schnurre lit a cigar. He leaned back and the sofa creaked. He puffed smoke up to the ceiling.

"Of course I know," he said. "It's why I wanted to speak with you. We've followed your struggle from afar. Ah, Jens. You might think Germany is on its last legs, but we still have sharp teeth. The German network in this country is quite strong.

"Nah, the thinking in this project resonates strongly with our own. Apart from where the Scandinavian countries come together to fight Germany, of course.

"Your king and our emperor were close. He told our emperor about the real outcome of the meeting in 1914. Then, in 1922, Sweden set up the State Institute for Racial Biology, the first country in the world to do such a thing. In many ways, Sweden has been a model for us. A model for the world."

Jens felt nauseous.

"But then, with the change of leadership, the three countries lost heart. They tried to appear holier than thou. Neutral." He gave a false chuckle. "Last time we brought it up with your king, he made as if he didn't know what we were talking about.

"*Nein*, it is true. Things have not stopped. Right now, two out of three Scandinavian countries are under our command— precisely because of this very idea. But, from what we can tell, a pseudo government in Sweden is running in the shadow of the real government—bureaucrats influencing the decisions and then implementing what they want to be implemented. We'd like to see this stopped. We cannot have anyone working with the intent of overthrowing the Reich!"

Never had he thought he'd find himself on the same side as the Germans. "Names." Jens didn't recognize his own voice. "I need names."

"I'll do better than that," Schnurre said and pushed himself out of the armchair. He walked to the wall and lifted down a painting. Behind it was a safe. He put his cigar in an ashtray on the desk, punched in the code on the safe, opened the door and took out a large folder. "I'll give you what you need."

"You have evidence?"

"But of course."

Jens didn't know what to say. If he took this, he was running Germany's errands. But if he didn't, this evil would continue. It was the only chance he had.

"What's in this?" he asked.

"Photos, names . . ." The German shrugged. "But I ask you to be careful. I gave it to one other person, and she ended up dead."

"Britta Hallberg."

Schnurre nodded. "She was very interested in the matter."

"You were her 'uneasy friend,'" Jens said, remembering Laura's words.

"She used to call me that." The German nodded.

"Did you not kill her?"

Schnurre's eyes widened. "Why would I kill her? She wanted the same thing as me. Besides, I quite liked her. She knew about people disappearing in the north. I just fueled her interest. The last time I saw her, she had found out the name of a person involved. She was very upset, but she said she had a plan. If only she had proof. And so I gave her the proof she needed. And then, they got her . . ." He shook his head.

He had to know: "What about Kristina? How do you know her?"

Schnurre wiggled a fat finger. "Are you a suspicious lover? I know Kristina's father somewhat, that's all."

"She doesn't . . . work for you?"

"God, no. But somebody close to you does. Do you know a Mr. Enander? Lives in the same house as you? Now I am telling you secrets."

From now on, Jens would be linked to Schnurre. There were no favors that didn't demand a return. Barbro had lied. And Kristina might not have had anything to do with anything, after all. Not that it mattered. He and Kristina were over. For many reasons.

"I'm guessing Barbro has been telling lies," Schnurre said. "She's probably scared of what she's gotten herself into. Britta was better than her." He sighed theatrically. "She never pretended to be something she was not. I respected her for it. 'I am here to spy on you,' she said when we first met. I guess it's the times. Most people have more than one master."

Poor Barbro, Jens thought. She had feared Schnurre finding something out that he already knew.

Schnurre leaned forward and held out the thick folder. "Be careful, Jens," he advised. "Lift stones carefully, when you want to see who or what pops out from underneath. You are being watched. As soon as you leave this building, you will be running against the clock."

As Jens left the German trade delegation, the folder under his arm felt too obvious. He stuffed it under the front of his jacket. A woman walking her dog followed him with her gaze. A couple of men came out of the Grand Hotel as he passed and jumped into a waiting car. Jens crossed the street to walk by the water. As he came to the famous restaurant, Operakällaren, someone shouted from the top of the stairs: "Jens!"

He just raised his hand. No time to stop.

A man began walking on the opposite side of Strömgatan, same direction as Jens, same pace. Was he one of them?

There was nobody else close by. Jens quickened his pace. The man on the other side did the same.

He reached the foreign ministry, figuring he'd go into his office, but then the man he had thought was following him

389

turned and jogged up the steps to the opera house, greeted a waiting woman and kissed her on the cheek.

Ghosts, Jens thought. He was seeing ghosts. He had to get rid of this bloody file.

He continued onto Malmtorgsgatan only to see three men walk in after him.

He began to run. Slowly at first then with all his might. Past Jacobsgatan, the tails of his jackets flying, into Karduansmakargatan. He didn't stop until he'd pushed open the doors to the office of the newspaper *Svenska Dagbladet*.

"Emil Persson, please," he said to the receptionist, breathlessly.

His heart was pounding. The street outside was empty. He walked to the window. Nobody was outside.

Emil came down. "You look like you've been running," he said.

Jens shrugged.

"Would you like something to drink?" Emil asked.

Jens shook his head. He only wanted to leave the folder and be done with it all.

Then the three men Jens had seen on Malmtorgsgatan entered the reception. Emil saw Jens's gaze.

"Come," he said. He opened a door and they walked into what must be the printing house. The printers were working full speed. The room smelled of oil and paper.

"Here," Jens said and handed the folder to Emil, who took it.

Emil opened the folder, flipped the pages.

"Whatever you do, don't relax," Jens said. "Stay alert. Look over your shoulder at all times. You get one shot at publishing this. One. Then they'll get to you. They'll stop at nothing."

Emil frowned.

"I mean it," Jens said.

The journalist licked his lips. "I'll go back to my office now," he said. "It'll be out tomorrow." He pointed to another door. "This door leads out to the back. You might want to take it."

60.

BLACKÅSEN MOUNTAIN

The director's living room was large and bright. Gunnar stood in the doorway. The curtains were a glossy yellow; the desk made of dark shiny wood. There was a cabinet with sparkling glass bottles on top of it and a patterned carpet on the floor. He had never seen a room like it.

"Enter," his father said, as if it were his house. Gunnar took a step to the side so as not to walk on the rug.

Behind him came miners who worked for his father. Just like Gunnar, each one paused in the entrance, taking in the cleanliness, the light, the pretty colors. Each of them avoided the rug.

The door kept opening and closing. The room became full of men in workers' clothes, and yet his father didn't start. He was waiting for something, Gunnar thought. Or someone.

Dr. Ingemarsson came downstairs. If he was surprised at all the men in the living room, he didn't show it. "Infection," he said grimly. "We have no penicillin. I have given him sulfa and now we must hope for the best. I will stay with him for now."

He asked the housekeeper to bring more hot water and then went back upstairs.

The men looked at the foreman, shuffled their feet, waited.

Then: a soft knock on the door.

The foreman walked to open it. They heard him greet some-one and then he walked back to show them in.

The Sami!

His father had been waiting for them?

They entered in their leather trousers, long woven shirts and those distinctive hats on their heads. A long line of men. A young boy much like himself among them.

The miners shuffled their feet and withdrew to the back wall.

"Well," the foreman said and began talking. He talked for a long time. Once he stopped, the room was so still, no one could have guessed it was full of men.

Gunnar thought about Mr. Notholm and the hare and felt sick. This was Sweden. Yet it was the same as what Hitler was doing. They'd read about it, his mother sighing and shaking her head. This was why his sister had died?

The room was still quiet.

The foreman looked out at his men and Gunnar could see what he must be thinking. Find it in your hearts. Find compas-sion. Find justice. His father had tried his best. He had laid out the facts and made his views clear. But some of his men still hated the Sami. They feared them. Feared anything that was different. Some of them might just subscribe to the view that the Sami were beneath them.

After what seemed like an eternity, Robert, one of the older miners, cleared his throat. "Well," he said in his slow, singsong voice, "we can't have that. Not on our mountain."

Then the men around Robert began to nod. "Right," some-one said. "Yes," someone agreed. The Sami raised their heads. His father exhaled. His men had come through.

TOGETHER THEY WORKED out a plan. They would try their best to avoid bloodshed.

"Do we have any idea how many there are?"

"No," the foreman said. "And we won't know until tonight. We are going to have to improvise as we don't have much time. Your people," he said to Nihkko, "need to make sure the captured Sami know what's going on. I don't want them to get themselves killed. We'll take the guards out one by one. The four men who arrived from Stockholm . . . I assume they're police or similar. We need to be careful."

"Just make sure Mr. Notholm is there," the young Sami boy said and, beside him, Gunnar nodded. "You need to take him first. Make sure he doesn't get away."

"We will," the foreman said, grimly. "We will."

"So what do we do with them once we've captured them?" It was a heavyset balding man who asked.

"Let's kill them," one of the other miners said.

"Then we would be no better than them," the foreman said. "Bill, do you have space in your prison?"

"For sure, but if what you've told us is true, wouldn't they just be released by somebody higher up?"

The foreman fell silent. Bill was right.

"Could we hide them?" he asked, finally. "Without anyone knowing?"

"For how long?"

The foreman shrugged again.

The room was quiet again. Then Bill spoke: "I don't need to remind you of the risks. If one of us talks . . ."

"I say we vote," the foreman said. "If anyone has any qualms, speak now. Otherwise we will all be equally at fault. All of those in favor, raise your hands."

There was a sea of hands before him. Unwavering, reaching high. There was no doubt.

"Will we tell the director?" Bill asked.

"No. We'll tell no one who wasn't part of the decision. You and I will take care of it, Bill. We will destroy this setup without anyone ever knowing what happened here. It will be as if it never was. And then we will pretend we know nothing. Or we will all be at risk. Understood?"

There was a hum of agreement.

"Well then, let's get going."

61.

LAURA

Laura avoided her father. He had only ever loved her when she was compliant. Everything she was, everything she did— even debating with him—had been alright if it didn't question his authority. She could see that now. As long as she didn't think for herself.

Was he right about Sweden?

She assumed, in some ways, yes. She was taking a side and it was ripping her family apart. If they succeeded, it would rip Sweden apart, too. It wasn't clear what she would be left with. She imagined that many people would act like her father: simply choose not to see. But she didn't feel she had a choice.

Britta and Karl-Henrik would have agreed.

She comforted herself with this. As if their moral compasses were stronger than her own and deserved to be heeded.

SUMMER HAD REACHED Uppsala. The town was green and lush. It was early morning. People walking to work or to school were dressed in light clothes. Professor Lindahl was around. She had checked with his office. Laura and Jens had agreed to simply wait for him until he came, no matter how long it took.

Jens had told her what Schnurre had given him and that Emil had promised the story would appear in today's newspaper.

"So what's the plan?" Jens asked, as they walked to the university building.

His blond hair was standing up. He looked drawn, tired.

"I don't know," she admitted. "I just want to hear him say it: confess it."

"You didn't bring Erik today?" Jens asked. "Or Matti?"

"No."

"Why?"

"I don't know . . . I thought . . . I couldn't see us confronting him together."

They passed the café where Britta had met with Sven Olov Lindholm. There was something about that meeting with the Swedish Nazi leader that still bothered her; something she ought to see but couldn't.

THEY WAITED FOR Professor Lindahl outside the classroom where they'd been told he'd teach next. There was a hollow feeling to the room without its students. Her heart was beating too fast. She was frightened. There was an odor to fear, she thought, and remembered where she had smelled it last: it had been on Britta, when the two of them met at the café in Stockholm. Now it was on her.

Jens glanced at her. Then he took her hand. They sat like that, hand in hand. The emotion made her want to cry. She longed to lean her head against his shoulder and forget everything that had happened . . . everything that had brought them to this point. But then there were muffled footsteps on the stairs, and they let go of each other.

As always, Professor Lindahl was dressed in black. His white hair was combed to the side, his lips were full, and his eyes with their different colors opened wide as he took them in.

"Laura Dahlgren," he said in his soft voice. "How nice." He looked at Jens. "And you're here, too," he said. "Welcome."

Laura got the impression that Lindahl was not taken aback that she had come, nor that Jens had come with her. He'd been told to expect them. He unlocked the door to the classroom and invited them in.

"So," he said. "Here you are. I'm surprised."

"Are you?" she asked.

"You never committed to anything, Laura. I would have thought that the obstacles thrown in your way would have stopped you by now."

Her heart sank. Then he did know. Of course he did. Dead friends, a blown-up apartment . . . To him, they were just "obstacles"?

"This time, the cause seemed worth it," she said.

He nodded. "Well, you should be proud of yourself. You've given us a good fight. In fact, you've helped us. You've shown us the weaknesses in our systems. We'll improve as a result."

"Why?"

He laughed. "You want me to talk about the many reasons underlying a program like this one? The fiasco of democracy, the weakening of our own race, the sullying of the elite, the continual decline of wisdom to sheer stupidity?

"You used to agree with the importance of an elite. After all, your own work, the one you did with your friends on Asatru, has

398

served as our inspiration. And do not forget, Laura, you are a child of this."

"A child of this?"

Professor Falk had been right, she thought. He had feared what Lindahl had been up to; seen the influence he had over them. Perhaps he had tried to protect them.

It dawned on her.

"It was you in my flat every night! You read our paper."

"I did," he said. "I was not displeased."

"You groomed us," Laura said.

"You met all the requirements. I just didn't think you'd be so conventional. Your group was so close: I didn't realize this close-ness could mean I might lose all of you at once." He tilted his head, reproach in his voice.

He had given their names to Inspector Ackerman, Laura thought. He had told him about their interest in Norse faith, about them falling apart. To him, it was all a game. He had never doubted he would come out on top.

Jens had been sitting there in silence with his head down, but now he looked up. "You do realize you'll pay a price? Just like Germany will when it falls."

"Perhaps."

"It will be all over the newspapers later today and there is nothing you can do to stop it."

Lindahl nodded. "I heard about that, yes. However, if you buy the paper, I think you'll find there's nothing in it. Emil Persson left on a long holiday this morning."

Beside her, Jens's face was white.

"He has gone traveling," the professor said. "Nobody knows when he will return."

"We'll find someone else."

"Ah, before he left, Emil handed over all his material. He could see that, for his own good, he shouldn't be hanging on to it. No, there will be no article. Not now. Not later. You gave it your best shot. It was not enough."

Jens opened his mouth, but Lindahl held up a finger. "And I think you'll find that your German connection will no longer cooperate. He's gone out on a limb for this matter twice now to no avail. We've had to remind him what it means to interfere in another state's business."

"We'll get you," Jens said.

"It will be harder now," Lindahl said. "But I do look forward to seeing you try."

62.

JENS

Jens was in a café on Östermalm. He was on his fifth beer, or perhaps it was his sixth. There had been whiskies, too. I need a drink, he'd thought. Once he'd begun, he'd realized that what he needed was to drink himself into oblivion. Try and forget all about what was happening, if only for a while.

"They got away," Jens said to himself. Again.

The room reeled and Jens frowned. He tried to concentrate on his glass. It went in and out of focus. He was drunk.

He put his head down on the table and breathed. The wood felt cool against his forehead.

"We're closing now, sir," the waitress said.

He sat up again. "Alright," he said. "I'm fine."

"And there's a man in a car outside waiting for you."

A BLACK VOLVO was parked at the curb. Jens recognized the car. The window rolled down and Christian Günther looked out.

"I'll drive you home," he said.

"I'm drunk," Jens said. "A bit drunk."

"I don't blame you," Günther said.

"Very drunk, actually," Jens admitted.

Günther opened the car door.

"I haven't been to work much lately," Jens said.

"I don't blame you for that, either."

Jens wiped his mouth with two fingers.

He got in the backseat beside the minister. He must reek of alcohol and smoke. Günther was looking out the window at the water. He turned to Jens.

"You did well," he said. "Everything I had hoped for and more."

Jens's mind felt fuzzy. "What?"

"You've done well," Günther repeated.

His words cut through the fog. "It was you," Jens said. "The materials on my desk."

"I was trying to help you."

It was Günther! He was on their side.

"Tell me about the phone calls," Jens said.

"We were discussing this," Günther admitted. "Or rather, how to stop it. All the current foreign ministers in the Scandinavian countries came in after the fact."

"We failed."

"You got close to exposing it. Closer than any one of us has done."

"What happens now?"

"We continue," Günther said. "And we want you to join us."

Jens could have cried: Christian Günther was not a part of the evil he had seen; they had done well. And it was not finished yet. And he was not alone.

They had arrived at Jens's apartment. The car stopped.

"We'll find a way," Günther said. "We will not let this evil win."

Jens nodded. "Thank you."

"Now try to get some sleep."

63.

BLACKÅSEN MOUNTAIN

Taneli lay behind a large rock. Close to him were Olet, the foreman and a few other men. Just like the previous night, the area was busy, with Sami prisoners carrying boxes out of the mine opening and loading them onto horses. The sun just over the horizon gave the scene a surreal feeling.

Taneli counted the armed guards. There were six of them on horses, guns lifted high. Two local men and four men in suits he'd never seen before. Another couple of men by the entrance to the mine. How many there would be inside the galley they didn't know. And he couldn't see Mr. Notholm.

He half rose. Where was he?

There! On his horse at the entrance to the forest. Why was he so far away? Watching over it all but not partaking.

Notholm rode up to the guards. "I'll head back," he said. "See you later."

Back where? To town?

"Don't mess up," one of the men in suits said.

Notholm frowned. "Of course not," he said.

The foreman wrinkled his forehead. "I'll go after him," he said. "Peter and Hans, you come with me. The rest of you are on your own here. But everyone knows what they're supposed to do." Then he and his men went to find their horses.

Be careful, Taneli thought. Notholm is vile.

"Are you sure about this?" one of the suits said to the other. "Would have been better if we did it ourselves."

The other one shrugged. "He's motivated enough," he said. "And the man's sick. How hard can it be?"

A wolf howl. Nihkko, Taneli thought.

"What was that?" one man asked.

"A wolf." One of the others laughed. "You scared?"

"It just sounded close," he muttered.

"Well then, go have a look if you're worried," his friend said. "Right."

The man kicked the side of his horse and rode toward the sound, where Nihkko and the others were hiding, where they'd pull him off his horse and silence him.

"John?" his friend asked after a while. "John?"

"Gone wolf hunting," another one sniggered.

"Taking a shit, more like it," someone else muttered.

There was a kerfuffle from the wood, wings beating, a cry, branches breaking.

"John!"

"That's just a grouse taking flight," one of the local men said. "Your friend must have disturbed it."

The men were looking in the direction of the thicket now. Taneli held his breath for what was to come. Olet left his side. He made his way in among the captured Sami, grabbed a box and hoisted it onto a horse's back. At the same time, three of the guards were pulled down from their horses and replaced by three miners. It was so quiet, only shadows moving. The three new guards took their horses farther away and made sure to keep their faces turned so as not to be noticed.

"Hey, you!" one of the remaining guards suddenly shouted; one of the local men.

Taneli held his breath. The guard was pointing his rifle at Olet.

Olet approached, head down.

"I haven't seen you before," the guard said.

"Come on," another guard said. "How could you possibly say that?"

"No, it's true," the first guard said. "Look at him. He's fatter than the others, too."

"You're seeing things. How would we suddenly have a new prisoner?"

The first guard muttered something but lowered his weapon.

Nihkko and his men rushed to pull the two down but not before one of the guards managed to let out a shout before being silenced.

"What's going on down there?" A guard at the mine entrance was looking over at them.

"Nothing!" one of the miners shouted back. "John here is unsteady on his horse, that's all. First it's wolves. Now it's his horse." He laughed and the other miners chimed in.

Please, Taneli thought. Please don't come and check.

"Bloody amateurs," the guard at the opening replied.

Taneli exhaled.

A line of Sami joined the prisoners. Don't react, Taneli thought to the prisoners, and they didn't. The way they looked . . . Perhaps they were beyond reacting. The tribesmen walked up the slope, heads bent. The miners watched intently.

A quick attack. Two more guards down. Two more tied. Now, the only ones remaining were the ones inside the mine.

The miners joined the Sami, running up the slope to the opening of the mine.

Taneli ran with them. He needed to be there. He needed to find his sister.

As he came closer to the prisoners, he saw they had been starved. Their ragged clothing hung off them. Their heads had been shaved and their eyes looked like black buttons in their gaunt faces.

"You can sit down now," one of the miners said to one of the Sami prisoners. He lifted his box off his shoulders.

The man stared at him with empty eyes.

"It's over," the miner said. "You're free."

TANELI FOLLOWED THE Sami and the miners into the depths of the earth. The path was sloping downwards. It was getting cooler.

Soon, the ragged mine path turned to cement. A floor. An antiseptic smell; same as at the doctor's clinic. There were side rooms, hospital beds, surgical instruments, shelves full of jars.

The corridor opened up into a larger room. The room was full of cages. All were empty apart from the farthest one. Inside were four girls. Their bones protruded so sharply that it hurt to look. They were filthy dirty, and they were naked.

Around him, men were wrestling other men. Taneli ran for the cage. And his sister.

As he approached, she lifted her head. She made a croak that didn't sound human. A thin scream. A bird's cry.

Using his fingers, Taneli tore at the chain securing the door.

"Here." One of the miners had found a pair of bolt cutters. He cut the chain and they opened the door to the cage. Javanna crawled out first. She tried to stand but couldn't. Taneli put his arm around her waist and held her up. There were no words.

"Javanna," he whispered.

Gunfire. They froze. A man ran out from a side door, carrying a rifle. One of the miners fell to the ground. Two. Then Nihkko leaped at the man. A flash of silver, a gargling sound, and the man fell.

After that, all was quiet . . . until someone began to cry.

64.

LAURA

Laura was sitting on the dock by the water outside her father's house. The evening was warm, with a blend of apple blossom and seawater in the air. The dark water moved slowly, clucking when it hit the wooden pillars.

There was nowhere to go. No hope. The evidence was gone again. What had they threatened Emil with? Professor Lindahl had won. How could she not have seen what he was like? They had talked about the elite a lot. It had all sounded right to her.

"Most Swedes were caught up in the rhetoric," Jens had said on the way home when she tried to express her feelings of guilt to him. "Nobody ever imagined it would go this far."

"They think we're beaten," she said.

"But we are not." But then he sighed and fell silent.

She wished Karl-Henrik was still with them. He was so good at seeing a way forward.

She didn't think she could face her father. Now that she knew what he thought of her, how could she? Somewhere in her mind, she had always hoped he would admit to having driven her mother away. It would have been easier. Instead, her mother had simply left and not tried to bring Laura with her.

For years, Laura had secretly thought that, one day, her mother would seek her out. Perhaps when she turned eighteen. *I'll explain everything. This is why I've been absent . . .*

On her eighteenth birthday, a thick white envelope had indeed arrived, addressed to Laura. It had been lying on the table together with the presents and the cake. Her heart had bumped in her chest. Thoughtlessly, her father had snatched it up and opened it—as if all mail that arrived at the house was for him. "Would you believe it?" He'd chuckled and waved the pages in the air. "You're invited to buy shares in L.M. Ericsson. What do you think?"

That was when she'd understood it would never happen. And something had broken inside her—she had felt it crack. Her mother had not once looked back. She might even have forgotten what day her daughter was born.

Time had shown her again and again that her mother was not going to come back for her.

Time . . .

Wait . . .

That was what was wrong about the meeting between Britta and Sven Olov Lindholm. Britta had met with him on the Thursday and died on the Monday. After months of researching and digging for her thesis, she had, after that meeting, taken actions that led to her death just four days later. And it had begun with her seeing Sven Olov. She thought about what he had said he told Britta: "Rumors of a project . . . Highest levels . . . Stop at nothing."

It wasn't enough. Britta would have had no idea where to go after that. Just like Laura hadn't. Something had happened that weekend that got her killed. Perhaps he had told Britta more. Something that he hadn't told Laura.

SHE FOUND SVEN Olov as he was getting ready for a late-night speech in a gloomy conference room with gray walls.

He exhaled noisily when he saw her. "I told you, I won't talk to you again." He began unpacking his briefcase, throwing bundles of paper down on the desk in front of him.

"You told Britta more than you told me," she said.

He remained silent, continued unpacking. A newspaper. A pen.

"You gave her a name," she guessed. "A starting point."

Sven Olov stopped moving. He straightened to look at her, folding his arms.

"That name got her killed," Laura said. "And then you got scared."

Still nothing.

"Sven Olov, I will not leave you alone until you tell me."

"They'll kill you."

She shrugged. "That's not your problem."

"They'll kill me, too."

"I don't think so. Nobody came after you after you spoke to Britta. Nobody needs to come now. *I* won't tell."

He sighed and shook his head as if wondering how he got himself into this situation. Then he met her gaze. "I told her about a Dane who was seemingly fixing things for this organization."

A Dane?

"An Erik Anker," he said, grudgingly. "For some reason, that name really upset Britta."

LAURA FOUND ERIK at the Grand. All the way there, she tried to deny it. It couldn't be him. He'd loved Britta. He was with Laura when her apartment blew up. He . . .

But for every argument there was a counterargument.

This time, his eyes didn't light up when he saw her. She walked over to stand beside him at the bar. The women around them were dressed as if for a summer party—beautiful dresses, flowers in their hair. They were drinking champagne. Champagne!

"I'd offer you a drink," Erik said, "if I thought you'd come for one."

"How could you?"

He leaned close to her and wrapped his fingers around her wrist. A gentle grip, but one that hurt, nevertheless.

"Look at the world we live in, Laura," he said. "Professor Lindahl showed us that we have to safeguard what is Scandinavian. Otherwise, in a few decades, there will be nothing of us left."

"Those people . . ." She choked. "God, Erik . . ."

"The world is falling apart. The current systems aren't strong enough. The Scandinavian race has a chance, but not if it is sullied by other races. Scandinavia could become a powerful nation once again. Can you imagine that? Can't you see how crucial this is?"

"Our project," she said.

"Once we started, it was obvious. Professor Lindahl agreed. He said the project could add value on a much greater level."

"How could you?" she repeated, crying now.

"It's easy for you," he said, and his face was bitter. "You've never had to work for anything."

"And Britta?"

He let go of her, grimaced, rubbed his forehead with his knuckles.

She felt light-headed . . . nauseous. "Tell me you didn't," she begged. "Oh Erik, please say it wasn't you!"

She put her hand on the bar to steady herself. She looked at him: his drawn cheeks, the black eyes. She couldn't believe it. He had killed her. *Tortured* her. Britta's lover, the boy who adored her, had turned into her worst nightmare.

"It was that bloody thesis," he said. "She was obsessed. I tried to get her to stop, but she wouldn't. Someone kept supplying her with clues about the network and then, in the end, provided her with proof. She also got my name—from him or somebody else. She went crazy! Luckily, she took it all to your father. He called me . . ."

"My father?"

Erik sighed and lowered his head.

The room fell away from her. There was a buzzing in her ears, and she couldn't see clearly.

"I don't believe you," she said shakily.

"Believe what you want," he said. "*Your father* called me and told me to get rid of the problem."

She couldn't even understand his words. It couldn't be true. It just couldn't. But it explained so much. Her father's refusal to get involved. His attempts to quash her. The fact that she was still alive . . .

"But we couldn't find her thesis. We were convinced she'd written about what we were doing in there, but the thesis was gone. We thought she'd sent it to you."

"The bomb," she said.

He nodded. "My job was to keep you away. I almost didn't

manage it. She should have listened to me, Laura. You all should have," Erik said. "We had the truth in our project. Instead, you tried to close it down." His eyes were glittering now.

"The eye . . . Her body at the Historical Society . . . They were messages for us," she concluded.

"You never saw," he said, and now he sounded bitter again. "You had everything from the beginning. You refused to see how important it was for Scandinavia and the rest of us."

She shook her head. "Britta didn't have it all from the beginning," she said. "You know this. She was born in a mining town to a miner, for Christ's sake."

"She latched onto you as if it were her right," he said. "As if she belonged with you." He scoffed. "I wasn't good enough for her and yet we were cut from the same cloth."

She could see it all laid out in front of her now. Her father taking the evidence from Britta, promising to help. The phone call to Erik. Erik at the university, smiling at the women working in the administration office, taking the key to the Historical Society off its hook.

"Where did you kill her?" she asked.

"At the Institute," he said. "I said I needed to see her one last time—for old times' sake."

She shook her head. Britta had still trusted him, perhaps still loved him. She had come one last time, never thinking he might harm her. She visualized Erik carrying Britta across the square, unlocking the door to the Historical Society.

"Who killed Andreas?"

He shrugged. It was him. Of course it was, she thought. Erik had been in the military. That was when he had learned to shoot.

"And Karl-Henrik?"

He shrugged again. "I like you, Laura," he said. "I had hoped you'd come around, or at least understand to leave well enough alone."

He looked different now. He was no longer Erik the student, the friend, the drinking buddy, but Erik the policeman. A soldier. Ready for everything.

He shook his head. "I could have killed you a thousand times, Laura, but your father wouldn't let me. A thousand times, he said no. In Lapland, I had you in my sights. It would have been so easy. I told him you were getting too close, but he said you'd never make it all the way. Not without him. And here we are. Now look, Laura. Look what you've done."

She straightened.

"Leaving already?" He nodded. "Well, I'll see you around. Perhaps sooner than you think."

His eyes were on hers, steady, cold. As she walked away, she could feel them following her.

She walked downstairs, then ran. She pushed open the heavy doors, hurried down the steps. At the side of the hotel, she vomited. When there was nothing left to bring up, she sank down on the pavement, head on her knees, chest still heaving. Erik had tortured Britta while she was still alive. And then he had killed her. All with her father's approval. And she . . . she *was* a child of this. She remembered the scribbled note in Britta's room: *Worst is that evil which could be normal;* the crossed out *normal* replaced with *good.*

SHE WALKED. SHE walked through Stockholm and the warm night, along the water, out to Djursholm. She cried the whole way. Sometimes she had to stop to lean against a wall, she was crying so hard. And then, in the early morning hours, she was there, outside her father's house. And she took the wide avenue of elm trees and walked up to the white villa, smelling the apple trees, smelling the sea. She'd been so happy here; felt so protected. She had had it all.

She wasn't certain why she had come. She wouldn't be able to make a difference. And yet she had to speak with him. She had to tell him that she knew and how he disgusted her.

She walked up the steps to the porch.

Then someone moved in one of the chairs and she gave a small shriek.

"It's me." Her grandfather's voice. He was sitting with a blanket around him.

"What's going on? Where's my father?" she asked.

"Oh Laura. He went to his office and locked the door. I heard a gunshot. Laura, what has he done?"

65.

JENS

When Laura called, Jens had a pounding headache and swore at himself. He got up and dressed. He swigged three big glasses of water and ran down the stairs. Laura had sent her father's driver to pick him up and the car was already on the street below his apartment. He wished he'd taken the time to brush his teeth.

As the car entered the driveway, Laura came out to meet him.

"They've just taken him away," she said. "His body."

Her face was swollen, her eyes red, and he put his arms around her and pulled her close.

"What happened?" he asked.

She withdrew. "Erik is part of this—Sven Olov Lindholm told me. When I confronted Erik, he told me about my father. I was going to talk to him . . . I think. But when I got here, it was too late."

Erik. Somewhere Jens felt relief. Not sorcery. Not an all-seeing evil. That was why the network had been one step ahead of them all the way. Erik.

It was too early, but he had to ask. "Do you think there's anything in his office?"

"No." She shook her head. "I already went through it. Before I called the police. I didn't want anyone to take anything away."

He cringed at the image: Laura stepping over her father's body to search his belongings. She'd already had to endure too much. But then she was stronger than she thought.

They sat down on the porch steps. There was twittering coming from the elm trees. Birds shouting that they had survived yet another night.

"Jens, my father . . . He must have felt he had no option," Laura said, wiping away tears. "Erik must have told him I knew. And then he—"

Laura sobbed and covered her mouth with her hand. Jens put his arm around her back.

"It couldn't have gone any other way," he said. "Once he chose this path, this was how it had to end."

He held her until the worst was over. Then he told her about Christian Günther.

"It feels good knowing that it isn't only us who are working against this," she said.

He agreed. The grown-ups had finally gotten themselves involved.

"I can't believe he would do this," she said, returning to her father.

"Were there any signs?"

"Never. He had this saying: 'And we go on.' He never gave up. Ever. And a gunshot is crude." She shrugged. "He liked neat. *And* he didn't leave a note. I would have expected him to try to make sure I knew he was right."

"I'm sorry."

"It's like my identity is gone. His daughter . . . that's all I've ever been my whole life."

"You are much more than just his daughter," Jens said. "Perhaps," he spoke carefully now, for he didn't want to make things worse, "his death will open things up for you. In ways you never thought possible."

She didn't respond. But he could feel her sitting up straighter. Getting ready, he thought, to face the day.

66.

BLACKÅSEN MOUNTAIN

The local hotel, the Winter Palace, lay dark. The front door was locked. Hallberg gave a sign to one of his men and he kicked the door in.

Dust whirled as they pushed open the door. The hallway was empty. There was nobody at the reception desk. A ghost house, the foreman thought, though he didn't believe in ghosts.

"Notholm?" He called. The man must already know they were there.

All was silent.

"Perhaps he left?" one of his men said.

But Hallberg thought not.

"The director!" he suddenly realized. "That's where he's gone."

The three men sprinted through the village. They turned into the director's garden, gravel scraping under their feet.

They found their friends lying on the ground. It looked like they were sleeping, but Harald was bleeding from his head and Ivar's body was lying in a strange position. Notholm had arrived first.

Hallberg raised a finger to his mouth. "I'll go," he whispered.

Once inside, carefully, he walked up the steps toward the director's bedroom.

He pushed open the door to the bedroom with one finger, gun aimed, and found himself facing another gun.

"Drop your gun," Notholm said, "or the director dies."

Hallberg obliged. Notholm turned his weapon back on Sandler. "Wake up," he said and poked him with his gun. "Wake up!"

"He's sick," the foreman said.

In the corner of his eye, he saw the door behind Notholm open. *Dr. Ingemarsson.*

"Shut up!" Notholm cried and turned his gun back on the foreman. "I want him to know what's happening. I want him to know he lost."

He turned back to the director.

The doctor was approaching Notholm, something in his hand. A walking stick? The doctor stuck it in Notholm's back. "Drop your gun," he said.

Notholm's eyes grew large and he dropped his weapon. Hallberg was on him at once, wrestled him down and shouted for his men.

"A STICK," HE said to the doctor later.

The doctor laughed. "I wouldn't have let him kill a man I'd just saved."

"The infection?"

"He's lucky. He's responding to the sulfa. I think he'll make it."

Hallberg nodded. "We'll take care of Notholm."

"Meaning?"

The foreman hesitated.

"Actually, I think I'd rather not know," the doctor said.

"He won't be staying in Blackåsen," Hallberg concluded.

"Let me go," Notholm demanded as they took him outside. "You have no idea who you're up against. They'll come for you. You'll see."

"Shut him up," the foreman said.

They found Dr. Öhrnberg at home, fast asleep.

"We have Notholm, too," they told him as he got dressed.

"You don't understand," Öhrnberg said. "It's for the sake of science. It's for Sweden."

Hallberg understood only too well. Notholm was just a sadistic person turned evil because he was given the opportunity. This man, however, was a true ideologist: a man at service of a cause—all in the name of science.

THEY BURIED THE dead miners in the graveyard just behind the church.

"I'll go and see their widows in the morning," the foreman said. "I'll say there was an accident in the mine."

His men nodded. They wouldn't talk. The things they had discovered during the night would haunt them for years. But they wouldn't talk.

He longed to tell their families about the cause for which their men had died, but it was a slippery slope. He could tell no one. They had buried the men in unmarked graves and he planned to tell the families there were no remains. This bothered him, too.

"I'll discuss it with the director," he said. "Maybe we can set up a fund for the widows . . . There are a few."

Then he looked at Bill. It would be hardest on himself and

Bill. It wasn't over for them, by any means. Bill met his gaze and it didn't waver.

"Notholm, Öhrnberg, and the men who came with the train have left," Hallberg repeated. "Before leaving, they told people they were heading south."

The doctor joined them.

"Accident in the mine," Hallberg said, clearing his throat and nodding at the new graves.

"Anybody else hurt?" the doctor asked.

"No." Hallberg shook his head.

"The director wants to see you."

"He's awake?"

"Yes. Just woke up . . . I didn't tell him about Notholm."

"Good idea," Hallberg said. "Might set him back."

"Right."

The doctor raised his hand. "Well, I'll be heading home now. Let me know if you need me."

SANDLER WAS PROPPED up on pillows. His upper body was bare and his chest was heavily bandaged. His face looked ashen, but there was a glint in his eye.

"I'm told Taneli . . . the young boy who stayed here . . . has left," he said.

Hallberg nodded. "Moved home. It was time. He got what he needed. You'll see him around."

"What all happened while I slept?" the director asked.

"Not much." The foreman shrugged.

"Not much?"

"Notholm left," he said. "Dr. Öhrnberg, too."

"Really?"

Hallberg nodded. "Said they were going south, that they didn't want to rent land on the mountain any longer."

Ah, so. The Director lifted his chin.

"Things will be easier now," the foreman said to his director.

"You think?"

"I know so."

67.

LAURA

She had searched the whole house twice before she found the box. It was hidden in her father's office—behind the books in his bookshelf. It contained letters to her. To baby Laura. Then, later, to Laura the child, Laura the teenager . . . Thick white letters. Just like the one that had arrived on her eighteenth birthday.

I just want to see you, the letters said. *Just a short visit. But he won't let me. I think he might hurt you or me if I try . . .*

Before we married, he was sensible, charming. I fell for it. I can only hope and pray that he loves you enough not to do the same things to you . . .

We were his possessions. I tried to take you with me, but you were his and he wouldn't let me . . .

Page after page of her mother's handwriting, the ink blotched with what might have been her tears, and now she was adding her own.

Her grandfather had read them, too.

"I'm so sorry," he said. "I didn't know about these. I really didn't."

All these wasted years.

Her tears came when her grandfather went to bed. She had

cried so much she felt drained. Her hands were trembling, and her arms were weak. How could he have done this? She was sitting in the bay window in the living room as dusk fell. The lights were off in the room and the darkness swam in and out of the window from the garden.

There was an address on the letter. A street in the south of Stockholm. She would find her mother—if it wasn't already too late. The last letter was dated over two years ago.

Something scraped on the upper floor. She stiffened. Her grandfather's bedroom was on the main floor. None of the servants slept in the house. Perhaps she'd been mistaken? No. She had heard it, she was certain. Coming from one of the bedrooms on the upper floor.

She held her breath. Her skin broke out in goose bumps along her arms and down her back. Someone was here . . . they had come for her.

She felt with her hand and found the gun on the settee beside her. Not the gun her father had killed himself with—the police had taken that. The other gun. The one he hid for emergencies. She had loaded it. Now she released the safety catch. She made her way to the door as silently as she could.

The hallway lay somber and quiet. The stairway to the second floor curved upward at the end, the corners of each step shrouded in darkness. She walked closer.

She should stop. Call the police. Wake her grandfather. Get out. But there was an intruder in the house, right here, right now, and there was no time.

She took the first step on the stairs, gun aimed upward, and the next. Every couple of steps she paused and listened. All was still. But there was a presence on the upper floor, as palpable as if she'd seen it.

Upstairs, she paused again. There were five bedrooms and her father's office. She carefully opened the door to his office. The moon shone in through the window onto the desk, but the room was empty.

My bedroom, she thought. He's in my bedroom.

She walked down the hallway toward her own room. The door was slightly ajar, and she looked in. By the window—a shape.

She pulled the trigger. Again, again, again.

ERIK HAD GOTTEN in through her bedroom window by using the fire escape to get onto the roof, then climbing to the balcony outside her room. But he had brought nothing: no weapon, no rope. Nothing. She didn't understand. If he'd come to kill her, he'd come unprepared. And he must have heard her approaching. It was as if he wanted to die, she thought. *The one among us who could kill is probably Laura.* Britta toasting her in her mind. *Likely better to be killed by someone you know.* Erik. As she saw the blond man lying on her bedroom floor, looking like nothing but a boy, she felt a huge sense of sorrow. For him, for Britta, for herself . . . for all of them who had been touched by the network and its deeds.

68.

They met in a basement room in a building in central Stockholm. Twenty men and women. The prime minister was there, the minister of social affairs. The leader of the Opposition, too.

The foreign minister stood at the front.

"All our information gathering tells us the same thing. Professor Lindahl was part of the team who set up the network in 1914—a young professor with a brilliant mind who was brought in to help. He assisted with creating the State Institute for Racial Biology. When the project was officially stopped, he continued. He had the connections, the information. In active circles, they speak of their leader as "the Teacher." It is him. We are certain. His closest supporter appears unfortunately to have been Dahlgren at the Central Bank. That is, in roundabout ways, where the money came from."

Christian Günther paused, took off his glasses and wiped them with a cloth. "I never thought we'd find ourselves in this situation," he admitted. He sighed, then put his glasses back on again. "Today, we arrest Lindahl using those sections of the Security Services that are still loyal to us. We start with him,

427

and then we wind in the network quickly, resolutely. We force him to give us other names. We stamp this out for good."

There was an excited muttering from the people listening.

"But for now, we wait."

The tension in the room was extreme. The prime minister and the minister of social affairs went to join Günther at the front. Three new kings, Jens thought.

He thought about the organization they were up against. It astonished him: how entrenched it was in society, its tentacles spreading everywhere. There was no knowing if a person was "trustworthy," he thought. Not really. Laura's father and Erik had shown him that.

After an hour, the phone rang. Günther answered it.

The room was silent as he listened. Then he said "Thank you" and put the receiver down.

"Professor Lindahl is no longer with us," he said.

The room broke out in clapping and cheering.

"No longer with us?" Jens asked.

Nobody heard him. Jens made his way to the front. The foreign minister was standing in a circle of people who were busy congratulating him.

Jens touched his sleeve. "No longer with us?" he repeated. "What does that mean?"

Günther was smiling when he turned to Jens. "He was already dead when they got there. He'd committed suicide."

"Suicide?" Jens frowned.

Günther nodded. "It will make it harder to find the others, but as long as he no longer continues with the project . . ." He turned back to the group around him.

Professor Lindahl hadn't seemed suicidal, Jens thought. And

Laura had been surprised that her father killed himself with a gun and hadn't left a note.

Jens could feel his knees weaken.

He looked at Christian Günther's stern face, with the round, steel-rimmed glasses, at the prime minister's blunt features, eyes looking up from underneath bushy eyebrows, at the social affairs minister, with his dark hair combed flat and the deep crease between his eyes. The faces, normally serious, weighed down with the burden of responsibility for their country, now smiling and relaxed.

There is someone else, he thought. Behind all this, there is someone else. Someone much more powerful. And this someone knew we were coming. Now he's cleaning up.

Around him, the conversations were excited, the voices deafening. A champagne cork popped.

Jens could see it now, the network: a fat cable conveying a current underneath them; black, quiet, sparking slightly, but still there.

It's not over, he thought. They've changed shape and we might not recognize them next time, but they are all still there.

Javanna came home, her brother by her side.

The Sami rejoiced for those who had returned. Then they mourned those who had been lost. For this time Stallo had taken many.

He's changed shape, Javanna thinks. Taken on the worst one yet. But one thing merits celebration more than any other: the settlers had stood by them. And that will never be forgotten.

Part of her wants to shout from the rooftops about what happened to her. The memories that still make her scream at night. But Nihkko and the foreman won't let her. The war is not yet over. It's only moved away from their town. And so she remains quiet. They all remain quiet. Soon, nobody even whispers about the events.

Taneli wants to go and say a proper goodbye to the director. The two will meet again, of course, but he says he needs to do this. Javanna says she will accompany him to town. Her strength is returning and she is able to cover the distance on her own. And so there she stands, waiting for her brother, by the empty hotel, the Winter Palace.

She looks at Blackåsen Mountain. At the black shelf raised above the ground.

And that is how it will be, she thinks. Together we will master you.

And the mountain responds: *We'll see about that*, it says. *We'll see.*

THE END

AUTHOR'S NOTE AND
HISTORICAL BACKGROUND

I knew I wanted to write about Scandinavia during World War II. It fascinated me how countries that had been in unions with each other ended up taking such different stances. The more I read, however, the more horrified I became. Race thinking was prevalent throughout the world at the time as an accepted science. In 1922, Sweden was the first country in the world to set up a racial institute to study eugenics and human genetics, but it was by no means alone. Some things really surprised me (for example, Jews' passport being stamped with a red *J* on the insistence of the neutral countries, Sweden and Switzerland, so that Jewish travelers could more easily be identified and refused entry at the borders; Sweden's work camps for communists and Finland's for the Russian prisoners of war). And I wondered, under the "right" (wrong) circumstances, how far would people have been prepared to take their thinking? Where would people draw that line in the sand?

An amazing installation was made in 2016 by Finnish artist Minna L. Henriksson in collaboration with the archaeologist Fredrik Svanberg for the Swedish Historical Museum in

Stockholm. Called "Unfolding Nordic Race Science," it depicts the organizations and people involved in race science in the Nordic countries from 1850 to 1945. The extent is remarkable. There are pictures online, and I urge you to see it—in person if you can. Seeing it in Stockholm in the spring of 2017 was one of my highlights of researching this book.

The plot in this book is pure fiction. The two meetings of the three kings happened, but their aim was only to declare the neutrality of their countries. Some of the historic persona existed, but they were not involved in a project like this. No experimentation is known to have happened in Sweden. Here are some of the facts:

THE SAMI

In the nineteenth and early twentieth centuries, Norwegian authorities suppressed the Sami culture, dismissing it as backward. Land was made state property. Sami settlers had to prove they spoke Norwegian before they became eligible to claim land for agriculture.

In Sweden, the attitude was perhaps less militant, but the Sami were deemed racially "less" than the rest of the population and not capable of managing their own destiny. During this period, Swedish teachers followed Sami reindeer herders to provide education for the children according to the policy "Lapp shall be Lapp"—i.e., children should not be taught enough to become "civilized" and not in Swedish schools. Sami areas were increasingly exploited by the then new mines in Kiruna and Gällivare and the construction of the Luleå-Narvik railway. The Sami who did not have reindeer herds were refused Sami rights. They were not allowed to hunt and fish where their ancestors had always lived.

In Russia, Sami life was brutally interrupted by the collectivization of the reindeer husbandry and agriculture in general.

During World War II, the Sami were used as guides, by both the Germans and the Allies, as they were very familiar with Lapland and were able to cover long distances on skis.

KIRUNA MINE

In the book, I have chosen the name *Blackåsen Mountain* to represent the Kiruna mine, as *The Historians* is a (very loose) continuation of my previous two books—each depicting this mountain at a time in history. But the history of mining in the novel is that of the Kiruna mine. During World War II, the ore from Kiruna went largely to Germany; Jacob Wallenberg was managing the negotiations with Germany together with Gunnar Hägglöf from the Swedish government; Sweden was indeed under huge pressure both from Germany and the Allies.

When it comes to the town surrounding the mine, I have taken liberties.

THE STATE INSTITUTE FOR RACIAL BIOLOGY

The Institute was set up, as the first of its kind, to study eugenics and human genetics in 1922. Its task was to study the inhabitants of Sweden from a racial perspective. The scientists tried to draw conclusions from the effects of biological heritage and the environment. Measuring of skulls, photographing and examinations took place to try to find evidence of the negative effects of mixing races. Its first director became increasingly anti-Semitic and the Swedish government took over in 1936.

Forced sterilization in Sweden took place between 1934 and 2013, sometimes by direct force, but more often by administrative coercion or persuasion. Those who were sterilized were psychologically ill, mentally disabled, people with physical disabilities and those deemed antisocial. The objective was racial hygiene, economic savings, public health and control of those deemed antisocial.

ADDITIONAL DETAILS

Christian Günther was Sweden's foreign minister during World War II. In 1940–1941, he worked on a Swedish-German rapprochement to the extent of becoming a Swedish security risk. One year later, he offered Jews a refuge from the Holocaust.

Karl Schnurre was a Nazi diplomat central to Sweden's relationship with Germany; he was sometimes described as "Hitler's special representative."

The expression "able artisans" was coined by Harald Hjärne, one of the history professors at Uppsala University, 1889–1913, and chairman of the Historical Society, 1884–1914. The *nachspiele* were where he seemed to feel most at home.

The Historical Society in Uppsala held lectures in Ekermanska's House toward the latter part of the 1940s. After the meetings the participants often went out for dinner. Gillet Hotel's restaurant was one of the favorites.

SOURCES

Arnstad, Henrik. *Spelaren Christian Günther* [*The player Christian Günther*]. Malmö: Arx Förlag AB, 2006, 2014.

Bergman, Jan. *Sekreterarklubben—C-byråns Kvinnliga Agenter under Andra Världskriget* [*The secretary club—The C-Bureau's female agents during World War II*]. Stockholm: Norstedts, 2014. An amazing book about something that is largely unknown!

Boëthius, Maria-Pia. *Heder och samvete* [*Honor and conscience*]. Stockholm: Ordfront Förlag, 1999.

Grant, Madison. *The Passing of the Great Race, Centenary Edition*. Whithorn, UK: Ostara Publications, 2016.

Hagglöf, Gunnar. *Svensk Krigshandels Politik under Andra Världskriget* [*Swedish trade policy during World War II*]. Stockholm: P.A. Norstedt & Söners Förlag, 1958.

Lindgren, Astrid. *Krigsdagböcker 1939–1945* [*War diaries 1939–1945*]. Stockholm: Salikon Förlag, 2015.

Lindholm, Ernst. *Byn på grytbottnen* [*Village on the pot bottom*]. Arbetarkultur Förlag, 1953. The portrayal of continuous noise in a mining village comes from here.

Ludvigsson, David (ed.) *Historiker i vardag och i fest—Historiska föreningen in Uppsala 1862–2012* [*Historians at work and leisure— The Historical Society in Uppsala 1862–2012*]. Department of History, Uppsala University, 2012.

McCoy, Daniel. *The Viking Spirit: An Introduction to Norse Mythology and Religion*. CreateSpace Independent Publishing Platform, 2016. Mimir as "the Rememberer" comes from McCoy's website, https://norse-mythology.org/.

Acknowledgments

The Historians has been three years in the making, and I am so grateful to so many people!

Thank you to my agents, Janelle Andrews and Alexandra Cliff, and the team at Peters, Fraser and Dunlop: your advice is priceless, and I am amazed at how you know just when to push and when to leave be.

Thank you to Jennifer Lambert at HarperCollins Canada for being so supportive and such a brilliant editor. I am so grateful for the time you've spent on this book and so thankful you'll still have me.

I am indebted to the hugely talented Sara Sarre at the Blue Pencil Agency for reading many versions and critiquing, as well as to the steadfast Lorna Read for catching all the mistakes I had not.

During the research period for this book, I was blessed with the most amazing conversations. I think getting to learn things and talking to knowledgeable people is one of the best things about writing. An especially big thank-you to Emir O. Filipovic, medievalist at the University of Sarajevo; Ivar Grahn, actor, Sweden; Henrik Hallgren, *gothi*, Samfundet Forn Sed, Sweden;

Gunnar and Elma Olovsson, founders of Geoprodukter, Kiruna; and Professor Emeritus Rolf Torstendahl, Uppsala University. Thank you to Carina Adolfsson, who took the time to read an early draft. All mistakes are my own.

Thank you to my writing friends: Mary Chamberlain, Vivien Graveson, Laura McClelland, Saskia Sarginson and Lauren Trimble for reading the many drafts. Your creativity and wise feedback have been invaluable, and I can't believe we are still together after so many years. In fact, I can't imagine life without you! Ten years is coming up!

I am grateful to Fergal Keane, as always, for letting me borrow his desk in London, for *sagesse*, and without whom I wouldn't be writing in the first place.

Thank you to those without whom normal life just simply wouldn't work: Monika Linder, Sofia Fredriksson, Raquel González and Miguel Duarte, the gals on my street: Amy, Jenna, Karen, Lemonie and Tanis—I get to see you *every day*! Erin and Erik in Calgary.

Thank you to Anna and Maja for being so patient all the days your mum was writing and traveling for research. ("As long as you are done by the summer.") Thank you to my father-in-law, John Taylor, for reading early drafts and helping me with the medical science. Thank you to my husband, David, for always covering the bases at home and for being my true partner in crime. At the end of the day, nothing would happen without you.

About the Author

Cecilia Ekbäck was born in Sweden in a northern fishing town. Her parents come from Lapland. Her first novel *Wolf Winter* was published in 2015. It won a High Plains Award and the 2016 HWA Goldsboro Debut Crown. She lives in Canmore, Alberta, Canada